Twisted Beauty

AMELIA J. RIVERS

UP CURRENT PRESS

-- To those always underestimated

Content Warnings: Consensual romantic encounters, mention of sexual assault and domestic assault, attempted sexual assault, blood, violence, death, family death, drowning, and murder.

Chapter One

Rosella's fingers curled over the parchment.

Taxes were due earlier and higher than before. They'd already suffocated her and choked out what little profit she had.

She rubbed a calloused hand over her cheek, stopping momentarily on the raised scar that ran from her earlobe to her chin. The rough ridge was a constant reminder of her mother's death. With a swallow, she forced her attention elsewhere.

She stared at the till and absentmindedly ran a finger over the dull coin that remained. There was no way they'd have enough gold for the coming winter. Not with the lack of sales from the town struggling with a weak crop. She had three other mouths to feed, too. Growing mouths that complained.

She grasped the necklace around her neck, running her hand down the thin gold chain until it landed on a familiar comfort. Her mother's ring. It'd been her mother's grandmother's and so on. It was also the only item Rosella had been able to safely ferret away and save from pawning until her father had been imprisoned. The gold band held three emeralds and two diamonds. It was a symbol of what her family had been and would never be again. Her father had once been a prosperous merchant, her mother the daughter of an earl's brother. Drinking had stolen her father's fortune and her mother's life.

A familiar bitterness tanged on her tongue and twisted tight around her heart. With a frown, she swallowed back the revulsion and blew a wavering breath from her nose.

Rosella's attention snapped to the jangle of the bell above the door. Giselle bounded into the room, her blonde hair dancing in a thick braid down her back, arms wrapped around a bundle of wood. It'd be enough for the night. Rosella should have questioned where it came from. They didn't own land with forests, they didn't have money for timber, and Giselle didn't know how to splinter wood.

Instead of questioning her, though, Rosella watched her take the load through the door into the small living section of the shop. Once it was burned up that night, there'd be no evidence and thus no repercussions as long as the real owner didn't show up before then.

Giselle, fifteen, was her youngest sister. Contrasting Rosella's auburn hair and freckled cheeks, Giselle had sun-kissed golden hair and fair skin like their mother's. She was constantly courted by the local men and loved to flirt with them, but never took them seriously. She shouldn't, either. Despite local belief, Giselle was too young to be wed. Too young to be a mother, even though their mother had been fifteen when she had Rosella.

And too young to be starving. Besides, Giselle's heart was already filled with thoughts of Odette.

"Hey, Roz," Bridgette called as she pushed into the selling room. Although the second youngest at eighteen, she was the tallest of the four sisters. Her tidy dark brown hair was pulled back into a coronet braid that wove around her head. Her gray eyes shone brightly with intelligence and mischief.

"What do you need?" Rosella asked, closing the register's door and shoving the tax notice into a nook by the register. She'd focus on the taxes tonight, when her sisters were asleep.

Bridgette cast Rosella a suspicious glance but continued into the room, maintaining eye contact. She peeked over the counter to see what Rosella was doing and furrowed her brow at Rosella's empty hands.

"What do you need?" Rosella repeated. She leaned back against the counter that once held expensive perfumes and liquors but now sat barren, catching dust. No one in town had funds for the finer products.

"What's the matter?" Bridgette pressed. She came around the polished counter to look for what Rosella could be hiding.

"Nothing's the matter," Rosella offered. She stilled her face, a practiced look, showing none of her trepidation as her heart pounded furiously in her chest. "You came in here to talk to me."

Bridgette rolled her eyes. "Did you hear there's going to be a festival?"

Rosella sighed, her body slumping. More money they didn't have. "For what, now?"

"You're such a spoilsport," Bridgette huffed.

Rosella bristled as Bridgette neared the nook, but kept a passive look on her face. "What's the festival for now? Didn't we just have one?"

Bridgette groaned and clasped her arms around her torso. "Roz, that was months ago, for the kickoff of the harvest. Now, we are celebrating the *end* of the harvest."

"We're celebrating by squandering what resources we have to celebrate a dismal harvest?"

Bridgette pursed her lips to the side and scanned Rosella. "What's up, Roz? You normally don't care."

Rosella waved her away with a hand. "It's been a slow day."

"What else is new?" Bridgette quipped.

And that was the problem. The harvest had been sparse, and without the surplus that was sold to the neighboring towns, the locals didn't have spare dollars for the novelties and luxuries she sold at the shop. A bad harvest for the town meant low sales for her. Low sales meant little food.

"You know, Benson was asking about you," Bridgette said, hopping up on the counter and dangling her feet in the air. Her boots showed their age with shined-up wrinkles and weathered gray spots.

"So?" Rosella forced herself to stand. She smoothed over her white blouse and black trousers, then moved away from the register to draw Bridgette's attention away from the nook. Her heart thudded in her ears. Benson shouldn't be asking about her. She didn't need the town thinking something was going on. There wasn't. She simply had a prime parcel of land, and others wanted it. Taxes hadn't taken it, yet. Her father's drinking hadn't taken it. Her mother's death hadn't taken it.

Now the town was trying a new tactic. Marry her off. If she married, the groom would get her land by law. Only if it was the last option to protect her sisters would she consider marrying.

"So? Roz, you're twenty-one. It's time you start thinking about getting married. Benson is nice."

"Married? Ha! I'd have to be courted first." Rosella held up a hand to stop Bridgette's normal rhetoric. "And I don't want that."

"Roz, we'll be fine," Bridgette said. She lifted her chin in the air and met Rosella's hard glare with her own.

"Fine with what?" Camilla asked as she stood up from a chair behind the shelf of preserves. She stretched and yawned, her tangled red hair ratted from her nap. She semi-straightened her rumpled cotton dress, which had patches stitched over worn spots to appear intentional instead of necessary, and strolled over to lean on the counter. She batted Bridgette's hands away when Bridgette tried to untangle her hair.

"I like my knots," she barked and shoved Bridgette backward.

Bridgette tumbled from the counter and landed with a thud. Red clawed at her face.

"I'm going to kill you," Bridgette roared and launched over the counter, grabbing Camilla, digging her nails into her sides, and yanking at her hair. Her normally calm and polished manners vanished as she tussled with her sister.

"What are you doing?" Giselle screamed, hurrying back into the room.

"Combing Camilla's hair," Rosella said as she tidied up Camilla's napping chair. She ran a hand over her own red locks pinned up in a bun.

"Camilla, you're nineteen years old," Giselle scolded. "Grow up." She pulled her sister upright and swatted away Bridgette's attempt to continue the assault.

Bridgette sucked in air and clutched her side as she leaned against the counter. Strands of hair frizzed from her braid, and her dress shifted off-center. She panted, "Did you two know Benson is asking about Rosella?"

"Ew," Camilla said. She scrunched her face up and stuck her tongue out with an "ack" sound.

Rosella chuckled and nodded.

"I don't know," Giselle said, forcing sincerity. After taking a quick step back, fanning her fingers under her chin, and batting her eyelashes, she added, "I think he's pretty handsome."

Rosella rolled her eyes but couldn't stop the laugh that burst out at Giselle's comment.

"Too bad he doesn't have brains to match those looks." Camilla hopped down from the counter. "I still don't mind looking at him, though. Wouldn't mind getting my hands in his hair, either."

"I don't know what you really see in him," Giselle said. "He's muscly and hard. I think Odette is much more attractive."

"She is lovely," Rosella nodded. Giselle had been interested in Odette for two years. Odette and Giselle often spent alone time together pretending to do chores, but Rosella had found them kissing several times. One day, Rosella hoped Giselle and Odette would be able to live the future they wanted together and not just when they were old widows.

Giselle blinked repeatedly and looked away, fidgeting with her hair.

"She still won't tell her parents?" Rosella asked. She strode over to Giselle and wrapped an arm around her.

Tears rimmed Giselle's eyes. "She's still planning to get married to Louis like her parents want." Giselle's lip trembled as tears rolled down her cheeks.

Rosella pulled Giselle into her embrace and ran a hand over her hair. Her chest constricted. She could do little to protect her sister's heart. Odette was a spitfire who matched Giselle's passion for life and exploring, but her parents' plans included her marrying into Louis's wealthy family. His family's estate sat south of the village with sprawling yards and fields. Somehow, the drought hadn't hit them as hard, and they used it to move their standing forward in town.

"I'm sorry, sweetie," Rosella murmured, tightening her hold.

The two other sisters joined them and threw their arms around the duo. The four swayed rhythmically in their customary embrace.

"Well, she's being a ninny," Bridgette said. "She'd be much happier with you."

Giselle shrugged and sniffed. "Like Dad would give me a dowry for it, anyway."

Rosella snorted a humorless laugh. Her stomach curdled. "He doesn't get a say in it."

"Because we don't have dowries?" Bridgette teased. She leaned back, offering Giselle a sympathetic smile.

"Because he's not getting out of his cell," Rosella said through clenched teeth. Even without running a hand over it, a phantom pressure traced the rigid scar on her face.

Camilla snorted and then giggled, the sound breaking the tension. "Leave it to Rosella. So, what is our dowry then?" She released her sisters and danced around the shop, sending her skirts twirling around her. She stopped at different displays, picking items up as she sang their name. "Dust aplenty, cobwebs, jam jars, or pickles—no wait, a horse grazing bag?"

Rosella rolled her eyes as the other sisters giggled. She had scant dowries for each of them, but she'd had to borrow from each over the past year to pay taxes that were due despite the lack of sales. With the newest raise in taxes, it was likely they wouldn't have any dowries or backup plans to pay the taxes.

Their father sat in the county seat's jail, withering away. His demise wouldn't help, as his breath meant a male was still connected to the shop and house even though Rosella was the executor of the property until his release or death. With him alive and taxes paid, no one else could buy it or claim it unless both he and Rosella agreed.

As the oldest and with no male heirs, it'd be hers fully when he passed, but then everyone would be out to swindle her land. Trying to claim it. The suitors would be unending. More than just Benson. Even if they were lacking in sales, she owned the parcel of land that the shop and house sat on. She'd paid her father's fees to ensure the land remained hers and wasn't auctioned.

Owning the land was the one thing that had kept them afloat. There was no rent due, just taxes. The heirloom property was highly sought after, nested squat in the town square. It was centrally located and spacious and seemed all the more spacious with so few items. Rosella wondered how much he had swiped from her mother's family to keep it going when his drinking worsened.

"Ah, Roz, we're just teasing," Camilla said, her large smile flattening and worry lines parenthesizing her face after seeing Rosella's expression.

"I have dowries for you," Rosella whispered.

"You do?" Giselle and Bridgette said in unison, sharing a look.

"I had..." Her voice trailed off and her gaze went to the floor.

"We weren't expecting you to do that." Camilla crossed her arms. "It's not your role. You're our sister. We'll figure it out."

"Not my role?" Rosella snorted. "I am the oldest."

"Roz," Bridgette started. Her fingers twisted in her skirts and her lips curled down.

"You're not our parent," Giselle said, but her blue eyes went glossy.

Rosella grunted. She'd taken on the role of being mom, sister, and father to the three younger ones the instant her mother had passed eight summers ago.

She ran a finger over her scar and licked her lips.

A loud rap on the door drew their attention. On the other side of the window stood Mister Deboteaux.

"Oh great," Giselle muttered and rolled her eyes. She crossed her arms over her torso and anchored her feet to the ground.

Rosella looked at Giselle and sighed. It must have been his lumber. They'd have a cold night, at minimum. Hopefully, she could smooth over the incident without a passing of coins.

"Mister Deboteaux," Rosella sang as he stepped in. His short stature was accentuated by his oversized coat and large wig. His buttons gleamed extra bright with fresh polish, and his stockings were starch white. His narrowed eyes matched his pinched lips. "What a... pleasure."

"Rosella," he said curtly and narrowed his gaze as his perusal passed each sister until his blue eyes landed on Giselle.

"Mister Deboteaux," Giselle snarled, not bothering to soften her stance.

"You know why I'm here," he snapped and pointed a finger at her.

"Can't fathom why," she said with a shrug.

"Giselle," Rosella warned. They needed to keep his ire minimal.

Giselle met Rosella's gaze and her eyes softened. "I honestly don't know." She pulled her lip between her teeth.

Rosella frowned. Giselle looked genuine. What else had she done beyond taking his lumber?

"What is the matter?" Rosella asked. She stepped in front of her sisters, establishing her place as the matriarch of the family. Even if the town looked down on them, they would respect her ranking when addressing her family.

"Her remarks to my son, Bertraud," he said without looking back at Rosella. A lecherous smile slithered across his face as his eyes traveled down Giselle. He licked his lips.

Rosella moved to stand directly in front of Giselle, blocking his entire view and causing his eyes to jolt to her.

"What did she say?"

"She said he was beneath the scum on her boots!" he roared. Spittle flew from his mouth.

A laugh choked in Rosella's chest, but reality stifled it. Mr. Deboteaux held clout in the town. Familiar numbness settled on her chest, forcing her to focus on another situation her sisters created.

"No, I didn't," Giselle said, moving her hands to her hips without leaving the shadow of her sister.

Rosella swiveled to glance at Giselle over her shoulder, her eyebrow cocked. "You didn't? What did you say then?"

Giselle feigned insult and put a hand to her chest.

Rosella rolled her eyes and asked again, "What did you say?"

Giselle huffed but answered. "I said, he was beneath the scum on HIS boots since mine are clean and he walks in manure."

Rosella closed her eyes for a beat and stilled her breath. Maybe she could will this away. She opened her eyes, but the shop still sat clean and empty. The hum of evening insects intensified, the heat of the day dampened her clothes and streaked the walls, and Mister Deboteaux still stood in front of her. Too bad it hadn't worked. Giselle still stood in defiance and pleasantly happy with herself.

The blood pounded in Rosella's ears, blocking all sounds. Inciting Mister Deboteaux would only bring more of the town's scrutiny. She shook her head and the sound of her other sisters laughing crowded the room, darkening Deboteaux's face.

"Girls!" Rosella yelled. Her voice drowned theirs and brought instant silence to the room.

Bridgette and Camilla stood embracing each other, tears of laughter rimmed their eyes on their flushed faces.

Giselle continued to stare forward; a small, prideful smile curled her lips at her other sisters' amusement at the situation.

"Sir," Rosella started, unsure how she planned to finish. "Giselle was inappropriate, and for that, I apologize." She held a hand up to stop her sister's tirade and still Deboteaux's response. "However, Giselle is only fifteen. Your son is ten years her elder."

"Jealous, are you?" he asked. A grin cracked his face and his beady blue eyes trailed over Rosella.

"No, sir," Rosella spat and cursed inwardly for sending yet another insult at the influential man. He was a swine and could make their taxes higher or even challenge her role as executor of her father and the estate. None of which she had the funds to afford legal counsel. "I just do not think it is appropriate for a man of twenty-five to be alone with a girl of fifteen without a chaperone, let alone allowed to speak to her about courting. I should have been the first person in our family he spoke to about his intentions. I am her guardian."

Her steady voice hid the trepidation she felt, but her growing anger gnawed away at the latter, bringing to mind the inappropriateness of his son's gesture and what it could do for her other sisters.

Deboteaux sputtered, his face darkening.

"Now, sir," Rosella continued. "I am sure that was not his intent."

Deboteaux flinched and his mouth twitched, the argument dying on his tongue as he wanted to keep face.

"I am sure this was a misunderstanding that we can work to rectify for both families and save face on an improper courting and what the implications would mean."

"Are you threatening me, girl?"

"No, sir," Rosella said, a small smile tugging on her lips. "I am offering a truce. Why don't you bring your son and wife over this evening for dinner? We'll have simple stew, bread, currant wine, and rice pudding."

"We have that?" Bridgette whispered to Camilla.

Camilla made a raspy throat sound in response.

Rosella stilled her face. Annoyance burned in her veins. They didn't have the food to spare, but her sisters' social standing was more important. They would not be treated as cattle.

"You're inviting my son over to court Giselle?" Deboteaux's face lit up and he shifted to see behind Rosella. "She'd be lovely at our family's dinner table in the future."

Rosella suppressed her gag. His interest in her went beyond dinner and likely involved sharing her with his son. There was no way she'd allow his son to court Giselle, but she couldn't allow his public display to go uncorrected and she had to tread carefully with the prominent Deboteaux family. She spoke with measured words. "No, I am not inviting him to court Giselle. I am inviting you over so I can properly be introduced, and your son can ask permission to court my sister and ward. As is our country's tradition."

Her sisters gasped and twittered behind her.

Rosella tightened her fists and gestured to her sisters to remain quiet.

Deboteaux narrowed his eyes, but as he turned to leave, he said, "Dinner will be nice. We'll bring a ham, don't worry about a peasant stew."

Chapter Two

Rosella stood at the door to greet the guests. Instead of the formal family tunic she wore to town events, she'd opted for black breeches and a simple faded maize shirt. Her sisters stood behind her in descending order of age, freshly scrubbed and hair braided: Camilla, Bridgette, and then Giselle. They had each donned their second-best garment, sparing their best for village events.

Rosella had managed to get them good protein for the evening: a ham courtesy of the Deboteauxes, instead of leftover stew. Even if it was from Mister Deboteaux's rejection and scorn of their "peasant stew." Camilla had baked fresh bread, following their mother's recipe. The golden floury aroma coated the room and made Rosella's stomach rumble. Bridgette had made the rice pudding, using fruit as the sweetener. Deboteaux's family would likely notice the lack of sugar and mention it to the townspeople.

She sighed.

Yet another slight she'd endure and ignore.

The currant wine was always on hand, though they never drank it. The luxury item had once been a nightly treat but now was used on the rare night company joined them. The sisters also knew to pour their glasses back into the bottle when the guests left.

Mister and Madame Deboteaux strolled through the entryway.

Madame grimaced as her eyes surveyed the clean but worn room. Her gown crinkled as she walked, the fresh crinoline rustling at her feet. Perched on top was a brocade skirt with a gold and blue pattern. Her bodice matched it and had white lace piping.

Mister Deboteaux also wore black breeches, as Rosella did, to mark him as the head of the family, but he wore a crisp white shirt with a black overcoat in the latest fashion. The brass buttons gleamed in the fading sunlight. Despite the dismal crop, his family thrived on special dealings. His eyes fell to Giselle, and his lip curled to the right. Rosella clenched her fists and rolled her lips between her teeth to keep the retort from coming forth.

Their son, Bertraud, walked behind them, freshly cleaned in starch-white trousers, a blue dinner jacket, and his hair slicked back into the latest style. He wore a matching leer to his father, but his gaze fell on Rosella. His hands twisted the yellow ribbon tie on a bouquet of spring flowers.

Bertraud paused before Rosella. He took her hand and bowed.

Her fingers stiffened so as to not retract from the unwelcome embrace. She'd scrub her hands with a wire brush that night to remove his touch.

He thrust the lush bouquet at her, the heady smell making her blink as she pulled her head back. His face never lost the lechery as he said, "I want to offer my most humblest apologies for my behavior earlier. I should never have approached Giselle without your consent. I would never want to sully the reputation of such a… fine family."

His last few words he said with a hitch in his eyebrows.

Rosella willed herself to not smack his face for the insult. Her father had ruined the family's reputation, and despite her best efforts, her sisters were able to keep their family in the gossip mills. All but Giselle should be married per the local traditions. Rosella had avoided the traditions by caring for her younger siblings. She'd accepted the spinster persona and wore it like a badge of honor with her black breeches and tunic.

She ignored the whispers and pitying glances from the town. Despite that, their father's infamy still plagued them with lesser standing in the town and common rudeness and lesser manners from the townsfolk. It meant she had to listen to Bertraud's insulting offer instead of considering gentler men with finer manners and houses, even if she had no intentions of accepting his courtship of Giselle.

A maid scurried behind the Deboteauxes, one of the several from their estate, a cooked ham in tow. She placed it on the spot Bridgette patted as she smiled at the maid.

The maid curtsied, her crisp dress and apron billowed around her. Her blue eyes drifted to the floor, awaiting direction from the Deboteauxes.

"I can grab you a place setting," Camilla said, her red tresses already escaping their braids.

The Deboteauxes froze and shot her a bewildered expression as red crept up the maid's cheeks.

"Or not," Camilla breathed through her teeth.

The sisters waited as the guests were seated, Madame careful with her silk brocade skirts as she sat. She rested ramrod straight, her displeasure puckering her face and stilling her actions.

Deboteaux sat next to his wife, but his gaze remained on Giselle. With each breath she took and each rise of her chest, he'd lick his lips and furl his fists.

The table was absent of conversation as the food was served by the Deboteaux's maid. Rosella, remembering the time with her mother's family at their estate, didn't offer to help but instead folded her intertwined fingers on her lap. Her first decade of life had been spent learning proper etiquette from her mother's family until they felt her father, and thus all of them were no longer fit for their company.

The Deboteauxes sat displeased by the setting of simple porcelain plates and cups. Madame picked at imaginary dirt on the silver setting and pursed her lips into a thin line as the bread was passed around.

Giselle reached for the breadbasket, her torso angling over the table. Sir Deboteaux's eyes darted to her chest, his mouth open, and a whimper sounded. His face flushed and his eyes darkened.

Unable to stomach his disrespect, Rosella slammed her cutlery too hard on the table and scraped her chair back. The long scream of wood on wood, prolonged and agonizing, silenced the others.

"Giselle," Rosella barked.

Giselle swiveled to look at Rosella, the bread scrunched tightly between her fingers, her large blue eyes wide.

Rosella growled softly and nodded. Despite everyone's attention, her cheeks didn't stain with crimson splotches. She inclined her chin toward the kitchen. "We need to check on the pudding."

Giselle's brow furrowed and she stared a beat at Rosella. But she didn't argue as she pushed her chair back. She kept the bread firmly in her grasp and took a nibble despite Rosella's eye roll. Giselle's gaze darted to Bridgette, who glowered back and nodded to go.

Upon seeing Rosella's expression, the maid scurried out of the kitchen to check on the table.

"I didn't make the pudding," Giselle seethed as she pushed into the kitchen. She whirled around to face Rosella and the expectant lecture.

"I know." Rosella finished guiding her into the kitchen by gently pushing back on her shoulders and forcing her to walk backward.

Once the door swung shut, muffling the silence, Rosella sighed and rubbed a hand over her cheeks. The rough ridge of her scar was a reminder of her responsibilities.

"Did you not see how he was ogling you?"

Giselle waved a hand in the air, batting away her words. "It's how he and most of the men look at me. I just ignore it."

Rosella leaned against the counter, the worn edge rigid and unforgiving in her back. The sharpness like the unpredictability of her sisters' futures and how they'd be used by the town and men.

"It's not okay," Rosella growled.

"You can't protect me from everyone," Giselle said. She stuck a finger in the pudding and pulled back a glop to taste.

"Giselle," Rosella moaned but didn't swat her.

"Bridgette makes the best pudding," Giselle said around her finger and smiled.

A smile skittered across Rosella's face, and she swiped a taste, too.

"Are you two coming back?" Bridgette pushed the door open and leaned in the room. Her glossy dark hair shined in the flickering candlelight.

Both Rosella and Giselle shoved their fingers into their mouths to hide the evidence of their thievery and giggled.

Bridgette rolled her eyes, but a smile spread across her face. With a quick glance over her shoulder, she reached into the dish, too.

Camilla's sharp laugh pierced the room, and the three sisters froze.

Rosella's face fell and her chest shuddered with a heavy breath.

"Uh-oh," Giselle giggled. "She was left alone. We better get back."

Giselle swiped another taste and jumped off the counter and darted around Bridgette back into the room. Bridgette met Rosella's gaze with an apologetic smile for leaving Camilla unattended before following Giselle back out.

Rosella left the pudding and braced herself for whatever Camilla had done. She slackened her face to indifference and entered with her chin high, as her mother had taught her. *No matter the situation, always show confidence until you believe it yourself.*

To Rosella's horror and expectations, Camilla was leaning back in her chair, tears of amusement streaming down her face. Splotches of red blossomed on her cheeks and her hand smacked the table.

During the time in the kitchen, Bertraud had currant wine splashed across his starched pants, dripping from his nose and chin. A look of murderous intent and embarrassment stained his pale skin a purple hue. Madame looked faint from anger. Sir's gaze was locked on Camilla's chest. The maid dabbed at his shirt, providing no aid in removing the stain.

Rosella pushed her other two sisters back into the kitchen, hoping to spare Bertraud further humiliation. His dark eyes darted around the room, seeing nothing until they fell on her. His eyes bulged and his jaw worked but no sound came out. He clenched his fists, and wine bubbled between his digits.

Giselle and Bridgette pushed against her trying to see the spectacle, voicing their displeasure and confusion in grunts and murmured curses.

"Don't," Rosella seethed to her sisters, but Bridgette pushed back Rosella's rigid arm. She stopped midway through the door and braced her arm against Rosella, stopping Giselle's entry. Despite her prim posture, her arm vibrated with held-in laughter and small whispery gasps escaped her lips.

"This is unacceptable," Madame said, standing abruptly, rattling her porcelain dish and sending her roll tumbling across the table. More than applied rouge reddened her cheeks.

Mister Deboteaux's gaze cut to Rosella. "This is how you invite my son's courting?"

Rosella's eyes darted to his, words trapped on her tongue. She hadn't invited anything. She held her words and breathed a few seconds from her nose before drawing out, "As we discussed, tonight's dinner was for us to get to know each other better and for me to decide if he may court Giselle."

Madame sputtered, turning on her husband. "Her permission?" Her shrill voice echoed off the walls.

Mister Deboteaux's gaze darted between the two women, his mouth gaping like a fish.

"I will bundle the ham for you to return home," Bridgette said, her gaze diverted to not start laughing. "I'm sure you want to tend to Bertraud before the stain sets if it has not already. I'm sure he'd be more comfortable once changed."

"Why would we bring a half-eaten carcass home?" Madame sneered, her lips puckered.

Though she should feel embarrassment from the comment and despite the irritation of the entire situation, for the briefest of moments Rosella had to force a smile from her lips. That 'half-eaten carcass' would feed her sisters for a couple of days.

Bridgette nodded politely. Camilla clapped her hands and her eyes lit with delight staring at the large amount of leftover meat. The clatter brought Rosella back to the reality of the situation and the Deboteauxes.

Rosella breathed through her nose. Her body vibrated with annoyance. Everyone in town would know about the evening. If anything, it might bring in a few gold coins so the gossips could have the sisters' side of it.

"Mother, Father, I will follow you out, I'd like a minute with Rosella." He swallowed, his Adam's apple bobbing. Despite his ruined attire, he stood proudly.

The two parents started their protests, but Bertraud gestured to the door. "It'll just be a moment. We were guests after all, and we haven't forgotten our manners."

Rosella nodded behind him. "Bridgette and Camilla, help Giselle with the dishes."

Camilla huffed and squinted at Rosella. "Is that... were you... the rice pudding!" She screeched and headed to the kitchen.

Bridgette turned from Bertraud to Rosella, meeting Rosella's eyes. She passed a questioning glance, making sure it was a good idea to leave her with Bertraud.

"Best to resolve this now," Rosella said and nodded, dismissing Bridgette.

After the sisters departed, Rosella folded her arms over her torso, tilted her chin toward her chest and waited.

Bertraud puffed his chest up, regaining his pompous air. "I am the *only* one willing to... accept this family and its needs."

Rosella raised an eyebrow at him but remained silent. She doubted the 'only' if someone else thought they could have access to her property or her sisters. Whatever he said, she didn't want his help or acceptance. He was like *all* the others.

"I am your last chance," he said, his gaze devouring her form from hips to face. As his father had done to her sisters.

"Giselle has many offers," Rosella said, stepping toward the table to stack dishes.

"I'm not talking about Giselle."

"Then what are you talking about?" Rosella gritted out, annoyance finally clipping her words.

"You, Rosella. Giselle is a child. You are not."

Rosella blinked at him, reality slithering through her and churning her stomach. He wanted their property, too. "You mean...?" She couldn't finish the sentence.

"Yes, I am here for you."

Chapter Three

ROSELLA TOSSED IN HER BED, THE DAY REPLAYING IN VIVID detail. Even if his intentions were unwanted, Bertraud made a valid point. Her sisters had little hope of marrying into an affluent family. Their father's sin still hung on them like a discarded spiderweb, invisible but sticky and impossible to shed.

She had enough remaining saved for one and half of her sisters to have a decent dowry. If it made it through the year's taxes. The rest had been whittled away in the previous year's tax hike. That meant two sisters would go without.

Camilla was more interested in slumbering and having fun than worrying about matrimony. Although Rosella had resigned herself to being a spinster and matriarch, keeping the family business afloat as a landing place for her sisters, she doubted Camilla wanted that life long-term. She'd likely dabble with men and women, adding to the family's name, and bearing illegitimate children.

Bridgette, although she hadn't mentioned much, had her eyes set on Gavin, a local merchant's son. With his social standing and the fact that he seemed to reciprocate her feelings, the half-dowry would be a fair amount. However, Bridgette, with her good manners, beauty, and pose, could easily wed higher up in society. The viscount wasn't likely, but there were others in town from old families and wealth that she'd meld into well. She could have a very comfortable life. If she sought it.

Even if it meant not associating with her sisters.

Camilla's choices could affect Bridgette's chances unless she excommunicated her sisters. As troubling and heartbreaking as it was, it was probably for the best. If Rosella could convince Bridgette to be self-helping instead of the family's voice of reason.

That left Giselle. Her beauty put her in the sights of many locals. Giselle could probably wed many of the locals with a small dowry, but Rosella knew Giselle's heart. She was in love with Odette. The sisters supported Giselle and offered to speak to Odette's family, but Giselle had begged them not to. She would need a decent dowry, then.

On top of her sister's individual needs, taxes were increasing, and the festival was coming. Her family would be required to contribute, as all families were, or they were at risk of further severing their societal standing.

Maybe she should consider Benson's interest.

The scamper of a rodent across the roof drew her attention. The wind howled in the gaps of the siding, loose of mortar, promising of a cold winter. She shoved the wool covers off and tiptoed across the floorboards, careful to avoid the squeaky ones. Her sisters remained silently in their beds. Their snores and murmurs were a normal night melody she fell asleep to but tonight it played as a taunt of their unknown future and her inability to provide for them.

Easing the door open, she paused when it squeaked. She held her breath as the silent night pulled on, making sure they remained in bed. Rosella slipped into the main room, sectioned off by doors for the coming winter when they'd sleep in there by the fireplace. The cold dark room, layered in a shimmery haze of filtered moonlight through the threadbare curtains, chilled her skin. She stared at the doors, one to the kitchen and one to the shop at the front.

In the kitchen, the scurry of rodent feet broke the still air as her presence unsettled them. She unhooked the latch on the breadbox and, reaching down to the bottom, plucked out a piece of bread and reclosed the container, denying the rodent tenants an easy meal.

After breaking off pieces of bread, she meandered back through the house to the chilled shop, rubbing the ring under her shirt between her fingers. With the dwindling matches in the drawer, she lit the lamp by the till, the only beacon of light and heat, and pulled out the crumpled notice. She stared at it as the light flickered from her breath. The slow creep of the moon dimmed as the coming sun chased it across the sky, bringing its threads of light and oppressive weight as the world woke up.

A knock rattled on the window, startling her. She looked to the clock first, the dial still saying everyone should be asleep. For a moment, her gaze flickered to the rifle. Her heart thudded against her ribs. Scrunching her brow, she moved closer and noticed the form of an elderly woman through the window.

She licked her lips and looked back to the door leading into the house. She could move back in there, back where she kept a rifle, and ignore the person. It was the wise thing to do, but the person had to have noticed her solitary light. Either they were concerned about fire, looking to make an urgent purchase, or going to rob her. Since she had nothing to rob, and she didn't want to turn away a possible customer or be timid in her own home, she sauntered to the door, pausing with a hand on the handle and one on the frame. Her breath came in a pant, filling her senses.

She flipped the lock and, pushing the door only a few inches open, hung her head outside. The sting of the crisp pre-dawn air stung her face and flared her nostrils.

A hunched-over woman stood in a threadbare dress and shawl with moth-eaten patches, feet wrapped in rags instead of shoes, and propped on a crooked cane. Her knotty fingers twisted at a lock of stringy gray hair. A tattered cloak shrouded her gnarled, leathery face, but her haggard features told of her years.

"Sweet child," the woman croaked. Her voice was thick and scratchy, sounding as if she hadn't spoken in years.

Rosella's grip tightened on the door. She'd never seen the woman before in the twenty-some years she'd lived in the town. Her brain screamed at her that it was a witch and to shut the door, lock it, and swing her rifle toward the door until she left. She puffed a humorless chuckle out at the childish thought of a fairytale witch. Real monsters didn't need magic. "Can I help you?"

"May you spare a bite to eat?" the woman asked. Her dark eyes tracked up to meet Rosella's. The flame of the candle reflected off them.

Rosella pondered the question. She could mean a bite of food or of her. She stared at the woman for several beats, assessing the risk, then again chastised herself for letting her imagination jump to a fairytale. Magic may exist, but only in distant, far-off lands. Like hope. The town and her life were void of it.

The clatter of wheels on the cobbled road tore her attention away. The milkman turned on her street and his sons darted from the cart, leaving bottles in the milk doors of the homes. She let out a breath. They wouldn't receive one of the deliveries. The woman had even less. And they'd been fortunate the night before to get a ham.

"Sure," Rosella said, pushing the door open. "I have some bread. There might be rice pudding if my sisters didn't eat it all."

The woman smiled, revealing brown crooked teeth, and stepped into the room with Rosella.

Rosella closed the door and relocked it. She flinched at the unexpected warmth of the room. She snuffed out the candle and led the woman to the kitchen.

Rosella lit the lantern in the kitchen even as the weak sunlight filtered into the windows, warming the room. She unlatched the bread box and blinked, seeing it full of rolls. She hadn't remembered there being that many rolls. Even at the start of dinner last night. She plucked two out and handed them to the woman.

She opened the icebox and pulled out the small jar of fruit preserves. She set it before the woman with a knife. "Sorry, we don't have butter."

The woman only moved her eyes as she watched Rosella. Finally, she said, "What about you? Won't you eat?"

"I already had a roll," Rosella said, ignoring the rumble in her stomach.

The woman hummed, smearing jam on the roll and then taking a large bite. "This is delicious."

"My sister is a good baker."

"You sure you don't want one? The jar looks plenty full."

Rosella nodded, unable to say the lie out loud.

"It's okay to take care of your needs," the woman said, taking another bite, catching the crumbs with her other hand, and popping them back into her mouth.

"My needs are met," Rosella said. She rubbed her arms and looked unseeing around the room.

"Are they?"

Rosella blinked and looked back at the woman. Her sisters were fed and warm. She had food, most days. She had a roof. What more did she need? The luxuries of the wealthy weren't needs.

The woman smiled again, her blue eyes now visible in the lightening room. She patted Rosella's hand, her boney figures bent with age. Despite her gnarled, calloused hands, her touch was soft and warm. "You're a good person," she said and stood.

"Would you like another roll?" Rosella scanned the crumb-less table.

"I'm filled," the woman said. She patted her stomach for emphasis. "Thank you. I should be on my way."

Rosella's stomach tightened, and before thinking, said, "Do you have someplace to go?"

The woman smiled and her eyes gleamed in the dim light.

"We don't have a ton, but we can help," Rosella said, unsure how she'd manage it, but she couldn't turn away someone less fortunate. She had a roof and her sisters.

The woman chuckled and strolled to the door. "You have a soft heart but a wall of iron toward yourself."

"Excuse me?" Rosella sputtered.

"You protect others at the expense of yourself."

Rosella stared at her.

"Thank you again for the rolls," the woman said and stopped by the door. "Oh look."

Rosella followed her gaze through the window. A bottle of milk was perched on her stoop.

"They must have gotten the wrong house," Rosella said. She started for the porch to flag down the milkmen.

"Maybe it is your good fortune," the woman countered.

It'd been months since they'd had the treat. Although the milk would be nice, it wasn't theirs.

"Someone's misfortune is not my gain." She wasn't her father.

The woman snorted.

Unfazed by the common derision, Rosella unlocked the door and peered down the road void of traffic.

"Perhaps there is a note," the woman said as she shuffled past her. "Oh look, there is. Can you read?"

"Yes," Rosella replied automatically. She blinked. The milkman was illiterate, but she accepted the scrap of paper from the old woman.

The note read: "Some good deeds just are. Enjoy the milk."

"What?" Rosella asked. Her eyes fluttered up to look at the old woman, but she stumbled into the doorframe, realizing she was alone on the stoop. She picked up the bottle and headed back to the kitchen after locking the door.

"Hey, Roz," Bridgette muttered as she yawned behind her. Her eyes grew at seeing the milk. "We got milk?"

"It was a gift," Rosella said. She handed Bridgette the slip of paper and milk.

"From who?" Bridgette said, smiling as she took the jug and paper from Rosella. They joined the other two in the kitchen.

Rosella shrugged, unwilling to explain and unsure she even understood what had happened. She'd have thought it a dream if the milk wasn't in hand. "It'll go with the rolls."

Bridgette nodded and sat it on the table.

"Who made more rolls?" Camilla demanded as she peered into the container. She shot a dark gaze over her shoulder toward her sisters.

"More?" Rosella asked, glancing at her.

"There were five left over from last night."

"How many are there now?' Rosella moved to stand by her sister.

"At least a dozen," Camilla said and grabbed two.

"How'd we get more preserves?" Giselle asked. "This was almost empty."

Rosella looked at the jar still on the table in front of where the woman sat. The jar was brimmed with jam.

Her mind jumped to a thought she had dismissed earlier. Then the note.

"Some good deeds just are," Rosella muttered as she grabbed two rolls and sat down at the table with her sisters. Something twisted in her stomach. Hope or fear. Nothing could explain the extra food. Like the firewood Bridgette brought home last night that they burned, she could ask more questions about it. But she couldn't explain the good fortune and she wasn't going to take food from her sisters already in hand. Especially since the milk would spoil.

Rosella eased in her chair, her eyes dancing between her sisters. Though they rarely complained about empty bellies, each day was a struggle to supply them with enough. As she watched Camilla slide ham between her biscuit halves, her muscles relaxed. Her sisters had eaten their fill the previous night and, by luck or something else, they had enough for the current day and more.

It'd been years since Rosella could remember having days' worth of food accessible. Not since her mother had been alive had she not had to worry about food. Somehow, her mom had always managed to provide enough for the girls.

For the few days between her mother's death and her father's arrest, her sisters hadn't had food. Too afraid to ask their father, they had gone to Rosella. Since that time, she had made sure food was on the table, even if she skipped a share. She had considered following her father's example from his libations, borrowing trinkets from others without permission or returning them, but she refused to follow any example he set—theft or murder—to get what she wanted.

If only she could figure a way to make sure they always had food. She snorted. She'd need more than magic for that, she'd need a miracle. At least they had a few days' reprieve.

Each in their normal spot, Giselle to Rosella's left, Bridgette directly across from her, and Camilla to her right, the sisters ate until full. Each had two rolls, jam, and a thin slice of ham that the Deboteauxes had left.

"Roz, what's this?" Giselle asked, hunching under the table to pick something off the floor. She righted herself, a gold chain and locket in her hand.

Rosella reached out to take the item. The bauble shone brightly in the dim light, and the cold metal chain pooled on her hand. The thick chain held a two-inch-sized locket. Gems encrusted the gold face in an elaborate design. Chips of gems showed a mountain with a rose on top, the rose petals made of tiny rubies and the stem of emeralds. The mountain was gold with stubbles of peridot for grass. At the base of the mountain was a river made of sapphires and sitting on the land with her fins dipped in the water was a mermaid, her scales a rainbow of gems. Racing away from the mountain was a stripe of blue gems that wrapped around the base of the mountain and ended in a pearl moon.

"It's a locket." Rosella rubbed a hand over the gleaming face. The piece would fetch an impressive price. She'd be able to provide dowries and help ward off the detriment of the tax hike for years. It was a glimmer of hope. It could solve so many of their problems. Her heart hammered with each possibility. So much was possible...

"Where'd it come from?"

Rosella's mouth dried thinking of the haggard woman. It had to be hers. She closed her hand over the piece, its cold form now heavy in her hand. It wasn't hers to sell. Its possibilities weren't hers. Her stomach tightened and the sensation of lead filled her. She wasn't her father.

"Is it Madame's?" Giselle asked, scooting her chair closer trying to peek at the locket.

"I don't think so," Rosella mumbled.

"If you don't know, let's sell it," Camilla said and took a big sip of milk. She eased back in her chair, her hands rubbing her stomach in satisfaction.

"It's not ours," Rosella said. Her lips pressed into a thin line.

"So? It's in our house. We found it." Camilla shrugged.

Bridgette looked between Camilla and Rosella; her face pinched in confusion. "Roz? Whose is it?"

She didn't have a name.

Giselle's delicate hand clasped Rosella's. When Rosella didn't respond, she prompted, "Roz?"

Rosella flinched and looked up to her sisters. "A beggar woman came by this morning."

"A beggar?" Bridgette parroted.

"This morning?" Camilla said, sitting forward. "When? Why did you let her in? Did she threaten you with a curse?"

The other sisters rolled their eyes.

"She was hungry," Rosella said. Her hand tightened over the bauble, and she ran a thumb over the raised face, the metal warm to her touch.

"So are we." Camilla pointed to Rosella's hand. "That'd end our hunger."

"It's not ours," Rosella said, and her fingers tightened over the face, the gems pressing into her flesh.

"I say we vote." Camilla stood and placed her hands on her hips. "Who agrees we should sell it?"

Bridgette again stared between Camilla and Rosella, her face blank.

Giselle tightened her hand on Rosella and hummed in contemplation.

"This isn't a vote," Rosella said. She stood, forcing Giselle to retract her hands. "We aren't thieves."

"What about the wood Giselle brings home?" Camilla countered. "It's not ours and she didn't pay for it."

Giselle whirled around, shooting a glare at Camilla.

Camilla shook her head at Giselle and then gave a shoo gesture with her hands.

"Wood is from the trees," Rosella murmured. "The forests. It's not the same thing."

"So, you're just going to rationalize it then?" Bridgette asked. She held her hands up, palms out to stop Rosella, and said, "I didn't say I don't agree."

"Do you know who the woman was?" Camilla challenged. She stepped between Rosella and Bridgette's line of sight and used her hip to bang the table for emphasis.

Rosella swallowed and looked at her hand.

"So how do you plan on getting it back to her?"

Chapter Four

Rosella stood behind the counter, watching the sun cross the sky as the door remained closed. The shadows of evening crept across the shop. The locket sat heavily on her collarbone, just above her mother's ring, tucked safely from view and Camilla's poaching hands.

The tax notice sat stuffed back in the nook, but her gaze was fixated on the spot. She was able to recite back word for word from it without looking at the damning document.

"Ready?" Bridgette asked as she pushed her way into the room. Her suspicious gray eyes scanned over Rosella. She wore a long dark gray dress with a high collar and swooping neckline, the same one she wore for all social gatherings. It'd been one of their mother's, worn for picnics on her family's estates. She'd adorned it with fresh pink flowers, but it'd do little to stop the gossips of the town.

"Why am I going?" Rosella asked as she locked the till and moved around the counter. A chill raced down her spine.

"Aren't you the head of the family?" Bridgette asked.

"Then why are you going?" Rosella said. She followed Bridgette out the door and turned to lock it. A warm harvest wind carried a hint of wheat and sun.

"We're all going," Giselle said, standing next to the shop, her lean form resting on the brick exterior. A smile curved her lips and her mischievous blue eyes stared at the people passing by. She wore another of their mother's dresses. The light blue satin dress with lace piping, no longer of fashion, had been modified to more current trends with yellow thread to appear gold, but it still garnered the town's scorn.

Rosella pinched the bridge of her nose and sighed. "Why?"

"We don't think you'll really go," Camilla said. Her floral cotton dress had been pieced together from material bolt scraps. The cream lace accents had once adorned a different dress that had been reworked into another design. "We're here to escort you."

Camilla cracked her knuckles and squinted at Rosella.

A smile flittered across Rosella's face.

Bridgette shot Camilla a dark look. "We think you'll go."

"And then sneak out," Camilla finished, sticking her tongue out at Bridgette.

"It'll look odd if we all go," Rosella protested, seeing her ability to sneak out early without unnecessary socializing evaporate. She curled her fingers at her side. Cold settled on her nerves as she schooled her face, readying for the town.

"No, it won't," Giselle said, rubbing her hands and smiling. "It's a meeting to discuss the festival, lots of families are coming. It won't look odd."

Rosella rolled her eyes but followed her sisters to the town square. The cobbled roads all led to it. The wide area flanked by shops, including theirs, had been swept clear with benches carried in for the gathering. Stone buildings tucked close together, most centuries old, were scrubbed clean. Boards ran the width of the buildings to catch dirt and sand before being tracked inside in the businesses. Freshly-pruned planter boxes adorned with mums brought color to the area.

Rosella ran a hand through her auburn hair, not bothering to tuck away the wayward strands. She wore her black leggings and black tunic. The tunic had once been her father's and was the symbol that she spoke for her family. He'd be livid to know she wore it, which was one of the only reasons she was able to don something of his. The frayed edges had been mended and beaded over with remnant trims from one of their mother's dresses they'd refashioned for Camilla.

Catching sight of Madame Deboteaux in her crisp taffeta dress and fresh wig talking to a few other ladies, Rosella steered her sisters in the opposite direction.

Giselle's blue eyes scanned the people as her lips pressed into a tight line. "I don't see Odette."

"Her family always comes late," Bridgette consoled, but wrapped an arm around Giselle's shoulders and pulled her in for a hug. None of them mentioned that they may be setting up plans for her and Louis's likely wedding.

"I see Gavin," Camilla loudly whispered while giving a finger wave to him.

He wore a crisp white shirt under a gray overcoat with silver piping overtop. Matching gray trousers and pale brown boots accentuated the red undertones of his brown skin. A small smile danced on his lips as he nodded back. His smile grew and he waved when he caught sight of Bridgette.

"Aww, look at that," Camilla sang.

Tucking an imaginary strand of hair behind her ear, Bridgette dipped her head and averted her eyes after smiling back.

"Oh, so smooth." Camilla shook her head and sighed.

"Shush," Bridgette hissed.

"Or what?" Camilla prompted. "Are you going to make a scene?"

"Enough," Rosella growled. Her brown eyes turned sharp on Camilla.

Camilla raised her hands in mock surrender.

"Rosella," a deep, warm voice carried across the open space.

Rosella stilled.

"Ohhh," the sisters whispered in mockery.

Rosella felt the sting of a blush hit her cheeks. Only her sisters could still illicit the unwanted response.

"Stop it," she seethed.

"Rosella," the voice called again. A tall man bounded over to the group, his brown hair falling from its style and across his forehead. He wore a starched white shirt and brown pants, his boots freshly polished. A black tailored long coat with white embroidery donned his shoulders.

"Benson," Rosella managed to say.

"I was hoping to see you here," he said, breathing heavily.

"Were you?" Giselle cooed. She batted her eyes at him and lifted her clasped hands to her chin.

His eyes darted to Giselle, furrowed in confusion before they darted back to Rosella. He licked his lips. "I was hoping we could talk."

Rosella schooled her face. Her stomach tightened. It could be about anything but was likely related to what her sisters were jabbering about yesterday. She didn't have the time for it. He was just one more person likely interested in marriage and their store. Granted, she'd known him since they were kids. He'd been nice and polished. He knew what to say. How to act. For their town, and likely any town, he was one of the best possible matches. Even if he was refined into a bored gentile.

The three other sisters stared intently at him, their eyes wide in interest.

"Uh, alone," he said and flinched. "I mean, uh..."

"He wants to court someone," Camilla whispered loudly.

Rosella blinked her eyes to fight the eyeroll. She couldn't just go back to her shop to avoid talking to him.

"How about after the meeting?" Rosella said. She reached back and grabbed the two sisters closest to her and dug her nails into their arms.

Giselle wrestled against the strain, but gritted out, "You should sit with us."

Benson's face lit up at the invitation, but his jubilation faded seeing Rosella's steely gaze fixed on her sister before turning a friendly but bland expression his way.

"It'd be an honor for you to join us, but I'm certain your father would want you to sit with him," Rosella said, nodding toward an older man wearing a black tunic with deep red vertical piping. The fresh seams were clean and pressed and the tunic's silk was deep black versus her faded black. His polished façade was the same as the group he talked with.

Benson's eyes fell and he nodded. "Okay, I'll catch up with you later."

"Come on, Roz," Giselle groaned. She slapped Rosella's arm half-heartedly as Benson walked back to his family. "Seriously."

"Leave it alone," Rosella said, tired of the old conversations.

"He's very cute." Camilla tilted her head to observe his buttocks. Her shoulders mimicked his walk.

"And sweet," Bridgette said and looked to Rosella. "He's also very interested in you."

"I'm not interested in him," Rosella said. Without looking at her sisters, she made her way to their normal row.

"But why?" Camilla moaned and stomped behind her, drawing a few stares from the other families. "He's one of the best in town. Boring, sure, but he'd be nice. You deserve nice."

"I don't have time to focus on such things," Rosella said. She sat down and patted for her sisters to join her. Her toes curled in her boots as she forced her focus forward.

"What? Why?" Camilla said and looked at her sisters for support. When they didn't readily jump in, she forged ahead. "Roz, we're all of marrying age."

Rosella snorted. "No, you're not."

Camilla rolled her eyes. "What else are we going to do? That's all this town has to offer."

Rosella sighed, knowing Camilla was right and hating her for it.

"It's okay, Roz," Giselle said. "You'll be the mean old lady that adults cross the street to avoid while children climb all over you as you give them candy you have tucked in the extra folds of your sleeves."

Rosella couldn't stop the laugh that rolled from her. "That's quite specific."

"And accurate," Bridgette mumbled and dodged Rosella's swat.

"WE'RE DONATING CURRANT WINE?" ROSELLA MUMBLED, staring into space after the meeting ended. They had one watered-down bottle that they'd poured their helpings back into.

"We'll figure it out." Bridgette patted Rosella's knee and offered her a smile.

"You know how to make wine?" Rosella asked, standing up and brushing imaginary lint from her tunic.

"We have bottles at the store," Camilla said.

"Three, to sell," Rosella said. She ran a hand absentmindedly over her cheek.

"We'll borrow from the store."

Rosella laughed. "We're going to run a debt up we can't pay? They are on consignment. We have too many of those now from the town. We don't need to be our own collectors."

"Rosella," a high-pitched voice rang out behind her.

"Oh no," her sisters muttered in unison. The three pushed together into one form.

Rosella grimaced and then forced a smile before twisting around to face Madame Deboteaux. She bowed slightly before taking a few steps toward the woman and from her sisters. After making sure Bertraud wasn't around, she made shoo gestures behind her back to encourage her sisters to keep their distance. The three turned and made a production of helping to clean up the town square.

Madame Deboteaux's gray eyes assessed her; her mouth pinched into a thin line. Her facial expression didn't change, but Rosella felt the disapproval waft off of her.

"Madame?" Rosella prompted, dipping her head.

Madame's eyes lifted to meet Rosella and she stiffened her already straight spine. "I see all four of you came tonight."

"Yes," Rosella said, unsure what Madame was implying.

"It must be hard to keep watch over such headstrong girls. Even in your own home."

Her commentary on the previous evening. Rosella's smile turned brittle, but she didn't otherwise react.

"I know you did your best..." Madame tapered off.

Rosella waited for the "but" that always came.

"I just think you'd have an easier time if you made matches for your sisters. Let someone take care of them properly. Mold them. You're blessed with Bertraud's interest and willingness to accept your hand without a dowry." Her face contorted in disapproval, her lip curling at the side. "He'll find matches and help you care for your sisters properly."

Rosella's eyes flashed. Interest and willingness to have her land. To have say and power over her sisters. "As opposed to the way I've cared for them."

Madame tutted and shook her head. "You did the best you could, but you were just a child. A headstrong one at that, not letting the town help."

"We were very thankful for anyone's generosity."

Madame's jaw twitched and her eyes narrowed.

Rosella knew well what she was referring to. Several had originally offered to house her sisters when their father had been taken away, but Rosella had seen it for what it was. They would use the girl around the house as they groomed her into a docile, obedient shell of a person, and then at the proper age they'd hand the sister off to one of their sons to pump out children and tend to their business, or they'd sell the sister's hand if she was desirable enough.

Generosity wasn't what the town had offered. They'd offered indentured servitude and being pawned off into marriage, willing or not.

She'd known when it'd been originally offered what it meant. Her lips upturned into a genuine smile, and she nodded toward Madame. "I hope you have a wonderful day, Madame Deboteaux. I wish you and your son the best. I'm sure he is swarmed by the local ladies of age."

Rosella bowed slightly again, masking her smile. Her son would make a match. His parents' wealth would see to it. It just wouldn't be her or her sisters.

Before Madame could respond, Rosella righted herself and, with a curt head nod, gestured for her sisters to follow. They fell in line with her.

Camilla walked backward as she stared at the bolstered Madame Deboteaux. "She's such a windbag."

"Sh," Rosella scolded.

"I'm only saying what everyone already knows." Camilla shot Rosella a cheeky smile.

Rosella rolled her eyes but couldn't keep the grin from her face.

Bridgette fisted her hands in her skirt. She averted her eyes to the ground before glancing back at Madame Deboteaux. "What did she want?"

"To remind me how unmannered you three are."

"That–" Camilla started, but Giselle slapped a hand over her mouth.

"Ow!" Giselle growled. She shook her hand in the air and then shoved Camilla. "That hurt!" she seethed, rubbing her hand.

"You taste salty," Camilla said, sputtering out her tongue.

"You two," Bridgette warned.

Camilla and Giselle stuck their tongues out at each other but fell in on either side of the other two sisters.

Then Giselle's face lit up, the spat forgotten. Digging her fingers into Rosella's arm, she breathed, "There's Odette."

A girl around Giselle's age stood next to her parents. Long curly black hair framed her face. Bored dark eyes scanned the group until they locked onto Giselle. Her lips curled into a smile. Her simple dress marked her family's recent struggles and willingness to marry her off quickly. With a quick word, she moved to join the group.

"I'll catch up." Giselle walked toward Odette without waiting for confirmation.

"Have fun," Rosella called.

"Hey, Rosella." Benson's deep voice cut over the chatter of those around them.

She groaned and felt the starting pangs of a headache. She released Bridgette but took a second to collect herself.

"Hi, Benson," she returned. She nodded toward her sisters to wait off.

"Hi," he said again. He shifted on his feet.

"Hi," she said, forcing a smile but didn't meet his eyes.

"I'm not certain how to go about this properly..." Benson said, running a hand over his reddening neck and staring at the ground.

"Do what properly?" Rosella asked. Sleep tugged at her eyes and pulled at her words. All she wanted was to go home with her sisters.

"You're the head of your house," he said and gestured toward her tunic.

She followed his gaze and took in her weathered garment. "Yes, I am."

"Who do I ask if I can court you?"

Rosella stilled her movements. Her eyes remained downward but unseeing. A whiny sound filled her ears and she stuttered. Red clouded her vision. He'd actually asked. She'd hoped her sisters had been joking or he'd come to his senses and realized it wasn't feasible.

She blinked and realized he was still talking but she had missed the words. "What?" she squeaked out. "What did you say?"

"I don't think it's appropriate to ask your dad," he rambled.

"Ask my dad what?" Rosella asked as her mind tried to catch up.

"If I can court you."

"No, don't ask him that." Rosella's eyes flew up to stare at him.

"So, who do I ask?" His eyes finally met hers. Fear shone brightly back.

Two had asked. More would likely ask as word spread about the offers and her family's struggle to pay the taxes. Could she fend them off? How long? Was it just a losing battle?

Too many thoughts spun in her head. About her sisters. About her.

"Rosella?" he asked when she didn't respond.

No matter what, she needed to see to her sisters first.

"No one," she said and shrugged. "I can't be courted."

"What?" he asked, pulling back. "Why?"

"I have to see to my sisters first."

His eyes darted to the two sisters a few feet back pretending they couldn't hear but were white-knuckling each other's hands in frustration.

"So, when will that be?" Benson asked.

Rosella shrugged and threw her hands in the air. "I have no clue."

Chapter Five

Rosella sat in the store watching the sun warm the sky. She'd been up for hours. More accurately, since the previous morning. After tossing in bed for several hours, she'd given up on sleep and moved to the dark store. The store was a reliable constant, a place for play as a child and then escape as her father's drinking worsened.

Her mind hadn't stopped since Benson's proclamation. In less than two days, people had tried to make courting arrangements for two of her sisters and two local men had stated their interest in her. It wasn't that she'd been avoiding the situations. They were always at the forefront of her thoughts. Moreso, she had wanted the time to rebuild the dowries for her sisters so that they didn't have to settle or make unwanted choices to help provide for the family. It seemed the town was tired of waiting. Tired of niceties. Tired of their independence. But this was their home. And they didn't have the funds or means to start over anywhere else. And it wasn't like other villages wouldn't be the same.

She scrubbed her face with her hands, gliding over her scar, and then hovered over her burning eyes before her hand absentmindedly fiddled with the found locket.

Rosella wasn't sure how to find the beggar woman, but she'd thought if she waited again in the early morning, she might reappear. It also provided her with something to do as her mind refused to slumber. As day broke and the streets filled with townspeople, she gave up.

She'd like to think she'd imagined the woman, but the rolls, jam, and milk they'd had for dinner were a reminder of the visit.

The locket could fix their needs and provide well into their futures. She'd have to go a few days' travel to a city with a fine jewelry store and wear the remaining velvet dress of their mother patched up with flowers and trims, but she could sell it. Feed her sisters.

Rosella took her hands from the pendant and ran them over the counter, removing the temptation. She wasn't a thief. Not as their father had been. She couldn't provide that example for her sisters either. Not if she wanted better for them.

A knock on the door drew her attention. Hope and fear warred in her chest. A frown darkened her face seeing a familiar silhouette. She didn't hide her annoyance as she unlocked the door and allowed Mister Trible in.

"Mister Trible, it's early," Rosella said with a nod and stepped aside so he could enter. Acid twirled in her stomach and slithered up her throat at the possibilities of why he could be at the shop before it opened.

Similar in stature to his son, Benson, Mister Trible had been a friend of her fathers in her youth. Her father's increased drinking drove a wedge between them until Mister Trible only acknowledged her and her sisters, it being inappropriate for him to speak solo to her married mother.

Likely one of her father's targets when funds ran low, her family had stopped visiting his home in her early years, but Mister Trible never intervened. Only cast her father from his circle. As the others had done. Unlike the others, he'd chaperoned their trips to see their father in jail. Had acknowledged Rosella as the matriarch of her family, even at thirteen. Treating her as such, he'd never offered a roof or room to them. As the town's treasurer, he saw to the tax collection. What at one time had been a comforting face, became one she avoided.

"Rosella," he said with a bob of his head. "Or should I say Miss Belle?"

He wore his black tunic and breeches. Freshly polished boots gleamed in the dim candlelight. Mister Trible came as the head of his family. His pin, nested below his brocade jacket he wore on top of his tunic, denoted his town's stature as an official. So not tax business. Family matters. She swallowed down her bubbling concerns. "Formalities? So this isn't a social visit?"

He snorted at her. "I saw Benson speaking with you yesterday."

Her spine stiffened, but she stilled her face. "Yes, we are friends. Have been since childhood."

He chuckled and shook his head, his hair the same color as Benson's but faded with gray. "My boy has hopes. You must be aware. I'm sure the town is."

"Oh, that's nice. Hopes propel us to do more," she said and moved to stand behind the till. "This feels like a social visit, though."

He sighed. "Miss Belle..."

"Back to formality." Even if not taxes, he had an agenda. If he was like his son or the others, he wanted her marriage to his son and the entrapments for her it came with.

"You received the notice."

Her eyes darted to the nook, but she didn't respond. Perhaps he put the pin on the wrong garment.

"The taxes are due."

"I understand." To busy her hands, she reached for the duster and ran it over the spotless counter.

"Can you pay them?" Mr. Trible tilted his head to the side, his eyebrows raised and lips pressed tightly together.

She flicked her eyes up to meet his gaze but didn't respond.

"The town will seize your property and sell it to pay your share."

"There isn't a need," Rosella said. She ran a trembling hand over the pendants at her neck. A decision made. "I just need a few weeks."

"Weeks? How many?"

Her mind scrambled at the distance and how long it would take on foot versus riding a horse.

"Four weeks," she managed to say without her voice faltering.

"No." He shook his head. "I must deliver the town's taxes in four weeks. I'd need to sell this land before then."

She bit back her retort. He'd already assumed she couldn't pay. He was already planning the auction. Already assumed his family would be the decision makers in the sale.

"Three weeks," she countered. Her voice cracked.

"Two weeks," he said. He crossed his arms over his chest and settled back on his heels.

She closed her eyes and grasped at the two chains around her neck. Her stomach knotted. She had no choice. "I need more. The travel time will be at least two weeks."

"Travel time?" he asked.

"I have a matter to see to that could help. If it doesn't, when I return, three weeks or not, I'll concede."

"You're just prolonging your pain," Mr. Trible said. He surveyed Rosella and pinched his lips. Finally, he sighed. "Fine. Three weeks. Not a day longer."

"Thank you," Rosella said, relief flooding her at the chance.

"Oh, and Rosella?"

Rosella lifted her gaze to his.

"When you sell your property, we'd be happy to welcome you into the family as my son's wife and buy the parcel."

ROSELLA'S HAND MOVED ABSENTMINDEDLY AROUND THE shelves with a duster. Camilla held down her chair, a dress in her hands to mend. She wove delicate, tight stitching across the neckline, bringing life to an almost rag. Giselle was in the kitchen cleaning. Bridgette had gone off to barter for flour and eggs.

The bell on the door rang and Rosella looked up, startled by the chance of a customer. Thoughts of Mr. Trible's comments tumbled in her mind.

As if summoned by her thoughts, Benson's large frame filled the door as he looked tentatively around. His jaw worked to steady his smile. The dark brown hair tresses around his face were recently slicked back. His clothes were freshly pressed and looked new. Instead of the casual brown breeches he wore to the festival meeting, today he wore gray breeches, shined black long boots, a crisp white shirt, and a fitted cropped coat.

"Benson?" Rosella asked before she could stop herself. Her fingers fisted against her side. She'd made it clear she couldn't be courted at the festival meeting. She also told his father she'd cover the taxes without selling her family's property. If not a customer, there wasn't a reason for him to be there.

Camilla popped up from her spot, her red hair in disarray, and Giselle pushed in from the house section drying her hands.

"Hi, Rosella, can we talk?" he asked. His hands fidgeted as he bowed his head and looked at her through his eyebrows.

Rosella looked at her sisters, both staring intently at them. Regardless of not wanting the conversation, there wasn't a way to avoid it without a scene from her sisters.

"Let's step outside," she said. She let out a breath and flicked her hands toward her sisters.

Benson nodded and opened the door for her. The sweet smell of sun and baking bread greeted her. Throngs of people milled down the road on their daily errands.

She walked with him to the edge of the building, out of sight and earshot of the door. A wooden overhang dipped above them, blocking the intense rays of the midmorning sun. Despite the warm air, she wrapped her arms around her chest.

"What's going on, Benson?" Rosella asked as she stepped into the shade and leaned against the neighboring building. The hard brick dug into her back.

He licked his lips before meeting her gaze. "I know my father stopped by."

Rosella curled her fists and swallowed.

"I understand..." he trailed off.

"You understand what?" she spat.

He sighed. "You fell behind and there is an increase in taxes. The bad harvest has hurt many, so it hurts you."

"So?"

"I know you don't want to sell your business," he said, his eyes glancing toward her store before looking back to her.

Rosella nodded once and waited, her stomach coiling. It wasn't Mister Trible's place to tell Benson, but it had apparently already happened. They'd known her since childhood, they all felt entitled to her business.

"I have an offer." Fear shone in his eyes.

"On my business?" She shifted away, rubbing a hand over her face, her finger finding the familiar ridge. The familiar numbness of disappointment swam in her veins.

He shook his head. "Not necessarily. I offer marriage. I will pay off your taxes. Your sisters can maintain the business. Camilla is nineteen and Bridgette is eighteen. You were... a lot younger when it fell to you. It will remain in your family, and with your sisters."

Rosella swallowed down her embarrassment and rage. "Benson, you are being kind," she lied.

"Rosella," he said and reached for her hand, but she yanked it back. He sighed and started again, "Rosella, I can make sure your sisters are taken care of. I can help them get married off. If you want to run the store... I guess..."

"You guess what?" she growled. He had it all planned out. He'd help arrange marriages for her sisters, "marry them off" as if selling livestock, have a deciding say in what should be their choices, allow her to run the store as an olive branch to boost her injured pride until... until what?

He shrugged. "You could until the first child came."

Anger blazed through her veins and her vision narrowed. "Until I squeeze out a kid? Then what? Be your little wife?"

"You don't want to be my wife?"

"No, I don't think she does," Bridgette said, stepping out of the shadows. Her gray eyes blazed as she looped her arm through Rosella's and tugged her toward their store. "Excuse us, Mister Trible, my sister and I need to see to *our* business."

"He said what?" Camilla bellowed. Her red hair flopped around her shoulders.

"That jerk!" Giselle pounded her fist on the table.

The four stood in the kitchen.

"And you didn't tell us about the taxes!" Camilla stepped forward while balling her fist.

Bridgette rolled her eyes and grabbed Camilla's arm, forcing her back. "Why didn't you tell us?"

"It's not your concern," Rosella said and stepped toward the ice box.

"Not our concern?" Bridgette yelled, her face reddening, catching them all off guard at her break in composure. "Roz, damn it, we are in this together."

Giselle and Camilla gasped.

Rosella forced a tight smile and moved around them, opening the ice box to remove the stew.

"You aren't our parent," Camilla said and stomped her foot.

"No, but I'm your guardian," Rosella replied, putting the pot on the stove.

"That doesn't mean you get to make all the decisions unilaterally," Camilla countered, pulling four bowls down from the shelf.

"Yes, it does," Rosella said.

"We can figure something out," Bridgette hedged.

"What is to figure out? I have to drain the last of your doweries and pray that I can refill them before your marriages or the next tax hike," she said. They'd need more than dowries. Taxes would only go up.

"We don't need dowries," Bridgette said.

Rosella waved her off. "You do if you want out of this life."

"What life? Out where?" Bridgette demanded. "What fantasy are you living in?"

"Bridgette, you're perfect," Rosella rambled. "You could marry a viscount's son or a banker."

"What are you talking about?" Bridgette huffed.

"You can get more than this life," Rosella said, moving in front of Bridgette to meet her gaze.

"That'd mean leaving you three behind." Bridgette crossed her arms.

"Yes, but you'd live a better life."

"I'm not leaving you," Bridgette said and pointed a finger at Rosella. "There's no better life without you three in it."

"Why not? You could have so much more. Comforts. Food. Luxuries. Wealth. It's the best thing for you."

"What about Gavin?" Giselle asked.

"Yeah, what about Gavin? Bridgette likes him. Shouldn't her happiness mean more than money?" Camilla said. She nodded at the idea, a smile breaking across her face. "Isn't that what you've also said? It's why you didn't peddle us off to others."

Rosella shot Camilla a dark look and Bridgette blushed. Rosella cursed at herself. She was doing exactly what the town did. Trying to make affluent matches with little regard for the feelings of those involved. She closed her eyes and steeled her breath.

Rosella sighed letting her breath out and relented. "If Bridgette wants to be with Gavin, I am in support of it. I just want you three to be happy and taken care of."

"Maybe we'd be happy if we got a say in our lives and yours, and you didn't act like a bossy ninny," Camilla said. "Maybe we'd be happy if you were happy."

Bridgette and Giselle stilled. Their gazes cut to Rosella.

"I'm happy," she choked out.

"Lies never fitted you." Bridgette rested her hand on Rosella's arm.

"Okay, enough on Rosella hiding stuff from us. That's normal. Back to Benson." Camilla clapped her hands.

Rosella listened as her sisters berated Benson, proclaiming her own arguments from yesterday as their newly-found truths, but she wasn't sure anymore. As the outrage of what he insinuated dissipated, she saw the merit in it. She didn't want to marry Benson, or have his children, but compared to the other prospects in town, he was the best. Bertraud had also asked for her hand, and although not as affluent as him, Benson and his family would be kinder and more pleasant.

It was a good offer. Benson was nice. He had enough means to support her and her sisters. She didn't need the business if she had other ways to support them. Nor did she have to sell her mother's ring. She could provide for her sisters through her marriage. She wouldn't have to travel to the other city. He could help with their dowries. She could set their futures. Benson would have a say in it, but she could provide them with the choice she didn't have. It was a good offer. A decent life.

It wasn't the life she wanted, but neither was being a shrew, fighting for a dying business while clawing her way through obstacle after obstacle to carve a life and choices for her sisters. But if she set her pride aside, married him, and took his offer, she could make sure in her agreement with him that her sisters would be set up as best as possible.

"Don't you think it," Bridgette said, shoving a slender finger in Rosella's face.

"Think what?" Rosella barked back. She stopped herself midair from swatting her sister's hand.

"You are not selling yourself to Benson!" Bridgette roared.

Giselle and Camilla nodded in agreement. Camilla's face reddened with anger while Giselle set her jaw.

Rosella sighed. "What? It's marriage. You three are thinking about it for yourselves. It's a good offer. It'd help the business and provide better dowries for you than what I can do."

"You're not cattle. We're not selling you off to the highest bidder."

"I don't have bidders," Rosella said, shifting on her feet.

"Bertraud offered, too," Bridgette snarled.

"What? How?" Rosella sputtered, staring between her sisters. She hadn't told anyone.

"I overheard." Bridgette smiled brittlely at Rosella.

"You didn't share that?' Camilla said, turning on Bridgette, her finger pointed in her face. "I should be told all these things, immediately. I'm next oldest."

Bridgette rolled her eyes and ignored her.

"We don't have many other options," Rosella said. Her throat dried as their futures hung like chains around her neck, searing her flesh and weighing against her.

"We can sell the locket," Camilla said, staring at Rosella's throat. "I know you're wearing it. You hate high-collared shirts, and you wore them yesterday and today."

Rosella rolled her eyes at Camilla's accurate observation.

"It's not ours to sell," Rosella said, grasping at her neck, her hand catching on to the two chains. The locket wasn't hers to sell. She wasn't her father; she didn't steal. Her finger traced the outline of the ring. If she married Benson, she wouldn't have to sell it. It was her last connection to her mother. To a shattered future. To a broken promise.

She blinked away the tears. Maybe it was the best. Sever the final connection. Let her mother provide for them in spite of her father, and in the same swift motion, remove the reminders of the burned dreams and "what could have been." The last lingering remnant of a life that wasn't theirs.

"We're not selling you into a loveless marriage," Bridgette shot back and raised her hands to stop Rosella. "Loveless on your side. I don't care if he's nice. He's not for you."

"You were pushing me yesterday to let him court me!"

"Court yes, not buy. This is just icky."

Rosella threw her hands up.

"We need to think of something else." Giselle tapped a finger against her lips.

Rosella's eyes darted to her. They were out of options. Her sisters didn't want her to enter a loveless marriage as she didn't want them to enter marriage to provide a path for the others' future.

"What about the locket?" Camilla asked, drawing the others' attention.

Rosella forced herself to not touch it or acknowledge her.

The acidic burn of guilt ate at her throat and she gulped. It was safe. Even from her. She wanted to sell it, provide them all the futures they deserved. But it wasn't hers to sell. But there was something that was hers. Something that would pay the taxes.

There was only one path left.

Chapter Six

Rosella lay on her bed, listening as the house descended into the normal nightly routine. Her sisters slept in their own thatched beds, their soft breaths the rhythm to her heart. The wind whipped against the house, the soft whistle breaking the silence.

Running a hand over the chains, she sucked in a calming breath before shoving the covers off and tiptoeing from the room. She cracked the door open, easing it so the moaning hardware grumbled quietly. Rosella took a last peek at her sisters before closing the door. The moon hung high in the sky, the brilliant light casting spindly tentacles into the room, providing her enough light to traverse the memorized room without a candle. She dug around into the nook and pulled out the note she'd written earlier over the tax notice, as they already knew about it.

She didn't want her sisters to worry, but she couldn't involve them, either. They'd never let her sell the ring, but its sale would provide them a year or two of food, taxes, and to pad the doweries. Their mother wouldn't want them to suffer for a relic of the past.

She didn't take any food. There were some bruised apples Giselle had retrieved with the nightly timber. Rosella didn't think too long on it, otherwise she'd be able to figure out the source of the contraband. Besides the apples, Camilla had baked an apple bread with the softer, overly ripe pieces. It'd keep them fed for a few days.

She'd walk to the town unless she could find a wagon headed in the direction. With so few travelers due to the dismal harvest, it was unlikely. It'd take her almost a week to reach the town and then another to return. She hoped she could do the transaction quickly. Time wasn't on her side.

She hadn't been to the town in almost five years, not since the last time she saw her father. He had to sign papers letting her be the executor of his accounts when the vulnerability of the shop and land became public interest. Despite the weight loss from the gruel diet, he'd still been the large, burly man she remembered. His wicked blue eyes had lost their luster from her youth. Stolen by booze and horrific choices. Her visit had been before his health failed and he was put on repair duty. Before then, he was on a labor work crew to pay for his sins, but nothing he did would bring back their mother or restore their future. All his work was for strangers' forgiveness.

Rosella took a passing glance at the shop, not sure if it'd still be theirs when she returned. She grabbed the satchel she'd left behind the counter. It contained a change of clothes, her mother's dress, a tattered blanket, two canteens, flint, and some rope. Slipping a knife into her belt, she crept outside.

The chilled night air bit at her face and she pulled her cloak up around her head. Despite longing to look back, Rosella steeled her gaze toward the path. Keeping to the shadows, she followed the cobbled town road to the dirt path that cut through the forest.

THE SUN CRESTED THE FOREST LINE, THE DIM LIGHT filtering through the fluttering green leaves. Rosella shifted her cloak back against her neck and ran a hand through her auburn hair. Her stomach rumbled, but she kept on walking.

The hours dragged on as the sun arched in the sky, slipping between the heavy foliage. Sweat dampened her tunic. She forced her breath to even, not letting it block the sounds of the forest. She thought about stopping, but tingles shimmied down her spine as she made ground. Nothing came into view as she scanned the forest line. The sentinel trees clawed at the sky, blocking most of the sun and rustling in the breeze. Shadows and thick foliage engulfed the area just a few feet from the path. She scanned the canopy when the forest floor and path didn't yield results, but nothing stirred. Despite the empty visage, she knew she was being watched. It could be animal or human. Neither were good options.

She licked her dry lips and her hand rested on her knife, her fingers curling around the handle. Hand-to-hand wasn't her strength, especially when she couldn't see the assailant. She'd prefer a sword or bow and arrows or a slingshot and distance to run, but her sisters needed the bow for hunting, and they no longer owned a sword.

With her gaze focused on the surroundings, she stumbled and landed on her knee. Her teeth nicked her tongue. The metallic taste of blood flooded her mouth and caused her to gag. She swallowed it down and ran a hand over her mouth. Lodged in the ground was an old piece of wheel. The metal fastenings had rusted, and the wood was faded and brittle.

She looked back toward her town that lay tucked miles back behind the thick forest and forward again. Such a piece shouldn't have had time to be buried in the ground. It should have been cleaned off the path. But then, with recent years' dismal harvests, there hadn't been much need for traveling to the larger city for luxury goods beyond what she could carry in the store. Only the wealthiest of them could afford trips to the inns and cities. Most of the town couldn't even afford wine or hearty food, and yet they were being called upon to pay more taxes.

She stood and dusted her pants off. A rock the size of her palm lay disturbed on the side of the path. She picked it up, checking its heft. She slipped it beneath her waistband; the weight was easier to carry there and provided her a free hand. It wasn't much, but she could chuck it at anyone approaching if she had time.

Continuing on, the sensation of being watched slithered down her spine, but the immediate predatory feeling had subsided. Her stomach rumbled again, reminding her she hadn't eaten since dinner the night before and that had been some bread and apples. There wasn't much easily accessible in the forest. She could hunt, skin, and prepare meat, all the necessary skills to feed her sisters, but she didn't have hunting gear or a place to build a fire. She scanned the treetops. It was midday by the sun's position, but in the forest, she'd only have a few more hours of dim light. She'd need to make camp. Even if it was sooner than she'd like, she'd rather have a good spot than travel farther and suffer.

A spot came into view an hour later. The land sloped up to a flat slab, providing protection from sitting rain, and a better outlook advantage with tree coverage.

With the fading light, she scrounged together branches, pine boughs, and some fallen bark from a tree and fashioned a lean-to against a tree. She settled on the forest floor, covered in pine needles and cones. The quiet surrounded her. The sensation of being watched had finally left, and it didn't feel close or urgent. Her muscles finally eased and she let out a long breath. Dust and sweat coated her clothing. She ran a finger over her tunic, confirming both the locket and ring were still with her.

She took a couple of swigs from one of her canteens, careful to ration it before she found a river to replenish it. She leaned back and stared at the darkening sky. It was too light for stars to appear even if the trees created a pseudo night canopy. Fatigue caught up fast, and she moved to get under the coverings. Doing so, she unsettled debris and unearthed a few twisty wild spinach plants. She smiled at her fortune.

Chapter Seven

Rosella slept hard, waking as the forest came alive with birds chirping and the scurry of forest creatures starting their day. She rubbed the sleep from her eyes. The area was still too dark to see clearly.

She wiped her arms, shaking pine needles from her clothing. Her leggings and cloak were dusted in dirt, her legs slightly damp from the unforgiving ground. She pushed off, hoping to make traction and clear the forest before the next nightfall.

The path sloped upwards, and her brain tried to unravel the years to the last time she'd traversed it. It had to have been this steep before, but she didn't remember the steep inclines or the towering pines. As if this was a different trail or forest. She shook off the image and continued forward. There was only one trail to the city, and there hadn't been a fork in the path that veered in the wrong direction.

As the path twisted, the scenery felt more and more foreign. The route she expected had been cut through pines, but the pines that towered above were different: spindlier, decades older, taller. The dark boughs danced in the increasing winds and thrashed together in their song.

She huddled her shoulders. Despite the coverage and lack of wind, cold chills skimmed down her spine and arms. Her eyes swung from side to side, looking for signs of something familiar, something dangerous. Back and forth, she looked, each step taking her deeper into the forest's belly.

Her stomach rumbled, breaking the trance of the woods. Her scouting turned into foraging as she scanned the edge for edible plants. It wouldn't be enough to satisfy her. She thought momentarily of the knife at her side, regretting again not bringing a bow and some arrows. She didn't have time to set a snare.

Catching sight of some berries, she pulled up to gather some sustenance. The sweet, plump wild blackberries crowded on the bush. After eating her fill, she plucked more and gathered them in her already-emptied canteen. She'd at least have another meal later if the forest was stingy with its offerings.

A distant howl cut through her thoughts, and her head shot up to survey the scenery. Nothing lurked in view, but she couldn't shake the feeling of being watched or stalked again.

Rosella didn't have the means to face a wolf or pack. Righting herself, she clutched at her knife in one hand and the rock at her waist in the other.

As she crept forward, her skin prickled, and her eyes darted around to find the perpetrator. Tingles raced down her spine. She wasn't alone.

The trees belied nothing, offering a curtain of leaves and trunks that blocked the view in most directions. She dared a look back, almost certain she'd find something, but the path was clear as the trees encroached the path, choking out the light and visage.

She looked ahead again, inhaling the scent of the trees tinged with moisture. She cringed. Rain. The smell danced on the breeze, tangling with the woodsy aroma. She looked above, curious about the coverage the trees would offer. They blocked the sun. Would they block the elements, too?

In addition to the howls and the sensation of being watched, she'd have to face the elements without proper protection.

Rosella pondered building another lean-to. She wasn't close to the forest's edge, but she'd get sick in the elements. She could fill her canteens with rain and possibly forage for more substantial food than the spinach she ate yesterday and the blackberries she ate today. If she could make a shelter, she might be able to hide or defend herself.

Finally relenting to common sense, Rosella scoped out a spot, again on an elevated plain with tree coverage but a view of the trail. As she started to climb the embankment, a faint laugh caught her attention. She stilled to listen but heard nothing. She looked at the spot and then the path. Maybe the rains were a better option. She wasn't in the safety of her village. In the familiarity of it. The laughter could be in her mind, an enchantment—she *was* in a forest—or someone in the trees, but she didn't want to find out.

A drop of water fell through the leaves, the cold bead splashing her forehead and sending a chilly spray into her eyes. She looked back at the spot, and again heard laughter. She couldn't stay. She darted up the path and rummaged through the fallen bark.

Finding a section of bark about three feet by four feet, she snatched it up and darted back to the path. She balanced it on her head, using her hands to steady it, and then took off at a run. She kept an even pace as she raced for the forest's edge. Cold bit at her hands as the rain set in. Her heart thudded in her chest. She steadied her breath, trying to hear if someone or something was closing in, but the hurried drumming of her heart in her ears droned out much around her.

Ahead, the path was dappled in gray light, signaling a clearing or the exit of the woods. She dug deeper and made a mad rush for the opening.

Ten steps away, nine, eight, seven, six. The rain pelts slashed at her skin, the icy barbs welting as she almost cleared the forest. She angled the bark to protect her eyes, forfeiting her arms to the onslaught, but before she made the clearing, something large rammed into her. She flew forward. Her breath escaped her. The hard, unyielding ground tore at her body as she landed and skidded several feet. Her arms, scraped and bloodied, throbbed in pain as dirt stung her eyes and blood tanged in her mouth.

Without thought, Rosella whipped around, brandishing the board as a weapon. She tried to scramble to her feet, but someone landed on her, pinning her legs down. A second person reached for the board she was thrashing around.

She growled as she tightened her grip and tried unsuccessfully to thrash her legs free.

"Rosella," a voice pierced the air. It sounded like Bridgette. Was a witch impersonating Bridgette?

Rosella didn't stop. The witch and her goons would wait for her to ease up before hauling her off. She knew what could happen to lone women or men. She'd go down fighting.

"Seriously, Roz, knock it off," a winded Camilla-sounding voice muffled from Rosella's stomach.

"Ow," Giselle's voice yipped as Rosella kicked her feet free, trying to make contact.

"Hey!" Bridgette's voice scolded, and a third set of hands lashed at her.

The board was ripped from her grip. Standing above and lying on her were her three sisters in flesh and scowls. Each wore old cotton dresses and their warm cloaks.

"What are you doing?" Rosella hissed and yanked her limbs from her sisters.

It was impossible for her sisters to have caught up to her unless they followed her immediately after she'd left, but she would have heard them. They weren't winded enough to have run and, judging by their appearance, couldn't have camped. A familiar, unpleasant numbness edged at her heart. But there weren't any horses, or a cart, or anything else her sisters could have used. Perhaps it was best if she didn't know. Feign ignorance as long as she could until she had to deal with it.

"Us?" Camilla bellowed. Her shrill voice echoed in the trees.

"Sh," Rosella said and scanned the woods.

The rain petered out, leaving a chilled dampness.

"SH?" Camilla yelled. "Who's going to hear us? No one travels this path."

"Merchants do." Rosella rubbed her arms. She didn't mention her thoughts on witches traveling the path or that she'd thought her sisters had been some. They'd only laugh at her foolishness.

"Not much anymore," Camilla said. She sat back and folded her arms over her chest. "So..."

Rosella met her eyes and lifted one eyebrow.

"What are you doing here?" Camilla asked, studying her fingernails.

"I left a note," Rosella said. Tugging her leg free of Camilla, she stood. Her wet clothes stuck to her, cold and dirty. A chill or worse could set in if she didn't get dry. She pulled her cloak around her to stay off the wind.

She scanned the trail and the clearing ahead. The patch of earth was void of trees, but the forest surrounded it, and the route shot off in two directions. She didn't remember a fork before in the path, but maybe she'd been too angry and grief-stricken the last time. Or hadn't noticed it with the others she'd traveled with. Unlikely, but possible…

"A note?" Bridgette said, stepping in front of Camilla. "You think a note was enough for what you did?"

"It is my job to take care of you," Rosella sighed. The rain continued and darker clouds stretched across the clearing's sky. They'd have to camp for the night and then she'd send her sisters back. She cursed at losing hours of travel, but she couldn't go on with them and she didn't want to risk sending them back so late, especially with the possibility of wolves or storms. "How did you know where to follow me?"

"Be back in a few weeks," Giselle recited, hand to her chest. "I have a plan. Eat well. Here are a few coins for food."

Rosella looked down. The coins wouldn't be enough, but it's what she had to provide them. Her sisters could collect fruit and timber for two weeks.

"The only place a few weeks down this path is the city." Cold blue eyes pierced Rosella. "Why were you going to the city?"

Rosella rubbed a hand over her face, smearing dirt and rain through her hair.

"Roz, what do you think you're doing?" Bridgette placed her hands on her shoulders.

"I'm going to get us the funds."

"How?' the three demanded in unison.

"I have a plan."

"Share it, ol' wise one," Camilla said.

Rosella considered lying to them, but they'd see through it. It'd only hurt them and cause more questions. She finally relented a partial truth. "I was going to sell something."

"We have something of value?" Giselle asked and looked at Camilla and Bridgette.

Bridgette shook her head while staring at Rosella, her brow pinched.

Camilla's face lit up. "Wait! I know! You're going to hawk the locket!" She punched the air and danced in place.

Giselle and Bridgette stared at Rosella. She kept her face stoic despite the heat clawing at her.

"No," Bridgette said, pulling out the word. "That's not what she's doing. It isn't ours."

"What?" Camilla stopped with her arms still in the air. "What else does she have? What would we have of value?"

Camilla's face darkened. Her mouth slackened and she shook her head no, wagging a finger at Rosella before the words tumbled out. "Uh-uh, no way. No, you're not!"

Camilla's shriek filled the air. Her fingers balled into fists.

"What?" Giselle asked. She stepped closer to Rosella as if the secret would divulge itself on Rosella's person.

"No, Roz, no." Bridgette crowded around Rosella and enveloped her in a tight hug.

"What?" Giselle's shrill cry racked her frame.

"Mom's ring," Camilla whispered, staring at the ground.

"Roz, no," Giselle said. "You can't. That's all we have left."

Rosella swiped at the tears forming at her eyes, but it didn't stop them from tumbling down her cheeks. "I have to," she choked out.

"No, no, you don't." Bridgette shook her head.

"Mom wouldn't want that," Camilla said.

"Yes, she would," Rosella said. A bitter laugh sliced through her tears. "She wouldn't want us hanging on to a ring when it could feed us."

"But—" Giselle started.

"You were barely seven, Giselle. She loved you fiercely."

"I know," Giselle sniffed. "I feel it in your embrace and care."

"Gah," Camilla said, stamping the ground and swatting at tears. "This is stupid."

"I can marry Benson, sell our land for pittance, or hawk the ring. Do you have a preference?"

Camilla shrugged. "I still say hawk the locket."

"Agreed," Giselle breathed. "Better than mom's ring."

Rosella shot Camilla and Giselle a dark look. They weren't their father.

A gust of chilled wind skittered through the path, rustling droplets from the leaves.

"What are we going to do for the night?" Bridgette asked. Her gray eyes took in the surroundings.

The other sisters surveyed around them.

"What did you three do last night?" Rosella turned to them. She'd have to face it sooner or later, anyway.

The three stared at the ground.

"What?"

The three continued to stare.

"How did you get here? What did you do?" Rosella gritted out. The answer was likely what she already suspected.

"We may have borrowed horses," Giselle said, rubbing her neck.

"Borrowed?" Rosella looked down the empty trail. "What happened to them?"

"The Trible's horses are old ninnies. When it was breakfast time, they took off back home." Camilla waved a hand in the direction.

With luck, they made it home before they were tracked back to her sisters. Otherwise, she'd hear about it when she returned. With the harvest finished, they shouldn't miss them for the short time. Hopefully.

"We waited for you to come back yesterday, and when you didn't, we left at night and traveled until the horses wanted to go home." Giselle rolled her eyes. "Should have let me talk to the groom. I could have gotten us better mounts."

Bridgette glowered at her. "They were just in the pasture. We don't need witnesses or more rumors."

Camilla waved her off. "They'll talk about Giselle, anyway."

Rosella sighed and walked toward the embankment and started collecting kindling. She wasn't shocked that they'd done it, but that she hadn't thought ahead of time that they would. They could never leave well enough alone. "We'll camp for the night and you three can head back in the morning."

"No," they said in unison.

"You can't start back tonight, it's too dangerous," Rosella said. "It's dark and raining."

"No, we're not leaving you," Bridgette said. "You can be headstrong all you want, but you're our sister. You aren't going on these paths alone."

"You know it's dangerous." Giselle scowled at Rosella. "Just like you wouldn't want one of us doing it. Even though Bridgette and Camilla are *adults*."

Camilla stuck her tongue out.

"Sometimes." Giselle choked a laugh.

"We're going." Camilla folded her arms over her chest. "It's final."

Rosella growled. "You need to watch the house and the store."

"No one's buying," Giselle said. She flinched at Rosella's expression.

"Besides, we may have talked to Benson and handled it already." Camilla clasped her hands behind her back as she walked in circles.

"What did you say to him?" Rosella sighed.

The three sisters looked at each other and giggled.

"What?" Rosella said, dreading their response.

"We may have mentioned needing to go to the city." Bridgette shrugged and averted her eyes.

"Did he ask why?" Rosella asked.

"Oh, yes," Camilla confirmed with a nod and roguish smile.

Rosella waited, but when she didn't elaborate, asked, "What did you tell him?"

"That we had to do some shopping." Giselle smiled at Rosella, a small blush darkening her cheeks.

"I'm not going to like this, am I?" Rosella moaned.

"We may have hinted that you are a traditionalist..." Camilla said.

"Okay, but I'm not."

"Well, he may be under the impression you wanted to look at gowns he could buy you," Giselle added.

"Gowns for what?" Rosella asked as reality set in. "He thinks I'm looking at wedding dresses?"

The sisters giggled. Camilla said, "He may think you are meeting with a tailor to discuss it."

"And he offered to watch the store so you could help me..." Rosella mumbled.

They nodded brightly at her.

"And when we return?"

"You didn't like anything." Camilla waved her concerns away.

"So, we'll just keep lying?" Rosella said.

"Do you want to look at dresses?" Bridgette said with a sly smile. "We can while we're there."

Rosella sighed and rolled her eyes.

"And it's not lying saying you didn't like anything," Giselle offered.

"He'll make sure everything is okay, or he knows you won't want to marry him." Camilla gave Rosella a bright smile.

"Did you say that?" Rosella asked, dropping the lumber she'd collected for a fire. Heat raced through her veins and her heart thudded in her chest.

"No," Giselle said scandalized, her hand on her chest as she fought a smile.

"I did," Camilla said, raising her hand. "I said you'd hate his guts and marry his brother if anything happened to the store."

Rosella stared at Camilla, mouth agape. "But his brother is fifteen."

"So? I'm sure his brother would go along with it."

"Benson seemed convinced by it." Bridgette shrugged and piled brush together for bedding.

Even if she wanted to throttle them for leaving the store and following her through the woods, a part of her heart swelled at the gesture. They'd devised a way to keep their home safe, even if it was a lie. Her sisters wanted to be with her. With the way events in town were turning, it was possible for one or more of them to be married soon. This could be their last adventure together, just the four of them.

"So, we go together?" Rosella asked the trees, realizing she wouldn't win the fight anyway.

"Yep," her sisters said in unison.

Chapter Eight

ROSELLA WOKE WITH A START. THE FIRE WAS BARELY EMBERS and a cold wind smacked her in the face and tangled in her hair. A howl in the distance pierced the night and was answered by more, the sound echoing in her veins.

"Girls," Rosella hissed as she scrambled to her feet.

"We heard," Bridgette answered from the dark.

"What do we do?" Giselle asked, her voice small in the vast wilderness.

"We lost the fire. We need it back," Rosella said.

A howl sliced the air again, closer than the last, sending tingles racing down her spine.

"I don't think we have time," Bridgette said.

"Did you bring any weapons?" Rosella grabbed her rock and knife in her belt and moved toward the fire.

"You know I carry a sword and shield with me everywhere," Camilla drawled. "Right here next to my unending pot of stew."

"Not now," Rosella said. She blew into the embers, trying to no avail to rekindle the fire. The orange glows bulged and darkened.

The brush swayed as something moved in it, and branches cracked beneath the weight of a creature. Chills ran down her spine. Rosella abandoned the fire and grabbed her satchel. It was all the sisters had.

"Roz, what do we do?" Bridgette moved closer, fear tinging her words.

"Grab hands, and don't let go." Rosella wrapped her cloak around her hand and grabbed a hot log.

She jumped when a hand grabbed her other arm.

"Does everyone have another's arm or hand?" Rosella asked.

"Yes," they responded.

"We're going to the path," she said, more confident than she felt.

"Where is it?" Bridgette asked.

Rosella swore as she strained to see in the faint moonlight. The trees grew close together, blocking their escape and depriving her of her bearings. The embers provided no additional support.

She took a deep breath and sent out a prayer. She tugged on the arm holding her and bolted away from the snapping twigs. Her sisters' heavy breaths filled her ears.

The branches clawed at her face and arms. Blood and rain lathered her skin. She closed her eyes to protect them since she couldn't see, anyway. Thrusting her arm out to protect her face and help avoid trees, she stumbled over roots and brush, which snagged her leggings and gashed her legs. Her body and lungs screamed for her to stop, but the primal drive to protect her sisters kept pushing her feet forward.

"Call off," Rosella said to stay the fear crawling up her throat.

"Camilla." Directly behind her.

"Bridgette." To her left.

"Giselle." Sounding farther back.

"Everyone have a hand?"

Three yeses called back.

Relief coursed through her. She still had them. She didn't notice when her feet found stable ground until she slid on the wet dirt road and stopped to get her bearings. The clatter of rocks rubbing together drowned out the other sounds.

"We're on the path," she said with disbelief.

"What direction do we head?" Bridgette asked, her voice close to Rosella.

A howl cut through the night again. The swish of branches sounded around them.

Tension settled on her skin and lit her nerves.

"Away from *them,*" Rosella said and pulled her sisters forward.

AHEAD LOOMED A MASSIVE CASTLE. ITS RUINS CLUNG TO THE mountainside, like shards piercing the sky, as the earth worked to reincorporate it back. The gray stonework of the structure twisted into fiendish creatures. The overgrown path was riddled with plants and odd human creations like wheels, planters, and statues.

Rosella stared at the isolated fortress. The mammoth structure should have tales and tongues wagging in the village. It was a two-day walk. Less on a horse. And yet. A shiver stole through her. It shouldn't be there. Or, more likely, *they* shouldn't be there.

A break in the clouds allowed the moon to shine down on it, the deep shadows drawing it more into the feral terrain.

Another shiver stole down her and her heart hammered in her chest. Where had she led her sisters?

"That place has to be haunted," Camilla said, staring at it.

Rosella stopped herself from nodding in agreement. She didn't want to feed into their fears or fantasies. It was just a castle. Where it shouldn't be.

She shook her head. There were probably a lot of things in the forest she didn't know about.

"Think we outran them?" Gisella asked, panting.

A howl sliced the night.

"Nope," Camilla shot back, rubbing her arms. Her eyes returned to the relic. "Ghosts or wolves? I vote ghosts unless they're banshees..."

"Do we go?" Bridgette interrupted Camilla. Her fingers tightened around Rosella's.

Rosella shuddered at the sight.

A call sounded closer. Wolves meant certain harm and likely death. The castle... Childish stories flittered in her mind.

Longer and closer, a second call cut the air. Without thought, she started moving toward the castle. To the human construct meant to protect them against the wild elements.

She wasn't sure they could even get to the castle with the rain-slicked path, and if they did, what forest creatures had already claimed it?

"Did we know a castle was out here?" Giselle asked, jogging next to her. Her teeth chattered.

Rosella shrugged and looked at the other sisters. She ran a hand along her cheek and a thumb against her scar.

"Do we know anything about the area, really?" Rosella said, "We only left town for dad, and that was years ago, and we had chaperones." It was more to ease her own mind, but even if she forgot a path, they should have known a castle was there. The path would need to be wide enough for carts. As the path they traveled now was. A castle wasn't something the town would keep secret. Nor something she would have forgotten, even with everything that happened with their dad. Nothing about the path felt familiar.

"So, some creepy castle is out here, just off the path, and we didn't know." Camilla's eyes lit up in the clouded moonlight as a smile grew. "I bet there is stuff inside."

"With the ghosts?" Giselle chided.

"The more ghosts, the better the stuff." Camilla rubbed her hands.

"What type of stuff?" Bridgette asked.

"Stuff we can hawk," Camilla squealed and sprinted.

"It's abandoned, I'm sure they took their stuff with them, or bandits cleared it out." Rosella cast her eyes back at the forest. Unease slithered down her spine. Too many childhood stories challenged her reason.

"It's worth looking." Camilla scoffed at Rosella and waved her off. "I bet it's drier inside there too."

Another howl sounded, closer than the last.

Rosella's stomach twisted and fear curled through her muscles. She felt the eyes tracking here even though only inky blackness surrounded them.

"Come on," Giselle said, running to catch up to Camilla.

"This is a bad idea," Rosella said to Bridgette.

"Yes, it is," Bridgette agreed as she sprinted to follow Giselle and Camilla. "But I don't feel much like getting eaten by wolves."

Rosella looked back at the forest below them, the vast expanses cloaking the land, masking its predators and secrets. She knew what lay behind. Wolves, physical and metaphorical.

A few hours in the castle, even an unknown, abandoned one, shouldn't cause trouble.

Rosella picked her pace up and paused at the rusted iron gate they strained to open. Intricate swirls raced along the top. Although close together, each iron rod twisted into a perfect spiral.

The gate was locked, and she questioned if it was a sign. Tingles raced down her spine as another howl filled the night.

"Help us," Camilla grunted.

Rosella studied the lock and pulled the hooked piece. Parts of the rusted iron disintegrated in her hand, leaving the lock dangling from the chain.

"Nice job," Camilla said and chucked the lock backward before pulling on the chains to create a gap big enough for the sisters to slip into.

"Come on." Giselle ducked under Camilla's arm and stepped onto the grounds.

Rosella turned back toward the forest and noticed the wolves slinking up the drive, their eyes shimmering in the moonlight as their bodies blended into the darkness. She hurried under the chain and helped Camilla shut the gate tight again.

The wolves stopped a few yards back and sat on their haunches, watching them. Their heads tilted in mockery. Then their eyes flickered to the castle. If possible, their mouths gaped in amusement at them. Without a look back at the ladies, they turned around and ran back to the woods.

"That's not ominous or anything," Rosella muttered.

Broken statues and toppled structures littered the overgrown court-yard. Darkened stone blocks and planters swirled in the yard. At greener times, it would have been dazzling with roses or other blooms. Walkways danced into the distance, with stone benches dotting the way. In full bloom, she could have lost herself in the gardens. Now it looked like a cemetery of forgotten days.

The castle twisted and turned with spirals and turrets. The grayed stone absorbed the moonlight, reflecting nothing as it stole the light of the area. Monstrous creatures encircled the roofs, battlements, and gutters. Though stone, Rosella had to shrug off the feeling that the eyes seemed to follow them.

Rosella's gaze swept over the vast grounds in its entirety. It was hard to imagine such a place could exist so close to town, less than a two-day walk—run without a horse—and she'd never known it existed.

A castle this size should have lands for miles and miles. Even an abandoned one should pique the interest of the town, as a means of wayward travelers or as warnings of despair used to keep the town in line. Not an unknown tombstone. What ghosts lingered inside? Instead of chiding herself for indulging in fanciful thoughts, the reality of the unknown settled hard in her stomach.

The previous couple of days flickered in her mind. The beggar woman she'd never met. The milk. The plentitude of biscuits and jam. The changes to the once-familiar forest. A shaky breath rattled her frame. It was just one night. Then they'd find their path back to what they knew.

"How long has this been abandoned?" Giselle asked, stopping to stare at a gargoyle with a fanged smile.

"Could be a decade or a century or more," Rosella muttered. "The earth hasn't really reclaimed big sections."

"Maybe it's afraid to." Camilla leaned her head back to stare at the spiraling towers that speared into the dark sky. More gargoyle statues dotted the towers.

"We could just camp here," Rosella said, eyes to the ground. Its bleak cement graveyard looked more welcoming than the castle.

A burst of lightning lit the sky and thunder rumbled, the sound vibrating through them. Clouds drifted in front of the sliver of the moon, casting them into darkness.

"I'd rather not," Camilla said and started for the castle.

"It's in ruins, the roof could fall on us, there could be rats or wildlife, or..." Rosella started but the sky split open, drenching them in a downpour and silencing her reasons.

"Yes, but we'll catch pneumonia out here." Bridgette pulled Rosella behind her toward the entrance. Her cold fingers silenced Rosella's retort.

The girls tromped up the steps. A wooden door wider than their home stood proud and strong against the weather.

"It's probably locked," Rosella said wistfully. She nestled under the overhang out of the rain.

"Do your touch thing again." Camilla nodded toward the door while wiggling her hands at the lock.

"I don't have a touch thing," Rosella growled.

"Try it anyway," Camilla said and nudged her gently.

"Yeah, at least try," Giselle whimpered. She wrapped her arms around her torso and shivered in the onslaught. "It'll get us out of the rain and wind."

Rosella grimaced and reached for the handle. The door gave no protest as she pushed against it and swung it open. A crash of thunder sounded behind them accompanied by a bolt of lightning that flooded the marble floor of the entrance before shuddering it again in darkness.

Silence descended on them. Rosella cast a glance back at the dark woods and the dangers that lurked, and then at the still castle.

It was one night.

And it was dry.

Her sisters waited for her to enter before crossing the threshold. Their footsteps and breaths were the only sound.

Closing the door behind them, a muted crash of thunder sounded, but the castle stood solid. Blackness enveloped them.

"I have my tinderbox." Bridgette's voice was small in the grand space.

"Is there a torch or wooden piece?" Rosella asked. Her own tinderbox was in her pack.

When another tangled vein of lightning raced across the sky, visible through the high windows, the room brightened momentarily.

"I see one," Giselle said. "Shuffle to the left when it lightnings again."

Once the torch was lit, Giselle swung it around to expose the space.

"Wow." Camilla's voice echoed into the void, calling back from the recesses.

"Sh," Rosella hissed. Her own hushed voice echoed off the walls.

Before them was a grand foyer. Marble floors spanned before them, uncluttered and ready for guests. A set of winding staircases flanked the room. Dark carpets ran the length of the steps. Shrouded paintings lined the walls, and metal lamps reflected the glimmer of moonlight between the clouds as the storm rolled through. Rosella's eye snagged on the oil still in the polished glass. A whisp of rain tinged the air, not dampness or stale air. Only the rumble of the storm and their breathing filled the space.

"We should start a fire," Bridgette said, eyeing Giselle as she shivered. Bridgette wrapped her shawl around Giselle's shoulders and drew her into a hug.

"Let's find some wood," Camila said. She rubbed her hands together as a large smile grew on her face.

Rosella looked around, her mind spinning from the day. Her imagination heightening her fear as she remembered fairytales of her youth. The ones her parents had told her to keep her from the woods and rivers. Creatures that lurked, waiting for humans, danced in her mind. They'd crossed into a forbidden area. An area barred, locked, tucked away, and forgotten. One she had seen the signs about. Ones that didn't make sense that they existed.

She just needed to keep her sisters safe for a few hours until the rains stopped. It wouldn't be that long.

"Let's find a fireplace," Rosella said. She steered her sisters deeper into the room but continued to watch the walls around them.

"Why?" Camilla said. "The place is abandoned. We can bust up furniture and burn it anywhere."

Rosella sighed. They'd mock her, but her core protested the action. "No, it's not our stuff."

"Oh, come on, Roz. It's garbage. People abandoned it."

"It doesn't make it ours," Rosella said. "Even if they're gone, we can respect what remains. If something is completely trashed, then maybe.

Besides, a fireplace is built to contain a fire and we'll do less damage. It'll be safer."

Camilla rolled her eyes at Rosella's restrictive manners but clung to Rosella's hand as they crept through the space.

At first, they circled the room, peering into the voids. A hallway encircled the room. The towering walls absorbed their sounds and muffled the rains.

If they screamed, no one would hear them. Rosella swallowed. No one would hear them outside, either. At least they were dry. A chill had settled in the space, but there was no dampness. Nothing that hinted at years of being unkempt. As they stood together, no other noises greeted but the faint pattering of rain and thunder. No animals stirred. No dripping water from the rain.

"Let's stick close to the front door," Rosella said, her gaze again drifting to it.

Crossing into the hallway, their torch's light reflected off the shined marble designed to illuminate the dark space. Silver-framed pictures glinted in the light, but the images remained in shadow.

"There better not be eyes in those paintings following us." Camilla whispered. Her fingers tightened on Rosella's arm and she stepped closer into her side.

"Sh," Bridgette scolded.

They paused before casting light into the first room. The arched door was large enough for all four to cross into, but instead, Giselle swung the torch in the space as a test.

The room had long tables and chairs covered in cloths. Cold clung to the stone walls. A faint hint of cookies and tea tickled her nose. Her imagination pulling her back to her mother's estate. The room was so similar in design, she was imaging scents from her youth. She shook her head. The aroma still lingered, the memory strong.

"It has a fireplace," Bridgette offered, though none of them stepped into the space.

"Let's keep looking," Camilla said. "I'd prefer more comfortable furniture."

Rosella' cocked an eyebrow but didn't argue.

A crash of thunder sounded above. Without a window in the hall, no light followed but the force rattled in Rosella's bones. Her neck hairs raised for a moment. She turned her head, expecting... She didn't know what. A person? A ghost? But the hall was empty.

"It's just the storm," Bridgette said and tugged Rosella forward.

She cast another look around, her nerves still alight, but it was just her imagination.

Another opening loomed ahead. Giselle swung the torch into the space. A dozen armored men reflected her light. The silver beings towered above, weapons at the draw.

Rosella's sisters' scream pierced the night. Her own shaking hand clutched at her heart. But the forms didn't move. Their posed frames stared forward, unseeing.

"It's just statues," Giselle gasped.

"Uh huh," Camilla agreed. She swallowed and eased her nails from Rosella's hand. "If there are ghosts, she just woke them up."

The sisters paused. Nothing sounded. No shuffling. Or voices.

"It's abandoned," Bridgette said, though her voice quavered with uncertainty.

"Do we keep looking?" Giselle whimpered.

"I'm definitely not sleeping in this hallway," Camilla said. "I'd take the tables over these things."

"We'll keep looking." Rosella extended her hand for the torch.

Giselle wordlessly handed it over.

Walking ahead of her sisters, Rosella swung the torch into each space before her sisters sided up next to her.

Finally, they found a cozy room with a fireplace as the storm eased. The vaulted ceilings towered above them in white marble. Heavy curtains framed the windows but had been left ajar as if someone had been watching out of them at one point. Through the slit, the forest was visible below as it sprawled off into the distance, the moon unfurling behind the remnants of the storm, bathing the land in an ethereal glow. The furniture stood draped in sheets like the other rooms, the rugs worn with time, and a fireplace sat center of the room. Rosella squinted at the arrangement. The room was dim with the moonlight streaming through the windows, but it looked clean. Protected, but not abandoned.

"Shouldn't it be dusty?" she asked.

"You're complaining it is too clean?" Camilla asked with her hands on her hips as she took in the numerous treasures around the room.

"Isn't it odd?" Rosella ran her finger over the surface of a table. There wasn't a trail of dust, and her finger was clean. As if someone had cleaned it that day.

"No more odd than finding an abandoned castle while being chased by a pack of wolves," Camilla said. Her eyes cased the room, delight flickering behind them.

"Sit down," Bridgette said, leading Giselle to the hearth and rubbing her shoulders. "We'll get a fire going."

"There's already wood in it," Camilla said, disappointed as she eyed up the furniture.

"How is that possible?" Giselle chattered.

"It must be left over," Bridgette said. She frowned as she met Rosella's gaze.

Rosella's jaw ticked. The wood didn't look brittle with age, nor were there signs of rot.

She ignored the knot in her stomach as she pulled her satchel around and dug out her flint. It'd just be a few hours and they'd leave. The wood was already there and intended for a fire. They weren't doing anything too wrong. Not much different than the wood Giselle found.

Abandoned—Rosella swallowed around a lump in throat—or not, they had nowhere else to go in the storm and they wouldn't stay long. They'd be gone with the first light.

"Look at us." Camilla plopped down on a sofa and leaned her arms against the frame. "In our own castle."

"It's not ours," Rosella said.

"Hey, it could be," Camilla said. A smile lit up her face and she snapped her fingers. "It's abandoned. We could claim it!"

"I don't think it works that way."

"Why not? Finders, keepers."

"How'd we get food out here?"

"Oh," Camilla said, slumping back but then shot up. "Maybe there's a garden. We all know how to hunt."

"If we have to sell our land, maybe," Rosella lied to stop the discussion.

"Just think about it," Camilla said. Once again leaning back, she gestured to the walls. "We could fix it up, hold grand balls, tell Benson he can be your butler instead of your husband."

Giselle chuckled and sank in closer to the fire, rubbing her hands together.

"Do we have any idea how to get to town or the city from here?" Bridgette asked, sitting next to Camilla on the sofa.

Rosella looked back to the windows. She shook her head. "I'm not even sure what path we landed on. I didn't know there was more than one path in the woods. It forked at the clearing, but I don't know how many options or what direction we headed in."

"What will we do?" Bridgette asked, snuggling into Camilla for warmth.

"When morning breaks, we'll figure it out," Rosella said. "For now, sleep." She nodded to the plush furniture and ran a hand through her hair. Even though they shouldn't be there, a part of her was glad her sisters were. She'd stand guard while they slept.

Chapter Nine

THE RAIN PATTERED ON THE ROOF, THE SLOW RHYTHMIC dance reminding Rosella of home. Her mom hummed in the kitchen and her sisters nestled with her in bed. The delicious scent of cinnamon and tea twisted in the air, taunting her nose. She snuggled deeper into the plush bed, burying her face in the velvet fabric.

She loved the dream.

Then she heard the giggles. She growled into the pillow at her sisters for disturbing her dream. When the giggles grew into laughter, she sat up. Her surroundings swam into view. Reality settled on her, hard and unforgiving. She was sleeping on a sofa in a castle with her sisters. They had escaped the wolves and storm. The weak rays of sunlight through gray rain clouds seeped through the stained-glass windows, the colors a kaleidoscope of shapes and collages on the floor.

She rubbed her eyes and looked around. The room in the morning light was grander than she realized. Only the sofas she and her sisters slept on were uncovered, but the other sofas with intricate arches and swoops draped in velvet covers instead of linen spoke of wealth. Art dotted the walls, grand oil paintings of the once-royal inhabitants, their eyes assessing and disapproving. Gold and silver statues and relics were displayed around the room. It hadn't been looted, even though it appeared vacant for years. It looked as if the castle slumbered and would awake at any moment to a bustle of activity.

Her sisters, already awake, milled around. They happily chatted and giggled as they moved about the room examining the treasures. Sleep still clung to her eyes, but Rosella stretched, feeling refreshed. She hadn't slept that well in years.

"Good morning, sleepyhead," Camilla sang as she swung a sword. The long blade sliced through the air with ease. The thick handle spoke of functional use more than just aesthetics although a carved sun and moon decorated the handle.

Rosella paused. Slowly, her eyes swept the room, taking in her sisters beyond their normal actions and noticed they were holding items. Items that didn't belong to them.

"Where'd you get the sword?" Rosella asked, afraid for the answer.

"I found it," Camilla said.

"Where?" Rosella gritted between her teeth.

"In a castle," Camilla sang and parried an invisible foe.

"Camilla," Rosella's voice echoed in the home.

Camilla shot her a dirty look. "Geez, Roz, don't wake the ghosts up."

"What are you ladies doing?" Rosella asked. Beyond what her sisters held, they had various items piled in the room.

"Well, we were talking while you slept," Bridgette said. She twisted her fingers together and licked her lips.

"Oh great, I'm so going to love this."

"Just listen," Bridgette said, sitting down by her and patting her leg.

Rosella shifted to look at her with brows raised.

"The castle is abandoned. There is no sign of life. No one will miss this stuff. We won't take much, but enough that you don't have to sell mom's ring, sell our home, or marry Benson."

"Isn't it odd it hasn't been pilfered?" Rosella stared at the various treasures. There were too many warnings. Too many odd happenings. "Shouldn't looters have stripped it, or the owners taken it with them?"

"Yes, a little, but it could have been forgotten or a plague took out the area." Bridgette shrugged. "It has to have been years, maybe decades. It's only a couple days' ride from our village and no one has mentioned a castle, abandoned or not. So, honestly, who will miss the stuff?"

"It's not ours," Rosella started.

"True, but it's no one's, like the lumber," Bridgette said. "It was on someone's land but not really belonging to anyone."

"Lumber is from the earth. This belonged to someone." Rosella sighed and rolled her head back and forth. Her sisters made valid points, but it wasn't right. It was too easy. Too tempting.

"Who left it, then?" Giselle sauntered over to join her sisters.

"It doesn't matter." Rosella rubbed her forehead. "The weather still looks rough, but maybe we can find something in the yard we could use for cover."

"So, you're okay with us taking from the yard but not the house?" Giselle asked as she plopped down onto the sofa holding a silver candelabra. The polished stem had a fluted design and delicate swirls for legs. The center head had small, embedded gems, to reflect color in the space. Each of the four arms held a similar head. The gems shimmered on Giselle's fair hand. The piece would fetch far more than their mother's ring.

Rosella sighed and shook her head. "I don't know. The weather could destroy anything out there. It looked like mostly rubble, anyway. It was behind a locked gate, but still left to rot in the elements. The stuff in here was behind a locked door. Who just leaves all this stuff around?"

"Locked door?" Camilla scoffed. She plopped down on the sofa, sweat beaded on her brow. "It just opened."

Rosella glared at her.

"Finder's keepers?" Giselle sang.

With a huff, Rosella turned her ire toward Giselle.

Bridgette scoffed. "You're also just playing semantics. Locked door versus locked gate. Everything here, outside and inside, was abandoned."

But the house didn't look abandoned.

Rosella's throat tightened as she took in the undisturbed treasures, the treasures her sisters had piled to take, and the general cleanliness of the room. Remembering the wood in the fireplace ready to be lit, she shoved off the blankets. Unease gnawed at her stomach. They should get started.

"This isn't right," Rosella said, shaking her head, trying to figure out the scene.

"As I said before, they probably caught pneumonia or something," Bridgette said. She sat up primly on the sofa and folded her hands. "If they passed away, there'd be no one to know."

"So, there're bodies here?" Camilla sat up, rubbing her hands. Her eyes skimmed to the darkened entryways that led to stairs.

"You're not looking for them," Bridgette said, pointing a finger at Camilla.

"Why?" Camilla pouted.

"That's morbid and you could catch something." Bridgette shuddered.

"Like what? They're probably all decomposed by the looks of the place. And there isn't a smell, so it's been a long time."

"Then why do you want to find bones?" Giselle asked.

"I don't know." Camilla shrugged and flipped her messy braid. "I just do."

"No," the other three said in unison.

Camilla stomped her foot but swung her gaze around the room.

"Then let's show Rosella our treasures," Camila said, clapping her hands and jumping to her feet.

"I'd rather not see," Rosella said. She started looking around for their few possessions to pack.

Camilla ignored her as she moved to the pile. "You've seen the sword I found. I couldn't find the jewels, but there is a picture of people wearing them, so they might be here. I'm guessing on one of the bodies." She raised her eyebrows.

"You went from robbing an abandoned castle to grave robbing?" Rosella asked.

"They aren't in the ground!"

"I'm with Rosella," Giselle said. "Not if they're on bodies."

"You're no fun," Camilla said. She lifted a golden cat and patted its belly. "Well, I also have this. It's kinda ugly, but it's heavy and I'm guessing solid gold. So, I'm looking past the ugliness and calling it a keeper to hawk."

Rosella started to protest, but Giselle jumped up. "That cat's fine, but I found a clock and two old-looking swords in a display box. You have to see the detail."

Bridgette and Camilla both leaned over to view it and made oohing sounds. The ornamental pieces held shined blades with silver and gold lacework around the pummel. Elaborate designs were set into the handle.

"Ladies." Rosella dug her nails into her palms. "These aren't ours."

"We heard you the first few dozen times," Camilla said. She flicked a hand dismissively in her direction and then picked up one of the rapiers. She swished it in the air and lunged forward at an imaginary foe.

"What about you, Bridgette?" Giselle asked, beaming over her treasures. She plopped back down on the sofa, spreading her arms behind her in triumph.

"Well," Bridgette breathed. "I found an old room, but it only had an entire set of silver."

Bridgette squealed as she pulled a blanket off a cart with a complete silver tea set.

Giselle and Camilla shrieked and jumped up to examine the items.

"We'll be set for years!" Giselle said and danced around the room. Camilla jumped into her line and, grabbing her arms, took the lead in an awkward waltz.

Rosella stared at her sisters. They were right. They could take the stuff and be done, but it was in someone's home behind a locked gate. Behind a locked door. A place that looked recently cleaned and had fresh firewood. A home that was odder with each new discovery. They weren't their father. They had their own means to pay their way without theft. They needed to vacate and leave the items behind.

She rubbed her eyes and stared around the room. The possibilities of the treasures were endless. They'd never have need or want again with just a few items and shrewd spending. Was it stealing? The place was abandoned, even if clean and odd. They hadn't heard or seen a person, there weren't smells outside of her dream that implied anyone had been there recently. But they also hadn't found any creatures scurrying about as she expected with the dilapidated exterior. Everything was clean and proper as if expecting the master to return at any moment.

Nothing really made sense other than the fact that it wasn't theirs.

They had one thing that was.

A ray of light flickered across the floor, the sun trying to peek out behind the rain clouds. They needed to get going, rain or not, if they wanted to make it to the city and back in time to protect their home. Their timeline wouldn't change even if they had veered off the path.

She turned around to face her sisters and braced for the fight.

"Are you three packed up?" she asked as she checked the contents of her knapsack and retrieved her flint.

"What? Why?" Camilla said, bringing Giselle twirling toward her.

"The storm is letting up. We should get going while there's still light to cover major ground."

"We need to find something to carry these items," Bridgette said. "Maybe there is a wheelbarrow or cart? Or maybe I should only bring some of the pieces to sell now. I can pick up the rest when we return home in case we need them in the future."

"Oh, that's smart!" Camilla said. "We can grab more on the way back. I bet we could buy a carriage and horse with what we take now and load it up on the return."

Giselle nodded in agreement. "We can finally have our own horse!"

"Are you hearing yourselves?" Rosella screamed. "This is not our stuff. We can't take it. For all you know, the stuff is haunted."

The three sisters peered down at it. Bridgette toed the silver set with her boot.

"Then we'll just need to sell it quickly," Camilla said, balling her hands on her hips and lifting her chin.

"No, no, no, no," Rosella chanted. A sliver of dread wove through her veins and settled like lead in her stomach. They were going to be more difficult than she expected. They saw the lure of the wealth and not the reality of taking it and explaining it. "It isn't ours and we need to leave."

"I say it's three against one," Camilla said.

Bridgette and Giselle flanked her sides, the three tilting their heads eerily in unison.

"Yeah, three against one," Giselle mimed.

"Besides," Bridgette said, smiling friendly at Rosella. "Who would miss it?"

"I would," a deep, masculine voice called.

Chapter Ten

Rosella whirled around, facing the entryway of the room. The rising sun did little to alleviate the shadows beyond the perimeter of the windows. The cloaked corners shifted with shadows descending toward them. Twisting arms reached for them, as if the furniture had come alive.

Camilla screamed, her voice shocking the others and echoing into the deep caverns of the castle.

"Who—who are you?" Rosella managed as she moved to stand in front of her sisters.

"The owner of the castle," the massive form responded. He kept to the shadows with a cloak draped over him despite the fact that the castle wasn't drafty. His hefty form blocked the doorframe and their escape. His breath heaved in his chest, each breath like a swish of a clock's pendulum toward their demise. Only shadows covered his face.

"We were just leaving," Rosella said, pushing her sisters back. "We wanted a reprieve from the storm. We'll grab our stuff and be on our way."

Camilla's wide eyes met hers. Her mouth moved, but no words came out. Her other sisters stood straight, their gazes locked forward.

Rosella's eyes flickered to Camilla's sword tossed haphazardly onto the sofa. She took a step toward it while gesturing for her sisters to back up.

"You aren't going anywhere." He bobbed his head, the billows of the cloak fluttering around him. Although mostly concealed, his eyes glimmered as they stared only at Rosella.

The shadows shifted around him as one form pulled from the darkness, but he remained shrouded. The new form was sinewy but had a wide chest and thick arms. Following it, a swarm of shadowed individuals moved to her sisters.

"No!" Rosella screamed and lunged for the sword. The cold metal was heavy in her hand. It was forged for battle, not decoration, stronger and better built than the one she'd practiced with since the day their father was led away in chains. She held it out, ready to strike.

Faster than humanly possible, dozens swarmed around the sisters.

Rosella swung the sword. The whipping sound sliced the air.

"NOW!" the master roared. The animalistic sound froze Rosella's blood and filled the room, echoing around them.

Eight forms lunged at her, staying clear of the sword. The others snatched at her sisters, a half a dozen per sister.

Her sisters screamed as they were dragged from the room.

Fear and hatred clogged her throat. Her vision tunneled, the edges dissolving to red. She sucked in a wobbly breath. Her eyes darted between those surrounding her. She'd never killed before, but for her sisters' lives, she would. They wouldn't be harmed if she still held breath. Even if it meant she'd crossed the line to becoming her father.

One shadow whispered something into the master's ear. A snarl rippled on his lips, but his yellow eyes glimmered.

The figure bobbed their head at Rosella.

"Drop the sword," the master growled.

"No!"

"Drop the sword, and my staff will see you out." Each word was forced through clenched teeth. His eyes narrowed on her.

"Out?" she repeated before thinking better of it.

"Take my kindness while it is offered. You're free to go."

Her breath caught in her chest. Did he mean...

"My sisters—"

"Are my prisoners."

Prisoners. Jail. Just as she feared.

Her hate-filled eyes moved to the form. Her mind reeled at what to say. What to do. They'd broken into his home. Used his stuff. Her mind raced, wondering where her sisters had gone and how they'd missed a person living there. Multiple people living there, she thought, as more shadows separated into human forms. What else had they done?

"If they broke something, we'll fix it," Rosella offered.

They couldn't end up like their father.

He said nothing, but his piercing gaze remained locked on her.

Rosella swung her gaze toward the eight still around her, out of reach of her sword. They, too, wore thick cloaks despite the warm temperatures, but their hoods appeared fur-lined to cover their faces. As they entered the sun's light, she realized the rest of them weren't quite human. They had misshapen limbs walking in a bipedal gait. They wore clothes, crisp and clean and formed to them under the cloaks.

What the hell type of place was this?

"We thought it was abandoned," Rosella tried. "We are really sorry to disturb you. We will leave."

"They stole from me. They will stay in my dungeon." His deep voice left no room for argument.

But Rosella didn't care.

"They weren't going to take it from the castle," Rosella pleaded. Her eyes enlarged and her fingers curled around the sword. Her heart rammed against her chest.

"You weren't planning to, but it was three against one," he corrected.

Rosella gulped. He'd heard their conversations. What else could he have possibly heard?

As if reading her mind, he continued, "They looted the rooms and planned to return with a carriage to haul my stuff away." With each word, he took a step forward until he cleared the entryway. Two forms sided up next to him, both covered in shadows.

"As you said." The cloaked form tilted his head at Rosella. The hood shifted ever so slightly to reveal a mouth of razor-sharp teeth.

Rosella's breath caught in her throat. A thousand thoughts

screamed to be heard. He continued speaking and she forced her mind to focus on him. Focus on the person who had her sisters.

"The home is clean, maintained. Odd. Rosella, I believe is what they call you. You will leave. They are just like any others who break into a home instead of knock. Coming to take what isn't theirs. To rob us like common thieves. And just like them, they'll pay the consequences."

Rosella's mouth went dry as tendrils of fear clawed at her throat and blurred her vision. She wouldn't leave her sisters. Couldn't leave them.

More figures returned to the room, likely from wherever they took her sisters.

"There has to be another way," she said as eight figures moved in. More remained lurking in the shadows and more slid into the room.

Ideas spun in her mind. She had to protect them.

Her sisters' actions weren't their father's. He'd done everything for himself. For his vices.

They just wanted food on a table. They didn't take wealth. The castle looked abandoned. Stuff to rot into the earth. They didn't deserve a dungeon.

"Can I stay in their place?" she asked before thinking.

"What?" he baulked, and the minions hesitated. He blinked, his yellow eyes narrowing in on her.

"I'll stay for them," Rosella said, standing taller and squaring her shoulders. This, she could do.

"There are three of them, and one of you. It's uneven and unfair. I also don't believe they'll learn by you protecting them."

"But they're my sisters." She stepped back from the encroaching servants, swinging her sword between them. "I can't let you hurt them."

"They won't be caused pain. They'll be released."

"When? When will they be released?" Rosella demanded.

"I'll be fair. Robbery is a ten-year sentence of hard labor per item. I'll let them go in ten years regardless of the number of items they have in their piles."

Rosella stilled, her world tilting, and she gasped for breath. Ten years?

"No, please," Rosella said, tears pricking her eyes. "There has to be another way."

"There isn't and you're free to go," he said, his voice resigned and distant. He turned, already dismissing her for ten years. "It's a shame they couldn't be like you. Maybe in ten years, they will be."

Anger spiked through Rosella. No one belittled her sisters. Even a large, entitled man who owned a castle. Even someone in a position to lock her sisters up. If they'd known anyone lived there, they wouldn't have touched the stuff, even without Rosella telling them not to. Even with what the items meant to them.

"They are my sisters, and although not perfect, they are good women," she said, her voice rising. "They'd have left the items. They aren't thieves."

They weren't their father.

"We both know they wouldn't have left them. Don't risk my anger."

"Or what?" Rosella taunted, the words tumbling out before she could consider the implications.

"Or." He turned back to her, his eyes glowing in the dim light. He stepped forward, his large foot elongated and covered in fur. His cloak slipped back, but instead of exposing his face, only fur showed.

Rosella stilled, her eyes widened as she took in the odd creature. This hidden castle held more secrets than just its location. She worked her jaw, her mind again slamming the images of the past few days through her vision. He wasn't truly a man, but a furry beast in human form. She wasn't in her safe village anymore. Or the familiar forest where she hunted for meat. She was truly in a horrendous fairytale. One that held her sisters as hostages instead of her.

"I could just toss you out to the wolves. I will currently send you in a carriage back to your village."

The air hung thick with expectancy. Rosella let out a shaky breath, the reality settling on her in a chill. Ten years. She had nothing to offer the beast. Going back would be pointless. So would going to the city to sell their mother's ring. Without her sisters, what did it matter?

"But…" Her voice faded off. She had no words to offer. No hope.

She'd failed them. They'd be in prison. Just like their father.

"What?" he finally asked.

"It doesn't matter." Rosella shook her head. A lump bobbed in her throat. "Not if you're imprisoning my sisters. It's all pointless."

"Fine, I'll have the carriage prepared." The man nodded toward one of the cloaked figures.

"Wait," Rosella said.

"What?" the man barked without turning around.

"Can I spend the day with them? If you're keeping them for ten years, it's the last I'll see them. What's one day to ten years?" She lowered her sword. It'd give her a few hours to plot something. Figure a way out. Find a way to save her sisters. Keep her close to them for a bit longer.

The figures encircled her. None touched her, but their faces turned to their master, waiting for his command. The same one that had spoken to him before sidled up next to him again.

The master's form heaved in a growly breath.

"Fine," he snarled. He turned. Casting a glance back at her over his shoulder, he said, "Take her to the dungeons. Let her have her goodbyes."

Chapter Eleven

Rosella stared into space and rubbed her cheek, her eyes fixated on the gold inlaid wallpaper. The floral pattern reflected the sunlight.

Those still lurking in the shadows shuffled out after the master. The four figures remaining darted around the room, lighting lamps and drawing the plush velvet curtains. The room flooded with light, showing the opulence in full grandeur. The rich rugs, velvet and silk furniture, paintings and sculptures lining the walls.

As one stoked the hearth with more kindling, Rosella found her words and courage. "Why do you wear such thick, fur-lined cloaks?"

The four stilled, sharing looks. Three seemed focused on one, who finally sighed. Stepping forward, he spoke, his voice aged, "I will remove my cloak, but only if you promise to remain calm."

Rosella stared at him. She'd already seen the master's furry legs and sharp teeth. What other fairytale creatures could there be? With everything else going on, she had little energy or fear to give to what they looked like. She'd never doubted that magic existed somewhere beyond her town, but she'd never imagined she'd witness it. And yet what else explained so much that had happened? She nodded in agreement.

The servant slipped his hood off, revealing a form both familiar and foreign to Rosella. His human form was distorted with curved thighs and knees bent in the opposite direction. Light red fur dusted his skin, and his head was oval with a taper in the front like a snout. His eyes were larger than normal and small whiskers protruded from his face. Although he had human fingers, long claws jutted from his tips, finishing his squirrel-like appearance.

Rosella blinked. Not knowing what to think or feel, she met his gaze. "You're half squirrel?"

He cast a look at the others. "Not quite," he muttered. Not averting his gaze, he stepped forward.

Rosella willed her feet to remain rooted. These creatures would be taking care of her sisters. She didn't need to offend them on day one.

"What's your name?" she choked out.

"Arthur," he said with a dip of his head.

She nodded back, staring expectantly at him. He must know her questions. And yet she remained silent.

Not wanting to offend Arthur, Rosella stopped herself from asking how he was a squirrel and human, whether this was their natural state, part of a mysterious castle, or was it something more. But she couldn't stop her eyes as she took in Arthur's visage in the light.

"You are taking this well," Arthur said. His lips curved into a tentative smile. "Better than most."

"Most?" Rosella echoed.

"Although rare, we've had other visitors, as the master said. It's been years since the last. They came to see what remained of an abandoned castle they stumbled across."

"I... we... didn't know there was a castle out here. I don't even know what *here* is called."

"Redrock. Castle Redrock."

Rosella tested the words on her tongue, but she'd never heard of it.

Arthur smiled flatly at her.

"And you, Miss Rosella? What town are you from?"

"Calla."

"Your country borders ours and was thus spared from what befell our kingdom."

"My town is less than two days' travel. How have I not heard of this place? Or that this was another kingdom?"

The four again shared a look.

"Please just tell me," Rosella sighed.

"We were once human," Arthur said. "Fully human, no animal resemblance."

When Rosella just stared at him, waiting, he continued, "We were a rich kingdom with expansive lands. We are cursed, as is our kingdom's lands and the memory of us. We've faded from everyone's mind as part of it. Even if only a few days away."

"Cursed like in a fairytale?" Rosella sputtered.

Arthur tilted his head to the side in a non-committal agreement. "We are the cursed staff of a cursed master."

Rosella's eyes turned to the rest of those with her. "You're all cursed to look like animals?"

"Yes," Arthur answered.

He nodded at the others and then moved about the room, righting the furniture and items she and her sisters had displaced. Guilt twisted her stomach at the mess they'd made in someone else's home. She rubbed her hands on her pants to clear the crumbs and moved to help tidy.

The squirrel scowled at her. His eyes flicked to the sword she'd retrieved from where she dropped it, and they narrowed. "You are a guest. Please sit. We will take you to your sisters once refreshments are readied."

Rosella pulled back at the reprimand but went to return the sword to the display. She allowed her fingers to linger on the jeweled hilt. Such an item would set them for years. She shook her head and turned back to the squirrel. "Refreshments? We are not guests. My sisters are set to be prisoners."

"You," Arthur said, narrowing his gaze further on her, "are a guest. You are free. And your sisters will need food and beverage to survive. As you do. They are in our care, and we will make sure they are tended to properly."

Rosella didn't bother to argue. She was still working on a plan as she moved around the room to right the items she'd touched.

The others removed the cloaks with Arthur's approval. A cat, fox, and wolf stared back at her.

She looked to the cat. "What's your name?"

"I'm Sofia," she whispered. She wore a black pinafore over leggings and a white blouse. Despite the tabby fur covering her body and distorting her features, Rosella got the impression she was young, possibly younger than Giselle. She smiled warmly at her, to which the cat returned it. Short fangs glistened, her green eyes shining brightly.

Something twisted in Rosella's stomach. Her sisters would be with these enchanted people for a decade. Would her sisters, too, be cursed after being sequestered in the castle? Would she return to find her sisters as cats, rats, canines, or rodents?

The fox and wolf stood at other points in the room, their furred bodies similar to the squirrel: fur covered their forms and their heads resembled the animals but blended in with their human features, their fur covered arms had human hands, and their legs resembled haunches, although still elongated as a bipedal.

Rosella turned first to the fox, and asked, "What is your name?"

"Merl," they said with a bow. Their lips curled into a smirk. "It is a pleasure to make your acquaintance."

Rosella stopped her eye roll and turned to the wolf.

"Lucien," he said with a head bob.

"Miss Rosella," Sofia said.

Rosella's gaze tracked to her. Two rabbit humanoids passed off trays to Sofia and Lucien.

"We're ready to take you to your sisters."

ROSELLA FOLLOWED THE FOUR THROUGH THE CASTLE. SHE was unsure why she needed so many chaperones, but wordlessly followed. Instead of trekking to the bowels of the castle as she expected, they took her through several passages that led to a spiraling staircase.

"Your sisters aren't in danger," Sofia reassured her with a gentle smile. "Instead of the dungeon cells, we're taking them where nobles would be kept for ransom in time of war."

The servants shared a look.

"The master approved?" Lucien questioned.

Sofia's eyes flicked between his and Arthurs. "He didn't specify where, and a cell is a cell."

Lucien's jaw ticked.

Arthur nodded his approval and waved them forward.

Although meant to reassure Rosella, her stomach twisted, and she had to swallow the rising bile. At the top of the staircase, a large, thick wooden door was propped open. A gentle murmur of conversation drifted out. Light spilled from the opening, bathing the top few steps in sunlight. Inside the chamber, cells lined the wall, three per side of the room. Metal doors sectioned them off. Instead of just a blanket, each one had a box for a hay bed. The three unoccupied rooms only contained the bed. The three occupied each had a rug, a bucket for waste, an out-of-place washbasin area that looked like it had recently been brought up, and a thick bed of fresh hay with several blankets and pillows.

"Rosella!" Bridgette cheered.

The other two swiveled in their cells.

Even though they were safe, something dark spun inside of Rosella. Her sisters were in cells like their father was, even if his was dank, dark, and smelly. Theirs weren't much different from their normal sleeping quarters save for the metal bars separating them. At the other side of the room from the door, a hearth burned with a fresh fire.

"Pardon," the fox, Merl, called next to Rosella. In their arms was a bundle of wood.

Sofia and Lucien followed closely behind with trays of food and beverage. A sweet, buttery aroma wafted off the plates, rumbling Rosella's stomach.

Her sisters didn't seem shocked by the animalistic appearance of the servants.

"So you mouthed off and he sent you up here?" Camilla asked, standing to shake the bars.

"I asked to stay the night with you."

Camilla's face screwed up. "You wanted to be in a cell? Aren't you the one always worried we'll be in jail like Dad?"

Rosella stared at her and lifted an eyebrow.

"Oh," Camilla muttered, a flush racing up her neck. She ran a hand through her hair and shrugged. "We have clean quarters and looks like delicious food to eat. Maybe we should just stay here forever?"

The other three sisters stared at her. Arthur met Rosella's gaze. Questions swirled on his face, but he held them at bay.

Sofia smiled, revealing sharp canines as she put a silver tea setting, grander than the one Bridgette had found, filled with sandwiches and cookies on a table next to the fire.

Bridgette whimpered watching the new set roll in. Neither the staff nor the master would have missed the other set.

Rosella's stomach rumbled again, matching her sisters'. Her mouth watered as she stared at the delicacies. Some she'd only seen in shop windows while in the city for her father. They'd been too expensive for the four sisters to share even one pastry, and now a tray heaped with them sat at their ready.

"I brought a selection of the master's favorite to choose from," Sofia squeaked. "It's been so long since we honored guests." Her eyes glistened with excitement.

"Prisoners," Arthur murmured but didn't stop Sofia.

Her sisters' breaths hitched, each leaning in to stare at the food.

Lucien pulled the door closed behind them, leaving Rosella, her three sisters, and six servants in the space. Then he withdrew a key and locked the door before pulling a different key to unlock the cells. He bobbed his head at the sisters. "We can't leave you unattended, but there is no reason you can't eat as a family by the hearth."

Despite the circumstances, a smile tugged on Rosella's lips. She met Lucien's pale yellow eyes. They burned brightly with curiosity. His lips quavered into a smile. She smiled back and said, "Thank you for this time."

Rosella swallowed hard as she took in the food, more than she'd seen or eaten in the past year, all beautifully displayed on the plates. Clenching her fingers, she bit her lip to stop herself from diving into the plates.

Sofia stared between the sisters, her brows furrowed, and nodded at the food. She provided a close-lipped smile and stepped back. "Please help yourself."

"Is it safe?" Giselle asked. She lifted a hand hesitantly to a cup of tea. The fine porcelain was nicer than any she'd seen previously. Gold etched the rim, handle and base, and a gold pattern wove around the floral design.

Sofia nodded eagerly, but Rosella didn't move closer to the delectable offerings, weighing the benefits of eating possibly enchanted food.

It's delicious," Camilla said around a mouthful of her sandwich as she reached for two cookies.

Rosella grimaced. They were trapped in a castle, her sisters possibly for ten years, with only the hospitality of the servants to care for them. Her sisters would have to eat what was offered or perish. She whispered, "Does it matter?"

Giselle snatched a cookie from the tray and popped it fully into her mouth. She closed her eyes and moaned as she chewed, already reaching for a sandwich and another cookie before she had finished her first.

The cat smiled and set about pouring more tea for each sister.

"What are we going to do?" Bridgette whispered. She edged closer to Rosella as she watched the squirrel add a log to the fire.

"I don't know," Rosella mumbled, selecting a sandwich. Taking a nibble, her mouth flooded with saliva, and she devoured a second. It was the best thing she'd ever eaten. Or she'd been so hungry for so long she couldn't tell. Either way, she reached for a cookie.

"Why are they cursed?' Giselle nodded toward the staff. She stepped closer to Bridgette and Rosella to keep her voice from being heard.

"They told you?" Rosella asked.

Giselle gave her an amused look. "Even if I'm young and sheltered, it's not hard to figure out."

Rosella offered her a sheepish smile in return. These cursed individuals would be looking out for her sisters. Caring for them. She needed to know if it would affect her sisters, too.

Facing Sofia, Rosella asked, "Why are you cursed?"

She cringed at her poor manners. Heat warmed her neck and cheeks.

"Rosella," Bridgette scolded under her breath.

Rosella gave her a harsh expression, silencing her.

The six servants looked at one another, none seeming shocked by the question.

Finally, the wolf stepped forward. "We've been cursed for years. We've lost track of the time."

"Years?" Rosella echoed.

"Perhaps a decade or two or more," he said.

"But why?" Camilla asked, eating another cookie. She settled in a pink-and-white striped padded chair next to the cart likely meant for the attendant.

The servants shared another glance. Something passed between them, and Lucien said, "His Highness's parents angered a witch."

Sofia made a throaty noise.

Lucien sent her a silencing look.

"His parents?" Rosella asked. Her gaze bounced back at the empty staircase hidden from view of the castle. The so-called master had slunk off after his servants had taken them to the dungeons.

"They slumber," the wolf said, his eyes flickering to the ceiling.

"Eternally?"

"No," the wolf said. His frame stiffened, and he frowned. "They'll awake if the curse is lifted."

"If?" Bridgette asked. "The curse can be lifted?" She looked to Rosella and swallowed.

Rosella's spine straightened, and hope turned in her stomach.

"It's not easy," Sofia interjected.

"We need more wood," Lucien directed to Sofia.

Sofia sighed as she sent a silent warning look to the sisters.

Arthur shook his head, not allowing Sofia to leave. His eyes sent Lucien a dark look.

"All curses should be able to be broken if someone is willing to do what is required," the wolf said, his eyes boring into Sofia before tracking to Bridgette. He stepped toward the sisters.

"Lucien," Arthur warned.

"It's the truth."

"A dangerous one," Arthur said. He smiled at the sisters, revealing large incisors. "Please, Misses, eat up. You must be hungry after the long night."

"How come you haven't tried to break it?" Camilla leaned over the chair to peer around Arthur at Lucien. She shoved another cookie in her mouth. "I wouldn't want to be trapped in a curse."

"Camilla," the sisters scolded.

"What?" she said around the cookie. "It's a valid question." She lifted a challenging eyebrow toward them.

The wolf, Lucien, snorted and folded his arms over his chest.

Arthur shook his head at Camilla but didn't stop Lucien.

Lucien replied, "You don't think we tried? In the first years, at least a dozen or so tried, our bravest and strongest, but any who have tried have met an unpleasant death."

Sofia wrung her hands. "It is too dangerous."

Lucien and Merl nodded in agreement. "We've accepted that it can't be broken."

The four other servants averted their gazes.

"How'd they die?" Camilla leaned forward, her eyes gleaming.

The wolf leaned back and glanced at the other sisters. His yellow eyes, dark with concern and wonder, assessed them.

Rosella shook her head at Camilla's back and offered a weak smile toward the wolf. She ran a hand along her jaw, her finger finding the familiar ridge.

"How do you break the curse?" Rosella asked. She picked up her cup of tea with her other hand, her thoughts already plotting.

"There are three charms required to break it," the wolf said. "A riddle for each. But each piece is guarded by a magical being."

"What are the charms?" Camilla asked, rubbing her hands.

"Where are they?" Giselle asked.

"What are the magical beings?" Bridgette asked.

The wolf shook his head. "We think we know where the first charm is but haven't been successful in retrieving it. The items are believed to be around the countryside. We are unsure what the magical beings are. We just know they are fierce."

"You don't know much," Camilla said. "Especially for a two-decade-long curse."

Rosella sighed.

"What about the other two?" Bridgette asked. "Maybe you could try for those first."

"We don't have them," the wolf answered. "According to the sorceress, the next charm's riddle is provided by securing the preceding item. All charms are in our kingdom. Protected by a local lore. Or so the sorceress says."

"What's the riddle for the first one, then?" Rosella asked.

The wolf shrugged. "The master has it, but we believe it is in the waters of the Dragon's Ravine."

"What is that?" Giselle asked.

"A ravine where the waters are so fierce, no one can cross. The water splash is said to be as powerful as a dragon's breath."

"Why doesn't the master go for them?" Rosella asked. "If he has the riddle."

Camilla snorted. "He too good and proper?"

The wolf's face fell, and he shook his head. "No, the prince cannot leave, or the curse becomes permanent. That was made clear by the witch."

"So those who attempted to get it have perished, and he can't go himself," Rosella asked. "So how is he supposed to break it then?"

"Find someone willing and able," Lucien said, smiling at her.

Chapter Twelve

Rosella sipped her tea, her stomach stretched and slightly uncomfortable from the vast amount of food she ate. Against her wishes, the servants had taken her to a private room. She'd requested to stay in the tower, but her request had been denied. By the master. Unwilling to come to the dungeon, he had sent the message through a servant. She wasn't a prisoner.

"We can hopefully take you again before you leave," Sofia offered with a smile.

Rosella growled in response. She knew she meant if the master allowed it. She paced the room, her long stride eating the ground.

The room was a smidge bigger than their store and house combined. The cheery yellow walls were contrasted with dark wood furnishing and white velvet drapes. Oil-painted forest scenes decorated the walls in bold carved frames.

Paying her taxes meant nothing if she lost her sisters for ten years. Nothing was worth not seeing them. She could ask to stay with them for the ten years, but she'd rather find a way to get them out. Free them now. She ran through the wolf's words again.

The castle was cursed, and no one could break it. Yet.

Cold twisted through her veins, tingling her skin.

Her thoughts played in her mind and on her umpteenth turn, she yanked the door open. Merl's odd fox eyes cut to her.

"Not a prisoner, huh?"

They dipped their head. "No, ma'am, you are not. I am here in case you request anything."

She stilled a beat at the unexpected answer. "May I speak to the master?"

Merl's mouth fell agape. "Pardon?" they finally choked.

"May I?"

"What is it you request?" Lucien asked silently, stepping down the hallway.

"May I speak to the master?" she repeated and turned to the wolf, meeting his gaze. His yellow eyes stared uncertainly at her.

He looked to Merl, working his jaw, but no words came out.

Merl's chin dipped, their eyes falling to the floor.

"I am sorry, miss, but he will not free your sisters," Lucien said.

"I know," Rosella confirmed. "May I still speak to him?"

"I will see if he's available," Lucien finally said, taking a prolonged look at Rosella before exiting.

Rosella lifted her chin and waited in the doorway. Merl settled beside her, their furred ears flicking toward sounds she couldn't hear.

"I am sorry, Miss Rosella," they offered.

She cut her eyes to them.

"You four seem very nice. I believe your sisters would have listened to you."

"It's nice of you to lie to me," Rosella said. Even she didn't believe her sisters would have listened to her. They saw the possibilities; they just couldn't see the possible consequences. They'd all been young when their father had stolen many pieces from their mother's family—jewelry, coins, baubles—but her sisters hadn't felt the sting of the rejection. The scorn from those who had once said they loved them. Their father's theft had alienated their mother from her family. Led her to lie to the villagers and created a situation that had killed her. She'd had no one to rely on when his drinking turned worse. Only Rosella, who never left her mother's side. The town and her family wrote her off because of her husband. Her sisters had been young, but more importantly, she and her mother had made sure the sisters weren't aware of what had happened. They made excuses. To her sisters, their father's thievery had been more story than fact and they hadn't heeded her warnings.

"You don't have to see him, Miss Rosella," Merl said. "Take Master's offer and leave. Protect yourself. He won't free your sisters. Not after— not with everyone hearing what he said."

Rosella snorted. "I know."

"Then why risk his anger?"

Rosella's dark eyes slid to Merl. They fumbled their lip as they met her gaze. "I have to try everything."

Merl's eyes flicked down the hall before returning to hers, their pupils already bulging horizontally. In a whisper, they said, "He's normally reasonable, miss. It's just—"

"Just what?" Rosella prompted.

They shook their head, their lips turned down. Silence fell between them.

Merl turned their attention to the east, the bright sun casting a warm glow down the hallway. Then Lucien shuffled into view. Gray fur tufted around his pristine uniform.

"He's agreed to meet with you," Lucien said. He rubbed his thumb over his fingers, gauging Rosella before asking, "Are you sure about this?"

"Yes," Rosella said without hesitation. Squaring her shoulders and lifting her chin, she started down the hallway.

Rosella followed Lucien into the large white marble foyer and up a winding staircase. With each step, her heart thudded loudly in her chest. The large staircase wrapped around the foyer, the opulent banister carved into angels. Each dark wooden spindle was polished until it glistened in the light streaming in from the bank of windows. A thick woven rug in red and gold adorned the steps, muffling their progression. The matching dark wooden chair rail on the wall was freshly polished, and above it was gold leafed trim.

The rest of the castle was as impeccably clean as the room she'd been in. Plush carpets ran the length of the walls, with accent tables displaying items that could pay her taxes tenfold. More oil paintings lined the walls, displaying more ancestors of the prince. Gold wall sconces held lanterns, each lit to accentuate the treasures of the hall as they passed.

The items her sister had planned to take were mere trinkets compared to the busts and statues in the hallway, each in a precious metal and several with gemstones embedded.

Such squander.

The wolf stopped in front of a set of doors. The ornate doors had carved designs around the border displaying angels and mythical creatures. Her eyes jumped to the wolf. *Perhaps not so mythical.*

Lucien wrung his hands; his eyes flickered to Rosella and then the door. "He's in here," he said and inclined his head. After a pause, he rushed out, "Don't be foolish. We'll be kind to your sisters. We'll feed them."

Rosella hesitated. They'd do more for her sisters than she could. The food they were fed today was more than they'd had as far as she could remember. The servants, despite the animal appearances, were well-fed and cared for. Her sisters didn't fare as well at home. Maybe she should let them stay. Put her pride away.

She looked up at the vaulted ceiling, painted in swirling gold designs and angelic images. It was beautiful. No. It was an illusion, and still a prison. Despite all the beauties and displays of wealth, he'd said they'd stay in cells, a dungeon. This was the glamour, the sales pitch. This wasn't their promised reality. They wouldn't be free. They'd lose a big chunk of their life, and if she freed them and sold the ring, she could feed them, too.

"Thank you," she murmured but nodded toward the door.

Lucien sighed but opened the door for her to enter. He did not follow her in as she walked into the room. Instead, he softly stepped inside the door, closing it behind him, and planted himself in the shadows of a corner.

"I'll be right here," he whispered. His yellow eyes reflected fear.

She swallowed her nerves down. Like with everything, she lifted her chin and settled her shoulders back, projecting confidence she didn't feel. Just as her mother taught her.

Like the rest of the house, the room was decorated in paintings and gold, but the select items around the room seemed to have a personal touch. Wooden figurines sat on a table, a chess set on another, and along a bank of windows that overlooked the forest, different colored glass items reflected the sun in a rainbow display.

Her attention was drawn to the open curtains. The forest sprawled below and petered away in the distance into grass. Rolling hills were mere dots in the background. A balcony made of gray stone jutted from the room and held planters with blooming flowers. Roses in shades of red, purple, and orange mixed with lilies, chrysanthemums, and other dainty blossoms covered the space.

"What do you want?" the master's voice called out, startling her.

She sucked in a breath to settle the jitters fluttering in her stomach.

Her eyes darted around for him. Despite the open window, the room was crowded with shadows. Large pieces of furniture dominated the room, blocking the light.

Movement to her left caught her attention, and she noticed his form cloaked in the shadows. Despite his face being mostly hidden, his eyes reflected the sunlight. His body heaved as he stared at her.

"Why do you stay in the shadows?" she asked.

"I'm hideous," he said flatly. "What do you want?"

"I came to talk about my sisters," she said, swallowing down the lump in her throat.

"I'm not freeing them." His gaze flicked to the door before resettling on her.

"I know," she conceded. She ran a hand through her auburn hair and scratched her cheek. Her finger traced the scar. "I was wondering if we could make a trade."

"A trade? What do you have to offer?" A chuckle rippled through his words.

Rosella bit back a snide comment. She inhaled a long steadying breath and with the exhale took a few steps toward him. She couldn't show fear. No matter that her legs wobbled and she had to focus on evening her breath.

His fingers curled as his eyes narrowed.

"I don't have material possessions. Well, a ring, my mother's, but I don't think you care about that."

"What would I need with a ring? We have dozens. You're wasting my time. Leave." He turned back toward the side of the room cloaked in shadows, putting more distance between them.

She recovered the distance. He lifted his head, his nostrils flared.

Lucien made a warning sound as she took another step closer.

Rosella dipped her chin toward Lucien, catching sight of his form over her shoulder. She wasn't one of the servants. She wasn't a prisoner. He could kick her out, but she was a guest for the night. She wouldn't waste her chance.

Easing her gaze, she took deliberate breaths. With each inhale, she took a step closer. Each exhale, she paused to gauge his posture.

He likely could hear her heart, the sound deafening everything else for her. But she crossed half the room's distance to him. She gulped back the trepidation burning like acid in her throat. Standing bigger than she expected, he towered at least two feet above her. With each step he had taken, he'd seemed to recess farther into his cloak, but he couldn't diminish his size and width.

"I can offer myself," she said and flushed at how the words came out.

"Yourself? What are you saying? A dowry?" He tilted his head as he studied her.

Lucien coughed a laugh from the corner.

Her cheeks flamed, and she said, "No, not a dowry. I can offer my services. I can help break the curse."

Lucien sucked in a breath.

The beast stilled. A rumble rippled through him, but something shifted in the air. He stood straighter, gaining almost another foot in height, his form seeming even more impossibly large and dangerous.

Rosella's eyes darted around, sweat beading on her temples. She waited for him to respond. To say something. The silence weighed heavily.

"What do you know about the curse?" he said, his voice barely above a whisper.

Rosella sputtered. Were the servants not supposed to tell her? But they were all under it. It was their story to tell, too. She opted for a part of the truth. "You are cursed. A curse can be broken. I will help break the curse."

He laughed, a growling sound that bordered on animalistic.

"Do you want the curse broken?" she snapped.

He stopped laughing, a snarl escaping him that rattled her bones as he stepped forward. One step at a time. Slowly bringing his form into the light. Slowly bringing him closer and closer until he was a mere few feet away. Rosella's eyes followed the motion up, drinking in each new piece of him. His furred foot, to the large hind legs, more pronounced than the staffs'. His chest expanded, surpassing the girth of any man she knew. His arms were human shaped and furred, as were his hands, like the servants. He took a final step forward, his swollen neck draped in a thick mane and his face, a mixture of creatures from a wolf to a lion and human. It was the human that stole her breath. Beneath it all, she recognized the pain and sorrow of someone not in control in their life. She gasped but held back any other sounds.

"What do you think?" he spewed.

"Then let me help you break it," she choked out. Her mouth dried and her heart hammered in her chest. Doubt flittered in her mind at the thought of those who died before her. How would she succeed where they had failed?

"And in exchange? What? Your sisters and their treasures? Our family jewels?" He scoffed.

Rosella shook her head, her resolve strengthening. "No. I don't want anything that is yours. I just want my sisters. They are mine, and I am theirs. I'll break the curse, and you give me my sisters immediately afterward."

"You'll likely die."

"If you keep my sisters, I'd die each day we were apart. A quicker death is more humane."

"They are thieves. They did this to themselves."

She bristled at his truths. "You do not know them. You saw them but one instance. When they saw a way to change their fortune. To not be saddled with the town's expectations. To not have to fight for every scrap of food. It was a moment of weakness."

He stared at her.

"You call them thieves but still feed them." Rosella's eyes narrowed.

"They are living beings, even if thieves. They need consequences, not starvation. I hardly think bread, cheese, dried meat, and wine are something to celebrate."

Rosella stared at him, forcing her gaze not to flick back to Lucien and what the servants had actually fed her sisters. Even the master's idea of dungeon food was better than what she provided them. Finally, she lifted her hand out to him. "If I break the curse, you will free my sisters."

"You'd risk everything for them?" he asked, his voice catching. "Certain death?"

"Absolutely."

His yellow eyes roamed her face, looking for something they didn't find. Suspicion darkened his features, but finally he reached out and took her hand.

"Then I will consider it."

She stiffened at the gentleness of his touch. She'd expected a rough grip. One meant to crush bone or show physical prowess much like the townsmen would do. He also didn't lift her hand to his lips as the men would do to her during a business transaction. Each time, Rosella would wipe her hand on her trousers as soon as they left. Instead, his warm fingers wrapped around hers and pumped a handshake. Then he retracted his hand, leaving her unexplainably cold.

For a second, they just looked at each other, the promise hanging between them. Chills raced down Rosella's spine. She swallowed at the odd sensation but didn't lower her gaze even as her mind screamed to break the trance.

Lucien cleared his throat and the moment passed.

Chapter Thirteen

ROSELLA WAITED UNTIL THE AFTERNOON, WHEN THE STAFF assumed she was napping, to sneak out of her unguarded door. Thick carpet cushioned her steps as she silently crept through the empty halls. Although the corridors twisted and turned, Rosella followed the mind map she made of the heirlooms to backtrack her way through to the tower. Just as when they entered, she didn't see anyone.

Her room, set on the east side, was one of many in what appeared to be rooms for the court. Behind thick, dark wooden doors more bedrooms with lavish spreads and carpets filled the space. White sheets were draped over the furniture to gather any dust. At the end of the hall the space opened into another hall lined with more treasures. Silver oil lamps lined the walls, unlit, but gleaming in the light. Marble tables lined the walls displaying various treasures of vases, statues, and swords. More paintings dotted the hall.

An alcove opened in the middle of the hall with a bank of windows that showed a dazzling display of forests and mountains in the distance. Rosella sucked in a breath, letting herself soak in the sight. She'd never seen mountains outside of books or paintings. The jagged gray mammoths broke across the horizon, unlike the docile paintings in her book. For a moment, she sat on the yellow arched-back sofa, with a gold design layered over the woodwork. A huge painting sat above the sofa, marking a forgotten time in the castle's history. Based on the crowns, Rosella assumed it was a king and queen, and since it was set so prominently in a visitor's section, she suspected it was the ones who slumbered somewhere in the castle. Between them, a child sat dressed in robes of fur, brocade, and a crown that dwarfed his head. His black hair matched the queen's, as did his yellow eyes.

Something sounded in the distance, breaking her trance. She scurried further through the mammoth home, retracing her steps until the aroma of baking bread and the tantalizing tang of smoked meat greeted her. Despite already eating to her fill and beyond, her mouth watered and her stomach rumbled for a taste. Pushing the thoughts down, she found the long-arched brick tunnel tucked between the castle and the tower. Checking over her shoulder, she settled her breath and tightened her body to not make a sound as she ascended the steps to her sisters.

The door sat shut, a beam of sunlight breaking free underneath. Her eyes snagged on a set of keys on the peg outside the door. Seven thick rodded keys hung from the metal loop. Rust and age clung to them, the time when they'd been used regularly forgotten. If it wasn't for the fact she couldn't outrace them, or hadn't given her word, she could free her sisters and disappear into the expansive forest. The fourth key she tried opened the door. It creaked, sending the sound ricocheting down the staircase.

Rosella cursed. If they weren't already aware, the staff was certain to come to the sound. But she had to tell her sisters, and she wasn't sure when or if she'd see her sisters again before the master either set her off to break the curse or changed his mind and sent her home.

"Roz?" Bridgette's sleepy voice called.

Swallowing her reservations, she entered the room.

A warm fire flickered in the hearth. Each sister had been given a sitting chair in their cell. Giselle and Camilla still lay on their beds, tucked beneath warm blankets. They scrambled to their feet seeing her.

Her sisters each donned a fresh new garment. The rich silks and velvets were of older styles but preserved as if new. Camilla wore a maroon silk and velvet dress meant for tea. Bridgette wore a cobalt blue brocade gown with floral scenes in pink and red. Giselle's green velvet dress had a high empire waist accented in gold cord and white lace.

Like her sisters, she too had new garments. Rosella wore a fresh pair of black breeches with a cream blouse, softer than the rough linen she normally wore. A thick brown belt hung on her waist. The servants insisted she needed fresh, clean clothes or she could catch something. Thankfully, they had obviously thought the same of her sisters.

"Your cells look cozy," Rosella said.

"They said we'd be here for a while and should be comfortable," Bridgette said.

She didn't question the servants' generosity or the master's unlikely knowledge of it. At least her sisters would be cared for as she tried to earn their freedom.

"I need to tell you something," Rosella said. She glanced back down the staircase. Steps echoed up. They'd found her already. Hopefully they hadn't told the master.

"What did you do?" Camilla demanded.

Her sisters shared a look.

"You're going to try to break the curse, aren't you?" Giselle sputtered.

Rosella licked her lips. "I offered my services to the master to try to break it."

"You did what?" Bridgette bellowed, pacing in her cell.

"NO!" Giselle cried.

"Interesting…" Camilla rubbed her chin.

"I can't stand here and let you be imprisoned," Rosella said. "I have to try something."

"It's ten years," Bridgette countered. "Not a lifetime."

Rosella snorted. "Ten days is too long."

"I don't like this," Bridgette murmured.

"What about Gavin?" Rosella pressed.

Bridgette's glossy gray eyes shot up to her. Her lips twitched in annoyance.

"Oh, that's a good point," Camilla said, nodding her approval.

"Rosella is our sister! Gavin can marry someone else." Bridgette choked on the last word. She sniffled and looked away.

"But why should he have to if I can free you?" Rosella said.

"Who says he wants to marry me?" Bridgette whispered. Her face contorted and she blinked, trying to keep the tears at bay.

"Anyone who has seen you two together," Giselle smirked.

Bridgette sent her a dark look, but her tears undermined the intensity.

"Even if we can't stop Odette from marrying the dud Louis, we could still help you." Camilla pointed a finger at Bridgette.

Giselle gasped. Her lip trembled but she didn't say anything.

"Really?" Rosella growled at Camilla.

"Hey, I'm helping you."

"Please stop then," Rosella said.

Giselle sucked in a breath.

Bridgette sighed. "Roz, those futures aren't promised. Yes, we love them, but that doesn't mean anything when it comes to marriage."

"It should," Rosella scoffed before thinking.

"They said everyone else died who tried it," Giselle choked out. "You can't do that. What will we do without you?"

"Destining me to fail?" Rosella forced a chuckle.

"Roz, if anyone can do it, it's you, but why are you doing it?" Bridgette asked.

"I can't stand by and do nothing."

"They'll grow tired of us in less than a year. Watch us less. I can manage the lock with time." Giselle sniffed. "And we have plenty of time."

Although she didn't doubt it, Rosella didn't want to know about Giselle's ability to pick locks and what it had meant in town.

"There you are," Lucien panted. His ears flicked back toward the steps. His furred hands gripped the doorframe.

"I wanted to see my sisters."

"We could have helped," Lucien said.

"I didn't want you to be in trouble."

He sucked in a breath. "Telling him you left without an escort would have been worse."

"She's free, remember?" Giselle said.

"Not to just roam the castle. Or visit the master's prisoners. He's very territorial."

"Isn't she going to break the curse for you?" Camilla yelled, fisting her hands on her hips.

Lucien cut his golden eyes to Rosella.

"I wanted them to hear it from me."

A soft knock sounded on the tower door followed by a muffled, "Excuse me."

"Yes." Rosella whirled around to face the newcomer.

"We have dinner prepared," Sofia said, bowing. Her brow furrowed. "I didn't know you would be here, miss. I sent Merl to your room with your meal."

Lucien stared at the sisters. "I brought her here. She asked to see her sisters."

Rosella stilled at the lie. He was covering for her?

Sofia cocked an eyebrow but didn't argue. "My apologies for the mistake."

"Dinner?" the girls echoed, sharing a perplexed look.

"You brought us dinner?" Camilla asked.

"Yes, the midday meal," the cat said. Her green eyes darted between the four.

"You mean we get another meal? One between breakfast and supper?" Camilla asked, fisting her hands at her mouth as she squealed in delight. "Roz, I don't care if you break the curse or not. I want to stay here."

Her heart panged at the words. A prison offered them more comforts than she could.

Rosella said, "You'll live in a cell for ten years with these two always in earshot. You won't have privacy and always have to hear their complaints."

"Such a spoilsport," Camilla grimaced. "I'm still eating, though. It'll be my reward for putting up with them."

Lucien shut the door and locked it. Then unlocked each cell so the sisters could eat by the fireplace. "I won't always be able to let you eat together. If the master finds out..."

His voice died off and his gaze flicked to the ground. He moved to the tray to serve food.

"We won't say anything," Giselle said, offering him a smile.

Sofia's brows pinched. "I don't think he'd mind."

"Don't lie to them," Lucien hissed under his breath.

"I'm not—"

Lucien cut her off with a curt stare.

Rosella smiled and followed her sisters to the hearth but paused when she saw Sofia's expression. Sofia licked her lips while wringing her hands.

"Is something wrong?" Rosella asked. "Will you get in trouble for me being here?"

New guilt wormed its way through Rosella. She would accept the punishment for what she did, but she hadn't considered the staff would be reprimanded for her choices.

"No, no, not at all," Sofia whispered. "I just, I just heard you were willing to try to break the spell."

"Yes," Rosella said. Lucien had spread the word quickly. "The master is considering my offer."

"He'd be foolish not to take you up." Bridgette glared at Rosella from the hearth, her jaw ticking. "How many out-of-luck people come here willing to help?"

The two other sisters stared between Sofia and Lucien.

Lucien shook his head.

Sofia said, "None now. The townspeople around here turned, too. Most of them are fully animal now. The wolves you met are part of them. Only the far border villages remain human."

"There's a town around here?" Rosella asked. She looked to her sisters.

"Remnants, yes. In the valley, opposite of the way you came. Hopefully, the curse will restore them, too."

"You saw us coming?" Rosella asked. Her mind flicked back to the askew drapes in the room.

Sofia nodded. "We always hope. Well, some of us."

"How come you're still mostly human if they're wolves?" Camilla asked. She joined the others, sandwich halves in each hand.

The cat shrugged. "I don't know. We are less and less each day. The castle is fading, and as it fades, we become more and more cursed. Soon we'll have nothing to return to. Soon we will transform completely. Lost to the curse."

"We never heard of a castle out here," Rosella said. "When was the last attempt to change the curse?"

The cat shrugged. "A decade, I think? Maybe longer. I've lost track of time. It means nothing here. The last attempt was a few years or so after it happened. We were still mostly human then. The last time, half a dozen young men left."

"If they didn't return, maybe they just fled?" Bridgette said.

The cat shook her head, her eyes darting down the hall and then they met Lucien's for a moment. Her lips twisted and her eyes rimmed in tears.

"Tell us," Camilla said, clapping her hands, leaning in. "What happened to them?"

The cat flinched and looked away, shaking her head.

"Can you tell us?" Rosella asked. "Will it help with the curse? Let me know what I need to watch out for?"

"The master has a mirror," Lucien filled in.

"So he can see how hideous he is?" Camilla huffed. "Big deal."

"That's mean," Giselle covered a laugh while she slapped Camilla's arm.

"What? We can see him. No one is giving us sympathy."

"Stop," Rosella said, pointing a finger at Camilla.

"No, it can show reflections like a regular mirror, but it can also show him the world." Sofia rung her fingers. "The world he isn't a part of anymore. It's meant to torment him. We watched the others try and fail." Sofia sucked in a sob. "We watched each one..." Her voice faded off.

"Oh, I am so sorry," Giselle said, embracing Sofia and stroking the fur on her head. She grimaced as realization lit her face that she was touching fur.

Sofia stiffened, but a sad smile tilted her lips as she patted Giselle's back and straightened.

"Yes, well, we have a new hero," Sofia said. She sniffed back her tears and gave the sisters a sympathetic look.

Giselle and Bridgette shared an uneasy look and slid a look at Rosella.

"Well, Roz can do it," Camilla said. She slapped Rosella's back and smiled at the others. "Roz can do anything."

Rosella made a noncommittal hum. She hoped Camilla was right.

Chapter Fourteen

Rosella paced in her room, her thoughts on her sisters still in the tower. Each time her mind cycled back to the impossibility of the task, she pictured them. Many had died attempting to break the curse. She had nothing special to offer to find it, break it, other than her determination. A wheezy breath escaped her. Those before her were probably also determined. But she couldn't think about that. She had to believe she could do it. Find it. Bring it back.

Her mother's words filled her. *Chin high. Shoulders back. Fake the confidence until you feel it.* So much of her life had been built on those words. They had gotten her through tough winters and droughts. Ten years wasn't a life sentence for her sisters, but it would rob them of the futures they hoped for. They'd be four spinster sisters, robbed of youth and future. No, she had to try. Like she always did.

Visions of both futures spun in her mind as the sun progressed across the sky. Servants came and went with water, a change of clothes, and snacks.

The sun hung bloated on the horizon, casting the room in a warm haze and reflecting on the gold decor. The forest bathed in the glow looked darker and more ominous with its hidden secrets and predators.

Rosella finally donned fresh black leggings and a black blouse, the castle still respecting her as the head of her household, even if she was a peasant with three sisters in their dungeon. In front of her was the satchel the servants had brought her. There were two canteens, dried foods, a dagger, fire starter, a wool blanket, rope, a slingshot, some coins, and a shortsword. She had more to travel with than she and her sisters owned. She had more coins in the rations than they had in the till.

Rosella's stomach twisted. It was nothing for the castle to give her. Mere pittance they could stand to lose if she died, and yet this would tide her and her sisters over for quite some time.

A knock resounded off the door.

"Yes?" Rosella asked.

Sofia pushed open the door and bowed. "The master is ready for you."

"Ready for me?" Rosella furrowed her brow.

"Yes, you'll be dining with him in the grand hall." Sofia nodded, her cat eyes widening.

"What about my sisters?" Rosella asked. She'd hoped to eat with them as a final meal. One last chance to see them before starting out. Especially as it may be the last. She swallowed and blinked back the emotion stinging her eyes.

Sofia shook her head. Her eyes flashed with sympathy. "Just you."

Rosella's face fell, but she followed the cat through the halls to the grand dining room. Narrow windows lined the wall with plush velvet drapes and gold and jeweled pulls. Even though she was still unaccustomed to the wealth on display, instead of ogling it, her attention drifted to the curse and her sisters.

"What about my sisters' supper?" she asked, glancing to the tower now basking in the late sun. The gray stone absorbed the rays, giving nothing back, but she knew what it held.

"They'll eat in their quarters," Sofia assured.

Rosella nodded and entered the grand hall. She knew how to get to them if the staff wouldn't let her go.

Sofia lingered at the door, her head bowed.

Rosella scanned the room. Several other servants lined the room, each cautiously watching her. As she neared the master, they stiffened in respect, their facial expressions going slack.

The master was already in the room, standing behind his chair waiting for her. He wore fresh trousers and a red overcoat, traditional finery even her relatives wore. Though the master's were finer silk and stitching. This time he didn't hide his face in the shadows, but he held a guarded expression. His hands rested on the back of the chair, tightening as she entered. Seeming to realize his stature, he pulled them back to his side. His gaze never left her.

The ornate table stretched the distance of the room between them but was dwarfed by the crystal chandelier. It hung suspended from the cathedral ceiling with five tiers of gleaming crystals. Two place settings were set up formally, one on each end. A sad smile flickered on her lips thinking of her grandparents' estate. The table was similar in design and setting. Years of manner and decorum came racing back, her shoulders and chin automatically going to proper position. Her fidgeting fingers stilled at her side, and she plastered on a small, demure smile she hadn't used in almost a decade.

Cold reality slithered through her veins. There was no point to pretend. To be something she wasn't. All these manners had done nothing for her. Her fingers were calloused and rough from hunting, gardening, and normal daily chores usually reserved for staff. Her hair hung behind her in a fresh braid, but still a braid. She'd refused the help the master's staff had offered. She was planning to head out on an unknown venture, not sit for tea and pleasantries. She eased on this reality. She was the head of her household, not a debutante seeking a perfect match with polished manners and gentile appearance.

Finding her spot, she nodded at him and then looked down at her place setting with fine hand-painted porcelain, sterling wear, and crystal goblets. She had questions, and the proper distance they'd been set apart wouldn't help. Decorum and propriety were reserved for those with wealth and time to spare.

She picked up her plate and setting and walked toward him. His face scrunched in confusion, his golden eyes following her, but he said nothing as she brought her place setting to the chair next to his. A servant made a "tsking" sound behind her, but she ignored it.

She started to pull her chair but was interrupted by another servant gently redirecting her. He resembled a mole, including a twitching nose. She didn't flush or apologize, but stepped aside and followed the gentle coaching of the servant. They wanted the pretenses, even if they didn't matter.

Finally, she looked to the master. Without the cloak, his rigid posture was noticeable. Somehow, his furred exterior made him more approachable than had he been in human form as a prince, resembling the people of her childhood. He didn't scrutinize her with the same fierce displeasure as her mother's family had.

"As you can tell, I am not used to castle life," Rosella said once seated. "Neither are my sisters. It's been years since I had to follow such rules."

His yellow eyes flicked to her. "What do you mean?"

"My mother's father was an earl's brother. They cared about such things. When she'd still visit them, we had to follow their rules. I've become rusty since that time."

"You don't see them anymore?"

Rosella shook her head. Her lips pressed into a tight line.

"May I ask why?"

Her eyes jumped to his. She hadn't expected his interest.

He lifted his brows in expectancy.

"We stopped seeing them when Giselle was still a toddler. They... didn't like my father and the visits became too strenuous."

He watched her, his eyes narrowing as he contemplated what she had left out.

"You have gentile heritage and yet are the head of your household. Tell me more about yourself." He nodded at her. His face flinched, and he added, "Please."

She shrugged. She was used to the townspeople prying into her life, but they knew all the scandalous details. Mr. Trible had even been on their escorts to the city. "What's there to tell? Does it matter?"

A servant placed an appetizer in front of them. A cream sauce covered a flaky pastry. Rosella had no idea what it was, but it smelled buttery and rich. Her full stomach rumbled in anticipation.

The master frowned at her. "For starters, why are you looking out for your sisters? Where are your parents?"

"Afraid they'll come looking?"

"No," he said and shook his head. "But it is odd for a woman of your age to be caring for three sisters. Especially if you have gentile relatives. Normally you would be married by now and possibly with children of your own. Why are you caring for your adult and almost adult sisters?"

She laughed a humorless laugh. "That's none of your business. But, as I'm at your mercy for my sisters' care, I need you to look out for them. Our mother passed away many years ago."

"My sympathies," he said, his voice gentle. He almost sounded sincere. "And your father?"

Rosella paused. She was used to everyone knowing her history. Now she had to share it with a stranger, relive it out loud, and see the birthed rebuke firsthand. She pursed her lips, but finally said, "He's in prison."

She stared at him, braced for the outrage. The flick of his nose and settling back in his seat as he stared down at her. Waited for his lip to curl into a snarl and the haughty intolerance to show her how unworthy she was to be in his company. Especially as he was a prince. Even if a cursed one.

Instead, he lifted an eyebrow. "Robbery?" he quipped.

Rosella almost retorted but noticed the grin tilting his lips. He was trying to joke. Trying to imply her sisters were carrying on a family tradition. It wasn't funny when it involved her sisters. Especially as it was true. "No, he murdered our mother."

"Oh," the master said. His expression morphed into one of horror. "Oh, I am sorry."

Rosella waved him off. Her stomach curdled. More than pity twisted his face, and she didn't know how to handle it. "I'm used to everyone knowing and pitying us for it. Don't. We grieve for our mother but not our father."

He nodded, his gold eyes surveying her. Understanding settled behind them. "They say we shouldn't be judged for the sin of our parents, but we are certainly held to their image nonetheless."

Rosella stared at him, his beastly figure baring so much. His eyes shuttered, giving her no emotion to clasp onto, but she saw the similarities of them to the painting. He was the child in the painting and looked like his mother. His parents had gotten him cursed. She bore the scar on her face and faced it in town. He wore his as fur and gnarled limbs.

"What about your parents?" she asked and then sipped her wine.

He looked away, sorrow darkening his face.

Silence stretched between them, but Rosella waited, for once not the subject of personal scrutiny.

"They slumber," he finally mumbled. His eyes flicked to the ceiling and his jaw ticked.

"The curse?"

"Yes," he said.

"Why do they slumber while you are in this form?" Her lips curled into a frown, taking in his sullen eyes.

"The witch cursed them, too."

"But they sleep?" Rosella pressed. "Are they also in animal form?"

He shook his head. "They are in human form. The only ones as humans in our area who are not passing through. I was a child when it happened. They are aware of what is happening but cannot move or speak. Their eyes open and they can weep."

"Oh," Rosella said. It'd been at least two decades based on his voice and size. Perhaps longer depending on the magic. His parents were trapped in their bodies, watching their young son grow into a beastly man. Watching him carry the curse they earned.

"It is their curse for doing nothing to protect the people when famine hit. They raised taxes. Now their fields flourish while they can't benefit, and the forest reclaims them as it does the people. You see the forests that loom in all directions? Yes, there were forests, but each day they consume more and more of the farmlands."

Even though there were no windows in the dining room, she could still see the expansive forests from the windows in her memories. They carried on almost to the mountains.

He continued, "They did nothing to prevent it and can do nothing to stop the curse from destroying everything in front of them. They watched me grow into this form. I've stopped visiting so they won't see it, but they know. They wept each time I visited. This spares their tears. When the castle is finally consumed, and we are all creatures of the woods, the curse will be irreversible, and they will perish watching us feast on them."

"Oh my," Rosella said and choked on her beverage.

The servants shifted in the shadows.

Rosella's gaze flicked to them. Their hopeful eyes belied their reservations. More than just her sisters' freedom rested on her ability to break the curse.

"Are you sure you want to try to break the curse?" He swallowed. His dull eyes met hers, already resigned to his fate.

"Yes," Rosella said. She nodded without thinking.

To her surprise, his hand rested on hers. His massive fingers dwarfed hers. The soft touch twisted something in her stomach and a flush threatened her cheeks. Instead of curling her hand into his touch as she wanted, she remained still, meeting his gaze.

He sighed. "All others have perished. *You* can go free. My carriage will take you home at daybreak."

"I won't leave my sisters." She couldn't. She had to face whatever lay ahead.

"They don't deserve you." He looked away in disgust.

She snatched her hand back, coldness twisting on her fingers.

His fingers curled on the tabletop.

Anger curled through Rosella. And something else she didn't understand or want to admit to. She pressed her lips into a thin line.

"It's not about deserving. You don't deserve your family, good or bad. Our father and mother proved that. My sisters do stupid things, but we all do. It's not who they are. They saw a chance to better our lives, even if it meant breaking the law. This much unused wealth is squandered, especially when it could feed starving people. It does nothing locked up here. I agree it wasn't theirs to take. They would have agreed, eventually."

He blinked at her. His eyes tracked across the room and the various items of grandeur.

"But their one choice doesn't have anything to do with what they deserve. You love and get love. I love them. I choose to fight for them. They choose to fight for me. We chose each other."

The master stared at her, uncertainty flickering across his face.

"I don't understand what you mean," he finally said.

"And for that, I pity you."

"You pity me?" he said, pulling back. His murderous gaze traced around the room at the extravagance and surplus. His jaw worked.

"Yes, you've known greed and curses. You have servants to serve you. They don't love you. Your parents care about watching their kingdom and wealth fall, not their son suffering. I'd take fighting for food with my sisters every day versus being in my father's care."

His growing anger stalled, his eyes widening, and his mouth opened and shut. His face scrunched for a moment. "You fight for food?"

Rosella looked away and rubbed a hand absentmindedly over her neck.

"Not for much longer."

He raised an eyebrow.

Rosella blew out a breath. Their conversation was pointless. She waved away the words. She rubbed her temple, her thumb catching the scar on her face.

His chest rose and fell with breaths as his eyes locked on her, waiting for her to continue.

"Tell me about the riddle," she said instead.

The room, if possible, fell more silent. Only their breathing and unspoken words filled it.

"You know there are riddles?" The words were soft but heavy.

Her eyes flicked to the shadows. "You're not the only one cursed."

He blinked. His eyes gauged her. "True."

Nodding, he leaned forward, resting his furry chin on his animal hands. He closed his eyes, and recited:

"THROUGH THY HEART OF COLD,
  Mercy has never been told,
  Walk in the breath of the ravine,

TO PRECIOUS GEMS UNSEEN."

• • •

"And you're certain which ravine?" Rosella asked, sitting back. The words twirled in her mind.

"Yes," the master said.

"How do you know?"

"The waters are cold and unyielding. They give no mercy. It's impassible. They bubble in the image of boiling water, and old lore said a dragon lived there and its breath caused the phenomena. All charms will be held at a place of lore. We have many, but only one that involves a ravine."

"So, the charm is at the bottom of the ravine?"

"We don't know. It has a guard, but no one has been able to get past it," he said. His gold eyes dimmed.

"What is the guard?"

"We can't see it in the mirror." He looked away. "The men scream and then drown."

"Oh," Rosella mumbled. Her gaze fell to her plate.

"Can you swim?" he asked.

"I don't think it matters," Rosella said. "If it can drown those men, it can drown me." Her throat tightened with fear. Would she even make it to the keeper?

"And you're still willing to risk it?" the master asked.

Rosella stilled, forcing her mind to picture her sisters.

"We have a deal, unless you want to release my sisters now."

He stared at her, his yellow eyes searching her face. His chest heaved, and he started to nod. "Perhaps it..." he started, but Lucien interrupted them.

"Master, it is so brave of her to offer to help break the curse," he said and bowed. His hands reached for Rosella's but stopped himself. "We are so indebted to you."

"Lucien," the master breathed.

She looked between the master and the wolf, unspoken words hanging in the air.

The master turned and looked away, and when the wolf left, he said, "If it were just me, I'd let your sisters go. But if you can break the curse, I need to try for them. They don't deserve this life."

Rosella stared around the room. She understood more than he knew. His need was greater than him.

He returned his gaze to her. "If you perish on the quest, I will immediately free your sisters. For each charm you bring back from the riddles, I will free one of your sisters until the quest is completed. You have three sisters. The witch said there are three charms."

She nodded.

"And," he said, his hand moving to hers again, but he stopped.

Rosella leaned toward him. Without thought, she took his hand in hers, willing him to continue.

His startled eyes tracked to their joined hands. For a beat he just stared, and then curled his fingers around her hand.

Her heart thudded in her chest. Unexplainable expectancy twisted in her. She wanted to chastise herself for the foolishness, but instead let herself enjoy the moment of a soft touch. She may never get one again.

"When you have completed it, I will give you the gold necessary so you don't have to sell your mother's ring you offered me."

Rosella ran her free hand over her neck. She sputtered, "You don't have to do that."

"But I will."

Chapter Fifteen

ROSELLA TOSSED IN HER BED. SLEEP EVADED HER AGAIN. THE clock on the mantel showed how early it was in the single flickering candle's light. There was no point in waiting for the first of the sun. She had little time as it was. If she left now, her sisters would be mad, but saying goodbye again would only crack her heart and distract her.

She didn't want to face goodbye, their pleads, or the lump in her chest. If she stole away at night, they'd be angry with her, but their last memory would be of sitting by the hearth enjoying a cup of tea and cookies. The servants had allowed her a quick trip to the tower before promising everyone they'd bring her by again in the morning. The promise had allowed Rosella to leave quickly, but her heart and mind hadn't settled. It would be one of their best memories and she hadn't provided for it. They'd stolen it and were given a last meal out of duty.

Rosella shook the image from her mind and crept down the foreign hall, shrouded in darkness, her steps light on the plush carpet. The moon shone through slit windows in the ceiling and torches lined the walls, every few had the wicks lit low and the light flickered in the corridor. The treasures cast eerie dancing shadows on the ground as she passed by. As if they were trying to snare her.

She made it to the front door before she heard other footsteps; the hurried sounds weren't trying to be stealthy. Unsure what was going on, she grimaced and ducked into a recess of the wall to not slow them down. The figures' shadows dancing across the hall had grotesque limbs and inhuman bends.

The two ran past her but pulled up, sniffing the air. They whirled around to her hiding spot.

She recognized the wolf and fox. Instead of the uniforms they typically wore, they each haphazardly tossed on nightshirts.

"Are you backing out?' Lucien panted, his golden eyes sharpening in on her. A snarl flicked across his wolf lips.

"No," Rosella said. She patted her satchel, heavy with the supplies they'd provided. She moved from her spot toward the door, but both Lucien and Merl blocked her path. "Can't sleep. Getting a head start."

"But we were going to provide you with a breakfast, and help you off," Merl said. "You were going to see your sisters."

A pang in her heart made Rosella pinch her face. "I would rather get a head start now. I can cover ground before the heat of the day."

"Give me a minute and I'll grab my bag," Lucien said and stepped back. He passed a look with Merl who nodded.

"Why? What do you need your bag for?"

The fox and wolf shared a look. Finally, Lucien said, "I will accompany you on the journey."

"That wasn't the agreement." Rosella shook her head and pursed her lips. She made the promise, not him.

"It was going to be a surprise," the wolf said. "I'll help get you there quicker."

"It's a path," Rosella replied. "How will you joining make it quicker?"

"I know the path," he insisted.

Rosella stared at Merl and Lucien. They fidgeted under her scrutiny.

"Does the master know?" Rosella asked, peering down the hall. She could use someone familiar with the woods to not get lost again. Especially knowing that the path could be enchanted. But she didn't want to risk his life with hers.

"Yes," Merl said without looking at her.

"Go get him and prove it. I don't need to risk stealing from him.

Even if you're volunteering, I don't want anything to be misunderstood."

"He's sleeping, miss," Merl said, rubbing their neck. "It isn't the best idea to wake him up."

Lucien nodded in agreement.

"I could start screaming. Then no one will be sleeping." Rosella raised a challenging eyebrow. "Either get him to prove it or let me go alone."

The fox licked their lips. "But you won't wait for us to return."

Rosella snorted. They were right, but she also didn't want to add more onto their debt list. "I'll follow you to his chambers."

The fox sighed and deflated. "Fine, follow me," they said and waved for her to join them.

The fox didn't take her the way she'd expected but instead came from the opposing side she was used to. A deep darkness sat on the area, drowning out the light, whispering of magic and nature. The candles, lit brighter than in her area, did nothing to dispel the darkness. Older artifacts, centuries old, dotted the walls but didn't gleam back.

"It's different here," she said, rubbing her shoulders.

"It's the first part of the castle that is being consumed by nature," the fox said. "His parents are in this wing."

"Oh," she said, her voice small and flat in the heaviness.

They passed a few more corridors before entering an area familiar to Rosella. The fox looked at her before they raised their hand and knocked.

Silence followed and Rosella wondered if it was really his room. It was too dark to tell for sure, and the framing was the same throughout. But a familiar intensity hung in the air.

"He's asleep," the fox said. They stepped back and went a few paces down the hall.

She looked at them and the door. She readjusted her satchel and pounded her fist on the door.

The fox flinched and shrank back.

A loud crash sounded on the other side followed by growling curses.

"What?" The master's voice boomed through the room and rattled Rosella's bones.

Merl grimaced and twisted their hands at their sides.

"It's me, Rosella," she said. Her throat tightened. She tried to swallow the lump forming.

The air shifted and silence slipped over them. Then the sound of heavy steps toward the door. Her heart hammered with each step.

The master yanked the door open. He wore long pajamas, and his thick mane was in disarray.

He blinked at her, his eyes trying to focus.

She licked her lips. Words failed her when she met his gaze.

"What's wrong?" he asked. Sleep deepened his voice.

He stepped closer to her, his frame brushing her arm as he peered around her into the hall. His eyes caught on to the fox and then slowly tracked back to Rosella.

His warmth seeped through his shirt and her tunic. She swallowed before she could form words. "Are you sending the wolf with me?"

"The wolf?" he asked.

"Yes. Sorry, Lucien, the servant turning into a wolf."

"Lucien..." the master said and nodded. His eyes were still full of sleep and he rested his back against the doorframe, his large form filled the space between them. "He volunteered to help you."

"Oh, okay," Rosella said. She rubbed her neck, the awkwardness of the moment catching up to her and staining her cheeks.

"Why are you asking now?" he mumbled.

"Oh." Rosella's eyes flew open. She hadn't asked to leave early. She didn't know she was supposed to. She'd agreed to go, and was going. "I wanted to get a head start."

His brow furrowed and he looked around the hall as if trying to find answers. "It's still night."

"The sun will be up in a few hours," Rosella said, shifting her bag on her shoulder.

"So leave then," he muttered. He slid a hand over his face, rubbing at the sleep in his eyes.

"I'm awake. I'll go now."

He stared at her for a few moments. His golden eyes sharpened as the moment drained sleep from him. He stood straighter. "Was the bed uncomfortable?"

The fox whimpered. They curled their lips toward their teeth.

"No, it was very comfortable."

"Then why are you up?"

"I'm always up," Rosella said and looked over her shoulder. "I'm sorry I woke you. I should have believed Lucien and Merl. I apologize. I just wanted to make sure there were no misunderstandings."

He turned to the fox.

"Sir," Merl said with a bow, their lip trembling.

"Where is Lucien?" the master asked, looking past Merl into the recesses.

"Your Highness, he's gathering his belongings. I was watching the room when I saw her creep out. I woke Lucien and we followed her to make sure she was safe."

"I didn't creep out." Rosella folded her arms over her chest, her chin tilted down. "I was just quiet so as not to disturb others."

"Did anyone know you were going or see you?" the master asked, a slight uptick to his lips.

"I didn't need to inconvenience them."

"So, you crept out."

Rosella rolled her eyes. "I didn't mean to cause such issues. I just wanted to get started now."

The master nodded, his expression sobering. "The ravine is about a two-day hike on foot."

Rosella closed her eyes and let out a breath. Her days were already ticking down. The first item would be four days minimum if everything went well. That would only leave her two weeks at most for the other two items.

"If you'd have waited until morning," the master said. He lifted an eyebrow. "You'd know we were going to send horses with you."

"What?" Rosella asked. If he had a carriage, it made sense he had horses. She just hadn't considered he'd let her use them.

"With the horses and leaving at the start of the day, you could be back by midday tomorrow. Just over a day."

She blinked. That would save her so much time. Before thinking better, she placed a hand on his arm. His fur beneath the cotton was wiry and rough. His eyes flicked down to her. When her own mind realized her foolishness, she withdrew her fingers. The dim light didn't allow for the crimson clawing at her neck to show. "That is very generous of you. I hadn't expected..."

Lucien sprinted down the hall, his breaths coming in pants. Instead of his nightshirt, he wore breeches and a tunic. His fur tufted out of his shirt and his ears flicked as he came to a halt.

"Sir," he wheezed and bowed.

"Are the horses readied?" the master asked. He squared his shoulders back pulling himself to his full height.

Rosella's gaze tracked up his form. He stood almost three heads above her.

"The groom is doing it now," Lucien said.

The master's eyes fell back on Rosella, catching her staring at him. He held her gaze for a moment too long. He cleared his throat and said, "Be careful, both of you. We don't know what holds the charm, and we don't know what the charm actually is. If it's too dangerous, come back."

Rosella's jaw ticked. She wouldn't come back without the charm. Lucien could come back; he hadn't made a promise. Too much rested on her success. Freeing her sisters depended on it.

Chapter Sixteen

THE CLOMP OF THE HORSE'S HOOVES echoed into the trees, the trail gobbled up by their quick trot. The sun brightened the horizon, promising a clear day and warmth. The trees arched over them, their dancing leaves blocking the heat from their backs.

"How far is it on horseback?" Rosella asked. She sat on a dapple-gray gelding.

While riding his dark bay gelding, Lucien lifted his shoulder. "It's been years since I've gone there, but it should be half a day or so."

"If it's so dangerous, why have you gone there before?"

Lucien's eye scanned the scenery before he replied. "It is a beautiful place. As a boy, sometimes my family would picnic there, and we would watch the rapids. But that was years ago. Before the curse."

"Did you see the keeper?"

Lucien frowned as his eyes narrowed and darted to the side, trying to draw on the memory. "Not that I recall, but we didn't go down by the water. Just watched from the cliffs."

"What do you know about what we will face, then?" Rosella asked.

"That something pulls you under the water." Lucien swallowed.

"Have you seen the charm we're after? Is it large?" Her fingers tightened on the reins.

Lucien shook his head. "The mirror has never shown us an item nor the keeper. We've only seen..." He licked his lips but didn't continue. A shudder stole through him.

Sofia had said the others who tried drowned. To watch people you know and love...

"Javier was just seventeen. It was a few months after the curse."

Rosella's eyes cut to him, her heart already clenching knowing the results.

"He went solo thinking maybe it was the large group that had failed." Lucien's shoulders lifted and fell. A snarl rippled over his furred lips. "He even packed gifts for the keeper thinking it would help."

It obviously didn't, but Rosella waited for him to say it. To release the tension in his shoulders even if it couldn't release the pressure in his heart. She knew the feeling all too well.

"His scream still rattles in my ears when the nights are silent."

"I'm so sorry." The words couldn't do anything. Rosella had heard them all before. They didn't ease the pain. They only offered the giver peace of mind that they'd said them.

He nodded. His eyes glossed, and with a few blinks, they cleared.

Rosella let the silence envelop them the rest of the way through the forest. Neither words nor time could heal some wounds.

The forest petered out, the path opening into a meadow in full bloom on both sides. A few paces ahead the trail veered wide before a section of rolling hills that led into another swatch of forest.

Lucien slowed, his face turning to the left. Rosella stopped, casting a glance to the side, but she saw nothing.

"What's wrong? Do you see or hear something?"

He worked his jaw before turning his glossy eyes to her.

"Spare a few minutes?" he asked, and without waiting for an answer, directed his horse into the grasses.

With a frown and glance in the direction they should head, Rosella followed him. A few paces in, Rosella realized they were on an overgrown trail.

"Where are we going?" Rosella asked.

Lucien nodded ahead. "This used to be a busy trail that intersected with other paths. Now it is overgrown like most of the lands."

Rosella stilled. Was this how she had missed the route to the castle the few times she ventured to the city? Had there once been one, forgotten with the curse, and overgrown to block anyone from finding their way to the castle?

Lucien pulled to a stop at the peak of a hill. His voice was void of emotion. Cold eyes swept across the land. Rosella rode to his side. Below, the remnants of a small village sat. The once quaint place now had trees growing through the windows. Roofs settled in on the homesteads. The town's center now housed plants and bushes. A small well peaked beneath the foliage.

Goosebumps rippled over Rosella's skin and her neck hairs raised. She cast a glance around, not seeing anything, but knowing she was watched.

"Did the villagers…"

Lucien nodded. "None remain."

"Wolves?"

"Most likely," he agreed.

"But not certain?"

Lucien turned his golden eyes to Rosella. Something flickered behind them, something animalistic.

Instead of prodding, Rosella stared at him, meeting his intense gaze.

A twig broke, snapping Lucien's attention away from Rosella. Their horses pawed at the ground.

"We shouldn't stay," he said and pulled on the reins.

Rosella followed. Her horse pulled at the reins for a faster gait. She gave it the space.

Had the villagers watched each other turn? Had fear and confusion been their final thoughts? Or had they been offered a quick mercy, unlike the castle's staff?

"When the curse happened, did everyone start to turn right away?" It was impolite to ask such a personal question, but Rosella didn't retract it.

Lucien shrugged. "We didn't look human, but we didn't have as much fur as we do now. Some of us were children when it took place."

Rosella blinked. They had never experienced a childhood. She'd had a limited one, but she still had one.

"His Grace immediately took on the image of a beast, torturing his parents with his fur and roars. The rest of us children, still looked children. As we matured, we changed, though. Each of us taking on an animalistic image."

"And the castle carried on?" Rosella's shoulders tensed. Whatever had seen them in the village continued on with them.

"What were we to do?" Lucien's ear flicked backward and his eyes narrowed.

"Didn't they try to send the children away? Perhaps save them from the curse?" Rosella searched the sides of the trail, but nothing wavered in the grasses.

Lucien nodded back to the village. "Yes, some parents did have hopes, but when they reached other areas of the kingdom, the villagers, too, had started to change. When we still resembled humans more than beasts, we could stay only a few days or risk infecting them. There are lands the curse hasn't spread to, yet. We watch it crawl across the kingdom. But hope vanished as we aged. To preserve what we could of the kingdom, we've locked ourselves away in the castle grounds. We stopped going out save for an urgent correspondence. Even then, we make many precautions with timing of day and location."

"I am sorry," Rosella said.

"You didn't do it, Miss Rosella. In fact, you are trying to save us." Lucien's wolfish lips curled into a smile.

As they neared the next forested area, the bold, harsh sound of rushing water filtered through the trees. Whatever had trailed them from the abandoned village held back. Rosella didn't know if she should be relieved or more concerned.

Chapter Seventeen

A few miles into the trail, the rush of water intensified until the path widened and the trees thinned to the right, exposing a cliff.

"We're here," Lucien said and dismounted. His wolf ears flickered toward the sounds below.

Rosella scanned around. Nothing looked sinister or alarming. Forests framed them from behind, a sharp drop to the ravine beneath them, and open fields further down. It could be anywhere. Yet below lay the chance at her sisters' freedom.

Rosella dismounted and joined him. "What do we do with the horses?"

"We'll remove the bit and loosely tether them to the trees. If we don't return, someone should come to retrieve them... I think."

Rosella swallowed and followed suit. She moved her satchel from the horse and put it on her back.

"Is there a path down, or do we have to climb?" Rosella asked, searching the rock face.

"There's some small ledges farther down. We'll have to scale some, and jump. It's the easiest way down. Are you good at scaling?" He tracked his yellow eyes over her, appearing satisfied.

"I haven't ever scaled a cliff, but I'm game for anything necessary," she said. Rosella walked a few feet from the edge and peered down at the ravine. She noticed some larger ledges jutting out farther down and headed that way. The area on her side of the river had a rocky, sandy floor. A plush outcrop of trees ran along the river on the other side.

"I'll go ahead of you and help," Lucien said. He hurried in front of her and turned to slide down. His hands trembled with each grip.

Rubbing her hands on her leggings, Rosella rolled her eyes but turned around and picked her way down the face, steadily finding hand holes and grips. Her foot hit a solid rock jutting out of the cliff face. She allowed her weight to rest on it and flexed her fingers.

"I said I'd help," Lucien said, panting as he came to rest by her.

Rosella ignored him and scoped out the next spot. The ledge was smaller and farther down. She rubbed her fingers together, dust falling off. Dirt was embedded in her fingernails, and she had scrapes on her elbow and knees, but otherwise, she was fine.

"So which part are we headed to?" she asked, taking in the water gushing over the rocks in the river, the frothy haze resembling steam.

Lucien turned to face the ravine and stumbled back, his face ashen, and slid against the rock.

"What's wrong?" she asked, putting a hand on his furry arm.

He jerked away. Realizing it was just her, he offered her a weak smile.

"It's so far," he murmured, his gaze lost to the scenery. "I didn't realize how far."

"You're afraid of heights?"

He nodded and gulped.

"Okay," Rosella said, rubbing his arm. "I'll get the charm."

"What?" he spat.

"I'll finish going down. You stay, or if you want to head back to the horses, you can."

He tilted his head up at the cliff and shrank back at the distance they had come.

"Okay, stay here," she said,. "I'll help you when I get back."

"But you can't face it alone." His conflicted eyes wouldn't meet hers.

She forced a shrugged. "If I don't make it, take the horses and run. No sense in us both dying." Her stomach coiled and bile burned her throat. Her sisters' freedom was worth the risk. She had to focus on them.

"I came to help," he offered.

"You got me here quickly," Rosella said, her muscles already easing without having to watch his awkward descent. "You're more of a help staying here."

His lips curved down, but he nodded.

Rosella blew out a breath and adjusted her satchel, ignoring the possibility of what lay below. One thing at a time. She turned to face the cliff and repeated her meticulous steps, inching farther and farther down. The sun beat on her back, burning her skin and offering a promise of pain if she fell. Sweat beaded down her face, dipping into her eyes and salting her lips.

She pushed on. Images of her sisters eating at the castle brought a smile to her face. If she succeeded in time, she could offer them a lifetime of food and comfort. He'd free them if she died, but without her return, they'd have nothing, not even their mother's ring to hawk. She should have left it with them. If she failed now, they'd be worse off. They'd return to an empty till, sparse shelves, and the loss of their home.

Rosella swallowed and pushed the image from her mind. Surviving was all she could do now to help her sisters.

She blinked back the sweat and finally closed her eyes and allowed her feet to skim the surface for a crevasse to dig into.

She landed on the next ledge about twenty feet from the ravine floor. The slosh of the water sprayed her a bit, the fine mist cooling her hot skin. The thunder of the rapids toppling over the rocks crushed all other sound. From the angle, with the sun filtering through the mist, the steam of the rapids resembled a dragon's fire. The master was probably right, and this was the spot.

At twenty feet, she couldn't really jump, but she didn't need to be as picky with her holdings. If she had something to anchor the rope to, she'd just slide. Instead, she took her canteen out and took a few swallows, the fresh water chasing the salt away. She poured a few splashes onto her face to clean her eyes and cool her sweat-dampened hair and head.

Rosella faced the cliff again and grabbed at what rocks and holes she could. She slid a ways, the rough face tearing at her knuckle's flesh. The sting made her grip tightened, the rock digging into her fingertips.

She tumbled to the ground. She allowed herself to lay there and gulp in air, the spray drenching her but also providing cooling relief. Her fingers smarted, the throb matching that of her speeding heart. The hot sun sizzled her skin.

"You made it!" Lucien called. He'd climbed back up while she had scaled down and now stood on the edge.

"Yeah, so did you." She took in ragged breaths, each one a reminder she'd survived.

"I'll wait," he said.

Rosella pushed herself up to a standing position and scanned the river. Digging out a dagger from her satchel, she crept forward to the river. Nothing happened. No creatures materialized, no object suspended from the air, and nothing tried to pull her under the water.

She let out an uneasy breath. Her nerves tingled.

After rolling the riddle around in her mind, and finally said out loud, "Through thy heart of cold, Mercy has never been told, Walk in the breath of the ravine, To precious gems unseen."

Again, nothing happened.

The rapids raced past her, bubbling and frothing as they bashed into the cold waters. The sting of the cold droplets danced on her skin.

"Walk in the breath of the ravine?" she asked the river. She bit her lip and took a tentative step into the misting river. The waters tugged at her feet, and she almost lost her balance.

"Do I need to walk closer?" Rosella asked the water and stepped another foot in. She dug her heels into the ground, anchoring herself to the sandy floor to not lose her balance. She wouldn't be able to walk in the fierce current, so she shuffled bit by bit as she neared the most tremulous part of the waters.

"Your heart is not cold," a voice called to her. The melodious voice cut above the water's rapids. "Nor have you kept mercy."

"Does that mean I can't have the charm?" Rosella asked. Did she have to live the lines to earn the charm?

"Why do you want the charm?"

Rosella searched the area, but there was no visible person or creature. She played the riddle again in her mind. *To precious gems unseen…*

"May I see you?" Rosella asked instead of answering the question.

"Why would you need to? To gauge me for attack?"

Rosella pulled back. "No, curiosity. I'm not sure if you are real or my mind willing something into existence."

The waters stilled around the rocks, the rapids bubbling gently over the worn, smooth surfaces. A green figure sat perched on the rocks on the other side of the river. Trees framed her. With one step back, the dryad would merge back into the woods, hidden from view. Her long hair, made of various shades of green and gold, trailed behind her and glittered with a swirl in the water by her feet. Her eyes were blue like the water, and her skin glistened green. The waves washed over her feet, shimmering like gems. Ruby-red lips snarled predatorily at Rosella. She wore a cape of leaves—greens, browns, reds, and purples—and a necklace.

Flashes of fairytales flickered in Rosella's mind, the surrealness almost too much. As if she'd stepped into a book. Instead of the dread and fear that should coil through her, awe grounded her feet.

"Hello," Rosella said instinctively.

The dryad chuckled, and said, "Hello to you. Why do you want the charm?"

Rosella met her gaze.

"I need to retrieve the charm to free one of my sisters," Rosella said.

"One?"

"Yes."

"Who has them held captured?"

Rosella sighed and looked at the water. Sunlight glittered in the currents, her image distorted and wavy stared back. Would the dryad give her the charm knowing it would be for the capturer, the one cursed? The magical guardian likely already knew but was testing her. "The master of a castle."

"Will he benefit from the charm?"

"I believe so," Rosella said. "But I'm not certain how."

The dryad hummed and tapped her chin.

"Many have come before. They have failed. Why are you different?"

Rosella's stomach dropped. Her breath stilled. She blinked and shook her head. "I don't know. I would think I am similar to them. I want to help my family. I will do all I can to help them."

"What riddle were you told?" the dryad asked, tilting her head.

Rosella recited it for her.

"That's lovely..." The dryad smiled. "...but incomplete."

"Incomplete?" Rosella echoed. That was all the master had told her. Was that why all had perished before her? The master only had part of the riddle? Her mind skipped back to her sisters and her heart hammered. Was this really it? Had she made the ultimate mistake? Her mind ricocheted thoughts around, not grasping on to one.

With her breath uneven, she forced her body to suck in a long breath. Focus. *Chin high. Fake the confidence until it is felt.* Her sisters needed her. The castle needed her.

The dryad nodded. "Yes. 'Through thy heart of cold, Mercy has never been told, Walk in the breath of the ravine, To precious gems unseen, A loss of true measure, Yields the greatest treasure.'"

"A loss of true measure?"

"Yes, one you must pay," the dryad sneered and lunged at Rosella.

Rosella hit the water; her breath ripped from her. Water surrounded her, silencing the living world and dragging her down. The waves crashed around, entombing her in their watery grave. She bit her lip to force her mouth shut, the last bit of breath still trapped in her mouth. The water stung her eyes and chilled her face, the numbness searing through her nerves, begging for the relief of breath.

The dryad's hands clutched her arms, her nails piercing flesh. Beads of scarlet blood bubbled to the surface. Rosella wanted to yelp, but held her lips tightly together, the pain burning through her face and body.

She pulled Rosella forward until she faced her. The dryad's eyes had sunken in, the blue orbs like gems embedded in a skull. Her smile displayed razor-sharp teeth and a forked tongue.

Rosella squirmed against her, but it only tore at her flesh; her blood floated away now in ribbons. Searing pain tore through her nerves.

Dots danced in Rosella's vision, the whiteness spiraling out.

The dryad's words became garbled. Rosella blinked but nothing came into focus. The silence around her drowned out her thoughts.

"I'm not done with you yet," the dryad hissed in Rosella's mind.

Rosella gasped, air rushing into her lungs, searing her throat. She blinked. Dots danced in her eyes, but her vision sharpened. Suddenly, Rosella was on the forest's floor with the dryad. The dryad floated before her. A wicked smile tugged her lips. Despite the fresh gulp of air, water still surrounded Rosella. The leaves danced around them, river water splashed on them like tiny emeralds.

"You'll stay until I'm done with you. I get so few visitors. I get so lonely."

Fear curled through Rosella. Yet her lungs had stopped aching. Had she died? Was she dreaming? The woman's claws dug deeper into her arm, the pain ensuring Rosella she was still alive. Somehow.

"My pearl is mine," the dryad spat.

Rosella's eyes darted to the necklace; the shimmering orb a white iridescent pebble laced in silver. Was it that easy? She wore it daringly around her neck?

"What do you want for it?" Rosella asked in her mind, hoping the woman could hear her.

"I want your soul," she said.

Rosella stilled. "No," she said, shaking her head in the watery ossuary. "But I will trade for it."

"Trade for it?" the woman laughed. "And what would you have to trade? What is the greatest loss you have?"

Rosella's mind reeled through all she had. The satchel had many treasures to Rosella, but their loss wasn't much to her. She'd have to return them to the castle, anyway. It'd be simple and easy, but not a measurable loss. As her mind screamed dozens of thoughts, she tried to slide her fingers across her cheek, to rub the ridge. And then, like normal, trace down to her necklace to her ring. But the dryad's embrace locked her arms in place. If she didn't succeed, the ring was her sisters' ticket to starting over. It was her last token of her mother. Besides her sisters and their home, it was her greatest loss.

"I have a ring," Rosella said, the words like a musket shot in her brain.

"A ring? Show me." The woman released one of her arms.

Rosella tugged the chain out, bringing both it and the locket out into view. "It was my mother's."

The woman's eyes lit up and she smiled. "I want the locket."

Rosella clutched at the hanging pendant. It'd be easy to give. There was no sacrifice. Her fingers tracked to it. The cold metal meant little to her. She could give it and be free. She shook her head. Her nostrils flared and her eyes stung with tears that wouldn't come. "I can't. It's not mine to give. Its loss isn't mine. And you know that."

"You wear it," the woman sneered.

"I need to return it to the person it belongs to. Its loss is nothing to me. You can have my mother's ring, though."

"Won't she be mad?"

"She passed away years ago. It's all I have to give."

The woman's smile faltered, and she tilted her head. "It's your mother's ring and yet you will part with it?"

"If it will free my sisters, yes. Their lives are more important than an object that won't bring my mother back."

"Yet you carry it by your heart?"

"It's my mother's. It's all I have left, and I miss her. I have nothing left but this. For all I have before you, this is my greatest loss."

Rosella unclasped it and held it out. The water snaked it away, the gems dull beneath the current. She swallowed the lump in her throat. She had no choice but to succeed now. Or her sisters would have nothing.

Long slender hands plucked the ring from the current. The woman blinked, her blue orbs sparkled, and a blue pearl wept from her eye. The gem glimmered and drifted into the woman's hand.

She looked at it and then Rosella. "It seems you have provided your greatest loss. All the others tried to give me something they could stand to part with. Or what I requested, taking the easiest way out."

With stinging eyes, Rosella took the blue pearl, leaving the decoy with the woman below the depths. She breached the surface, her lungs screaming for air. She took useless breaths as her body fought for life. The sun had dipped into the horizon, long shadows of the forest drenching the path and ravine. A cold wind skimmed her arms and she shivered. She clawed her way to the shore and lay gasping for air. Something hit her foot and she looked down to see her satchel.

She scanned the cliff's edge but didn't see Lucien. He probably headed back when she'd been pulled under water. She looked at the climb, her limbs fatigued from the first climb and the underwater battle. She'd have to camp on the ground and scale it in the morning.

She held the pearl in her hand. The cold pebble dug into her palm and she rolled it to increase the sensation. She'd found the first charm. She'd beaten the first riddle. Now, she just needed to get it back.

Chapter Eighteen

Rosella awoke against the ravine's wall, her back stiff and her skin scratched and sore. The moon was bright in the sky, backdropped by millions of glimmering stars, the swirls of colors recessing on themselves.

She patted her chest. The one necklace with the locket was still there beneath her blouse. Her fingers rubbed the empty spot her mother's ring normally lay and she swallowed. Her sister's freedom was worth the loss. She blinked back the emotion rimming her eyes. She had much more to do than to wallow in what couldn't be.

She grabbed the canteen looped around her neck. The pearl lay inside, padded with remnants of her shirt. The treasure. She uncapped it, verifying the pearl was still was inside.

The small pebble would free one of her sisters. She draped the leather strap over her neck and glanced up the cliff.

She rubbed her hands on her legs, bringing sensation to both, and started to ascend the face. Going up was quicker without the sun beating down on her or the trepidation of what lay in wait in the waters. Hand over hand, she pulled herself up the rock. Her hands skimmed the rocks, rubbing them raw, as her feet found footing.

She crested the wall and fell to the ground, the grass a cool relief on her aching skin. She leaned back, allowing herself a reprieve in the soft embrace. She guzzled water from the second canteen and looked at the woods. The trees laced together. Their branches, which had offered protection from the sun's heat earlier, now cloaked the path in blackness, capturing the moonlight high in the canopy. Real or imaginary, she felt eyes watching her.

She didn't have time to wait, darkness or not. She didn't want to risk using the flint on a branch; the light would make her an easier target for whatever prowled in the folds.

With the unknown lurking behind the trunks, she reached for her dagger and swore realizing it was gone. She looked around for a rock or large stick before grabbing the few rocks surrounding her. She took off at a jog as she entered the trees. The moon's brightness was snuffed out beneath the branches. Around her was stillness aside from her breath. The crunch of her feet. After her eyes adjusted to the darkness, she scanned the perimeter as she went. She strained to hear anything, but her rough breathing and beating heart drowned out most sound.

After about thirty minutes or so, Rosella finally strolled to a fast walk, but chills shimmied down her spine. She was being watched again. Or it never left. Whirling around, she tried to see what was watching her. The path remained empty but thick shadows swarmed in the trees. Hunching her shoulders, she picked up her pace.

The feeling grew, her stomach tightening, and adrenaline flooded her system. Entering the open field she and Lucien had ridden through before, her heart thudded louder. Images of the morning spurred her forward. Unable to contain the surge, she tore off running. The rough path tore at her worn-soled boots, driving into her flesh. She bit back the shards of pain piercing up her legs and continued. Stopping wasn't an option.

The howl finally came and was answered by one closer.

She whispered a prayer and tightened her arms around the canteen, pressing it to her chest. She had too long to go.

The brush crunched around her, the snaps drawing closer to her. Her breath came in long raspy grunts, increasing as the noises drew near. Her vision tunneled, the cacophony of her heart competing against the forest's warning.

She ducked at the skittering of feet behind her. There was more than one creature. She tightened her embrace around the canteen.

The first creature landed on her, nails tearing at her shoulder and catching the canteen strap. The leather cord cut into her arm as it tugged. Screaming hot pain burned her shoulder. A cry escaped her as she nestled the canteen closer and grabbed for the rocks but the weapons fell from her hands.

She balled around the canteen and fell to the ground, her body the last defense of the pearl.

"No," she cried. She was so close. She had the charm. She could free a sister.

A snarl cut the air followed by another. She looked up to see three wolves surrounding her. So close she could see their eyes and sharp teeth.

In desperation she clutched her belt again, habit driving her to reach for her weapon. The bite of her blade sliced her palm, blood weeping from the wound. She flinched and then stared down. It hadn't been there when she'd left the ravine. She didn't question the miracle—it was one of many that day—and pulled out her blade.

Rosella cautiously pushed herself up to a sitting position and eyed the wolves. The familiarity of the three wolves staring at her stirred memories. It was like her three sisters ganging up on her. She had to remain calm, focused, and in control.

Pushing a breath through her nose, she sucked in a steadying one, long and slow. Her body eased with the practiced breathing. Calm. Focused. In control. Fake the confidence until you feel it.

She brandished the blade and put her feet beneath her.

The wolves growled, their teeth bared, and stepped forward.

She clutched the blade tighter, the handle stinging her cut, reminding her she was alive. Bolting forward, she rushed the closest wolf.

The other two lunged at her. She caught the first wolf in the front leg with her blade. It yipped, stumbling backward.

The motion sent her onto her back. The two other wolves dove at her. She thrusted the blade at the charging wolves. She caught the next one on the belly, the gash shallow. Blood slicked her blade and hand.

The first two retreated but the third wolf bit her shoulder, the searing pain causing pops of light to burst in her eyes. It dug in, pulling her toward it to shake her. Her vision darkened as her body tightened in protest. It'd tear her flesh and snap her neck like prey.

She whimpered, the sound lost in the air. She lashed out with the blade behind her, catching the third one. It yipped.

The third one, still bleeding from the attack, grabbed at her. It snatched the canteen strap and pulled it from her. With the prize in its mouth, the wolf shook it, rattling the contents within.

"No," she shrieked and jumped at the wolf. Her shoulder screamed at the pain. Nausea coursed through her. But she landed on the wolf; her body draped over its back.

The wolf jerked at the contact, snarling and snapping to buck her off. It dug its teeth into the canteen, piercing the bladder. The long whistle sliced the air.

Rosella grabbed chunks of its fur, its ears, anything to get closer to the canteen. Her arm brushed the wolf's face and mouth. The teeth raked her arm, causing her to drop her dagger. Her blood dampened the wolf's muzzle.

Too focused on the canteen, she ignored the pain and dagger as she clawed at the wolf's eyes with one hand. With the other, she scrambled for the canteen. The wolf lurched back, tossing its head and jerking its eye out of her grasp. It snarled but held tight to the prize.

She finally slipped her arm through the loop. The leather rubbed harshly against her wounds, but she felt nothing through the adrenaline. She yanked her arm back, wrapping the leather around her fist, over and over, bringing her closer and closer to the wolf's mouth and teeth. Closer to her possible death. Closer to the vulnerable eyes.

The wolf held on, its teeth bared as they sunk deeper into the leather. Its head reared, trying to avoid her other hand as she reached again for its sensitive eyes.

It snapped at her arm around the canteen, its grip loosening with each readjustment. Keeping it distracted on the canteen, she wrapped her other arm around the wolf's neck and squeezed, clawing at the skin around the neck, digging her nails into the tender flesh.

With a yip, it released the canteen and turned its jaws toward her.

The motion rocked her. She crashed to the ground and the landing knocked the breath from her, but she rolled to avoid the wolf's teeth. Its snoot skimmed her arm, and she kicked at the wolf's side. She made contact with its chest, which only angered it.

"I don't want to hurt you, but I will," she screamed. Her voice cracked. Her hand miraculously landed on the dagger. Grabbing it, she slashed at the wolf, catching it in the torso. It was shallow, but blood darkened her blade.

The wolf jerked back in pain. With a whimper, it turned and darted away.

Rosella fell back to the forest floor, the canteen in her lap, her shoulder throbbing. She winced when she ran a hand over it. Withdrawing it, her hand was coated in her blood. Her clothes hung damply around her, from sweat and blood.

She laughed, unable to contain the multitude of emotions bursting forth. Salty tears streamed down her face.

She checked the canteen again and smiled seeing the pearl inside.

She used a tree to pull herself up and leaned against it. The movement tugged her wounds, and a trickle of blood ran down her arm.

Her stomach rumbled as her adrenaline fled. Tremors raced down her body and wobbled her knees. Exhaustion pulled on her eyes and slowed her muscles.

She could sleep now, but instead, she pulled out a bread roll and wedge of cheese, allowing herself the simple pleasure of eating. She couldn't stop yet.

"I'm coming," she whispered to the forest.

THE SUN WAS AT ITS ZENITH AND EDGING INTO THE HORIZON of the next day when the castle came into view. Fresh tears ran down her face, and her feet felt lighter. She ran the remaining distance, her hand bracing her shoulder as the vibration tore through her and her cuts reopened from the motion. Ignoring her body's pain, she focused only on making it to her sisters.

The gate remained unlocked, and the grounds were covered in debris and vegetation. Stumbling over the uneven terrain, the ground tore at her feet and knees, but she was undeterred and scrambled for the door. Before she could open it, the door was thrown open and her sisters and the servants darted out, all shouting at her at once.

The words blurred into one shrill drone.

She flinched. Her shoulder dropped and her body buckled.

Her sisters, somehow not in the dungeon, tugged at her, pulling her into different embraces.

"We saw you coming!" Bridgette cheered at her. "He let us out when Sofia saw you coming."

"I said you could do it!" Camilla crowed.

"I'm so proud of you," Giselle said.

The staff twittered around her, their hands clambering to touch her. To cheer her. Faces swirled in her view. The cacophony of applause rattled her mind.

"Quiet," the master's roar sliced through the celebration, silencing everything.

Rosella pushed forward out of her sisters' hold but fell to her knees. She'd made it. A sob lodged in her throat.

She couldn't form words, but with her bloodied hand she held the canteen out to him.

Then darkness enveloped her.

Chapter Nineteen

Awaking in a bed, Rosella snuggled deeper down, enjoying her dream. The plush comforter was warm and the pillow soft and heavenly. She was in a castle with food, a dry roof, and no looming taxes. There were no holes to plug or wood to scrounge.

The whisper of a soft snore tickled her ear. Her sisters must still be asleep despite the stream of sunlight flooding the room. She should get up. The store needed to be open to make money. Yawning, she pushed herself up. Her body protested, her muscles tightening against the strain. Stars popped in front of her eyes and with a gasp she slumped back.

The snores turned to snorts, and someone rustled nearby.

"You're awake," the master's voice rumbled from a chair near the bed. A large hand tightened around hers, warm and soft, but strong. A surge shot through her veins. His fingers flexed as he started to slide his hand away. For a reason she couldn't explain, she curled her fingers around his hand, staying his retreat.

The master. Not her sisters. Something odd twisted in her stomach and her heart hammered in her chest. A curl of embarrassment twisted through her at her foolish response.

Rosella closed her eyes and groaned. She remembered where she was. Why she was there. How her body was hurt. She took her hand back, freeing him from her odd reaction.

She went to speak, but her mouth was dry and her tongue like sandpaper. She croaked, "Water."

A glass was pressed to her lips, and she let him help her drink.

"Thank you, Your Highness," Rosella whispered.

"Grayson," he said. "Please call me Grayson." With gentle fingers, he brushed a lock of hair from her face.

A warm sensation followed where he touched. Tingles racing down her skin. She ignored it and nodded.

"I made it back," she said after pulling away from the emptied glass. The wolves' faces flashed in her mind. In the light of the room, she could almost see their lost humanness in the memory of their eyes. The snarls tickled her ear. Her heart pounded at the memory. Her shoulders curled around to protect her torso. She grimaced. They'd stay with her forever in her nightmares.

Grayson watched her, his yellow eyes assessing. He reached for her hand but stopped. He curled his fingers and pressed them to his leg. His disheveled mane matched his wrinkled silver-and-gold elaborately embroidered tunic and black breeches. His boots sat next to his chair, his feet donned in stockings. Based on the severity of the wrinkles, he'd been there the whole night.

"Yes, you made it back," he whispered. "You've been asleep a full day."

Unable to meet his gaze, she stared at the bedspread and the way the sun reflected off the metallic threads. Allowing her body to relax, she leaned back. Once Rosella eased back on the pillows, he settled back in the chair.

Grayson started, "We thought..."

Heavy silence filled the space between them.

Rosella turned to him, his gaze lost in something only he could see.

"You thought what?"

"We thought you were pulled under and... drowned." His voice cracked as his eyes fell to the floor.

"I was pulled under," Rosella confirmed, leaning back as the memories danced in her mind. Her lungs burned at the memory. She rubbed over her chest, feeling her heart through the shirt. She should have drowned. She shouldn't have made it.

"How'd you get out?"

"I shouldn't have," Rosella said, opening her eyes. "She pushed me back to the surface. She did something so I could breathe underwater and answer her questions. Then she pushed me back."

"She?"

Rosella nodded. "The guard was a woman, a tree dryad. She was stunningly beautiful. Shades of green. She had the rest of the riddle that I had to break."

"There was more to the riddle?" Grayson asked, leaning forward. "I'd never heard that in the other attempts. How'd you solve it?"

"I gave her a treasure," Rosella said. She rubbed her neck, her fingers toying at the empty spot. Hollowness from the lost contact with her mother threatened her chest, but her fingers curled around the pendant below her shirt. It had been the plan to exchange the ring. And now her sisters were closer to freedom. She just had to finish the other two for everything not to be in vain.

"A treasure? Did you give her the money in the satchel?"

Rosella shook her head. "No, it had to be a loss of measure to me. The money is yours."

"What did you have?"

Rosella swallowed, and said, "I gave her my mother's ring."

His eyes widened, and he sucked in a breath. "What?"

"'A loss of a true measure, Yields the greatest treasure,'" Rosella recited. She licked her lips and averted her eyes to the bedsheet. "I had to lose something of value to me."

"But you've lost..." His voice tapered off. "I'm sorry."

She flicked her gaze to him. Tears blurred her vision, but she kept them at bay.

He stared off in the distance, his eyes seeming to see through the ceiling.

"You promised," Rosella's voice broke. If he broke his promise...

"Yes," he said, returning his gaze to her. "Yes, you have my word. Your sisters will go free and you will get the money for your taxes if you break the curse."

Doubt sank in her stomach. So many had offered her help along the way, but at least now she knew the price. She was risking her life to break the curse. So far, he had honored what he offered. Her sisters were fed and clothed as she tried to break the curse. She had nothing if she didn't follow through on her end. She had no other option but to trust he'd honor his word.

"You've already done more than anyone has in breaking the curse." His yellow eyes found hers. Sorrow and cautious hope shone back. His jaw ticked and he looked to his furred arms.

"I wasn't alone," Rosella said, remembering Lucien. "Did Lucien make it back safely?"

"Yes, he'll be punished for leaving you," Grayson growled. "He confirmed you drowned, but he ran when you were pulled into the water. He didn't wait or try to help."

"Don't punish him. There was nothing he could have done. I heard about the others. I should have drowned. Besides, she pulled me under at midday and I didn't crawl out until sunset."

"How is that possible?"

"How is it possible you're cursed?"

He opened his mouth to speak but closed it.

"Where's my canteen?" Rosella asked. She finally remembered what she'd earned.

"I'll get you more water," he said and reached for the glass.

"No! Where's my canteen? I need it."

"You gave it to me," he said. His brow furrowed at her.

"Where is it?" she screeched.

"I brought it up with us." His eyes widened and his lips flattened into a line. He reached behind him and pulled out the scratched and torn bladder. "This won't hold water anymore. We'll get a new one."

"It doesn't have to," Rosella said and held her hand out.

He handed it to her.

She opened it and took out the cloth-wrapped pearl. She rolled it in her palm, the small bauble that offered so much, and then extended it to him to take.

"What is it?"

"It's the charm," she said.

"What do I do with it?" He reached for it, his brows pinched together.

"I'm not—" she started to say, but her eyes grew watching the magic unfold.

The pearl disintegrated on his touch, and blue swirls engulfed him.

The magic blazed and then dissipated into his skin. His fur glowed, then dulled. Rosella blinked, realizing his fur had been replaced with human skin momentarily before the fur covered him again. His body hunched closer to the ground, and he resembled more of a beast.

She reached out to touch his hand and rubbed a finger over the new fur. The soft fur bristled on her contact, and a charge shot through her. She pulled her hand back, rubbing her fingers.

"I'm sorry." Color stained her face.

His eyes enlarged. They stared between her and his hands, which were now curved with fur sprouting on his knuckles. He ran his hands over his arms and stood, touching his face and neck, the further transformation evident.

His form was still large, and his legs and head resembled a more canine structure. If she saw him in the woods, she'd assume him a beast, not a man.

He turned back to her, his eyes blazing. "It's worse!" he growled.

Her eyes widened.

He turned in the mirror, his breaths coming heavier and harder. "I never should have thought anything would help. I was a fool."

"No," Rosella stammered. "We followed the riddle."

"How did this make it better?"

Words rolled on Rosella's tongue, but none would help.

"I... I don't know... Why would she give me the wrong charm?"

"It'll never be broken. We're doomed to forever be like this. Our hope was just another part of it."

"Grayson," Rosella whispered. His harsh gaze fell to her. "I can go back. I can seek her out. See if she tricked me. I'm sorry, Grayson. It's what she gave me."

His eyes shuttered. With a blink, his face fell. "It's all part of her cruel curse," he muttered. "It has to be the charm you were to retrieve. It just makes it worse unless broken."

"Then I go for the next charm." Rosella moved her legs to the edge of the bed.

His eyes fell to her dangling legs. "You need rest."

She shook her head. "There isn't time." Flinching from a jolt of pain in her side, she went to push herself up. Before she could stand, he was in front of her. Despite his transformation, he laid gentle hands on her shoulders. Startled, her head turned to see his hands on her. His leg brushed her knees. A tingle raced through her. And when she looked up, little room separated them. Her mouth fell open, her breaths shallow. His eyes darkened as they tracked from her eyes to her lips and back.

A knock sounded on the door, drawing their attention. Grayson stepped back, creating a chasm of space between them.

"Come in," Grayson barked.

A wolf burst in. Images of the forest flooded her mind. She gasped and reached for her sword before realizing it wouldn't be in the bed with her. Rosella blinked and leaned back. "Lucien?"

"Yes," he said, a smile brightening his wolf face. "You found it? You survived?"

"Yes," Rosella nodded, staring at his golden eyes, long snout, and furred hands. He, too, had transformed more into an animal form. Had the dryad given her the wrong charm? Had she been tricked? Had she furthered the curse instead of helping break it?

She looked to Grayson, but his gaze was averted and distant.

"Roz!" Giselle squealed and pushed into the room. She bounded across the room and jumped onto the bed.

Camilla and Bridgette followed closely behind and crawled onto the bed with them.

The three enveloped her in a hug, rocking back and forth.

"You scared us to death," Camilla said, swatting her uninjured arm and then kissing her cheek.

Giselle pushed Camilla backwards. "Don't hurt her."

"Don't push me." Camilla shoved Giselle back.

"Knock it off," Bridgette ordered. She turned to Rosella. "How are you?"

"I..." Her voice faded off as she took stock. Her shoulder throbbed, her head was light, her stomach churned for food, and her hands and arms stung from the scrapes. "I'm okay."

"Liar," Bridgette said. A watery smile tugged on her lips.

Rosella stared between her sisters, words trapped on her tongue. Something was off with her sisters. She blinked, their images swimming into focus. Their eyes seemed larger, their faces more angular. Her wide eyes tracked to Lucien and Grayson, both more animal. Her sisters... were morphing too?

"Roz?" Giselle asked. "Your face..."

Rosella's hand flew to her face. Nothing new.

"You lost all your color. Are you going to be sick?" Giselle scooted back.

Her sisters had fallen into the curse. The words refused to roll from her tongue. They didn't seem aware, and she couldn't burden them with a truth she had to overturn.

"Rosella?" Grayson's voice startled her.

Blinking, she shook her head. Her sisters' appearances were once again normal. She'd only imagined it. The days of fear were catching up with her.

"Perhaps her sisters should return to their room," Arthur offered from the doorway. His squirrellish cheeks were larger than before, and teeth protruded from his mouth. "Miss Rosella needs more rest."

"Rooms? Aren't you staying in cells?"

"That'd be easier for you, huh?" Camilla said. "Keep us in one place." A cheeky smile lit her face. "His Grace is letting us stay in a room while you save everyone. He's posted guards outside of it because he still doesn't trust us. Still, nicest prison possible."

Rosella's attention jumped to Grayson, the voices a buzz around her. He'd been kind to her sisters, offering the comforts of his castle, while she brought back a charm that deepened the curse.

With his shoulders back and rigid posture, he met her stare, but his eyes were unreadable. The heated look from moments ago was gone. An odd sensation curled in her stomach.

"We're okay," Bridgette whispered, interrupting the moment. "We'll be here to help you heal up, too."

Giselle nodded.

"I need the next riddle," Rosella said. She leaned against the pillows, trying to distract her mind from Grayson.

"You need to rest," Bridgette scolded.

"There isn't time."

"We don't have the riddle," Grayson said, rubbing a hand over his morphed face. "Rest would be best."

Instead of protesting as she'd done earlier, Rosella set her jaw to save energy for when she would leave.

"Hey," Camilla exclaimed. "You have more fur! And your face..."

Bridgette growled and swatted Camilla to stop talking.

"If you don't have the riddle, how do I know where to go?" Rosella asked. She narrowed her eyes at Camilla and raised an eyebrow in warning.

Camilla mimed her but remained silent.

Sofia slinked in, her cat face ashen. She trembled as she handed a sheaf of paper to the master. "This was found on your parents."

"Found?" Grayson asked.

"It just appeared, sir," the cat said. "The castle, Master... the vines are retreating," She looked around and startled backward seeing the changes of the other cursed ones. "Master, Lucien..."

Sofia ran her hands over her face and gasped. She hurried to a mirror and fell back at the sight of her furry face.

"Retreating?" Grayson said and moved to the window to peer out. "The ground is healing?"

"Yes, sir," Lucien said. "Look at the gardens. There are blooms. She broke the first part of the curse. It is healing the land."

"So it did help?" Grayson asked, his gaze only finding Rosella's.

"But it's accelerating their change," Camilla whispered.

The words hung thickly in the room. The curse was unraveling on both ends.

"So each charm undoes something?" Bridgette finally said. "It's in layers?"

"We weren't told that," the master said. "It just required three impossible charms to find."

"Not impossible with Rosella looking for them," Camilla said, pride brightening her face.

Rosella rolled her eyes but smiled.

"A new riddle?' Giselle asked, gesturing toward the paper. "That must be for the second charm."

"I wonder what it does," Camilla said.

Grayson swallowed. His eyes cast to his staff and their more pronounced features.

"What does the paper say?" Rosella gestured her chin toward it.

His gaze flicked to her, guarded and raw, and then the paper. He shook his head.

"What?"

"You need to rest," he said. He furrowed his brow as he crumpled the paper in his paw.

Lucien squinted, looking between the master and Rosella. Not happy with what he saw, his lips curled into a snarl. "Sir, look at us. As the castle heals, we are transforming faster. We are running out of time. It is accelerating as she closes in. If she says she's ready, we should let her go. We can't waste time."

The others turned to him.

"Do your eyes not work?" Camilla asked Lucien. She shoved her way to the edge of the bed to stand up and place her hands on her hips.

"What? They work fine! The curse is eroding away the castle's servants. We need to hurry or we will be fully animals!"

And possibly her sisters.

"She's obviously injured and needs to recover," Camilla countered, sticking her finger in Lucien's face as her own flushed in anger.

Rosella cleared her throat, drawing their attention.

"I only have fifteen days to break the curse and return home to save our business and house." Rosella thrust her arm toward Camilla to stop her.

"She's in a hurry, too," Lucien spatted back at Camilla and nodded toward Rosella. "If we don't hurry, it may be too late."

Grayson bobbed his head and sighed.

"All right," he growled.

"Our house isn't worth your health," Bridgette said. She settled by Rosella to wrap an arm around her shoulders.

"She survived a drowning," Lucien said. "She's tough."

"We know that!" the sisters yelled.

He raised his palms up in surrender.

"Tell me the riddle," Rosella said.

Her sisters started to protest, but she shook her head at them. She had to do it. Her sisters and the castle depended on her to retrieve it. She could rest afterward.

Grayson unfolded the paper. Holding the crumpled mess, he read, "An opposing view it grows, Its beauty in repose, The prick to defend, Until plucked to mend.'"

"What do you think it means?" Rosella reached for the paper.

The master frowned, but begrudgingly handed her the paper.

"Yes, I can read," Rosella said and rolled her eyes.

His jaw ticked and he momentarily averted his gaze.

"Our mother was an earl's niece. She taught us." She flinched before her eyes cut to Giselle.

"It's okay, Roz," Giselle said. She smiled and patted Rosella's leg. "You taught me. You're the best mother."

Bridgette stilled and looked at Rosella. Sadness drooped her face, and tears rimmed her eyes. "I'm sorry you had to be."

"Oh, knock it off." Rosella swatted at her sister. "We do what we must."

"You don't have to do this," Bridgette said. She nestled on the edge of the bed, her fingers curling in her skirt. She sniffed and blinked away at the tears. "Really, you don't."

"Yes, I do."

"Roz," Bridgette whispered. She licked her lips and bowed her head in resignation.

"Did you pick yet?" Lucien asked her, interrupting the sisters.

"Pick what?" Rosella asked, giving him a quizzical look.

"You get to free one of your sisters," he said.

"Oh, yeah," Rosella said. The victory was small, but one would get freedom.

Camilla snorted and shook her head. "Don't pick me, I'm sticking it out until the end."

"What about the house?" Rosella said. "The business? You're the next oldest."

"Do you want me in charge?" Camilla challenged.

Rosella made a throaty sound.

"That's what I thought," Camilla said. A wicked grin danced on her lips. "Besides, they won't believe anything I say. I'll likely make it worse."

"Bridgette makes the most sense," Giselle said. She smiled brightly at Bridgette when she turned a dark look her way. "You're the next most stuffy, prudent, parent-like one of us."

"And she could go see Gavin," Camilla said with a smile. "With no chaperone."

Hot red flooded Bridgette's cheeks.

"Or wait." Camilla snapped her fingers. "Giselle could go and try to stop Odette from marrying Louis."

Giselle gasped.

"Camilla!" Rosella scolded.

"What?"

"I think we all stay until the end," Bridgette said, smoothing out her skirt, unable to meet anyone's eyes. "If any of us go back now, there will be too many questions and not enough... realistic answers. None of us but Rosella would go alone. They all know that. It would alarm the town. Their forced help would make things worse. Besides, Benson will watch everything for us so that Rosella isn't angry with him. He's hoping this helps his courting her. We have fifteen days to get back."

The master's golden eyes drifted to Rosella, searching her face.

Rosella swallowed hard and stared at her hands. "He's doing it because you coerced him."

"So?" Camilla demanded. "He'll make sure it's all still standing. It *not* standing would make you the opposite of happy. He doesn't want that."

"He's still doing it," Bridgette said. "We all want to be together."

Though they appeared fine now, Rosella couldn't shake the image of her sisters from earlier, their own faces changed with the curse. The town would seize them. Illusion or not, it wasn't worth the risk.

"Wait, an opposite view," Camilla said, snapping her fingers as she jumped. "Where was the first one located?"

"In a ravine," Rosella said.

"What's opposite of a ravine?"

"A desert?"

"No. Well maybe, but deserts aren't around and I'm hoping it's closer. What's opposite of a big cut in the ground?"

"There are no deserts in our kingdom, and all the charms are to be in our kingdom," Arthur added. "In an area of lore."

"What about a big pile of ground?" Giselle asked.

"Yes!" Camilla squealed. "A mountain, or volcano! Oh, a volcano would be so neat."

The three sisters stared at her.

"There aren't volcanoes around here, either," Bridgette deadpanned.

"It'd still be cool," Camilla said, folding her arms over her torso and sitting against the bedframe.

"None in our kingdom, Miss Camilla," Arthur corrected again with a smile.

"Are there mountains in the kingdom?" Rosella asked. The ones she saw from the window would take weeks of travel to reach. "One with lore?"

The master and Lucien looked at each other. Something passed between them.

Finally, Grayson said, "We're on a foothill. If you go over the hill, you'll be in the valley of a mountain range."

"Is there a lore associated with them?" Rosella turned her hopeful gaze to Grayson.

Lucien and the master shared another look.

"What?" Giselle asked. "What does that look mean?" She moved a finger back and forth between their faces.

"There's a rumor," Grayson said. "I guess lore..."

"Oh, I bet it's there." Camilla squealed and pressed her fists to her lips. "What is the rumor? I bet it's related."

"What's the rumor?" Rosella asked. She dug her nails into the comforter. Whatever it was, she was about to face it.

"There's a rumor of a troll."

Chapter Twenty

Shortly before mid-day dinner, Arthur ushered her sisters out with Sofia to the dining hall, which was readied with delicacies. Grayson retired with a stern look from Arthur.

"Miss Rosella," Arthur sighed. His warm eyes sparkled in the dim light.

She met his gaze.

"I want to change your bandaging. It has started to seep."

Rosella touched a gentle finger to her shoulder. Blood dotted her fingers when she retracted them.

"You don't have to go immediately," he breathed. "Your body needs to heal."

"My body can wait." Her sisters, the staff, and Grayson couldn't.

"It is very nice to have visitors again. It's been so long."

"How long have you served the kingdom?"

Arthur's brow furrowed, his gaze darting to the side in thought. "Since I was a boy. My father was the butler to master's grandfather."

"Do you have any children?" The words were out before Rosella considered the implication of them.

Instead of sadness, his lip quirked up in a smile. "I do not have my own, no, Miss Rosella."

"But?" she prompted, seeing his amusement.

"But, due to circumstances, the master has been like a son."

Something flickered behind his eyes, his gaze darting around the room.

"He didn't have a nanny? I thought royalty..."

"He did, ma'am, but when the curse happened..." This time his lips curved into a frown. "A spoiled human child is quite different from a spoiled child with claws and sharp teeth."

"He hurt his nanny?" Her breath caught in her throat.

"Oh, no, miss, no, no, no. There were some unfortunate and unintentional scratches, but nothing serious. Most were too afraid of what he'd become. Most of us still resembled humans with only the beginning of changes."

"When everything settled down, I took on the main care of the master. It wasn't proper, a butler raising the master and future king, but nothing about a curse is proper."

"That was kind of you."

Arthur's eyes found her. So many unspoken words skittered behind them. "Perhaps we have more in common than we know."

Rosella swallowed down her retort. Her curse lay in a prison cell.

"He's a good leader and a better man," Arthur said. "Sometimes— usually—duty interferes with his personal decisions."

When he gave her a knowing look, Rosella only stared back. He could judge her decisions all he wanted. But her sisters' needs outweighed hers.

"By now your sisters have probably already finished eating. I believe Miss Sofia will show them the gardens for fresh air. For you, I think fresh air is needed in a quieter area."

"I'll be okay."

"Yes, yes, Miss, but allow an old servant the opportunity to serve and tend to you."

Rosella rolled her eyes, a smile dancing on her lips, but she allowed Arthur to lead her through the castle after he changed the bandage. The wide passages tapered from the ones she'd traversed a few days prior to ones she'd never seen before. Based on the thick air and a heavy promise that clung to the older walls, she assumed they'd entered the royal wing.

Around her, the treasures glimmered in the dim light. Ancient swords lined the walls. Based on the size and wear, they'd been used in battle, likely when defining the kingdom's boundaries. Helmets and coat of arms stood in defense of an invisible army but defenseless from the curse. Jeweled goblets and trinkets covered the rest of the stone walls. A few paintings stared back at her, the clothes speaking of centuries prior. Their watchful gaze forced her chin higher and a ball to form in her stomach. Even with only a sword and without a shield and army, she was trying to free their kingdom.

Arthur stilled and gestured toward grand gilded doors. Its golden swirls topped leaded stained glass. Colors reflected in the dim sunlight but didn't breach the thin patch of sunlight. He pushed the doors open, exposing a large terrace that overlooked the gardens.

"Refreshments will be brought out shortly," Arthur said.

Before she could turn to him, he slinked back into the recess of the castle. Her gaze lingered down the hall, back to the safety and comfort of her room. A soft breeze tickled her skin, bringing with it the sweet scent of fresh flowers. She turned back to the terrace and a small iron table set under a pergola. With a sigh, she took a seat, letting her muscles relax into the plushily-lined chair.

Someone cleared their throat.

Startled, she whirled around in her seat to find Grayson stepping through the doors.

"I... I'm sorry, Arthur..." Rosella stammered, not sure why she was apologetic when she'd followed Arthur's lead.

Grayson dipped his head in acknowledgement, a weary smile dancing on his lips before disappearing. "You are welcome here, Rosella."

An odd warmth bloomed in her chest and she fought the smile on her lips. She was a fool, to be flustered over a simple sentence and smile.

"May I join you?" He inclined his chin toward the second seat.

"Of course, this is your castle," Rosella sputtered.

His eyes dimmed, drifting to the patio before returning to hers.

"But I would also enjoy your company," she added quickly. A blush threatened her neck. Unable to retain his gaze, she looked to the second chair and flicked her fingers. "Please."

Silence filled the space, heavy and stifling as he remained standing.

When Arthur appeared, a *tsk* fell from his lips with a look of dismay.

"Such a beautiful day," he said. "Perhaps your majesty could show Miss Rosella the new blooms we have thanks to her."

Grayson and Rosella's eyes found each other's before both looked away. Grayson's jaw ticked, his eyes narrowed. Before Rosella could dismiss the comment, Grayson offered his hand to guide her up.

"It would be my pleasure," he said.

A long sigh escaped Rosella's lips. His stilted manners odd after his early candor. Still, she accepted his offered hand. His fingers curled around hers, feeling right. Unused to the comfort and expectancy twisting in her stomach, Rosella swallowed down her reaction.

"What's wrong?" Grayson asked. He started to retreat his fingers.

She shook her head. Decades of lost training returned, and she slid her hand to his elbow, a respectful spot, severing the embrace and hopefully whatever burned through her.

He tilted his head toward her, his eyebrow cocked. "If you're tired...?"

"No," she lied. "Show me the new plants."

He guided her toward the massive, curved perimeter. His arm brushed her as they walked, his closeness new but familiar in an odd way.

"Thank you for taking care of my sisters," she said. "Letting them stay in rooms."

Hesitation stilled his step before he continued. "The sentiment is better suited for my staff."

"Aren't you the one who permitted it?"

He sighed.

"Whose idea was it?" For some reason, the answer meant a great deal to her.

"Does it matter?"

"Yes."

"You're doing so much for the castle. Risking everything."

"That didn't answer my question."

He chuckled humorlessly. "Mine."

Although she had guessed the answer, hearing it sent butterflies in her stomach. Subconsciously, her fingers tightened on his arm.

His gaze fell to her grip, confusion and something else warring behind his eyes. His eyes slowly tracked up to her face. The heat in them twisted in Rosella's core, her breath catching in her throat.

To stop the blush at her impropriety and the heated reaction, she blurted out, "They'll eat all your food and create chaos."

A genuine smile lifted his lips. He shifted, his body closing the small distance between them. Instead of shying away, she enjoyed the warm comfort he offered. "They do have impressive appetites. If Camilla gets her way, she wants to redecorate their room."

Rosella blinked. Despite everything, her sisters were being them. With taxes and the curse, they focused on making the best of the situation.

"How are you able to have so much food?" Rosella asked. "You're a cursed castle that doesn't have contact with the outside world."

Grayson swallowed, his eyes unfocused, seeing something only he could see. "We have a vast kingdom. As you know, more and more are cursed, more and more no longer remember us or our lands. The paths here have grown over. We cannot go long to other places, or we bring the curse with us. As my parents did, I govern through correspondence. We keep taxes and collection low which doesn't bring the ire of the country and not too low to bring the interest of the people."

"You've ruled since you were a child?"

Grayson flinched. "No, my staff helped me until I could make decisions. Although I had the final rule, even as a child, I relied on the experience of my staff. I was fortunate to have Arthur and Lucien. Arthur has been more than a butler and confidant, and Lucien was being groomed to be my attaché. It was just sooner than expected. He had Merl, who was—is, I guess—my father's attaché. I was lucky."

Rosella's startled eyes jumped to meet his.

"Yes, I'm cursed to be a beast, in lands that are being overgrown, but I had people who helped me."

Rosella nodded as hardness settled in her stomach. Her help had come in the form of others trying to use her and her sisters for land and marriage deals.

"Did you have others to help you when—" Grayson flinched. "What about Benson?"

The name sounded funny on his lips. Rosella's gaze flicked up to his. His guarded eyes stared intently at her.

"No. Well, we had offers of help, but they were only covers. They saw my sisters and me as a means to our property, and as either marriage candidates for their children or means to make affluent matches. Benson..." Her voice tapered off.

"What about Benson?" His voice was tight.

"He asked to court me, but I said no."

Grayson stared at her, his expression unreadable. Finally, he asked, "Why?"

Rosella shrugged. "Pride, I guess. I had two offers in two days. Benson and another. They are using the tax hike to drive me into a desperate agreement."

"Two offers?"

Rosella nodded. "The first I'd rather take my chances as a beggar, but it makes Benson's offer seem better."

"You're going to accept his offer?" Grayson's words were barely above a whisper.

"Not if I can pay off the taxes and save my land. Unless I need to for my sisters, I will only marry for love. But that is a fairytale."

Grayson stilled by her. His gaze scanning the lush grounds, greening and vibrant with new life. Her sisters' laughter cut into the air, like bird caws floating on the breeze.

"Your taxes will be paid," Grayson assured. "We'll make sure of it. Then your future will be your choice."

Rosella laughed. Her retort was interrupted by Arthur's return.

"I have dinner," Arthur said with a bow.

The cart was piled high again with delicacies and pastries. Releasing his arm, Rosella walked to the offered cart. Grayson lagged behind, creating distance, his promise hanging between them.

Rosella squashed the desire to reach her hand back out for his, to close the distance. Her foolishness was unwanted and distracting. Instead, she focused on the food. The sweet and savory treats watered Rosella's mouth. She took the offered wine chalice, glad to have something in her hand. A choke shook her frame as the full body of the drink filled her mouth.

"Are you okay?" both Arthur and Grayson asked.

Rosella choked a laugh back, nodding. "I haven't had real currant wine in so long. Ours is so watered down it's a travesty."

Arthur and Grayson shared a look, then Arthur excused himself.

Her lips curled in a smile. Butter cookies next to jams and preserves covered one tray. "These were my mother's favorites."

"Is it okay they were brought out?" Grayson dipped his head to catch her eyes.

Rosella nodded, still smiling. "Yes, they are a good memory of her. For the holidays, she'd make them and drizzle icing on them. She'd use preserved fruits to flavor the icing. Bridgette almost had the recipes perfected, but sugar is a luxury."

He took a step closer. "Do they taste like hers?"

Rosella nibbled on one. "They are very good, but they aren't like hers." Dabbing some preserves on one, she popped it in her mouth. She made a second and offered it to Grayson.

He stared a beat before gently taking it. "Interesting," he mumbled.

Rosella laughed at his polite distaste of it.

"What's your favorite, then?" Rosella asked.

His dark eyes jumped to hers and a slow smile spread on his lips. "Cinnamon bun."

Again, he stepped closer, his closeness eliciting a flush in Rosella. He selected two and offered her the one with more icing. Their fingers brushed at the passing, both of their hands lingering longer than necessary. He didn't step back, his hooded gaze only on Rosella as she sampled the offered pastry.

Arthur returned, a small smile quivering on his lips. Both Rosella and Grayson stepped back at his appearance. Arthur shook his head but made them plates to eat at the table.

Chapter Twenty-One

Rosella waited for night to fall. Her sisters were camped around her, sleeping in various spots. Her sisters laid strategic items around the room to stop her from leaving, but she'd watched them do it while they thought she slept.

As the moon crested the trees, spilling across the white comforter in a silver glow, she bit back the pain as she crawled out of bed. She gasped as her shoulder fought the movement, but she forced herself forward.

Beneath Camilla's legs were Rosella's boots. The worn soles hadn't provided much protection. Her sisters wore slippers instead of sustainable shoes. She'd forgo the footwear and possibly waking Camilla up and wrap her feet in cloth.

Her sisters had tucked away her travel items to deter her from leaving. Moving to the wardrobe, she inched the door open, going slowly to not jar the hinges. She waited for her sisters' snores to peak to move the door. Once open, and after allowing her eyes to adjust, she found bells on her items to warn her sisters when they were moved.

She tugged off her shirt and picked each bell up with the cloth to muffle the noise and placed them on the bed. Slipping a blouse and leggings on from the cabinet and grabbing two sets of leggings to wrap her feet, she snatched the satchel, leaving the door open.

Trying the handle, it made a small compression sound as it clicked open. Stepping out into the dark hallway, she waited again for her eyes to adjust. Instead of the normal dim flicker of the wall torches, they'd snuffed the light out of the hall to stop her possible escape. The curtains had been drawn on the windows, except for the ceiling windows that lit the walls above but didn't make it to the floor.

With her limited time, she couldn't wait. Her family had days and the curse was moving faster.

She crept down the hall, the shadows hugging her. Careful to not make too much noise, she became too aware of the sound of her labored breathing.

"Where are you going?" The master's voice cut through the silent night.

Rosella jumped and her heart pounded in her ears. She gasped for breath, clutching her chest.

"What are you doing hiding in the hall?" she spat, knowing he'd been waiting for her, knowing she'd try to sneak out. She cursed at herself for not thinking there would be another trap set. But her sisters hadn't left her. Nor had they shared secret looks or giggles. Had they not known he'd be out here either? Had he chosen to do this on his own?

"I asked, where are you going?" He stepped from the shadowed wall, his hand gently grazing her arm until his fingers rested on her elbow. His large form hovered above her, his warmth a contrast to the chilled hall.

She swallowed, her mouth suddenly dry.

"I was getting water," Rosella said. She pulled against his grip, but his firm hands stayed in place.

"And then what did you plan to do?"

Rosella growled in the back of her throat.

"You need rest," he said. The softness in his voice ignited something in her core.

He closed what little distance was between them. His hand trailed down her arm until it rested around her hand, his padded fingers calloused but warm against her fingers. He tugged her to follow. She hesitated but finally relented, following him down the hall.

Despite the lack of light, he led her to the study in his wing. The vaulted ceilings arched over book-lined shelves with large windows running the height of the room. The velvet curtains were tied back, showing the scenic forest view blanketed in moonlight. The moon shone brightly through the window, the moon high in the sky. White light flooded the room and pooled on the rug, robbing the room of color and replacing it with an ethereal glow.

"Your sisters can't hear us argue in here," he said, shutting the door behind them.

"How do you know we're going to argue?" Rosella quipped. She folded her arms over her chest and lifted her chin.

He tilted his head toward her and cocked an eyebrow.

"I can command you as the master of this castle, but we already see where that led to. You're not well enough to travel." He finally released her arm and moved toward the windows. He nodded at a wingback chair tucked close to the fireplace. A small fire kindled in the hearth, taking the bite from the air but not warming the room.

"We're running out of time," Rosella said, not taking the invitation to sit. She'd likely fall back asleep if she sat down again. Though bandaged, her shoulder ached. Sleep tugged at her eyes, but she didn't rub them.

Maybe her sisters had sent messages to him without her realizing it.

"The curse can wait," he lied. He flexed his fingers.

"It won't wait. You are transforming faster as the castle changes." The image of her sisters morphing pulsed in her mind.

"The castle is healing," he growled in protest and ran a paw over his head, the stubble of fur already filling in on his hands. "That's something."

"For how long?" Rosella whispered.

He snarled.

Rosella's breath hitched. His lip quavered over the large canine, his teeth glistening. For a brief moment, he looked like a lion from her mother's books. Sucking in a breath, she stilled her reaction.

"I have two weeks to save our home and you have less time by the speed of your transformation," Rosella said, taking a step closer. "None of us can return until I'm done. Bridgette was right, the town would ask too many questions if only one of them returned, even two. The town doesn't want us to succeed."

He turned to face her. His golden eyes shone in the dim light. "What do you mean?"

"They want our land. They already don't think I can bring the funds back. They've been looking for a way to weasel it away from us. Bribery, marriage, and taxes haven't been enough to get me to loosen my hold. Without the ring..."

"I already said I'd pay them if you break the curse. I could send a servant with them now..." He frowned. "A talking creature probably wouldn't help."

"No, but it'd bring droves of villagers here to burn the castle down."

He scanned her over, and then looked back out the window. "You could go pay it off first and then return here to try to finish the curse."

"What?" Rosella sputtered. She had a chance to save her home? Just like that?

He swallowed before meeting her gaze. "I trust you to honor your word."

His eyes flickered back to the countryside. With his face in profile, she was able to notice the larger protrusion of his snout and curving ridge of his forehead. He may temporarily still have human features, but the curse was quickly morphing him. If she did as he requested, the entire castle would succumb to the curse before she returned. Her sisters may be lost to the curse, too. She may lose her home, but they'd lose their humanity. A house could be rebuilt. A life could not. She knew that too well.

A pang pierced her heart, and she swallowed down the acid clawing at her throat. If she completed the riddles, she'd have her sisters, but possibly no house. If she died, they'd be free and homeless. No matter what she did, they couldn't have everything, but they'd have each other. And they were always enough. Her sisters and the castle's staff were the most important thing, not a house. Not a ring.

Before thinking, she reached out and took his hand.

Startled eyes shot to her.

She stepped closer. His breath hitched. His eyes darted between hers, trying to read her face.

Her decision was made. She needed to break the curse first, no matter the consequences.

She squeezed his hand and smiled.

He didn't return the sad expression. Instead, his eyes fell to their hands and the little space between them.

"Why aren't you afraid of me?"

"Why should I be?"

"I'm a monster."

Rosella shrugged, her smile brightening. "You have fur and resemble an animal, true. I've met many men with shining coats, perfectly groomed hair and skin, and polished manners all while hiding the monster inside. People see me as my father's daughter. They see me as a victim. A spinster. An obstacle to owning my land. They only care that I'm well enough to serve them. Yes, you locked my sisters away in cells, but they planned to rob you. You've fed them. Given them clothes."

"I think you credit me with my staffs' misunderstanding of *dungeon*."

Rosella snorted. "Are you saying you don't know what they've done for my sisters?"

He averted his eyes and sighed, his silence admitting he knew.

Without thinking, she cupped his face, drawing his attention back to her. Lingering too long, her fingers slowly fell away. His eyes moved between her lips and eyes, darkening.

Warmth coursed through her and twisted in her core. She tilted her head to the side, staring into his eyes. So little space was between them. If she closed it, would she regret it? Would he pull away?

The clock chimed on the mantel, breaking their moment and their embrace. The new day had started. She had fourteen left. She needed to hurry.

"How far is the mountain?" she asked, moving closer to the window and providing distance between whatever was brewing between them. The situation was complicated enough. She didn't need to add more expectations, more uncertainty.

"Walking, about a week or more," he said. His gaze fixed on her.

Rosella closed her eyes and slid her lips between her teeth. No matter what, there wasn't time for both.

"If you take horses, it'll be two or three days' travel," he said. Taking several steps, he closed the distance between them again. The fresh smell of lavender and lemons swirled between them. He'd recently bathed. Her mind hooked on the thought.

A curl flittered through her stomach. She blinked to clear the thought.

"Are you offering a horse again?" she asked, hope blooming in her chest.

"Yes," he said, the word stamping the finality of it.

"I'll head out now," Rosella said, and before realizing what she was doing, took his hand in hers.

He fastened his fingers around her hand, dwarfing it in his paw. He sighed in defeat.

"We both know I have to go now," Rosella said, placing her other hand on his clasped one.

His eyes met her gaze for several beats. "What should I tell your sisters?"

"That you never saw me, or they'll torment you."

A sad smile flickered across his face as he tightened his hand around hers. He swallowed and heaved a large breath.

"I'll have Lucien readied," he said, releasing her hands as his eyes drifted to the floor.

"He doesn't have to go," Rosella said, her hand cold from the loss of touch.

"He wants to," the master said, walking toward the door. "It's his choice."

"But why?"

"He let the sorceress into the castle," he answered without looking back.

Chapter Twenty-Two

Rosella sat in her saddle on the same dapple gelding as her last journey. A fresh pair of boots donned her feet. A gift from the castle. Beyond her satchel, both she and Lucien had a bedroll and travel bags tethered to their horses. Despite the additional weight, the horses trotted with ease through the path going east. Like the path she'd been on coming to the castle, ancient pines towered above them.

Lucien carried a bow and quiver. Rosella had opted for a short-sword, feeling it a better option after her encounter with the wolves.

The forest floor narrowed the farther they went, and roots snarled the route as the land consumed the forgotten trail. Slowing to a walk, the horses picked a careful pace.

When the sun crested the hill, winking through the canopy, they stopped for a lunch of bread, cheese, and fruit. They removed the horses' bits and tethered them to a branch so they could munch on grass.

"What do you think will be the charm?" Lucien asked as he sipped mead. His ears flicked at distant sounds.

Rosella shrugged, wiping her mouth. "I don't know but I am concerned about the guard. A troll, right?"

"Yea, the tales go back generations."

"So, the troll has been there for centuries?" No one had mentioned the water being, but with a known troll, they may be able to get information from the locals.

"I'm guessing there are multiple trolls. One would be easy enough for people to hunt down for the havoc it causes. I always thought it was a myth, or lore to keep kids out of the forest."

Rosella cocked an eyebrow. "We have to face more than one, then?"

Lucien grimaced. "I hope not. Do you have the riddle?"

"I copied it," Rosella said. She withdrew the paper with the riddle she'd already memorized from repeating it so many times. "'An opposing view it grows, Its beauty in repose, The prick to defend, Until plucked to mend.'"

"Beauty in repose?" Lucien asked, rubbing his chin.

"Something sleeping?"

"But a beauty sleeping? What could that mean?"

"I'm not sure, but it says, 'its beauty in repose.' It's an object with a dormant beauty? What could be a prick to defend something?" Rosella asked.

"A sword? A needle?" Lucien offered. "Until plucked?"

"You pluck plants."

"What plant pricks you?"

"Anything with a thorn," Rosella said. "Roses, thistles, and other plants all have thorns or needles."

"So, we need to fight a keeper to get a charm that will prick us?" Lucien asked. He frowned as he brushed his hands clean.

"I'm more concerned about the missing part," Rosella murmured, the memory of rushing water overwhelming her senses as she recalled the first guard's response. Her breath caught in her throat and her heart slammed against her chest.

"Rosella?" Lucien called. His yellow eyes narrowed in concern.

Rosella flinched, reality settling around her like a fine mist. She swallowed back the lump in her throat. "Sorry, what?"

Lucien's eyes narrowed. "Are you okay?"

No, but she wasn't going to dwell on it. She rubbed her forehead. Her shoulder throbbed but she let it. "I'm fine. What were you saying?"

"What do you mean, the missing part?" Lucien asked.

"When I found the keeper, I had to repeat the riddle, but she said it was incomplete. The last two lines were the key to getting it."

"Do you think the next one will be similar?"

"I'm sure the riddle's missing pieces, but I don't know what it will do," Rosella said.

"The first one freed the castle."

"But expedited your transformation. It's double edged. As you break it, it speeds up. What do you think the second piece affects?" She stood and put the bit back in her horse's mouth, readying herself for the next leg. Her mind splintered. A curse this cruel was in retaliation for something. She couldn't imagine what the prince had done to deserve a curse that required facing three murderous guards and solving ridiculous riddles. Especially when he was a child.

"I can only hope what it is," Lucien said, digging his boot into the dirt. He ran a furred hand over his face.

It all started with the sorceress.

"Why'd you let the sorceress in?" Rosella asked, the words tumbling out before she could stop herself. She blinked at the realization she'd sounded like Camilla, and like Camilla, she didn't retract her question.

"What do you mean?" Lucien asked, his eyes shooting up in alarm.

His cheeks burned, and she silently reprimanded herself. Rosella swallowed. She'd already offended him; she might as well finish her questions. "Aren't you the one who let her in?"

"Yes, but..." A dark look passed over Lucien's face. "It seems you spend time alone, unchaperoned, with His Highness."

He was trying to deflect. Just like her sisters. Something tickled in her brain. Instead of letting the question slide, she stared at him, unblinking.

Finally, Lucien growled and said, "Yea, I let her in."

"Why?"

"She was a beautiful woman looking for a place to spend the night."

"You offered her a room?" Rosella asked, her mind reeling. It wasn't grounds for a curse. Quite the contrary.

"Yes," he said and nodded. "I offered her a room."

"If you offered hospitality, then why did she curse you?"

"Master's parents found out," he said, blinking. He stiffly readied his own horse, his attention fixated on the bridle.

"They didn't want to offer her hospitality?" Rosella pushed as she mounted her horse. Her body ached at once again being in the saddle.

Lucien snorted and looked down the path. "I left a few bits out."

Rosella leaned in and nodded, urging him to say more.

"The king was welcoming..." Lucien said and lifted his brows.

"Did he force himself on her?" Rosella choked. She knew nothing of the king. His actions should be punished but they shouldn't be faulted on Grayson.

"No," Lucien said, shaking his head. "She cursed him first."

"But why the whole castle?"

"The queen had wanted to watch," Lucien said.

"Oh," Rosella let out in a whoosh, her mind going blank.

"The sorceress blamed the rest of us for not stopping them," Lucien supplied. He mounted his own horse and started off on a trot, putting distance between him and Rosella's questions.

"Even their son?" Rosella asked, matching pace.

"He was a toddler. She cursed him to grow into the monster they were inside."

"He seems sad," Rosella said. "Not a monster."

"He's holding your sisters captive," Lucien roared, whipping around to glare at her. His eyes narrowed and his lips quivered in a snarl.

Rosella sucked in a breath. Grayson trusted Lucien, said he was his attaché, but Lucien didn't agree with his choices? His laws? He thought him a monster like his parents?

Was he?

"They stole from him," Rosella offered. "Robbery is a crime."

"They hadn't left yet," Lucien spat.

Rosella nodded in agreement. She'd tried that argument the first night. But even she knew her sisters were likely going to leave with the items. Even if they hid small pieces in their skirts. They would have also traded them the first chance they got.

"He would have locked you away, too," Lucien seethed.

"Pardon?" Rosella said.

"I stopped him, and I convinced him to let you say goodbye."

Rosella's mind rolled back to the first night. The figure that had whispered to the master when he ordered her sisters to the dungeon. Had he simply listened to Lucien's guidance and not his own conscience?

"You shouldn't trust him," Lucien growled, setting his jaw. He sighed, and his body deflated. "You shouldn't trust him, but the staff will make sure your sisters are safe."

"He's not a nice person?" Rosella asked, a swarm of buzzing ringing in her ears.

"He's their son. He's like them. He's a monster inside and out."

Rosella reeled back the few days in her mind. His punishment had been harsh, but far less than the town would have done. Her three sisters would have been in a work gang or sold into marriage to the highest bidder. He'd offered the tax money to pay ahead of time. He'd offered a chance to go and come back. Her sisters were in bedrooms, not cells. They were well fed. What wasn't she seeing?

"We have a few more hours of sun and a curse to break," Lucien muttered. "Let's move."

Chapter Twenty-Three

Rosella tossed in her bedroll, the hard ground not the issue, but her reeling mind. Lucien's words played in her mind. The prince wasn't benevolent, but he wasn't horrible, either. He allowed her sisters to stay in a wing, fed them, and they were warm.

They hadn't officially taken anything, but Rosella knew they'd have pocketed something if they could. It wasn't to rebel against her, but their attempt to help. Giselle kept them warm with timber and fed with fruit. Camilla managed to get them meat several times a month, even if the cuts were low-end. Bridgette kept them in good standings with the commissions. She'd transitioned them from buying the more luxury items to selling them on commission. It kept more product in the store, even if it didn't sell, and made them appear more well-off. Even if they weren't and the town didn't believe the illusion. It did bring in lookers who sometimes bought basic staples.

The four of them had broken into his house. Abandoned or not, they'd gone past a locked fence and opened a door to a home that wasn't theirs. They'd built a fire and slept on the furniture. They should have left when she noticed it was clean. He could have held all four of them for breaking in. It'd have been his right, and yet, he'd offered her freedom.

"I can hear your thoughts over here," Lucien's sleepy voice called out.

"What?" she asked, worried that he could be a mind reader, especially as a sorceress existed.

"You're tossing around and sighing loudly," he said, propping himself up on an elbow. The moon reflected off his golden eyes. "Do you want to talk about it?"

"No," Rosella said. She scooted around on her roll, getting more uncomfortable.

"It's just the two of us. It could help you feel better to talk about it."

The night stirred around them. Insects hummed. The trees swished in the gentle breeze tinted with a chill.

Rosella shook her head. "Just thinking about my sisters."

"It was cruel of him to lock them up," Lucien said. He stretched, resting his hands behind his head. "They hadn't actually taken anything, just moved stuff around."

Rosella shrugged. Their intent was to steal, and they proclaimed it loudly and in great detail.

"The castle looks abandoned from the outside," Lucien offered. "It looks in disrepair, the courtyard is overgrown, and everything is broken. The temptation is justified."

Rosella looked to him, uncertain where he was headed.

"I think he overreacted."

"Doesn't matter at this point," Rosella said. Uncertainty twisted her stomach. She could bring up that he was Grayson's attaché, but he was allowed to have his opinions. He didn't have to blindly follow. He was cursed because of the kingdom. He had a right to not be happy. "You should sleep."

"I'm up now," Lucien said and smirked at her. Something flickered behind his eyes.

"Then let's move," Rosella said, standing up. She dusted her pants off and rolled up her bedroll.

His smile faltered as he looked around the dark forest. They'd found a clearing a few paces inside the forest line. Their small fire flickered like a beacon of light contained by a few rows of rocks.

"It's still night," Lucien said even as he sat up. "We can wait for light."

"Extra hours before the sun."

Lucien grumbled and his face darkened, but he rolled up his items.

As Rosella tucked her bedroll away, she bumped the saddle bag, unsettling the packed contents. Readjusting them, she found a small pouch tucked into the corner. It was too light to be gold, but it wasn't empty. While Lucien focused on his horse, she opened it up and peered inside. A note blocked the items. Pulling it out, she noticed a half dozen buttered cookies. A smile curved her lips. The note was written in Bridgette's neat script.

Rosella,

I pray a speedy and safe journey. The master thought these might help fuel your trip and bring you good luck. I'm not sure how he knew you liked Mama's cookies. I put icing on them like you two liked.

Tears welled in her eyes, but she blinked to keep them from falling. Unable to wait, she popped one in her mouth. A flood of memories danced through her mind, her mother's words wrapping around and comforting her.

They ate a light breakfast and reloaded the horses.

"How likely is it we'll see someone on the trail?" Rosella asked. They hadn't seen anyone outside of the castle or the dryad. With the local village transformed, maybe there wasn't anyone left to travel.

Lucien shrugged. "I haven't been on it before."

"But you know where it goes?"

"It only leads one way."

Lead rolled through her veins. She'd thought that of the path from her home, too.

Their horses' clops were the only sounds as they continued on. Warm golds and yellows bathed the sky, dimming the stars and eating the horizon.

The sun crested, bathing the land in light as they exited the forest and cut across a hilly field. Wildflowers dotted the terrain and splashed a rainbow of colors in all directions.

In the distance, the mountain range cut at the horizon like jagged teeth. The darkened rock was covered in trees and sharp cliffs.

"Where do we head to?" Rosella asked, looking at the expansive range.

"I don't know," Lucien said and scanned the visage.

"What rumors go with the troll?"

"They were just rumors of a troll," Lucien said and shrugged. "They aren't precise. Just common knowledge."

"Then let's see if we can find a person, farm, or village. If there is a troll, they should have a working knowledge of it."

IT WAS HOURS LATER WHEN THEY SAW THE FIRST SIGN OF human life. A farmhouse stood in the distance, the stone structure a tiny dot on the backdrop. Bales of hay were scattered around the field, and cattle moseyed in the pasture.

"Do you think it's cursed, too?" Lucien asked.

"There's livestock," Rosella said and steered her horse toward the cottage. "Someone must live here, cursed or not. I'll go up. They probably know about the tale."

"I'll come with," Lucien said.

Rosella turned to him, a sympathetic smile on her face. "I think you may frighten them if they don't know."

"Why?" he spat. "It would take more than a few minutes for the curse to spread." With those words he looked down at his fur-covered limbs. His jaw ticked. "Oh. I'm so used to it. You and your sisters don't shriek in fear from us."

Rosella's smile turned bitter. Their father was far scarier than hybrid creatures. "I'll be back."

Lucien nodded and waited on the path.

Rosella picked a fast trot. The sound should catch someone's attention while not appearing too threatening.

Before she reached the house, a woman emerged. Her gray hair was tied back in a bun, and she wore a long, faded dress made of patched-up cotton. She'd obviously avoided the curse so far.

"Who are you?" she barked before Rosella was near her.

"My name is Rosella."

"I don't know no girl by that name. Where'd ya come from?"

"I'm from a village over the hill and a few days' travel," she said and gestured a hand backward.

The woman's eyes bulged and she stared at Rosella.

"Did you cross from the castle?" the woman whispered.

Rosella hesitated with her brows knitted. She knew about the castle? "What castle?"

The woman eased. "You lucky girl. Don't you go back on that trail. There's a castle with beasts roaming inside. They'll eat your flesh while you scream. The forests are said to be cursed, too."

Rosella pursed her lips. So, others knew of the castle. How was that possible? If it was her village, they'd have stormed it with pitchforks and fire. Her eyes cast around. The farm stood alone in the fields. Perhaps the closest village thought the woman told fanciful stories. Or had been cursed, too, and it hadn't made it out to the lone farm.

She focused back on the woman.

"Thank you for the warning."

"Why are you traveling alone?" the woman said. Her sharp eyes scanned Rosella over. "It's not safe for even a man to travel in the forests alone."

"My brother is at the path," Rosella lied. She waved toward the lone figure. "He doesn't want to ask for help, so I had to come alone."

"I ain't got nothing to offer."

"Not that type of help," Rosella said quickly. "I just need information."

"Just information?" the woman said. Her eyes fell to Rosella's expensive gear.

Rosella returned the perusal, and then took in the worn dwelling, the lean cows. She patted around in her travel bag and felt the soft velvet of the coin pouch. She'd felt bad taking them originally. The coins together were more than she'd seen in years. They'd provide so much for her and her sisters and had been nothing to the castle to give to her. But looking at the farmer, she'd probably feel the same way about the coins as Rosella. They'd provide. Rosella's fingers slipped around one coin, and she brought it out nestled safely between her fingers.

"If you can answer my question," Rosella said, and flashed the coin, "I will give you this."

The woman's eyes flew open, and she licked her lips.

"Whatcha want to know?"

"We need to travel across the mountains but heard rumors of a troll. Where is the troll so we can avoid it?"

"Why are ya traveling there?"

"I can pay you for the information with an answer or a gold coin."

The woman narrowed her eyes and rubbed her hands on her hips. She took a few steps and turned toward the mountain range. She pointed to a valley between the peaks. "You see that dip right there, where the pass is really low?"

Rosella nodded.

"It's the easiest way to get across."

Rosella looked at it and back to her. "So where's the troll, then?"

The woman snorted a laugh. "Just go that way and you'll be fine."

Rosella squared her shoulders. "You answered a question I didn't ask."

"I provided you with better information."

Rosella turned to put the coin back.

"Hey," the woman shouted and stomped up to the horse, causing it to rear back.

Rosella gripped tightly with her legs and eased the reins. She slackened her face into the expression she used on her sisters.

"I offered a gold coin if you told me where the troll was, not what road to take."

"Just 'cause you have money you think you make the rules," the woman said.

Rosella didn't retort and turned her horse back toward the path.

The woman reached up and grabbed Rosella's leg. Her boney fingers dug into her tunic's fabric folds.

Rosella looked down to meet her eyes.

"You don't want the troll. It's a horrible, nasty thing. You got that look to ya, like you'll take on the world. Don't. Leave it. You owe no one nothing."

"Have a good day, ma'am," Rosella said and nodded. She urged her horse to walk even with the woman still clinging to her tunic. She'd find it herself if need be.

"Fine," the woman growled.

Rosella eased the horse to a stop. She lifted an eyebrow at the woman.

The woman pointed farther down. "You see that bare spot on the ridge?"

Rosella followed her finger and nodded. Her stomach knotted in anticipation, and she licked her lips.

"That's where it lives. Don't veer off of the path and only go in daylight."

"Why only daylight?"

The woman shook her head and folded her arms. "That's a second question."

Rosella bowed her head in agreement. She handed the coin to the woman and produced a second. "Why only go in daylight?"

"The troll patrols for victims at night. During the daytime men patrol with muskets."

Rosella handed her the second coin.

If they could make it to the trail by nightfall, she could have the next item before daybreak.

Chapter Twenty-Four

As they neared the mountain, tiny villages dotted the landscape on either side. Plumes of smoke twirled toward the sky as lights flickered and blinked into existence. The scent of wheat and cattle carried on the breeze.

The trail turned wider and better maintained. Roots and rocks had been removed, leaving a smooth road.

"You believe the woman?" Lucien asked as he scanned the winding path that disappeared into the thick foliage of the mountain.

"She tried to help me at first," Rosella said. "She could have lied, but we won't know until we get there."

Lucien sighed, the sound almost a growl. Silence filled the space except for the tromping of the horse hooves on dirt. Nothing stirred as night slowly crept across the sky, chasing home the people and animals.

"Are we hoping he grabs us both?" Lucien said finally.

Rosella's eyes flicked to him. His wolf ears twitched at sounds she couldn't hear, and his brilliant yellow eyes darted around the vista. The troll likely wouldn't be interested in a wolf-man.

"I don't know what trolls do," Rosella said. "If he grabs me, hide on the side of the trail and wait."

"Wait, what? Why?"

"If you don't see me by morning, go back home," Rosella said.

Uncertainty settled in her gut, acidic and bloated. It had been almost easier going in not knowing what to expect. Now, folklore and tales told to keep children from the woods flickered through her mind. She'd even read the stories to Giselle.

"No. The master was not okay that I did it before. I will not face his wrath again." Lucien swallowed.

Rosella rolled her eyes. "All the others drowned. She pulled me underwater. What did he expect you to do?"

"Jump in and get you."

Rosella turned to stare at him. Another death wouldn't bring back life.

Lucien shrugged. "I am not to leave you again, or I shouldn't come back to the castle. You are stuck with me."

Getting Lucien killed wouldn't help anyone. "I didn't ask him, but do you know what the mirror showed him?"

"You going under water."

Rosella furrowed her brow. "Nothing else?"

Lucien averted his gaze and resettled on the saddle. "He saw me escape. I was to be punished."

"I told Prince Grayson—the master—not to punish you."

Lucien's lip curled. A dark shadow passed behind his eyes. "The master told you his name?"

Rosella jerked back. "Was it a secret?"

"No. He just hasn't been called that since..." Lucien hesitated.

"Since?"

"Since he was human," Lucien whispered.

Rosella stilled.

"Be careful, Rosella."

Rosella cut her eyes to Lucien.

"Don't let his good manners fool you. He's up to something if he's given you his human name, likely to set you at ease for his next plan."

The words twirled around in Rosella's mind. Who was she really helping? Did it matter who Grayson really was if her help also broke the curse for the servants? Saved her sisters? Focusing on it now wouldn't help. And it wouldn't matter as long as he held up his end of the bargain.

The sun finally dipped below the hill, drenching the area in full darkness.

"Think the trail is clear of villagers?" Lucien asked.

"It's dark. The woman said they don't travel it at night. She warned me to stay off of it."

"The towns here are on the outskirts of our lands. We think the curse was a few months from reaching here until you found the first charm. Master communicates with the governor through letters. We don't travel out here so the curse doesn't infect them."

Rosella nodded. His entire reign had been as a beast and directed through letters, and yet, the towns maintained the trails. The human areas still flourished.

They started up the incline. The night song of insects and creatures bathed them. The cloak of night blotted out the scenery and the trees curved around their heads as they traversed deeper into the mountain. Wind whistled through the trees, making the branches lash above them like claws.

An owl's hoot cut the night and a wolf's distant howl echoed.

Rosella's spine stiffened and her neck tingled. Real and phantom curls of pain twisted in her shoulder. She closed her eyes and took a deep breath in preparation.

A thunderous crash broke the calm night. Trees bowed and snapped as grunts filled the air.

Fear heated her muscles and caught her breath.

Rosella grabbed her shortsword and braced her body.

Her horse reared and whined, sending her to the ground. She groaned as her sore shoulder collided with the earth. Stars popped in front of her eyes, and she swallowed as nausea crept up her throat.

Her horse pranced beside her. He shook his mane and nickered.

"Are you okay?" Lucien called, reining in his own skittish horse.

Rosella spat blood from her mouth and rubbed a hand across her lips. She scrambled to her feet, using her good arm to get up. Pain arrowed down her arm.

The ground vibrated beneath her with each thud that sounded earth-breaking.

Rosella grabbed the reins of her horse and handed them to Lucien.

"Aren't you going to ride?" Lucien asked.

"I can't stay on and fight with one arm," she said, gripping her shoulder and facing the coming danger.

Lucien furrowed his brow but didn't comment.

A horrific smell of mildew and death slammed into them as the trees near them shook. The grunts grew louder and angrier, as if a swarm of something was descending on them.

Every muscle in her body screamed to run. With each hammer of her heart, her fingers tightened more around her sword. Her heart still couldn't drown out the sound of what was coming.

There was no turning back. No hiding.

The troll broke the tree line, his swollen body brushing the trees' canopy. Animal skins draped around him, swishing as he ran. Bare feet tore at the ground, dirtied and scabbed. Perhaps Lucien's wolfish appearance wouldn't dismay him.

He didn't stop before he dove at her, his oversized, gnarled hand reaching for her. His mouth hung agape, showing rows of crooked yellow and brown teeth. His bulbous nose hung to the side. His black, beady eyes solely focused on her.

Rosella ducked. Adrenaline spiked through her. She watched his steps, and as the troll closed in to grab her, she kicked his knee. The force sent her back, but she caught herself with her good hand. He stumbled over her and rolled on the ground, but he was back on his feet in an instant and lumbered toward her.

"Hey," Lucien howled.

The troll turned to him and sneered. Drool dripped from his lip.

"Yum," he garbled. "More fresh meat."

"Leave him alone," Rosella warned and brandished her sword at the troll. She held it in her shaking right hand, using her injured left side to balance it. The weight dug at her muscles.

The troll looked back at her and chuckled. The sound rippled through him, his stomach and cheeks shaking with it. "Puny runt. I'll eat you later."

"Are you the keeper?" Rosella asked.

"I keep many things," he spat and licked his lips. His attention focused back on her. He hunched over and set his leg back, ready to charge. "I'll keep your bones in my tree."

Rosella lunged forward. Her feet dug into the ground, her new boots padding her feet. She sliced her shortsword up and diagonal, slashing the troll's arm.

He bellowed into the air and grasped his arm as blood gushed over his hand and down his arm. He bared his teeth and swung toward Rosella.

"Get out of here," she gritted at Lucien.

"But the master—" Lucien started.

"NOW!" she yelled.

The horses neighed in nervous response.

Lucien growled but directed his fidgeting horse farther up the trail with her horse following.

The troll pivoted between the two, his focus split between the two meals.

"Move and I'll cut you again," Rosella said.

"I'll eat you bit by bit while you scream," the troll growled and lunged at her.

Rosella jumped to the side, but he managed to wrap an arm around her. The force sent her sword from her hand. He smashed her torso to him, his arm against her collarbone, and he dragged her through the trees.

Searing pain clawed at her shoulder and radiated through her. Rosella fought to stay conscious despite the pain and struggled for air. Black dots danced in her eyes. Each breath, thinner than the last, burned her throat and lungs.

Her body bashed against bushes and trees as he ambled to his home. New bruises sprang up on her body and blood trickled down her arm.

He dragged her to a clearing ringed with roses and buckthorn. Without a second glance, he tossed her on the ground.

Rosella lay gasping for air, her vision swimming. She tried to sit up, but her body crumpled back down.

"What should I eat first?" the troll asked as he rooted around his stuff. "Your toes? Your fingers? Your ears?"

Rosella swallowed down the revulsion creeping up her throat. She blinked to focus, taking in the homestead. It was a crude structure made of broken planks. There was a firepit and bits of animal pieces strewn about. The rank smell of death clung to the air, causing her to choke.

"Are you the keeper?" Rosella asked again.

"I keep many things," the troll shot back. "I told you that before."

"Do you have the second charm of a curse?" Rosella asked. She willed her eyes to follow him and her arms to prop her shoulders off the ground.

He turned to her. His dark eyes reflected the flickering fire and a smirk curled on his lips.

"So what if I do?"

"I'd trade for it," Rosella said.

"I'm already going to eat you," he snarled. "You got nothing I can't already have."

Rosella licked her lips. She didn't stand much of a chance. To her left were the remains of a deer, the bones mostly picked clean. But they were still sharp. Keeping an eye on him as he built his fire, she reached out and grabbed a leg bone. She whispered a word of apology to the deer and forced her body to crouch. Running on adrenaline and willpower, she forced her mind to focus only on the moment.

She'd get one shot at it.

Protect my sisters, she willed through the air to Grayson.

"If you're going to eat me, can you at least answer my question? Are you the keeper?"

He cackled.

She took that as a yes.

The necklace on the woman had been a decoy. The pearl had to be earned to materialize. She was missing a part of the riddle. Only the troll had it.

As with the woman, she recited the riddle. "'An opposing view it grows, Its beauty in repose, The prick to defend, Until plucked to mend.'"

He turned to her, his eyes curious. "Is that all?" he taunted.

"You should know if it isn't," Rosella said.

His lips flickered into a growl. "You're missing lines."

"Maybe," Rosella said with a shrug. "Or maybe I just don't want to tell you so you can't go and break the curse."

"I'm the keeper!" he roared. "Of course I know the lines."

"No, no, I don't think so," Rosella said, blasé. Her stomach twisted and her heart slammed against her ribs.

"'An opposing view it grows, Its beauty in repose, The prick to defend, Until plucked to mend. Pardon shall be granted, When the fear is planted!' You stupid girl, I told you I knew."

Fear planted.

"I guess you proved me wrong," Rosella said and, using all her force, lunged at the troll. He stumbled back and fell to his knees. Still quick, he grabbed her arm, his grip like iron, and she dropped the bone. Rosella bashed into him with her full weight and used her free hand to poke his eyes and hook his nose with her nails. Having four sisters had its advantages.

He howled in pain and released her to rub his face.

Rosella kicked his groin, and he doubled over. She then kicked his knee, forcing him to the ground.

"I'm going to eat you," he roared, thrashing his arms around in his blind rage.

She grabbed the bone again and shoved it in his mouth.

He gasped and garbled and grabbed for the lodged item.

She kicked his chest, crashing him into the fire.

She couldn't watch his demise; the sounds alone would haunt her nightmares. She smashed her hands over her ears to dull the sound, but his cries ate away at her resolve and a sob rolled through her. Her mind flew to the castle and her sisters and the staff. Their freedom was worth ending his misery. How many lives had he ended? She would have just been one more had she not taken his first.

With a dirtied hand, she swiped at her nose. She blinked and took in a heaving breath to gather control.

"'Pardon shall be granted, When the fear is planted,'" she recited. The object of her fear lay writhing on the ground.

Planted.

She looked around and, finding his club, started to dig a shallow pit.

"You killed it," Lucien's voice cut into the air. He rode his horse into the clearing.

She glanced back at him, dirt and blood covering her face and arms.

"Help me dig a pit," she panted, her one arm unable to get much purchase.

"Why?" he asked as he dismounted and moved to help her dig anyway.

"It's part of the riddle."

Sweat beaded their brows, running rivers through the dirt on their faces. The moon arched over them, tracking through the trees in the few hours it took to dig the pit. Despite Rosella's exhaustion and muscle fatigue, they rolled the troll into the grave when it was deep enough and covered it with dirt.

"The town is going to call you a hero," Lucien said with awe. Dirt covered his fur and smudged his face.

"No, they won't."

"Why not?"

"They won't know." She stared at the mound.

"You're not going to tell them?" He grimaced.

"No. It doesn't matter. He killed others. He tried to kill me. I had to kill him for self-preservation." She licked her lips. She'd killed a creature. She'd hunted before, but never a human or a resemblance of one.

Had she turned into her father? A murderer? No. He'd killed in a drunken rage when his mother wouldn't let him bed his daughter. Rosella killed a troll that ate humans.

She ran a finger over her scar. No. This was different.

With acid in her throat, she recited the riddle. Red mist swirled above the mound, twirling and twisting in the air like embers. The glittery mist evaporated, and a single red rose grew from the ground, the sapling barely as large as the bloom.

"Is that it?" Lucien asked.

Rosella plucked the rose. The bush disappeared.

"Now, we just need to get back."

Chapter Twenty-Five

The sun heated the air and brightened the fields in a warm glow. They had traveled through the night to get distance from the mountain. Their horses clomping was the only sound that surrounded them. As the day wore on, the sun bathed them in heat, only the few trees dotting the path providing relief.

"I don't understand why you don't want credit," Lucien said, finally breaking their silence.

"What good would it do?"

"You'd be a hero."

"In a town I don't belong in."

"They might provide you an award, and then you could pay your taxes," Lucien said.

Rosella let the thought roll around in her mind. To do that, she'd have to convince someone to follow her, dig up the troll, and then return. It could be days or weeks. It'd be morbid. The troll could have disappeared with the charm. It may not even exist anymore, or it could affect the charm if the troll was dug up. She shook her head.

"I can take the rose back while you do it," Lucien said. He licked his lips. "That'd free you up some time. I can meet you back here with the next riddle."

Rosella's eyes narrowed on him. "That's very generous, but I've made a promise."

"But you could be a hero."

"Being a hero is short-term, and something that speaks of an ongoing promise. I'd have to keep going on hunts to maintain the status. I don't care about the glory or false accolades. I did it for nothing other than to break the curse. My reasons are selfish, not heroic. I wouldn't have killed it had it not tried to eat me. It was self-defense. I don't need to glorify it. It's borderline murder." Guilt wormed its way through her throat, and she swallowed against it. She rubbed a hand over her scar and stared forward.

"Murder? Are you serious?"

"We were on his property. I went to the area he was known to roam at a time I was warned not to go. I was purposely drawing him out."

"He eats people."

"Which is why I don't feel guilty about how it turned out," Rosella lied. "But intentions matter."

"So now what?"

"We return to the castle and get the next riddle."

"Your shoulder is banged up. You took a lot of abuse back at the troll's property after being dragged through the woods. You're bruised, bloodied, and your clothing is torn. You need rest. Food. Proper care for your shoulder and wounds."

Rosella looked down. The dark had hidden the effects of her battle, but in the sun, her wounds were on display. She ran a hand over her face and flakes of dried blood fell around her.

"Don't you want the curse broken?" Rosella asked. "Weren't you the one agreeing I should go?" She wanted to curl into a bedroll and sleep for days, but sleep never came, and she had more important matters. Her sisters' safety was priority. Then, breaking the curse.

"Yes, I wanted you to go, but I also wanted you to take a day or two to rest," Lucien countered, his look sympathetic. "Not rush off. Don't you ever take care of yourself?"

Rosella looked away, refusing to engage in the conversation. It was one she had with her sisters, though they knew more about her, and their opinion mattered much more.

The air hung thickly between them. Lucien pinched his lips into a thin line. His wolfish eyes flashed.

"Do you think yourself a martyr?" he spat.

Rosella snorted. "No, I'm not a martyr. I am a poor woman from a distant village who has three sisters who are all doing what's possible to keep our land and put food in our bellies."

"The castle has great wealth," Lucien hedged. "The master is alone."

"We have a home," Rosella said. Her gut twisted at the familiar suggestion even if the thoughts also sent heat through her. It was just the tension of the situation. The lure of the comforts.

She wondered what other lies she could tell herself.

"I'm sure one of your sisters would be willing to marry the master, fur and all, to provide for the rest of you," he finished saying what she expected.

"We don't sell each other," Rosella spat. Everyone's solution was so simple in their eyes, but Rosella witnessed daily what those marriages looked like. Her sisters deserved more. Grayson deserved more.

"Marriage of love is for the poor."

Rosella snorted a chuckle. "Then our hearts shall be overfilled. Aren't you the one who said he shouldn't be trusted?"

He pursed his lips. "Perhaps one of your sisters wouldn't mind a man of service, then," Lucien said with a cocked eyebrow.

Rosella cracked a smile. "Besides, two of my sisters have interests already. I'm not sure about Camilla. She has a new love interest weekly."

"You have lucky men in your village."

"Giselle has a girlfriend." Rosella stilled. Odette was set to marry within the month. Giselle hadn't mentioned it since arriving at the castle. Only Camilla had. Rosella had been so concerned about her sisters and their home that she hadn't considered their lives beyond destitution or being roofed. Giselle's heart was just as important. There was still time for her. Still a possibility for Giselle's long-term happiness.

Rosella would see to it immediately.

"Lucky men and woman of your village."

"That they are."

"What about you? Don't you have someone waiting for you?"

"No one I return the interest to." At least, no one in the village.

"Poor fools," Lucien said, a charming smile dominating his face.

THEY CAMPED AT THE BASE OF THE HILL. THE FATIGUE OF traveling for two days with no sleep had caught up to them.

The dark forest blocked most of the moon, casting long shadows over the trail and blurring the area beyond.

Exhaustion weighed on her muscles and mushed her mind. Rosella struggled with her bedroll and clambered into it. She snuggled down and patted her ribs. The rose was wrapped in a shirt inside of her shirt. She'd done it when Lucien had used the forest beyond for a rest stop. Despite his help, she didn't want anyone but her knowing where the charm was. Even if it was foolish paranoia, she followed her gut. She'd made the promise to return it, and she would.

A nearby howl startled her awake. The moon dipped low on the horizon, ready to cede the sky to the sun. She glanced around, sleep slowing her motions.

Lucien wrestled in his roll, whimpering in his sleep.

The howl sounded again, closer still.

"Lucien," she hissed. "Wake up."

He startled awake and blinked, trying to get his bearings.

"What's going on?" he grumbled.

The howl sounded again, just a few feet away. The horses skittered around and neighed.

Lucien scrambled to get his feet beneath him. He sniffed the air and growled.

The low rumble ripped through Rosella's bones and she shivered.

Lucien's eyes flashed and his body shifted to four legs, his head swinging at the invisible attackers.

Rosella stiffened, taking in the change. His human fingers curled into fists, giving him the illusion of paws. His muzzle rippled with a snarl. He looked more wolf than man. *Sounded* more wolf than man.

A stick cracked, and Rosella whirled around. A scream stuck in her throat.

Lucien growled again, and then launched forward. He disappeared into the thicket. Yips and cries filled the air.

Rosella cringed. She gripped a dagger from her satchel, her short-sword still back on the mountain, lost in the shrubbery.

She turned in Lucien's direction and jumped back when a wolf walked toward her. Blood smeared its gray fur. Golden eyes locked on to her. It took a moment to realize it was Lucien.

Movement sounded behind her, and Lucien launched in that direction. There were more fighting sounds before Lucien crept back to her from the bushes. Blood covered his muzzle too and he limped.

Upon seeing her, his hackles raised. He growled and tilted his head, his fangs glistening in the dim light. His fur bristled as his haunches rippled.

"Lucien," she whispered. The breeze ripped the word from her.

He stepped forward, his eyes squinting as he snarled at her. He bared his teeth and coiled back as if preparing to launch forward.

"Lucien?" she breathed over a lump in her throat, her muscles tightening.

The wolf blinked and looked away, shaking his head before returning his gaze to her.

"Lucien, are you in there?" she asked, her voice more shrill.

He took another step forward, his canines jutting out.

"Lucien, we are so close to breaking the curse. LUCIEN!" She screamed, her cries echoing into the void.

A rough growl ripped from his throat as he rocked forward with heaving breaths. He flinched and shook his head, sitting back on his haunches. His hands uncurled. He dropped his head and ran his fingers over his forehead.

"Lucien?"

"Yea," he choked. "I'm back."

She stared at him, unsure what to do next.

"I'm okay now," he said, more to himself.

He wasn't. They both knew it. But there was only one way to fix it.

"Do you want to start back?" Rosella asked.

Lucien looked at her, his golden eyes giving her a peculiar look. He finally said, "Yes, maybe it'll be best if we just head back now."

Rosella packed up, patting her shirt to make sure the rose was still safe.

Chapter Twenty-Six

The path wove through the dark trees and mist clung to the ground, providing a dreary backdrop despite the high sun. When they crested a hill, the castle sat in view. The previously-crumbling castle sat in pristine shape with white brick, blooming gardens, and the buzz of life.

Rosella wouldn't mistake the castle as abandoned.

Before they'd made it to the castle, the grounds were teeming with animal-folk lining up for their return.

Rosella scanned their faces, her heart swelling at seeing her sisters and an odd sensation twisting her stomach seeing the master. Her sisters wore new dresses again, sparkling with golden threads and soft silks. Prince Grayson wore black breeches, a black tunic, and a silver embroidered black jacket.

The horses pranced into the grounds, heading for the stables. Rosella and Lucien jumped down, handing their reins to stable hands.

"You made it," the master said with a smile. His eyes solely focused on Rosella.

"We did," Rosella said. Despite the ache in her body, she smiled back. She held his gaze for a few seconds longer than proper, the heat in her stomach matching that clawing at her cheeks. When his eyes took in her appearance, they flashed in anger and fear. His jaw worked. Unable to stand the scrutiny, she flicked her gaze to her sisters.

"You look awful," Giselle said, pushing through the throng. "You're covered in yuck."

Her sisters were worth everything.

"Whose blood is this?" Bridgette's cautious eyes scanned over Rosella. "And your shoulder..."

"You messed it up more," Giselle's light touch traced a long gash already crusting over.

"I bet the troll looks worse." Camilla's forced smile didn't match her words as her green eyes darkened with concern.

All three looked to her. Their unspoken words filled the space with love and fear.

Rosella shrugged. Emotion made her blink. "I'd love a bath."

"It'll be seen to immediately," Grayson said with a nod to Arthur before he returned his gaze to Rosella. As he continued to stare at the injuries, his furred fingers curled into fists.

"Roz, maybe..." Bridgette started but then her gaze flicked around the castle courtyard teaming with animal folk.

Rosella gave a small smile. Her injuries would have to wait. They all knew it.

"We love you," Bridgette sniffed. She shoved her way through her sisters and embraced Rosella. Giselle and Camilla huffed at being pushed.

"You're going to get filthy," Rosella chuckled. She returned the hug, careful to not smash the rose.

"I don't care." Bridgette held her tightly. "I love you."

Giselle and Camilla crowded around them causing Rosella to laugh. They rocked in their normal embrace. Her sisters were worth everything.

"You do smell, though," Giselle said, pulling away from the group and giggling. She pinched her nose and waved beneath it.

"I bet you do now, too," Rosella said, noticing some of her dirt had transferred to her sister.

"What was the charm?" Bridgette asked.

"You didn't see it in the mirror?" Rosella's gaze flicked around and settled on Grayson's again. She swallowed.

"I did," he said. His golden eyes met hers, dark with concern. Something skittered behind them. "We should see to your shoulder, now. Arthur should have everything ready soon."

Rosella waved his words away. "It is fine for now. There will be time for it later." At least, she hoped so. Her shoulder needed more than a few stitches.

He worked his jaw. His face warred between concern and pride. When he caught sight of her sisters' concerned looks, he forced a smile. True awe tinged his voice. "You were amazing."

Color crept up her neck, but she kept her expression natural. Heat twisted her stomach and she finally looked back to her sisters, unsettled by the unexpected reaction. His praise was unearned for killing the troll, even if it felt good to hear.

Bridgette and Camilla's gazes bounced between Grayson and Rosella's blush. Despite sharing knowing smiles, they remained silent.

"What did you do to get it?" Giselle asked.

Rosella's jaw ticked and guilt spiked her heart. How could she admit to her sisters she killed someone?

"What did you do?" Bridgette whispered as she leaned in, her gray eyes searching Rosella's face for the truth. "Roz?"

"She destroyed a troll," Lucien shouted behind them to the crowd with his arms up high. He twirled around, making eye contact with his audience. He jumped in the air and took a prowling stance. Acting out each bit, he said, "She killed a monster in self-defense, with her bare hands and an animal bone! Then buried him. She even dug the grave with his club!"

Nausea crawled up Rosella's throat. She blinked and stepped back from her sisters.

"She also doesn't want credit for it," Lucien whined at the crowd, bowing forward dramatically in exhaustion and disappointment.

Bridgette narrowed her eyes at Lucien. "Then let's drop it," she demanded and slipped her arm around Rosella's stiffened shoulders.

Giselle and Camilla sided up next to them. Both shot Lucien a silencing look.

Lucien's smile faltered at the reprimand, and he turned to face Bridgette. She stared him down until he looked at the ground.

The crowd stared uncertainly between Lucien and Rosella, happiness and confusion warring on their faces.

"You've completed two of the riddles," Sofia the cat said, stepping forward from the crowd. Her genuine smile dominated her cat face.

"Yeah!" Camilla said. "Give him the charm so we can see what part of the curse is undone."

Those around them nodded feverishly. Expectant eyes stared at her.

Rosella looked around at the faces, and then settled on the master. Unease stiffened his posture and concern flickered across his face.

"Let's get inside first," Rosella said. "It's safely tucked in a spot I don't want to dig into in front of others."

She maintained eye contact with Prince Grayson. She ignored the tingles racing along her spine. His jaw ticked and he nodded.

The staff swirled around, off to finish their chores, disappointment at the delay dampening their smiles.

"Oh, fun," Camilla cheered. She winked at Rosella.

A smile flicked across Rosella's face before she trekked inside and headed directly for her room. Her sisters, Grayson, and Lucien trailed behind her.

Her eyes caught on the reflection in the mirror in her room. The aftermath still painted her skin in darkened blood and dirt, and debris snarled in her hair. Her image in contrast to the thickly twisted silver mirror sparkling with fresh polish. She swallowed and stepped behind the privacy screen and pulled the rose out. She unwrapped it from its swaddle and held it to the master. The red bloom arched over the stem, the aroma wafting around her.

He stepped forward, his body close enough that she could feel the heat radiating off him. A swallow stuck in her throat as warmth coursed through her veins and core.

He looked at it and then to her. "Thank you," he whispered. "Though it doesn't feel like enough words for what you did."

She cast her gaze to the floor.

Bridgette slipped her arm around Rosella's shoulders. "I'm so proud of you."

A smile flittered over Rosella's lips. Her sister said that even after knowing what she had done.

"It looks like just a regular rose," Camilla said, leaning in closer and pulling Rosella's attention away from her thoughts.

"The pearl looked like a regular pearl," Rosella said.

"We didn't see it," Camilla said accusatorially.

"We saw its magic, though," Giselle said.

Camilla waved her off. "Not the same thing," she groused.

"Ready?" Rosella asked Grayson. Her eyes narrowed in on her sisters, sending them a "be quiet" message.

Grayson licked his lips and nodded. His nose flared as he reached for the rose and grasped it in his paw.

Red magic swirled from the rose into him. Hope hummed through the room. The magic stopped as the rose vanished. The master again flashed human, his long dark locks ragged around his shoulders, his yellow eyes still piercing. His muscled bodied rippled and fur sprouted over him, consuming all his flesh. His mane grew and his canines jutted out, longer, sharper, thicker. His body lurched forward, trying to go to all four limbs.

Her sisters' gasps filled her ears.

He was almost all beast, his eyes the last visage of his humanness.

Rosella sucked in a breath. Had both ends of the curse unraveled again?

Grayson's head bowed as he resigned himself to the next transformation.

"Okay, I guess you brought the right magical rose back," Camilla said, her eyes large as she watched the display.

"Oh, thank you for your approval," Rosella said, but her gaze never left Grayson.

"So, what happens?" Giselle asked. Her gaze bounced to Rosella and Grayson. "Was something else restored?"

"Holy cow, you are stunning." Camilla whistled.

The three others turned to see.

Lucien's wolf face and fur were gone. His human flesh and stature had been returned. His long blond tresses hung loose around his head and shoulders. His human form stood tall, thickly muscled. His rigid jawline was lightly stubbled, and his eyes were crystal blue.

He stared back at Camilla and reclined slightly from her. Worry skidded behind his eyes, and his gaze darted to Rosella.

"Lucien," Rosella said, her voice caught in her throat. "You're human."

"What?" he stammered and turned for her mirror. He shrieked and ran his hands over his face. His body trembled. Tears streamed down his face and his shoulders rocked in sobs. His knees gave out and he knelt to the floor, allowing the emotions to consume him.

"Lucien?" Rosella questioned.

His watery eyes shot up to her. He reached out for her hand and trembled at the feeling of skin-on-skin contact. He caressed her hand, causing her sisters to chuckle.

"Thank you," he gasped. "Thank you, Rosella, for breaking this curse."

"I haven't finished," she said. Her eyes darted back to the master, who still held the features of a water buffalo and wolf. He was still cursed. "There's still a third charm to get."

The master opened his mouth, but instead of words, a garbled roaring sound came out.

The others stared at him in shock.

"Each time you break a layer of the curse, the other parts expediate," Bridgette said, taking a step back from the master. Her fingers furled and unfurled.

Her sisters showed no new signs of transformation.

Rosella swallowed. She needed to get the third charm. The thought clenched her muscles and her shoulder throbbed. Her body was broken and battered. She had less than two weeks to find the third charm and return home if she stood a chance at saving their home. Less than that for Prince Grayson. A tremor rippled through her and she slumped against the wall.

Grayson struggled to talk again. His mouth moved around his jaw in grunts and growls. With strained control, he managed to say, "Thank you, Rosella."

Rosella snorted. He thanked her and yet he was more cursed.

"That means two of your sisters are free," Lucien said, turning a charming smile to them.

Camilla stared at his muscled form, his clothes drooping and ill-formed to his completely human form. He winked at her when he caught her staring.

"He's right," Grayson said. His eyes narrowed in a faraway look.

Rosella nodded and scanned over her sisters. "I was thinking. Isn't Odette set to marry Louis soon?"

Giselle's smile crumbled. She bunched her shoulders up and trembled as tears sprang to her eyes.

"Why are you bringing it up?" Bridgette scolded and wrapped her arms around Giselle, pulling her in tightly.

"I was thinking one of you could go back with Giselle and talk with Odette."

"I'll do it," Camilla said and cracked her knuckles.

Rosella lifted an eyebrow to Camilla.

Giselle pushed back from Bridgette. Hope brightened her teary eyes.

"I'll do it," Bridgette said. She frowned at Camilla and shook her head.

"I'm second oldest," Camilla countered.

"If you go, there won't be three meals a day or soft beds," Bridgette said, folding her arms.

"Oh, yeah, go right ahead," Camilla said, flicking her hand toward her sisters.

"Thanks for your approval," Bridgette deadpanned.

"It's settled," Rosella said. "Bridgette and Giselle will head back immediately to talk to Odette."

A woman came running into the room, her blonde hair trailing behind her lithe frame. She appeared no more than twenty at most.

"Another riddle appeared," she said breathlessly.

"Sofia?" Rosella asked, recognizing her voice.

The woman blushed and bobbed her head. She ran a hand over her face and hair, a smile brightening her human features.

"Are all the staff back to being human?" Rosella asked.

"Yes," she said with a little squeal, but her amusement faded looking to the master. "Sir, you're not?"

He licked his lips and shook his head.

"Oh, why?" she asked. "His parents are still stone. They should be it."

"I think he's the last piece of the curse," Rosella said, her eyes darting to him. "Him and his parents."

"But Lucien said it's your parents who—" Sofia started but stopped.

"Master is their son," Lucien cut in. His form towered above Sofia, but she met his dark gaze.

Squaring her shoulders, Sofia spat, "But he's not like them."

Grayson's eyes dimmed and a sigh heaved his frame.

"He's their son, and we often pay for the sins of our parents," Rosella said.

"Ma'am?" Sofia asked.

Rosella shook away the question.

"Roz, it's okay," Bridgette said. She saddled up next to her and draped an arm around her. "The town is wrong."

Rosella snorted.

"You really do stink, though," Bridgette whispered.

Rosella smiled despite the situation and bumped her shoulder against Bridgette's.

"What does the riddle say?" Rosella asked.

The master took the slip of paper and scanned it, his brow furrowing as he mouthed the words. He worked his jaw. Finally, he read, "'At the shoreside, Fractions will divide, Feats have been met twice, But freedom's found with sacrifice.'"

"Sacrifice?" Bridgette echoed. "Haven't you already sacrificed enough to do these?"

"You've only done two feats?" Giselle said, rubbing Rosella's arm, her own worries on Odetta put to the side. "Those seemed impossible."

"The wording is vague on purpose," Rosella said. "Each riddle is missing the last two lines, which actually say what needs to happen."

"But a sacrifice isn't enough?" Giselle asked. "There'll be more?"

Chapter Twenty-Seven

After two days, Arthur finally drove her sisters from her room with the promise of a large meal and trip to the private part of the castle.

With thoughts of jewels and treasures, Camilla and Giselle jumped at the chance. Bridgette resigned herself to be the voice of reason. Rosella watched them leave through slitted eyes.

Once they were gone for more than a few minutes, Rosella shoved off her blankets. Stretching, her shoulder screamed in protest, but no new blood blossomed on her shirt. Her travel gear had been tucked away and hidden from her. The goal was to stop her from leaving and give her time to heal. But there wasn't time, not for Grayson, not for the taxes.

The door creaked a soft protest when she slid it open a few inches.

"Ma'am," Merl said from the other side.

Rosella blew out a breath, her shoulders slumping. With a yank, she opened the door to display Merl on the other side. Their once-foxlike face was clean shaven. Their brown hair was shot with gray and warm hazel eyes sat on olive skin. Outside of their fox form, their weathered lines belied their years, though their eyes remained youthful and curious.

"Are you always saddled with watching my door?"

They chuckled. "No, Miss Rosella. We do rotate."

Her face fell, the idea of having a guard watching her bristling her nerves.

"Arthur asked me to let him know when you awoke so he could rebandage your shoulder."

"It's not necessary. No blood." Rosella rotated her arm to prove her point. She tried to suppress the grimace, but Merl flinched at her expression.

"Yes, Miss. A walk anyways?"

"Are you accompanying me?"

"Is that an issue? I can ask for Lucien or Arthur to escort you."

"That's not what I meant, Merl. I meant, do I have to have an escort?"

"Yes, Miss. His Majesty's orders."

A heaviness settled in her stomach. She wasn't a prisoner and yet he was trying to control her motion.

"It is his castle, Miss," Merl said as if reading her thoughts.

She blew out a sigh. "Doesn't mean I need an escort."

"No," they said and nodded toward the hallway. "But the master wants to make sure you are okay and not pushing yourself."

Their words spun in her mind. A few days ago, she'd sworn fear flickered across their face when talking of the master, and now, they defended him. Lucien and Arthur's conflicting words danced in her mind, each shouting to be heard over the other. She'd had little contact with Merl save from their occasional escort and didn't know who her comments would end with and what could be the consequence of talking to them. Still, they were well respected.

"May I ask you a personal question?" she said before she could think better of it.

Their brows lifted in surprise, and they flicked their eyes to hers. "Personal?"

"You can say no," Rosella said.

"But you've piqued my curiosity on what you would want to know."

She snorted a chuckle. "You've served the prince for decades. You've known him since he was a child."

"None of those were questions, but accurate statements."

"Now that you are human, do you plan to leave the castle?"

They stiffened, their head pulling back. Confusion twisted their features. "Why would I leave?"

Rosella pursed her lips. "If you wanted to leave, could you?"

Their brows quirked. "Yes, Miss, I could. Are you asking if you can leave?"

"No," she said too quickly. "As a fox you seemed... cautious." Rosella chose her words carefully, afraid of pushing too much.

Merl's gaze shifted to the side. They lifted their head. "Miss Rosella, I served the master's father, King Lyleford, for three decades before the curse. There were choices in the last few years of his reign that didn't align with how he and Queen Artemis had ruled prior. When they were blessed with a child, after twenty years of marriage, I thought it would change their new course. It did not. When the curse fell on us, and they fell to it, I continued to serve King Lyleford. He is, after all, still with us. I report to him daily, hoping my words reach him.

"I have only respect for Prince Grayson. He carries more than a person should. Any caution shown is from years of hard work with King Lyleford. Prince Grayson may be a different person with different expectations and requirements, but I am still in service to the king and my actions are congruent with that."

"I did not mean to imply you were disrespectful."

Merl smiled. "And that was not the message I received. You are concerned for the safety of your sisters. You leave them in our care with the master overseeing us. You have hesitations based on my requirement of traditional decorum. You..." Their brows pinched as they searched for words.

Rosella waited. Finally, she prompted, "I what?"

Merl sighed. "You understand the traditions but don't care. It is both refreshing and frustrating."

A laugh bubbled out of Rosella.

"You are good for His Majesty."

"Pardon?" Rosella choked. What were they implying? Did they think she was doing this for something other than the agreement?

Merl froze, their eyes wide and blinking. They stammered, "I mean, you have been good for His Majesty. You brought hope back. You broke two parts of the curse."

Arthur appeared, his graying red hair neatly styled back. His eyes bounced between the two. Settling on Merl, some invisible message seemed to be sent before Merl bowed and excused himself.

"My shoulder is fine," Rosella said. "You don't need to worry."

Arthur tsked. "Lying isn't a flattering look on anyone."

Rosella leveled her gaze on him.

"How about a stroll, then? Loosen up your muscles and help with the stiffness?"

Resigned to a chaperone, Rosella nodded.

"Perhaps you'd like to choose a book to read?" Arthur asked, leading her down a familiar hall.

She cut her eyes to him before looking at the oversized door. There wasn't time for reading, but perhaps if she played along, she could figure a way out of the castle.

Warm sun flooded the room, the bookcases purposely carved to protect the books from the rays while also providing ample light to read. A fire flickered in the fireplace to offset the chilled air of the large windows.

Grayson sat in a wingback chair, papers on a side table while he scrutinized one with columns of numbers. His fully beast form bowed the chair.

"Your Majesty!" Arthur breathed. "I hadn't expected you in here."

Grayson's eyes narrowed and his lips lifted in confusion.

"I'll come back at another time," Rosella said. Despite her best efforts, her eyes sought out Grayson's. When his met hers, her stomach twisted with butterflies.

"Nonsense," Arthur rebutted. "There's plenty of space. Since you are both here, though, I will have tea and biscuits brought in."

Without another word or room for argument, Arthur darted from the room.

Rosella watched him go without turning. When the door closed behind him, she stared at it a beat before slowing tracking her focus back to Grayson. His gaze had never left her, and tingles raced up her spine.

"I'll just choose a book and get out of here," Rosella mumbled. With her heart hammering in her ears, she turned to stare unseeingly at the thousands of books lining the walls.

"I believe Arthur is fetching us tea." His voice was rougher than normal, but more controlled each day as he practiced speaking in his new form.

She licked her lips. Uncomfortable with her reaction, she sucked in a breath and slowly released it. No one elicited this type of response in her and she wasn't about to start acting a fool. They had an agreement and nothing more. Once she broke the curse... she chided herself for the gall to assume she'd finish it. She needed to stay focused. Anything could happen along the way. But *if* she broke the curse, she'd return to her life, and he would continue to rule his kingdom.

"Any recommendations, then?" she asked, gesturing to the books.

His curious gaze watched her for a few seconds before turning to the tomes. "Do you have a preference?"

She shrugged. "I didn't have much choice in the books we had. I read fairytales and fables to my sisters as children. I read husbandry books at my mother's family estate. Since... taking over the store, I haven't had time except for the necessary notices."

He stood and silently joined her. Despite the vastness of the room, he chose to stand a few feet from her, his presence both enticing and unsettling.

"Like adventure?" He ran a finger along the spine of some books.

"I'm living one now," she said. "Maybe something less relatable."

He smiled. "Poetry?"

"Working with riddles."

He nodded, his smile dimming.

"Grayson, I—"

He tilted his head toward her. A smile curved his lips. "I know, but perhaps reading it would help us decipher the riddles better. It's all metaphorical, flowery, confusing ways to say something instead of the direct approach."

"I prefer the direct approach."

His smile grew. She found herself smiling back.

With a long blink, Grayson sucked in a breath and focused his gaze back on the books.

Rosella's heart twisted, a coldness dusting her heart, but she turned her focus to the books, too.

"What about this one?" Grayson asked, plucking a title from the shelves. The cover displayed hand painted animals on it.

"What's it about?"

"A bunch of talking animals." Grayson smiled. "It's meant to be fantasy."

Rosella laughed.

The door opened, a rattle of wheels drawing their attention.

"Find a good title?" Arthur nodded toward them.

Rosella followed his gaze to the book Grayson held. Somehow, they had closed the distance between them. Their arms had aligned as they looked at the book. If she tilted her head back, their faces would almost touch.

"Yes," Rosella breathed, unable to look up from the title.

Grayson shifted, drawing away from her. Clearing his throat, he took three steps to the side and set the book on a large oak table, silencing their conversation and creating a chasm of distance between them.

"Please sit by the fire," Arthur said. "You could get a chill from being by the windows for too long."

Rosella didn't bother to remind him she spent nights sleeping on the ground.

He laid out a spread for them of pastries and tea.

Once seated, her body's fatigue caught up with her.

Heavy silence lingered between them as they sipped tea. The crackle of the fire the only other sound.

Harsh whispers cut into the air, drawing both of their attention. Lucien stood at the door with Arthur, both animatedly whispering toward each other in disagreement.

"What is it?" Grayson barked. His voice had taken on more of a growl than words.

"I was reminding Arthur we need to begin the tax collections and were to meet with you today."

Rosella stilled. Her mind reeling back to her own owed taxes. Unlike Grayson's, her kingdom kept increasing taxes.

"That discussion can wait for tonight," Grayson growled. "You are dismissed."

"Yes, your Majesty," Lucien said with a bow. His blonde hair glistened in the sun. His piercing blue eyes snagged on Rosella's before he turned to leave.

Intentional or not, it was a good reminder of her own taxes due.

"May I ask," Grayson started but stopped.

"Ask what?" Rosella said, realizing she was rubbing the familiar ridge again.

"Nothing," Grayson shook his head.

"Please ask it," Rosella encouraged. "We know I haven't stopped myself from asking questions."

"The scar... How did you get it?"

Rosella swallowed. Acid curled in her stomach and crept up her throat.

The night came flooding back. Acid turned to nausea.

He'd tried to cross into their room again. Her mother's voice rang out, filling her ears. Images flashed in her mind. His stumbling footsteps. Half-said words that slurred into a disjointed tirade. The blood. So much blood.

After he'd plunged the knife into her mother's heart, Rosella had used the same knife to slice his shoulder, rendering his arm useless. In prison, he had to toil in the sun for years with an arm that wouldn't aid him.

He'd used his bottle to slash her face in retaliation. The sting of the cut, the smell of the expensive wine, the pops of light and wooziness came rushing back.

Wordlessly, Grayson picked up her free hand, cradling it in one of his paws. With the other, he gently laid it across the one cradling her face.

"From that night?" his words barely a whisper. "Did he do this to you?"

She could only nod. Tears stung her eyes and her nose flared.

Rage flickered behind his eyes. In contrast, his touch was soft as he curled his fingers around her hand, drawing it away from the scar.

"Rosella," her name was like a prayer on his lips.

Her watery eyes lifted to meet his gaze. She worked her lips, until she managed to say, "I don't want your pity."

"That, you do not have. You only have my respect and admiration."

Chapter Twenty-Eight

Rosella stood before the dining room, her hands fisted at her hips. Although not completely healed, her body was better, her mind agitated, and she was desperate to move. Her arm, still sore, could hold a sword. She had the last riddle, the bargaining tool to free her sisters and save their home. Yet trepidation coursed through her.

Soon, her family's debt would be paid, and they'd all be permitted to leave. They'd return to their normal life, void of magical dealings and curses. They'd return to their shop, friends, and survival. The castle wasn't permanent. The surplus of food and comforts weren't theirs to have. But freedom would be theirs.

Raising her hand, she steadied her nerves and rapped on the doorframe before entering the room without permission. It was not customary and belied her humbled upbringing. Her mother had taught her and her sisters proper etiquette and manners, but they didn't help them survive when trying to scrounge together food and lumber nightly. The swirl of buttered cod, her father's favorite, clouded the air and brought back a stampede of memories.

The town had helped. In the beginning, families offered them a roof, offered them food. They'd taken the food, but Rosella's pride kept her from joining other's homes. She knew her and her sisters would be separated. Four mouths were a lot to feed. She'd wanted them to stay together and had made an oath to do what it took.

The town's charity dwindled as harvests came and went, and as Rosella continued to run her family's store. Bitterness from the town built over the years. She'd made good on her promise and proved them wrong; she could take care of her sisters. But still the town tried to treat her like a scared and starving child, pitying her and her sisters.

Her father's side of the family was in the wind, no known whereabouts, but her mother's side resided along the countryside. It was a few days' ride, but it may as well have been years. Their mother had two brothers and a sister. None had wanted to take in her children from a commoner, much less a merchant, especially after everything her father had done. His sins were as good as their sins. As far as her mother's family had been concerned, they'd died the night their mother had.

With that declaration, Rosella had purged herself of the need for decorum to follow the customs of the nobility and gentry. She was a drunken merchant's daughter. A merchant in prison for murder. She hadn't lived up to the namesake, save for the death of the troll, but she wore his mark as the scar across her face. She didn't bother to cover it. It was as much a part of her as her breath. Even Grayson's notice of it didn't make her want to cover it.

Had her mother lived, Rosella would have been scorned and shunned for the ghastly mark on her face. She still would have had meals with the townspeople, who would have taken in her mother and sisters in attempt to get claim of the land, remaining fortune, and the use of her and her sisters for strategic arrangements. She'd have been groomed and plucked until her beauty shone and then married off to an affluent man with money her sisters could have used for dowries while Rosella pumped out his children, forever tied to him as a means to support her family. It seemed a fate that clung to her like a spiderweb.

With her changed future, she was still the lynchpin to her sisters' futures. Instead of being traded into marriage, she'd been traded into servitude to build dowries and trying to save her sisters from the shame their father had gifted them. With the gold from Prince Grayson, she could manage for a bit longer as she waited for harvests to turn for the better again.

The dining room, bare of others, even servants, except the master, was a mockery of her life. Her empty dreams. Her empty future. She didn't belong here. Like before, she went to gather her place setting, purposely set up parallel to his for proper distance and decorum. As Merl pointed out, the staff still tried to encourage the formal manners.

"Wait," the master called, his hoarse voice still fighting for its last shred of humanity.

Rosella's eyes shot up to him, curiosity burning brightly. He wore black breeches, and instead of his normal embroidered tunic, he donned a coat that cut across his waist and draped with tails. The edging was in gold swirls that ran up the front and circled his collar. If possible, he looked even more animal today than he had yesterday in the library.

He had no time to wait for her body to heal. She needed to go now.

He took his place setting, clattering his silverware on the fine porcelain. Taking his wine goblet, he moved down toward her. His beastly legs lumbered, pronouncing he had morphed more into a beast.

She smiled at his unexpected gesture. Her heart thudded in her chest with each step he took. Something unexplainable twisted in her stomach that both delighted and confused her. She couldn't wrap her emotions up. Once she got the last charm, they'd leave and never come back. *If* she got it, she had to remind herself. The third charm required a sacrifice. Unsure what it could mean, her mind reeled between her life, something with her family, or something else that would destroy her.

He placed his items down and stared at the pile.

Focusing on his gestures, Rosella chuckled and pointed to her own setting. He nodded and moved his pieces around to mimic hers.

She pulled her chair out, but he stopped her with a lift of his hand.

"I may not look it, but I was raised with manners," he growled and finished pulling her chair out for her. "The staff saw to it."

She gave him a skeptical look but accepted the gesture. He helped her sit, his paw brushing against her. A heated jolt shot through her and she stifled a surprised gasp. She needed to get ahold of herself.

"Thank you for joining me," he said and dipped his head as he returned to his seat.

Rosella gave him a tight smile and diverted her eyes. She ran a hand over her black tunic. The staff had replaced her previous one, using some of the fabric to weave in intricate braiding at the hems. The faded black appeared intentional as an interesting piece. They'd woven red ribbons to match her hair and small gold threads wove down the center in vertical accents. It was the most stunning tunic she'd seen, and she felt odd wearing it, but it was her mark of status. She spoke for her family. She was the matriarch. Although often worn by men, a few other women in town wore them once their husbands had passed and they chose to not remarry.

"I want to thank you," Rosella said, color creeping up her cheeks as she fought the words she wanted to use.

"Thank me? You're breaking the curse and I'm holding your sisters —well, now sister—prisoner."

"In name only," Rosella said. A small smile claimed her face. "You say prisoner and yet they stay in rooms larger than our house, have fresh clothes and baths daily, and three meals a day with real wine and hearty food."

He laid his paw on hers. Despite being startled, she eased her hand within his, twisting her wrist so their palms touched. His eyes flicked up to her, bright with hope.

With a sigh and complete disregard for decorum, she rested her elbow on the table and her chin on her hand to meet his gaze. Even as she warned herself to not mix her emotions up, she slipped into the comfort of his touch. How the town would mock her. She rebuked the advances of some of the most eligible men in town and yet held hands with a beast.

He dropped his eyes to the table before speaking. "You've done much for your sisters. It shows in how they respect you."

"I wonder if I should have let them live with other families after our parents left us. I was so set on keeping us together, I didn't consider the implications of it. They could have had more food, been raised with proper manners, and not have a mark in our village. They'll forever carry that stigma. I let my pride lead me."

"Your sisters would not have been respected in the other families as in yours. They'd have been indentured to the families, seen as less. They'd have been married off as soon as possible."

Rosella met his eyes. His truths were spot on.

"Food and comforts aren't always worth the cost," he said and toasted her, his beastly head towering above her.

She swallowed and nodded and raised her glass in toast.

His jaw worked before he asked, "How are you? I saw what the troll did. My staff says the cuts were deep, but they say it is getting better."

Lies and truth rolled around on Rosella's mind. She settled in the middle. "I am much better than I was. I can use a sword."

His face scrunched. 'That didn't answer my question."

"I am better."

His eyes narrowed. A protest darkened his face.

After sipping she cleared her throat and said, "The riddle."

"Yes, the reason why you're here," he sighed.

She nodded.

His smile faltered. He withdrew his hand from hers, bringing instant cold to her.

He wrestled in his pockets and produced two copies. "I had a copy made for you."

She smiled, and said, "'At the shoreside' seems specific, but the closest sea is quite a bit away."

He nodded and rubbed a hand over his neck. "The closest shore is a week away."

"A week?" Rosella stammered, her mouth drying. There wasn't enough time. She barely had more than a week left. She couldn't do both. Her heart and stomach sank. Perhaps with the funds he gave her for the taxes, she and her sisters could start a new life. Uncertainty twisted in her stomach and choked her breath.

Seeming to read her thoughts, he asked, "How much time do you have to pay the taxes?"

"We'll be okay," Rosella lied.

"Don't lie. I'll send a driver with Giselle and Bridgette to your village. They can pay your taxes. They are human, again."

Rosella blinked. Could it work? Doubt wiggled in her stomach.

Even with a servant, the town wouldn't trust the funds, assuming them stolen and the servant was in on it, especially if only two sisters returned. If the three returned without her, claiming she fell ill or something, perhaps the town would buy it, but even so, it was unlikely.

Maybe a servant accompanying them would provide more of a distraction. More time. It wouldn't likely work, but it was the only thing she could think of that would provide her time to go after the third charm and protect their home.

But the town wanted her property and would use anything to get it. Without her giving the money, they'd say *she* failed to deliver the funds as promised. But it didn't matter. Not anymore. Not with Grayson on the line. They could start over if they had to. Grayson couldn't.

Acceptance rested heavy on her throat. She would send her two sisters to clean up what they could, hide what possessions they had so they could reclaim them when they returned. Perhaps Bridgette could convince Gavin's family to house them for a few weeks while they figured out their affairs.

Rosella blinked. She would be exploiting the relationship Bridgette possibly had with Gavin. Or perhaps she could send word back to Benson that she would accept his marriage proposal if he sheltered her sisters until her return.

Numbness settled in her heart. She was right back where she had started, but this time, she saw the reality of it. Not the starry ideals of protecting her sisters. Her pride had led to her sisters being locked up. No, this time, she would agree to marry Benson and protect her sisters as she had always promised to.

"I appreciate the offer, but the town will not take the funds from my sisters without many questions and scrutiny. I don't know if a servant would help or create more doubt."

"Let them come here," Grayson said, spreading his arms out. "My staff can vouch for anything your sisters say."

Yet, if the curse hadn't fully broken yet and the castle remained a mystery, the town would think her sisters unhinged. She had to finish breaking the curse in order for her and her sisters to return home, free and clear. And for Grayson.

Giselle and Bridgette could return and claim Camilla and Rosella were finishing out preparations for the marriage. The talk of marriage would settle the villagers and draw attention away from what had happened.

Rosella laid her fingers on Grayson's arm. His eyes fell to her touch before jumping to her gaze. Suspicion burned behind his eyes.

"Giselle and Bridgette will return to talk to Odette's family. If you want to send someone with my sisters, you can. I appreciate the offer. I am going to go after the third charm now. Camilla and I will go back after I return with the third charm and break the curse."

"If," he breathed.

Rosella stilled.

"If you return," he growled. His frame heaved, each ragged breath increasing the intensity. "There is no guarantee you will return."

She blinked. "I have finished the two. If I come back, you will free Camilla. If I fail, you will witness it in the mirror and free Camilla. Either way, my family is free."

Grayson roared. The sound echoed off the walls and rattled the china. Footsteps scurried behind the walls.

Rosella's heart froze before ramming in her chest. Her vision tunneled and her breaths became shallow as she stared at him.

His paws curled on the table, his nails carving large divots. His eyes flashed, the humanness vanquishing, and the predatory eyes of a lion shone back.

"Grayson," Rosella breathed, forcing the word out.

"Master," Lucien called, coming to stand beside Rosella. Merl and Arthur had joined them, the three servants flanking Rosella.

Grayson's eyes jumped between the four.

"Grayson," Rosella yelled. She stood, and despite the protest of the other servants, placed her hand on his. "Grayson."

A long breath escaped his nose, his lips quivering.

"Master," Lucien pressed.

"Grayson," Rosella repeated, stepping closer.

Grayson flinched, his body recoiling. After several large breaths, his eyes dimmed. He worked his jaw to find his words.

"Fine, then. I absolve you of your promise. You are free to go." He swept his hand toward the door and the forest beyond the windows. "You do not have to come back. I don't want you to come back. Your sisters can go with you, all three of them. You are all free. Go."

The servants shifted behind her.

She stilled. The idea was not an option. She gave her word. It was almost done. She couldn't stop now. She couldn't break her promise. He didn't have time for her to go to her town and come back.

"Please leave," Rosella said over her shoulder to the three.

"Ma'am," Arthur said. "Are you sure?"

"Yes," Rosella said with a nod and waited until they departed.

"Go with them," Grayson barked, pulling his arm from her. "Go!"

Arthur stalled at the door, his gaze jumping to her.

Rosella inclined her chin for him to leave.

"We're so close," Rosella whispered. "It's the last one."

He stepped back, lifting his head to stare down at her. His dark eyes canvassed her face as if looking at her for the last time. He took another step back, widening the distance between them.

When Rosella took a step toward him, a snarl rippled over his lips.

"No. I forbid you from going for it."

"What?" Rosella sputtered. "I promised."

He shook his head. With another step, he shifted away from her, the gesture severing their connection and leaving Rosella brittle and cold. "You have nothing left to sacrifice for me other than your life."

"We don't know that."

"And we won't find out. I am not worth your life. You freed the staff. That is what mattered. My family and I deserved this curse."

"You were a child," Rosella yelled, pressing her fingers on the table to stop herself from taking another step and causing him to retract further.

"A nasty child, and I haven't done much better now." He raised his hands to stop her. "I don't say this for sympathy or rebuttal."

"I promised," Rosella said. "You are worth it. I'm going to follow the riddle. I'm going to finish this."

"No, you're not," the master roared, pounding his fist on the table, the sound animalistic as it echoed off the walls. His body heaved and his eyes darkened.

Rosella blinked at him, shelving her fear behind a bland expression. Her breath hovered in her throat.

"You're going back to your village with your sisters," he growled before he ambled out of the room without looking back.

Chapter Twenty-Nine

Rosella leaned against the brick castle wall. Her eyes flickered above to the white turrets, the sun reflecting off the alabaster.

The staff loaded the cart with food and clothing. A few items glinted in the sun; extra gifts of the castle to see them through the lean harvest.

Arthur walked up to her and handed her a velvet pouch of coins. He wore a black and silver livery. Streaks of gray wove through his busy red hair.

"The master says this should be enough," he said and handed it to her. Curiosity burned in his kind blue eyes. He'd seen Grayson's tantrum the day before. Had come to her aide.

Rosella raised an eyebrow at the weight of the pouch. It'd be enough to cover the taxes and keep them fed for a few years, and they gave it to her like it was nothing. Her family's taxes and more would be covered, and yet her heart sat heavy.

"Thanks," Rosella mumbled, taking another glance above to the windows. She wasn't sure why, but she hoped for a glimpse of Prince Grayson. He was absent from the sendoff. She hadn't seen him since he stormed out of dinner. She frowned and turned back to Arthur. A pang twisted in her heart.

"No, thank you, ma'am," Arthur said and bowed. "Without you…" His voice faded, and he looked away.

A breeze skittered through the thick leaves. The towering trees stood sentinel against the wind, blocking everything behind their curtain. The path renewed, disappearing a short ways into the forest, obstructing the view as it had done when they first arrived at the castle.

"Arthur," Rosella said. She leaned close to the man, a smile curving her lips. "Can you do me a favor?"

His eyes bulged and he nodded rapidly.

ROSELLA WATCHED THE CARRIAGE TURN AT THE FORK IN THE road, her sisters tucked inside with gold and a letter from her. With all three sisters going instead of two, the town would think she was recovering from a fever in the other town. It'd buy her a few days. The town would likely try to find their lie, but hopefully, the extra gold she hadn't expected could delay them. She could argue she'd sent the money on time. As she had. The town would fight her sisters, maybe her, but if need be, they could take their treasures and go elsewhere. Start fresh. Somehow.

She would honor her promise to Grayson. As she always did. He had honored his and then some. And most importantly, he was worth fighting for.

She turned her horse in the opposite direction, heading for the city, where she had originally planned to go at the start of her journey. She'd turn off a bit before the fork into town if the directions she had were accurate, and then head right until she saw the sea. It was a fool's errand, but she had to try.

The silence of the forest surrounded her, and she eased back on the horse. The prickly feeling from the other trips through the forest was absent. She carried a shortsword, another from his collection. One he'd personally gifted to her. The saddlebags were loaded with food, additional small weaponry, fire starters, a few coins, a blanket, and a change of clothes. Arthur had made sure she was prepared.

She'd push each day into the night and travel until the horse needed rest.

The morning wore on to afternoon and then evening. Gusts of wind brought the smell of manure and grass. She was close to farms and therefore close to the edge of the forest. She pushed further as the sky turned black above the canopy and the brightest of pinprick stars shone through the foliage.

As she neared the edge, she steered the horse to the bank and found a leveled spot to set camp. She spread her bedroll down and gathered logs and rocks to build a firepit. She settled in, waiting for the horse to be rested.

The night droned on. Her mind was too active to sleep. Around her, the music of cricket chirps and croak of toads mingled with the rustling branches.

A twig snapped. Then another.

She stilled her breathing and grabbed the shortsword she'd bundled in the roll with her. She pushed herself up and scanned the forest. The inky darkness beyond her fire belied nothing. No shapes moved, no eyes glowed. Nothing.

"Rosella?" Lucien's voice called out.

"Lucien?" Rosella said and slumped back down. A rush of relief flooded her. "What are you doing here?"

"I was concerned," he said. "We were concerned." His voice neared as did the sound of his horse climbing the incline and the crack of sticks. "We don't know what you'll face. Your body is still healing."

"Why'd you come, though?" Rosella asked. "I've done two already. You can't just leave your post. Won't you get in trouble?" She settled back on the bedroll and pulled her knees to her chest as Lucien moved around the foliage to find a spot to camp.

She tilted her head as she watched his lithe form. She had grown so accustomed to his wolf appearance that his human one was like looking at a stranger.

Over the fire, he eyed her up, his blue eyes dark in the dim light, his handsome features swoon-worthy.

"I don't care," Lucien said and picked at the dirt around his bedroll. Instead of the livery he'd worn the last she saw him, he now wore brown britches and a white shirt with a leather traveling jacket.

"Lucien," Rosella said.

"He shouldn't have made you promise to do this," Lucien said and stabbed the dirt with a stick. "He should have done it himself."

"I thought he couldn't leave the castle," Rosella said. Her brow furrowed.

"He can," Lucien said.

Rosella's eyes flickered to him. Had it all been a lie? Her stomach twisted, waiting for the unsaid words.

"He'd just be cursed forever," Lucien said.

Rosella rolled her eyes. The twisting eased but her gaze focused on Lucien.

"Wouldn't that defeat the purpose of breaking the curse?"

"He could have done it for the castle, for us."

"He was a child when it happened," she said.

"He's not now," Lucien said. His jaw ticked and he scowled.

By his logic, any of them could have tried to break it.

"Does he know you came?" Rosella asked. Her voice caught on the implication.

Lucien looked away and shrugged.

"Does he?" she whispered.

"By now, probably," Lucien mumbled.

"So, then he knows I didn't go back to town," Rosella said. Disappointment warmed her veins. Her plans blew away with the wind.

Lucien whipped his head around and looked at her. His blue eyes blazed. "What?" he barked.

"He sent me home."

"But..." Lucien furrowed his brow. "You had a horse, and supplies..."

Rosella shrugged.

"The groom?"

"Believes I had permission," Rosella said, nodding.

"But the master doesn't know?"

Rosella shook her head.

Lucien groaned and flopped back.

"You can go back," Rosella said.

Lucien pushed himself on his elbows and shook his head. "That'd be worse. I'm going to be punished for either leaving the castle without permission or going back without you. I'd be better off dying with you on this quest."

"I appreciate your vote of confidence," Rosella said, folding her arms.

Lucien waved her off. "You've beaten two of them. I'm just saying, returning without you after I left would be worse than a fate with a keeper. A keeper would be quick."

Rosella frowned. The troll had no intentions of going quickly. Although the master was short tempered, he'd never shown violence toward anyone, especially her or her sisters after breaking into his home.

"I'm surprised I caught up with you, then," he said around a yawn.

"I was waiting for the horse to rest before starting again," Rosella said. She nestled down into her bedroll to wait. The hard ground pressed into her back.

"Do you sleep, ever?" Lucien asked as he flopped back on his roll, his voice thick with sleep.

She didn't answer as soft snoring filled the air.

Chapter Thirty

Over the next couple of days, they rode from sunup well into the night. By the start of the second day, Lucien gave up trying to start a conversation. Silence stretched between them most of the time. They rested for breakfast, lunch, and dinner and to provide the horses a reprieve.

"How much farther do you think it is?" Rosella asked as dark clouds loomed on the horizon.

Lucien blinked at her words.

"We've traveled faster than a normal person would, probably double," Lucien said, chuckling. "I'd say a day or so."

Rosella nodded; her eyes still fixed on the approaching storm.

"I think we'll stop early tonight," she said. She inclined her head toward the thunderstorm.

"We won't find adequate cover," Lucien said. "There aren't forests, and the outcrop of trees will still get us wet. We're likely to catch cold. It's not good for the horses, either."

"What do you suggest?"

"We're close to the shore, but it's still near farmland. Let's see if we can find a barn or livestock covering. I can smell livestock, so we're likely close."

Rosella nodded.

The winds shifted a half hour later, bringing in salty air as they neared an old barn similar to ones that had dotted the horizon in the past days. Soft moos filled the air, which hung with the stench of manure.

They made it to the structure as the sky cut loose. They pulled the horses inside and closed the door behind them. The cows blinked at them but didn't protest the intrusion.

Rosella pushed her drenched hair out of her face and wrung out her tunic. A bite of a cold wind whistled through the planks.

"We should change," Lucien said. "We don't want to be in wet clothes."

Rosella raised an eyebrow at him.

"I'll turn around," he said with a toothy grin. "I won't look."

"I'll go behind the bales of hay." Rosella grabbed her dry clothes. "You can change here. Let me know when you're done."

"I'm not shy," he said.

Rosella rolled her eyes and ducked behind the bales. She quickly changed clothes and pulled her hair back into a braid.

"You finished changing?" she called out, refusing to look.

"What? You're done already? Just hold on." He grunted and then said breathlessly, "Okay."

She came out, taking a cautious glance first to make sure he was clothed.

"Yes, I'm dressed," he said, annoyed.

She eased. Her stomach twisted with uncertainty, and she kept her distance in the small space. Even if he'd been a wolf, his animal form felt safer. Now, he reminded her too much of the gentry she'd grown up with. Cocky and arrogant. His blue eyes held the same sharpness as the predatory suitors.

"We'll rest until the storm blows over."

"What if it takes days?' he asked.

"Then I'll get us covers," she said and yawned. "But riding in a thunderstorm is dumb."

"Wow, you're actually tired," he said. Lucien leaned against the rough wooden wall, his blue eyes casually tracing over her face.

"It's been a couple days since I slept much," she said and shrugged.

Fatigue tugged at her eyes and her muscles ached. She had ignored her body for so long, but stuck in the barn on soft hay, her pains caught up with her.

"How do you do it?"

She shrugged.

"Did you pick it up when your parents died?" he asked.

She shook her head and picked lint off her clothes. Her sleeplessness went back much farther than that night.

"What, then?"

She looked back to him, erecting an imaginary wall.

Her past wasn't shared beyond what the town knew and threw back at her. Even her sisters didn't know, and never would. The night their mother died wasn't the first time their father had tried to come into their room while he was drunk.

He never got to lay a hand on her or her sisters. She'd lost sleep many nights to make sure.

When the murder had been discovered, and her mother's body found, there'd been questions about what he did to her sisters before and after the murder. He hadn't touched them. That wasn't a lie. She'd been able to stop any attack, but even she knew it was only a matter of time. Still, the town looked at her funny afterwards. They saw her as darkened and spoiled, not caring what the truth was. With time, the incident had become a faint memory, almost myth. He was locked away, and she had taken on head of the family. Her sisters were seen as the young and frivolous ones. She'd been treated more as a respected widow until recently, when locals wanted her hand in marriage, but even that was common with money or land-wealthy widows.

"Rosella?" Lucien whispered. His voice was gentle and his eyes soft and filled with concern.

"What?" she croaked. She blinked back the memories. The barn swam into focus. With a final swallow, she shoved the past back down.

"What about the scar?" he asked and reached to trace it with his finger. "Is it part of the reason you don't sleep?"

She swatted his hand away and jerked back. The line pulsed with phantom pain.

"Sorry," he said. His eyes widened.

"Don't touch it," she said, unashamed of her reaction. It was her face, her scar, and none of his business.

"How'd you get it?" he asked and met her gaze.

"It was a long time ago," she said. "Time to sleep."

Lucien's jaw ticked and his face scrunched, but he didn't argue as he lay down on his bedroll.

Rosella scooted down into her mat, relieved for the diversion of sleep.

"WHAT ARE YOU DOING?" A SHRILL SCREAM PULLED ROSELLA from her dreamless sleep.

She bolted up and looked around for her bearings, her shortsword already in her grip.

"You nasty things," the woman's voice said again and a broom came close to her head.

"What?" Lucien grumbled, sitting up.

"You are copulating in my barn!" Hunched over, the woman wore patched garments, but her boots were newer despite dirt and more caked around the edges. Her leathery face spoke of a hard work life, but crow's feet and wrinkles from laughing parenthesized her face. Gray hair fell past her shoulders in a tight bun.

"No, we're not," he said diplomatically. "We were sleeping until you roused us."

"We'll be leaving," Rosella murmured. She struggled to stand up on her wobbly legs, tired from days of unrest.

"We were caught by the rain," Lucien said. He flashed the woman a brilliant smile.

She pulled back slightly, a smile almost flickering across her face before she scowled and swung her broom at him. "You rogue! You scoundrel. Using my barn for your illicit deeds. I should call the guard!"

"No, nope, no need for that." He gave her a sheepish grin. He ran a hand through his light tendrils. "My wife and I were trying to make it home before the storm, but it let loose. We were so happy to find cover. We can pay you for the hay we may have spoiled."

"Wife?" the woman said while Rosella mouthed it.

"Oh," the woman said. Her eyes softened and a small smile danced on her lips. "Oh, that's sweet. You were looking out for your wife."

Rosella rolled her eyes. She dug in her saddle bag for his offered promise. It wasn't hers or his, but it'd help pave the way.

"Oh, no," the woman said, her eyes widening at the piece.

"No, please," Rosella said, holding it out. "We insist."

The woman pocketed the coin while Rosella and Lucien exited the barn with the horses. The woman stayed inside, checking on her cows.

"What was that?" Rosella seethed through her teeth.

"It stopped her rant," Lucien whispered. He winked at her. "It isn't a stretch for how we looked."

Rosella shivered and forced her feet forward.

The chilly sea breeze carried the smell of salt and brine. The overcast morning was streaked with pockets of sunrays between the clouds. Seagulls squawked in the sky.

"Well, we made it to the shore," Rosella said. She brushed her hand over her horse, removing the bits of hay and straw. Excitement and fear curled through her. They could face the keeper today. She would break the curse or perish.

They both saddled their horses and mounted. Reality hung heavily around them.

"Any idea where to go?" Lucien asked. His gaze bounced in the direction of the vast shoreline.

"The others were based on local lore," she said and turned back to the barns. She sighed, stopping her horse. She hopped off and handed her reins to Lucien.

"What are you doing?" he asked.

"Figuring out where to go," she said and walked back to the barn.

The woman mucked the stall.

Rosella knocked on the frame startling the woman.

"Yes, lovebird?"

Rosella forced herself not to roll her eyes and continued with the charade. "My husband and I were considering visiting the shore and grabbing a bite at a shop. Is there any place we should stay clear of?"

The woman pondered the question, rubbing her chin. "I wouldn't go to the bakery. They overcharge. The butcher carries their day-old bread at half price. Tastes fine."

"Thank you," Rosella said. "Is it safe to walk on the shore for a bit?"

The woman furrowed her brow. "On a day like this?"

"We'll never see it again," Rosella said, shrugging. "Might as well walk in the sands if we can."

The woman smiled. "Ah, young love. Stay by the town and you'll be fine. Don't go to the cliffs in the bay."

"Oh, why?" Rosella asked, keeping her voice light. "Is it a rough current?"

The woman snorted. "No, they're cursed waters, and it's best not making today your last."

"Thank you," Rosella said, smiling.

She returned to her waiting horse, and after mounting it, headed toward the cliffs in the bay.

Chapter Thirty-One

THE WAVES CRASHED ON THE SHORE, THE FROTHY, ANGRY white caps licking at the sand. A brisk wind carried the sea air, moist with rain and salt.

Rosella took a moment to stare at the water. She hadn't lied. This would be the first and likely last time she ever saw the sea. The angry dark gray waves toiled in the wind. White seagulls dotted the bleak smokey clouds, their caws in contrast to the rumble of the waves.

"She said the cliffs?" Lucien asked. His gaze traveled over the calm, sandy beach until it curved into the water and then up a steep cliff that ran into the horizon. The sharp edges jutted against the raging seas, promising death.

"Yes," Rosella said and looked at Lucien. Each location was harder. Each keeper deadlier. She had made the promise, not him. "You don't have to go."

He rolled his eyes at her and steered his horse toward the cliffs.

As they neared, the sand drifted to rocks and then boulders. The slippery surface was too much for the horses, and they jumped off to continue on foot.

"Will they stay here?" Rosella said. She petted her horse. It nickered and whinnied toward the cliffs, the warning weaving into her veins.

Lucien found a log and, after removing their bits, tethered the horses to it.

They pranced in place. Their unease rattled Rosella, but she tightened her toes and fists to steady herself. She needed to stay focused if they were to succeed and break the curse fully.

"What do you think we're facing?" Lucien asked.

Rosella looked at the sea and shrugged. "It could be anything, aquatic or land. Creature or human."

"What do you think we have to sacrifice?"

Rosella swallowed.

At the shoreside, Fractions will divide

Feats have been met twice, But freedom's found with sacrifice

She'd played that verse around in her head many times, but with nothing left that'd be a true loss, she hadn't been able to move past a life for sacrifice. When asked for the sacrifice, she wasn't sure what she'd do. If she was capable of just surrendering without a fight.

After scrambling over large boulders and creeping around a sharp corner, they found themselves on a rock shelf. The flat base sat suspended above the water, having an unobstructed view of the sea. Water slicked the surface, residue of the large waves that crashed against it.

"It's gorgeous," Rosella murmured, taking in the whitecaps, rippling navies and grays of the water, the splashes of the sea, and the breach of a creature farther out.

"Do we jump in the water? Wait? Continue on?"

"This feels like the spot," Rosella said.

"Feels like it?"

"The seas are here. We're on a platform dividing the sea from the land. We've met two feats."

"All we need is a sacrifice?" Lucien said and smiled at her. His eyes darkened.

Rosella backed up from him, her hand dropping to the ready for her shortsword.

"What?" Lucien asked and looked at her with alarm. "What did you think I was going to do?"

Rosella narrowed her eyes but didn't relax or give an answer.

"Where do you think it is?" Lucien asked.

As if in answer, a laugh sounded below.

"So, you found me," a melodious voice called from the waves.

Rosella stepped back as Lucien leaned over the rocky edge. His features softened, and his grin grew.

"Hello," he crooned.

Rosella inched closer, looking over the edge. Below them swam a woman with raven-black hair, brown eyes, and red lips. She wore multiple strands of pearls, necklaces, rings, and bracelets. Diamonds sparkled from her ears and were woven into her hair.

The woman cut Rosella a sly grin. Her eyes sparkled like gems.

Rosella looked to Lucien, who had a dreamy look as he reached toward the woman, with his hand extended and fingers dancing.

Rosella nodded at the siren and said, "You are the keeper?"

"Of so many things. You must be more specific." The siren arched from the water, bringing her closer to Lucien. Her long tail glittered in the sun, the scales a kaleidoscope of rainbow gems.

He reached further out for her, stumbling, and almost tumbled off the ledge. Rosella grabbed his shirt and pulled him back. They toppled backwards. He landed on top of her and air escaped Rosella's lungs.

His eyes cleared of the siren's lure and then darkened as he looked at Rosella.

"I've been hoping," he whispered. He dipped his face toward her. His lips almost brushed hers.

"Get off me," Rosella sneered and shoved him back. He fell back on the ground. He grunted and he rolled his eyes. His hand ran over his forehead and into his hair.

"Lover's quarrel?" the siren called. A laugh chimed on the air.

Rosella shook her head, grimacing.

"I heard you two were married," she said and raised an eyebrow.

"How did you..." Rosella's voice trailed off. Either she was the old woman, or she had a magical mirror. Or something else disturbing and unexplainable.

"Or were you just pretending?" the siren asked. A funnel of water lifted her up onto the ledge so she could rest her elbows on the rock. Droplets of water rained on them.

Rosella stood and brushed the debris off her shirt. She didn't want more games. Too much time had been wasted already. A curse had infected the land and transformed people into creatures. The being before her was likely capable of much, including watching them.

She recited, "'At the shoreside, Fractions will divide, Feats have been met twice, But freedom's found with sacrifice.'"

"Right to it, huh?" the siren said with a laugh, the musical sound clouding Lucien's eyes again.

"What are the other two lines?" Rosella asked. She tapped Lucien's leg with her foot to get his attention.

"You sure you're ready?" the siren asked, looking between them, licking her lips.

Dread curled in Rosella's stomach. She had to be ready to react. Both times, the keepers had lunged at her. With Lucien distracted, he could get hurt.

"'The impossible is near, Even if only in a tear.'"

The siren remained calm, her eyes following Rosella. Only the sound of crashing waves broke the stillness.

Rosella flinched. They needed a tear? Whose tear?

"So, one of us sacrifices our life and you cry?" Rosella asked. "Or the other cries and gathers the tear?"

"The sacrifice has been already done, child," the siren said with an evil grin.

Rosella blinked. Her eyes jumped to Lucien, but he still lay breathing.

It had to be a trick. What sacrifice had been made? "Then may I have the tear?"

"Did either of you sacrifice for it?" the siren asked.

Rosella stared down at Lucien and then at herself.

"No, but if it's already done..." Rosella muttered. There hadn't been a sacrifice unless she meant sending her sisters home. Had she sacrificed their home for her word? For Grayson? But her sisters had the money for the taxes and a letter. It couldn't be that simple.

"If you want the tear, *you* need to make your own sacrifice," the woman said, tapping her chin. "Hurry, though, or it will be too late. Hm... How about a trade?"

"Trade?" Rosella parroted, fisting her hands at her side.

"I'd take the locket you have tucked beneath your tunic," the siren said.

Rosella's eyes shot open at the proclamation. The siren shouldn't know. Her hand fell to the locket, grabbing it through the fabric. She shook her head. "I can't."

"Can't? Or won't?"

"I can't. It's not mine."

"Is it his?" she asked, turning to Lucien, her smile growing. Razor-sharp teeth glistened in the dim sunlight.

Lucien's blue eyes lingered on the Siren, a soft smile curving his lips.

"No," Rosella said. "It's not mine to trade."

"You said that in the river, too," the siren said, batting her hand in the air. "Aren't you willing to sacrifice it to end the curse?"

"What? You were in the river?" Were the curse's keepers just an illusion? Had she been watching? "How is this possible? Have you been watching us?" If the master had a magical mirror that showed him where they were, it made sense another existed and someone else watched them. Even if it was creepy.

"Were you the troll, too?" Lucien asked, coming out of his daze.

The woman gave him a disgusted look. "So much ambition and looks, but not much common sense."

"What do you want for the tear?" Rosella asked. "I can't give you the locket."

"Will you kill him?" she asked and smiled sweetly at Lucien. "A sacrifice?"

Rosella stuttered, shaking her head.

"What about you?" the siren asked, turning to Lucien. She tilted her head. "Would you kill her for the tear?"

His eyes darkened and his lip curled up to the side.

"Yes," he said and lunged at Rosella, catching her off guard.

She hit the rock hard, lights popping in her eyes. Her vision grew hazed, everything distant and blurry. Warmth covered her chest. She moved her hand to touch it, and pain shot through her from the pressure. Her hands trembled as she touched her torso. When she lifted them into view, they were reddened by her blood. She tried to breathe, but her lungs burned.

"What are you doing?" she croaked out to Lucien, most of it inaudible as blood gurgled from her mouth. He had sacrificed her for the curse. The master would be right. She wouldn't return. But if Lucien broke it...

"I'm protecting the staff. He's a monster. You broke the two most important layers. You should have gone home and forgotten all about us. Now you're making me finish this. Had I known it was layered, I could have changed my approach through the years."

Hatred and fear welled in her, but she could do nothing. Her broken body refused to move. Refused to fight. Rosella's eyes grew heavy as the pain spread. Fire scorched her lungs, and breathing became too painful. She thought of her sisters and a lump lodged in her throat. They could at least carry on. Grayson would forever be cursed.

She'd failed.

She'd made it to the end and failed.

Lucien turned toward the siren, his hands and dagger smeared in Rosella's blood. He didn't bother to wipe his hands as he asked, "Do I get the tear?"

"Oh yes, darling," she said, and a single silver drop fell from her eye, the metallic sheen unnatural on her skin. She pulled a locket from one of her necklaces and put the tear inside. She closed it and handed it to Lucien. "You earned it," she said, grinning.

Lucien sneered at her. "We can't have you doing that again."

As Rosella's eyes shuttered shut, Lucien dropped the locket into the sea and then stabbed the siren.

Chapter Thirty-Two

"Rosella," a soft voice murmured.

Rosella licked her lips and pressed deeper into the bed.

"Mommy, is she awake yet?" a voice lost in memories squealed.

"Sh, Camilla, she's sleeping," the warm velvety voice said, wrapping around Rosella's heart and squeezing.

"But Mommy, she's missing everything," Camilla pouted. The voice drew near until the bed was indented beside Rosella's knee.

Rosella strained to open her eyes, but pulses of colors danced across her lids as her eyes remained closed.

"Mom," another voice called out. Younger but more mature than Camilla's.

"Bridgette, love!"

"Mom, I'm worried about Rosella. She's been asleep too long. Way too long."

"I'm awake!" Rosella screamed, but the words remained trapped in her mind.

Her body refused to acknowledge her strain to open her eyes, tighten her fist, bolt up, scream. Instead, it held her prisoner as her sisters shifted on the bed and her mother's gentle hand laid across Rosella's forehead. Her tender caress sent warm curls through Rosella's veins, warming her soul, and increasing her fight to wake up.

A silent sob racked her body.

"Mama," a third voice said. "Can I join, too?"

"Of course, Giselle. We'll all sit with Rosella. She'll know we all love her and want her to wake up."

Words lodged as a lump in Rosella's throat. Her eyes burned from unshed tears. She clawed at her limbs to move, to do anything.

Finally, a scratchy word escaped her throat. "Mama?"

"Rosella, my love," her mother said, her words a soft whisper in her ear. Gentle hands brushed across her forehead and tucked a lock of her hair behind her ear. "You've done so much. You've done so well. I am so proud of you. I love you. I will see you one day, but not today. You must wake up now."

Rosella gasped as air rushed into her lungs. The burning sensation singed her throat and her body lurched forward.

A warm damp cloth slid across Rosella's cheek. She flinched and pulled back. Her eyes refused to open, the blackness an uninviting void.

A soft hum tickled her ears, and she fought her eyes to open.

The cave was dark, the soft trickle of water binged in the lulls of the humming.

"Welcome back, dear," a soft voice whispered. The familiar voice was no longer her mother's.

Rosella thrashed against her body's fatigue to force herself awake, to move, to protect herself. Her head spun and with pops of light in her vision, she fell backwards.

"No, no," the woman said. "Don't strain yourself."

"Where am I?" she croaked.

"We're inside the cave now," the woman said.

Rosella blinked, trying to focus in the dark of the chamber. A single candle cast light into the unending shadows and her vision swam, adjusting to take in the moving form. Rock walls surrounded them, slick with moisture. The area they nestled in was a makeshift camp. A table with two chairs, a few chests forming a half-wall from the dark expanse, and two cots to sleep in. Despite the dampness, the air was warm. The scent of stew and bread filled the air.

"You're the siren."

"I'm many things," she said.

"But he stabbed you," Rosella said, rubbing a hand on her neck. Tendrils of phantom pain shot through her shoulder.

The woman waved off Rosella's concern. "I've had worse."

"He stabbed me, too," Rosella croaked. Her hands flew to her chest, running over the healed wound. A small red sliver remained.

"Your body is healed," the siren said. "Other wounds take longer."

"You helped me?" Rosella choked out.

"You needed it."

"But you've tried to kill me all along."

"I've tested you, where it matters beyond the physical. You didn't succumb."

Rosella shot her a dark look.

The siren laughed.

"Do you always speak in riddles and vagueness?"

"Hasn't stopped you."

"But I failed," Rosella said, the thoughts tumbling forth. "He dropped the locket into the water and tried to kill you and me."

"Yes, he did."

"But why?" Rosella croaked.

"He doesn't want the final piece of the spell broken," the siren said.

"Why? The only thing left is the master and his parents. He made sure the servants were freed from the curse."

"Have you seen the treasures in the castle?" the siren asked.

"You know I have," Rosella said. "What does it matter?"

The woman chuckled. "Your sisters saw them but a few short hours and were already focused on their luxurious futures."

"So, Lucien plans to rob Grayson?"

The siren tipped her head. "More than that. Lucien wants to rule."

"But the other servants..." Rosella said, her eyes darting around.

"Will find out too late to help," she said. "Lucien has wanted this longer than the castle curse. Why do you think he let a sorceress in? He knew they were never to let a wayward in."

"What?" Rosella breathed out.

The siren's ruby-red lips curled into a smile.

"Lucien said Grayson's parents wanted to..."

"You think that was his first lie?"

Events from the previous weeks rolled through Rosella's mind. From the cloaked figure talking to the master, to the ravine when he disappeared, and all the warnings he spoke of the master. All meant to turn her against Grayson. From locking up her sisters to a horrific perverted lie about his parents.

"But you cursed the whole castle. The King and Queen! You punished the villages. You turned the townspeople into wolves!"

The siren shrugged. "Punished? I did so quickly to those by the castle. They felt no pain. No bite of fear or starvation that their royalty caused. They are suspended in animal form, like the land. It was merciful compared to if they were allowed to live in fear of the castle or chaos. Lucien wasn't wrong about the King and Queen being selfish and stingy. They weren't welcoming and shunned anyone not of nobility. They had raised taxes and demanded more of their people during hard times. They had a lesson to learn, too."

Taxes. No matter the land, the wealthy seemed to want more from the less fortunate. To drain everything to keep those beneath them in their place. To provide themselves the same level of luxury while the people starved. It was why she was even on this journey to begin with.

"And Lucien's going to use this as an opportunity? He plans to take over the castle?"

"I believe so, yes."

"Is there any way to stop him?"

"I believe a solution will arrive soon."

What solution could arrive? Could she still break the final piece of the curse and save the castle? Rosella furrowed her brow. "It was a magic tear. By chance is there another?"

"No, I am sorry, there is not."

"Did you catch the locket?"

She shook her head. "The tear is gone."

"So I can't break the curse," Rosella said and covered her face with her hands. Fatigue filled her muscles and mind. Everything was for naught.

"No, you cannot," the woman said and patted Rosella's shoulder.

Somehow, she still had to protect the castle, protect the staff. Even if she couldn't help Grayson. A sob rippled through her. She'd done so much only to fail at the end. Everything had been... not worthless. The servants were free. But... Tears rimmed her eyes. A hard lump bobbed in her throat, threatening to steal her breath. Rosella slumped back. "How will I tell him?"

"Why do you have to?" the woman asked and gave her a curious glance.

"I promised I would do it."

"He absolved you."

Rosella shook her head. "I made the promise. He only absolved it so we could get back in time to pay our taxes and save our house."

"Yet, you let your sisters handle it?"

Rosella bowed her head. "They have a letter explaining my absence." She could only hope it'd be enough.

The woman clucked her tongue.

"I made a promise," Rosella said. "He honored his end."

"Maybe he thought the risks outweighed his gain. As you did. Maybe he was willing to sacrifice being human so you could have what you wanted."

ROSELLA PICKED AT HER PORRIDGE, THE TAN SLUDGE dripping from her spoon back into her bowl.

"When did you become a picky eater?" the siren asked, nodding toward her bowl.

Rosella lifted a brow as her gaze flicked to the siren and then back to the lump of porridge that plopped into her bowl. "Pardon?"

Shifting into a human façade, the siren leaned back in her chair. She crossed her arms over her bare chest as her gaze perused Rosella. The corner of her mouth ticked up. "Maybe you've always been picky. You don't eat a lot."

Rosella shrugged and averted her gaze. Her stomach felt like lead again. She had been with the siren for almost two days. For one, she had been completely asleep. She would need to return to her sisters. On foot, though, it would be weeks. She would miss the tax deadline if she had started yesterday, today, or ever. If the town didn't believe her sisters, they would lose their home. And there was nothing she could do about it.

"Or is it you've trained yourself to eat less, think you need less, so your sisters can have more?"

Rosella stared at her bowl, not bothering to answer. Her cheeks didn't stain under the scrutiny nor the accusations. She'd heard them all before. Understood them but didn't care.

"So far you've been concerned with feeding your sisters, keeping them from marrying for food, protecting them for their inevitable theft, and now you're trying to break a curse you didn't create for a promise you were absolved of."

Rosella lifted her eyes to meet the siren's. "What is your point?"

"You have deprived yourself for so long, the only way you feel is to give to others. You experience emotion through them."

"That's ridiculous," Rosella sneered and shoved her bowl away.

"You live off your sisters' happiness, but they want more than anything else for you to be happy."

"I'm fine."

"Fine isn't happy."

"It isn't miserable, either."

"Oh, but isn't it? 'Fine' is that boring line of depriving yourself from emotion. Status quo. Little pain, but then little joy, too."

"What do you care?" Rosella spat. "I'm just part of your little game you've been watching. You could change everything. You could break a curse that is consuming humans, but you don't care. You've punished them for decades. But you don't want it broken, do you?"

"Oh, don't try to turn this on me. The rules to break it were simple." The siren's lips pressed into a thin line. Her eyes blazed with fury.

"But they weren't, and you know it!"

The siren smirked and dipped her head.

Anger rolled through Rosella, hot and fierce. "Are you mad that I was succeeding? Were you upset I solved the first two riddles? I was too close, so you had to do something else? Lucien helped me. Well, tried to.

Did you pollute his mind?" Rosella's eyes widened and her nostrils flared. "That's it, isn't it? You had him attack me."

The siren tilted her head to the side, *tsk*ing as she shook her head. "We both know that's not true."

Rosella sighed and rubbed a hand over her face. Her emotions swirled. She knew it wasn't true. But that meant she'd been used. Lucien hadn't wanted to help her or the others. Just himself.

"You have choices ahead of you," the siren said, interrupting her thoughts.

Rosella stared a beat before replying. A wiggle of hope bloomed in her chest. "I have choices? I can still break the curse?"

The siren sighed and slumped back. She shook her head. "You cannot break the curse."

"Then what choices are left?" Rosella spat.

"What do you want?"

"It doesn't matter."

"Oh, but it does. What is it you really want?"

"To protect my sisters, stop Lucien, and free the master from the last of the curse."

"Is that what you really want?"

"I already want the impossible," Rosella chortled. She chuckled humorlessly. "Why not tack on happiness?"

The siren's lips curved into a grin. "There are always paths to our wants."

Rosella snorted. "What path is there?"

"Oh, one's coming, about now..." the siren said, staring into the distance.

Chapter Thirty-Three

Grunts carried across the wind followed by long scrapes against the rocks. As the noise drew near, a large mass moved against the shadows, scrambling across the uneven terrain. The clumsy lope didn't stop its progress and it charged forward.

Rosella swallowed. Her eyes skidded around the cave looking for a weapon. Was this a new part of the curse? Had the siren tricked her again? Had Lucien sent something?

"Rosella," Grayson's voice rang out, more of a growl than words. The deep baritone echoed on the cliffs and into the sea and vibrated in her core.

"What?" Rosella said, scrambling to her feet. "Is that him?"

"Yes," the siren said. A smug smile tugged on her lips.

"What is he doing here? He can't leave the castle."

"Why don't you go ask him?"

Rosella swallowed, looking down at her crusted, blood-soaked shirt. She'd failed. Lucien was out there and yet the master was here. The curse... it wouldn't matter now, anyway. He'd left the castle. The tear had washed away.

It was over.

Rubbing her hands down her sides, she swallowed back the unease in her throat. She had to tell him she failed. Her body, healed by the siren, didn't protest as she scampered down the rocks of the cave to meet him on the boulders outside.

"What are you doing here?" she yelled, emerging from the cave, the wind ripping her words from her.

He charged forward, his hulking form even larger than before. Tusks jutted from his mouth and a full mane tangled around his head.

"Rosella?" he stammered, confusion darkening his face. "Is that really you?"

"Grayson, what are you doing here?" she yelled, closing the distance to him, his form dwarfing her. Her heart thudded in her ears as she stared up at him. His yellow eyes frantically darted around her face.

He pulled her into an embrace. His body trembled as his paws tightened around her and his breath came in ragged pants.

Rosella nestled into the warm hug. His heartbeat thudded in her ear. She curled her fingers into his shirt, pulling him closer.

Sucking in a breath, he ran his trembling paws over her hair. Forming the words carefully, he said, "I couldn't let you do this. I saw you turn from your family. I saw Lucien follow you. I saw him..." His voice cracked, but he finished, "...stab you."

He pushed her back to examine her and his nostrils flared at seeing the blood stains on her shirt.

"She fixed me," Rosella said, and nodded in the direction of the cave.

He followed her gaze but didn't release her shoulders.

"Why did you leave the castle?" Rosella asked. A sob threatened to come out. "You'll be a beast forever."

"Some things are more important. I didn't trust Lucien. Not after the ravine. He tried poisoning my food after you were to leave with your sisters. He left without a word before I could confront him. I was afraid he'd hurt you... and he did."

Poison. Lucien had used her to make sure Prince Grayson would stay a beast. Stay cursed. Pave the way for him to claim the castle as his.

"She thinks he wants to claim your title," Rosella said.

"Who's the 'she' you keep mentioning?" Grayson said. His eyes narrowed and his paws tightened on Rosella.

"That'd be me," the siren said, walking out of the cave. No longer nude, she wore a gauzy gown of lavender. Strings of pearls hung loosely around her, and diamonds twinkled in her hair. Her body shimmered in the fading sunlight.

"She was the last keeper," Rosella said.

"I saw what Lucien did," Grayson said. He kept his arm around Rosella. "I thought he stabbed you, too."

"He thinks so, too," the woman laughed, the sound like chimes.

"He dropped the tear," Rosella stammered and lowered her eyes. "The curse..."

"I know," the beast said and forced a smile, his fangs jutting out. He tightened his arm around her shoulders, pulling her again into a hug. "I made it permanent when I left the castle. I'll be okay. I'm just sorry I am too late."

The woman chuckled, her eyes dancing in mirth, and snapped her fingers. Her form morphed into the old haggard woman who had eaten rolls with Rosella and who dropped the locket.

"Wait, it's you," Rosella said, her mouth falling open. Somehow, she wasn't surprised by it, but more surprised she hadn't thought of it.

"You know her?" Grayson asked.

"She visited my shop one morning," Rosella stammered. "She... ate bread, and left us with more rolls, jam, and milk. She also dropped a locket."

"So generous," the woman smiled and then turned a sharp eye to Rosella. "And skeptical. You passed my test in your home. When you went out to save your family, I switched the path you were on to one that had grown over with the curse."

"You mean, you sent me to the castle on purpose."

The siren chuckled, her gem eyes twinkling. "May I have my locket back?"

"Yes," Rosella said and slipped it off her neck, the small locket's weight like a burden gone. "If you'd shown me before, I'd have given it to you."

"Yes, but this was more fun," she said, taking the locket and inspecting it. "You never opened it?"

"It wasn't mine."

"Smart girl," she said and rubbed a hand over it.

"Thank you for the chance to break the curse," Grayson said and bowed to the siren. He turned to Rosella, and said, "Thank you for breaking the curse. I'll help you get back home. Your sisters miss you fiercely."

Rosella let out a dejected breath. Her lips trembled but she nodded. "I'm sorry I didn't finish it," she managed to say.

"You solved each part. Lucien made his choice," the master said.

"I made the curse," the woman said, eyeing them.

"Yes, my parents were disgusting." Grayson nodded.

"Hm," the siren mumbled noncommittedly. She fanned her fingers out, inspecting the glittering rings on each. She plucked one with diamonds and emeralds. "I believe this is yours," she said and handed Rosella back her mother's ring.

"But..." Rosella started. Tears welled in her eyes, and emotion clogged her throat. She managed a watery, "Thank you."

She slipped the chain and ring back around her neck. The familiar comfort returned.

"Now, for the curse," the siren said with a nod. "My requirements were met."

"But he left the castle." Rosella furrowed her brow.

"To sacrifice for you. He did not plead or beg. He accepted his choice."

"The tear is gone," Rosella said.

"It was what *you* needed to break the curse by yourself," the siren said. "I do not need the tear to break it." She handed the pendant back to Rosella.

When Rosella wouldn't take it, the siren lifted Rosella's hand out, palm up, and placed the locket in her palm and then closed her fist around it. She clasped Rosella's hands between hers. A dark scowl dampened the siren's face when Rosella tried to push her hands back.

Rosella looked at her skeptically.

"It is yours now. I give it to you freely, but do not open it until you are in a winless situation."

"I can't take it."

"You must. It is yours. I don't want it back. It would be a great offense." She waited until Rosella slipped it back around her neck and then turned toward the beast. "And you. You are not like your parents. Even if you do not know their true nature but the lies Lucien has told you. You are a kind, considerate man who seeks to help others."

He stared at her, his yellow eyes shining with uncertainty. He flicked his gaze to Rosella, who nodded and smiled at him. With his canines jutting out, he returned it.

The siren flicked her hand, reciting, "'A curse in the past, To bind the heartless, Now at its last, With freedom to harness.'"

Gold magic swirled from her hand and engulfed the beast, absorbed through his fur and skin until he radiated with golden light. With a chime it dissolved, and in place of the hunched over animal hybrid stood a tall, broad man, with long, disheveled black hair, yellow eyes, and over-sized clothes. It was the same visage that appeared before each level of the curse worsened. The man who looked like the paintings in the castle.

"Grayson?" Rosella questioned. Her eyes raked over his form, her cheeks staining in color.

He held his arms out as he took in his human form. He twisted around. He looked back to Rosella and smiled.

"You broke the curse," he said, pulling her in for a hug.

His warmth soaked through her, and he tightened his hold. Her heart hammered in her chest and heat curled in her stomach. She never wanted to let go.

Rosella shook her head but hugged him back. "I didn't."

"You both sacrificed, each in your own way," the woman said.

She patted their arms and pushed them apart to walk between them. Grayson scowled and looped his arm around Rosella's shoulders. She wrapped her arm around his waist, her fingers curling in his loose shirt.

The siren smirked at the two. "You two need to hurry back. You have a castle to defend."

Chapter Thirty-Four

Rosella stripped out of her bloodied shirt and donned a clean one provided by the siren. She ran a hand over her face, trying to force the lingering smile from her lips. Despite all that happened and what remained, her stomach fluttered watching Grayson move around the cave. His large form filled the cave and her mind. When she looked to him, she expected to see a furred body, an almost-lion. Instead, he struggled to keep his oversized garments on his muscled and hard human form. Large hands pushed a lock of black hair from his face. Stubble already dusted his jaw. Yellow eyes greeted her with the same intensity, stirring her core. His sight and touch still sent heat sizzling in her veins. At the castle, so much had stood between them. Now, it was on her to create distance. They had separate lives ahead of them, and no matter what she felt, she had to remember it.

A blush crept across her cheeks when he looked up and caught her gaze. Again. He smiled and warmth coursed through her, destroying her thoughts.

"Even out of the beast form, you're still... big," the siren said, raising an eyebrow as a smirk curved her lips. She tilted her head toward Rosella, and whispered, "Lucky you."

Rosella froze, her eyes locked on the siren as heat shot up her neck and face.

"I don't have much for you," the siren said, shifting through different piles of treasure. "I don't normally host men. I just drown them at sea."

Grayson's eyes widened, but he accepted a shirt and trousers from her.

"Before you two play fools," the siren said, her gaze bouncing between them, "you two must stick together. Through it all."

Grayson opened his mouth, but the siren held up a finger to cut him off.

"She's healed. She solved three riddles and faced keepers. Do not coddle her or play pompous hero in the final stage. You'd still be cursed if not for her."

"I…" Grayson started but shut his mouth. He shot a guilty smile to Rosella. Taking her hand in his, he nodded toward the siren. "I understand."

Rosella rubbed her thumb against his hand, the sensation sending tingles through her. It was something she could get used to. She shook her head to stop the wayward thoughts. They both had different lives. She helped break the curse and he paid her taxes. The curse was broken. Their arrangement was done. The tingles turned to sharp curls in her stomach that sent acid to her throat.

"Are you okay?" Grayson asked, stepping closer as his fingers tightened around her hand. He tilted his head to meet her eyes.

His hand felt so right in hers. But it wasn't hers to have. Swallowing hard, she nodded but her gaze darted away from his. She met the siren's fierce stare.

"Is it safe for him to go back to the castle?" Rosella asked, her voice cracking.

Grayson stiffened by her side as he scrutinized her rigid posture. Confusion furrowed his brow. "It's my castle," he started.

"We don't know what Lucien will do," Rosella said. His fingers tightened around hers again, and she wanted to squeeze back, lace her fingers with his, but it'd only make saying goodbye harder.

"No, but you both need to go," the siren said. "It will take both of you. Now go, before it is too late."

Rosella and Grayson walked back to the shore. Streaks of sun speared through the gray overcast sky, shimmering off the sea and sending ripples of light toward them.

Rosella had to stop herself from staring at his human form and focus on the rocky terrain. He moved his hand from hers to her elbow. Together, they supported each other down, he unsteady on his human legs and she fatigued from the healing.

Her eyes darted around the shore. The horses she and Lucien had ridden were gone, as she expected. They'd be forced to walk if they couldn't find horses to trade for or borrow.

"I know I was down for at least two days," Rosella said, breaking the silence. "He has a lead on us, and the horses and all our supplies."

Grayson looked around the shore, a frown darkening his face. His hand dropped from her arm. She rubbed her arm where his hand had been, but it remained cold with the absence of his touch.

"How'd you get here?" she asked. Images of him loping through the forest as a beast crossed her mind. He would start more myths to carry on for centuries.

"I rode my horse," he said. With his unfurry, human finger, he pointed past the sandy shore to a horse at least eighteen hands tall waiting in the shade at a distant outcrop of trees. It was the largest horse Rosella had seen. His gaze cut back to Rosella, his yellow eyes bright as he took her in. "I think the two of us together weigh less than I did as a beast. Even so, I think Henry can hold us."

Rosella stared at the draft horse, loaded with gear and a traveling lantern. She looked at Grayson with a knot in her throat, but she nodded in agreement. They'd have to ride together. Her stomach flipped and she licked her lips. "How much farther ahead do you think he is?"

"We can find out," Grayson said and walked to his horse. Rosella trailed behind him, staring at the path she'd come with Lucien. It was clear of people and storm clouds blotted out the horizon in the distance.

He dug out his mirror from a saddle bag, and said, "Mirror, show me Lucien."

The mirror image shimmered in waves of silver before Lucien came into focus.

Rosella recognized the farm in the distance behind Lucien.

"Based on the forest line, he has about a day's lead," Grayson said.

"He always sleeps late and needs lots of rest," Rosella said, realizing they stood a chance. Perhaps she hadn't been asleep as long as the sluggishness of her body felt like she had.

"What?" the beast snorted.

"He always wanted to sleep instead of ride," Rosella said, a smile cracking on her face. What had annoyed her before was now her advantage.

Grayson hid a grin, but his eyes brightened in amusement. He said, "No, you just don't sleep. I think you get two to three hours at most. Even when injured."

Rosella narrowed her eyes and crossed her arms over her chest in defiance.

"If the horses didn't need rest, I doubt you would have stopped," he said, slipping the mirror back into the bag. He moved around the horse, tightening the girth and checking the straps.

"I stopped to eat," Rosella challenged.

He rolled his eyes. "Only breakfast and dinner, and if he whined."

"How do you know this?" Rosella asked, moving her hands to her hips. A curl of embarrassment twisted through her.

Grayson stilled, his eyes large as he stared at her. Finally, he said, "I kept tabs with the mirror. I wanted to make sure you two were okay."

She eyed him, her eyes dark with suspicion.

"I needed to make sure you were all right. I didn't watch you too much. I checked in to make sure you weren't in danger."

"You saw the troll try to eat me," Rosella said.

"And you kill him," he said. His jaw ticked and he looked away.

Realization tingled like mist on her skin. His odd behavior at dinner and trying to send her home made sense.

"Is that why you didn't want me to go on this last one? You thought I'd kill it, too? You didn't want murder to break the curse?"

He threw his hands in the air, and said, "No! You needed to see to your family's needs. And you're not a murderer. That thing..." He shook his head and rubbed a hand over his forehead. "No, you'd done more than enough. The castle and my staff were free. You almost died twice. I was the last one left. I wasn't worth... You couldn't die to save *me*."

Grayson growled and bowed his head.

"But you matter," she said. She reached a hand toward his shoulder, but let it hover between them.

He grimaced and refused to look at her. Red blotches raced up his neck.

"Your parents' choices weren't yours." She closed the distance between them. He flinched at her touch and his muscles rippled beneath her fingers.

"I was theirs. My curse was to punish them. It's all I've remembered being. My human form wasn't as important."

Rosella smiled sadly. Her fingers tightened around his arm. Heat slid through her and she blinked at the sensation.

"I should have intercepted you as soon as I realized you'd left your family," he muttered. "Lucien..."

"He made his choices. They aren't yours. I made mine, and you made yours. Now, we need to stop him."

A large breath racked his frame. He nodded slowly, until he lifted his head and met her gaze. His yellow eyes shined with emotion.

Rosella's breath caught in her throat. They could do this. She'd faced three keepers and a curse. And her own death already.

"You want the lead or back?" Grayson asked as he untethered the horse and put the bit back in.

Rosella sucked in her cheeks and stared at the ground. Both options were pleasant and unpleasant at the same time. She didn't have time or desire to think about such things as attraction or how he felt against her. It was only a distraction and she needed to stay focused.

"I'll start with the lead," she said, turning around so he couldn't see her blush as she mounted the horse. "We can switch after each rest."

"Deal," he said and sat behind her.

Chapter Thirty-Five

The moon arched in the sky, the white beacon casting long shadows around them, basking their path in light and silhouetting them on the trail.

The horse galloped with ease with the two riders. Grayson sat back, his hands gripping tightly to the saddle as if trying to stop himself from pushing further into Rosella. Rosella clutched the reins as she steered the stallion toward the road.

His hard, muscular body was pressed against her back. Despite the urgency and gravity of the situation, her body responded to the touch. Heated spikes shot down her spine, gripping her stomach. She clenched her body to stop the reaction to no avail. Need wrapped around her core, and she tightened her hold on the reins. All her thoughts of creating distance between them had evaporated.

If this was what Bridgette felt toward Gavin and Giselle toward Odette, no wonder they were so shaken, so distracted. Fortunately, Benson nor her other suitors elicited such a response. She'd be able to stay focused on her business and tend to her sisters. It would be a simple, safe life. Even if her thoughts may linger on Grayson until they faded with time.

She stiffened, caught in her thoughts, when his hand curled around her waist, and he leaned in. Instinctually, her body arched into his touch. His voice was soft and warm on her neck. She squirmed, bringing her ear to her shoulder. He chuckled at her response which vibrated her neck again causing her to squirm in a different way.

"We should rest," he said. "Lucien probably pulled off a few hours ago. We're probably a day and a half behind him."

"We could keep going," Rosella said. She licked her lips. Her body didn't want to keep going but listening to her body would be foolish. Especially with her current reactions and thoughts. "Take him over tonight."

"The horse needs rest, as do we," Grayson said, his voice gravellier. "We'll be better prepared for him after a rest."

With his words settling on her, the heaviness in her eyes came into her focus. She nodded and scoped out a spot. Maybe she could shake the weird sensations if they weren't touching.

They pulled off into a thicket of bushes and tethered the horse after removing the bit. Away from the horses and Grayson, the cold air caught up to Rosella. Winter was coming, dancing on the breeze. Perhaps this year with some of the gold, they could fill the holes in their house to block the draft.

"Fire or not?" he asked. He rubbed his arms, his brow pinched.

"Not used to being cold?" she asked as she pulled out the bedroll and blanket. She missed his touch and warmth but busied herself with tasks to ignore the sensation. Keeping her distance would help her focus and make it easier to part later.

"No." He frowned at his body and straightened his shoulders. He took the roll from Rosella to set it up.

She stifled a laugh.

"Small fire," she said. Leaving him to the bedroll, she gathered some sticks and branches.

Following Rosella's guidance, he made a small pit with rocks and started a fire with a flint.

She handed him a canteen, some bread, and dried meat from the sack the siren had provided.

They ate in silence until Rosella leaned back and nestled into the ground.

"What are you doing?" he asked. He tossed more kindling into the fire, the embers flickering in the black sky.

She yawned. "I'm going to catch some sleep."

"Use the bedroll," he said. He nudged her with his foot and directed his chin toward the roll. "I set it up for you."

"It's yours," she said. She curled into a ball next to the fire, snuggling in close. The heat met her face and she sighed.

"I'm not using it," he gritted out.

"Then be cold," she said before letting sleep consume her.

WHEN ROSELLA AWOKE A FEW HOURS LATER, THE FIRE HAD reduced to embers and the first rays of light streaked the sky. She nestled against the bedroll and then frowned. She wasn't on a bedroll. It was draped over her. She looked to Grayson, and saw he had the blanket from the saddle draped on him. He shivered as he slept.

She brushed the roll off, and fetched sticks to add to the fire.

The prince snorted and tossed in his sleep.

Rosella dug out some rations and started to munch as she sat by the fire.

His eyes flew open, darting around. He jolted to the side, hunched, ready for an attack but then was caught off guard by the sight of his human form. His wide eyes darted up to find Rosella.

She raised her eyebrows in amusement, and a smile tugged on her lips.

"Morning," she said and tossed him a hunk of bread.

"Morning," he groused and sat up. "It's still dark."

She nodded toward the horizon. "Sun says it's not."

"Those are rays, not the sun. The sun is still hiding. We should still be sleeping."

"We should get a start now."

"Why?" Grayson yawned and laid back down. "It's still night."

"Lucien is lazy. He'll still be asleep."

"He's not lazy," the prince snorted. "He may be a murderous traitor, but he's not lazy. You just don't sleep."

"Either case," Rosella said. "We can cover the distance while he's sleeping."

Grayson sighed in defeat and helped pack up camp.

Rosella sat behind him on the horse this time, unsure how to settle in. The horse's gait was steady, but she was off-balance, not in her normal position. He hadn't needed to hold on to her for support when riding behind her, but she struggled to find her balance on the larger section of the horse.

Her family didn't own a horse, but she'd ridden others' in town. But she'd never ridden in tandem. She forced herself from gritting her teeth, the vibrations sending painful jolts in her mouth from clenching too hard. She held the edge of the saddle for security, but her fingers ached from clasping on the rim and her arms screamed from being held at the awkward angle. It was worse than fighting the keepers.

They traveled for an hour, the sky streaked in bright pinks and yellows. The rising temperatures already promised a hot day. Grayson sighed before he slowed the horse to a walk.

"What are you doing?" Rosella asked. She took in the surrounding landscape, but nothing seemed unusual. Unlike in the past, she didn't feel watched.

"Hold on," Grayson said. He reached behind him with his free hand opened, palm up. He turned to catch her gaze.

She felt the unwelcome burn of a blush flood her cheeks.

"Give me your arm," he said.

"What?" she squeaked.

"Give me your arm. You're doing weird things back there and you're unsettling the gait."

She scowled and mimicked him. She wanted to fold her arms over her chest but was afraid she'd fall off the horse.

"Arm," he demanded. "Now."

She growled, but released her grip on the saddle and tightened her legs as she reached forward.

He fumbled to get a grip on her hand, still adjusting to his human size, but pressed her hand against his abdomen. He switched the reins to the hand he held against hers.

"Now, the other one," he said, reaching backwards with his other hand.

She didn't argue, though she felt ridiculous, and heat curled in her stomach and face.

He pressed her hands against him with one hand in finality and held the reins with the other.

"That's better," he breathed. His chest lifted and fell before he urged the horse into a trot.

His fingers still pressed on hers, sent tingles through her.

She didn't voice her agreement but eased down into the more comfortable position.

Chapter Thirty-Six

Night swept over the sky, the sun fighting in a display of colors before finally relenting. The bright moon drowned out the stars and lit the path long after they should have stopped.

With the cover of night, Rosella's reservations lifted, guarded by the protection of the darkness.

"How does it feel?" Rosella asked. Her fingers fisted his tunic as she leaned to peer up at him.

"What?" he asked, cocking his head to look back at her. His hand still rested on hers, warm and inviting, as the pads of his fingers rubbed circles.

Rosella licked her lips, the closeness in the darkness too real. She willed her mind to focus. "Does it feel different to be in a human form than the other one?"

He snorted a humorless chuckle and turned back, his fingers still tracing hers.

Rosella swallowed. A ball of embarrassment twisted in her stomach. "I apologize, that was rude to ask," she said. She tried to slip her fingers off his side, but he tightened his hold.

He grunted and rubbed his thumb along hers. She nestled her hand against his warm flank, the contact more delightful than she would want to admit.

"I was stronger in the other form, but less agile. I still think I need the space I did before. I am not used to the feel of the cold. I miss the protection it brought. Others stayed away, and I could barge my way through things. I have to relearn my space. Relearn how I fit into the world around me."

Rosella waited as he paused and fidgeted with the reins in his free hand.

His voice was barely above a whisper. "I like feeling again, though, even if it means I'm vulnerable. I like the feel of skin. I like the way the breeze feels. The cold of night and the warmth of the sun."

He rubbed his calloused hand over Rosella's wrist, tingles racing up her arm.

"I miss clothes that fit," he said and pulled at the fabric stretched around his chest. The clothes the siren had provided were a better fit than his beast clothes he now swam in, but the new garments were cut for a trimmer frame.

Rosella chuckled. "I have an idea."

"What?"

"See that barn?" she asked and pointed in the distance.

"Yes, so?"

"Head for it."

"Why? It's off the path."

"Not by much, and we might be able to sleep in it and out of the elements."

"You're offering to rest?" he asked. His eyes widened and he glanced back at her.

Rosella rolled her eyes. "Just go there."

He begrudgingly turned the horse toward the barn, but before they made it a few paces, a whistled filled the air followed by the sound of fabric tearing.

An arrow pierced the prince's arm.

He howled in pain, causing the horse to rear. Rosella tumbled off backwards, hitting the ground hard, the air knocked from her lungs. Dots danced in front of her eyes. She gasped futilely for air as her back arched from the pain.

"Rosella," Grayson yelled. Quickly settling the horse, he

dismounted and ran to her. Blood from the arrow wound soaked through his shirt. He grimaced as his movement opened the wound more.

As he knelt to her, another arrow flew over his head, missing him by less than an inch.

"You're bleeding," she choked, fighting for air. She pushed at the sleeve material to see the wound better.

With gentle hands, he brushed her off. His hands cupped her face and moved down her neck and to her arms, searching for injuries. "I'll live. Can you move? Did you hurt your back? Are you bleeding?"

Despite the pain, Rosella laughed and then coughed. She wheezed out, "Just the air. You're bleeding. Let me look."

"Oh, what a sweet moment," a voice jeered. The person stood between them and the path, shrouded in the shadows of the night. She'd missed them crouching in the shrubbery when they'd veered off the trail.

Grayson turned toward the voice and pulled the sword from his scabbard. A growl rippled from his throat. He remained crouched as he scanned the foliage.

Rosella forced her arms to push her up. Scorching breaths clawed at her throat and her eyes swam to focus. Her fingers curled around where her shortsword pummel should be. She cursed upon realizing it was with the horse.

"I'm not coming closer, but if you don't stand up, I'll shoot her, too," the voice said. "I only want you."

"Who are you?" the prince demanded.

"Nobody. Like you."

"Why are you here?" Grayson asked.

"Waiting for you," he said. "I get one hundred gold pieces for bringing you in."

"From whom?" Grayson spat.

The voice chuckled. "It doesn't matter."

"How much do you get for me?" Rosella choked. Her breath came in wheezy uneven pants.

Grayson held up a hand up to stay her.

She rolled her eyes as she sat completely up. She blinked, forcing the world into focus. The moon lit everything up in dark silhouettes. Nausea threatened her stomach.

"You weren't supposed to be here," the man said. "Just him. I have no need for you."

"Maybe we're the wrong people, then," Rosella tried. She pushed Grayson's arm away as he tried to block her from view.

"His horse and gear match the description. As does his height and big form."

"Henry was the only one that could carry me," Grayson murmured.

"Lucien," Rosella growled.

"If he moves away from you, I'll let you go. Otherwise, you're just collateral. Why don't you encourage him to move?"

Grayson shifted to move away, but Rosella grabbed his arm. He scowled at her.

"Help me up," she seethed.

"Stay down," Grayson growled and brushed her hand from his arms. "Please."

Grayson stood, leaving Rosella on the ground. "I'm here. I'm moving away from her. You're getting your way. Don't hurt her."

Rosella stayed her retort and pulled her feet up to her butt. Her back tweaked from the motion. A snarl escaped her lips. She felt around and grabbed a few rocks.

"Good," the voice sneered.

Another arrow soared at the prince but went wide, nicking his arm. Grayson quieted a roar and jerked backwards from the sting.

Rosella chucked the rocks in the direction of the voice.

"Ow, what the stars was that?" the voice said. "I'll get you, you bitch."

Grayson used the distraction and charged forward, colliding with the figure before he could loose another arrow. His large frame rammed into the man, throwing him to the ground. With lashing hands, the man clawed at Grayson's face and neck.

Curses filled the air.

Rosella pushed her arms and legs to crawl toward the brawling men.

A roar, eerily similar to Grayson's beastly one, filled the air.

Although he'd pinned the man to the ground, his size in his favor, his hold swayed as he assimilated to his new form.

Unused to fighting, his grip slackened as he readjusted. The robber took advantage, thrashing his head and legs, digging his fingers into Grayson's vulnerable flesh.

Grayson yelled and scrambled to get a better hold, but the man threw dirt at his face. Instead of loosening his hold, Grayson pushed down, smashing the robber's arms to the cold ground. A yelp tore from the robber's lips as his arm cracked.

"You won't touch her," Grayson spat in his face.

Rosella made it to them, dirt and grass embedded in her nails. The moon shone off the pale face of the assailant. His eyes squinted tightly, and his teeth bared as he fought against Grayson, his arm unable to provide help.

An evil grin lit her face. With a seasoned grip, her fingers grabbed at him. He bellowed when she yanked on his ear, tugging his head toward her.

Grayson stared at her in bewilderment, not loosening his hold.

"Stop," Rosella demanded. With a jerk she yanked his head to an uncomfortable tilt.

"Ow," the man wailed. His good hand flew to her attack, but Grayson forced his hand back to the ground by putting pressure on the broken arm.

"Stop fighting," Rosella said and yanked both of his ears.

He screamed. His body arched, and his head scrunched close to his shoulders. When he tried to pull his head away, Grayson held his torso firmly and Rosella twisted her hold on his right ear and used her other hand to pinch his underarm along the muscle, as she did to her sisters when they wouldn't stop fighting.

He bucked against the pain, and whimpered, "I'll stop."

Rosella released her grip and he fell quiet.

"Don't ease up," Rosella told Grayson. "He'll wait for you to loosen your hold and bolt."

Grayson nodded, his focus on her as his hands tightened on the thief.

Their haggard breaths filled the night. Nothing sounded around them.

"Who sent you after him?" Rosella demanded. She pushed her hair from her face and sucked in air.

The man whimpered, and started to say, "I don't know," but stopped when Rosella grabbed his ear.

"I know many painful spots," Rosella said, smiling. "I am happy to show them all to you."

The master chuckled, an amused smile tugging on his lips.

"He was a blond man," the man said. "He had two horses."

"Lucien." Rosella confirmed her suspicion. Disappointment settled in her stomach. "Why did he send you?"

"I don't know."

"How'd you come under his employ?" Grayson demanded. "I don't recognize you and Lucien doesn't normally leave."

Rosella doubted that, but she left her thoughts unspoken.

"My group tried to rob him," the man whimpered, letting his head fall back and his body go limp. His free hand cradled his broken arm.

"Group?" Rosella repeated.

He nodded.

"Are they here, too?"

He shook his head. "He sent us to different locations."

So more would be in wait.

"What were the terms of your arrangement?" Rosella asked.

"He gave me twenty-five pieces and the bow and arrow. The rest on delivery."

Rosella's mouth hung open. She didn't know he had carried that much gold on him. She looked to Grayson who shook his head but his face was dark.

"Where were you to meet up for the rest of the gold?" she asked.

"Some castle over the hill." His face pained when he moved his arm.

"You agreed?" the beast asked.

"He was good for the twenty-five. That's more than I've gotten in a year. I figured the rest was worth trying for." The man whimpered.

"He was never going to give you more," Rosella said. "He'd kill you as soon as you delivered him."

His eyes widened and he swallowed. He shook his head feverously. "That's not true," he said, but his tone was uncertain.

"All of us know it is," Rosella said. "I, however, can guarantee you fifteen gold pieces."

"Fifteen? I want a hundred. You broke my arm."

Grayson snorted. "You shouldn't have threatened her."

"We could go with none and just take what we want," Rosella offered. She settled her hands around his ears.

"What do I have to do for the fifteen?" he squeaked.

"Give us your clothes and head in the opposite direction."

"That's it?" he asked, his eyes darting between the two.

Rosella knew it was a risk. Killing the troll had been hard enough, but he had planned to eat her. Had eaten others. This man was desperate.

Grayson didn't move his focus from Rosella when he nodded.

"You follow us," Rosella said, "and what happened here will seem enjoyable to what I'll do to you next. If I see you again, I'll take it as a sign you're not just desperate, but a murderer. You'll face his wrath too." She inclined her chin toward Grayson.

The thief gulped and looked at the prince.

Grayson finally met his gaze. His yellow eyes narrowed in annoyance. "If you go away and don't follow us, I won't pursue you and kill you. Any other choice, and you don't survive. I'll make sure of it."

The man's eyes bulged but he nodded.

Chapter Thirty-Seven

With thread and needle from a small pouch in the saddlebags, Rosella stitched up Grayson's wounds. When daylight broke, she'd clean it out and restitch it but the strip of cloth from his shirt worked as a bandage.

The new clothes were still too short on Grayson, but the boots covered most of the difference. The shirt had more room than the other, but still stretched across his torso.

Rosella chuckled as they moved away from the man and the barn at a fast clip, her hands absentmindedly rubbing against his shirt. His muscles rippled beneath her touch. He held the reins with his uninjured arm and rested his other hand against hers.

She rested her head against his back, stifling a yawn. All she wanted to do was ease into him and rest. His warmth was inviting and promising. She frowned at her thoughts. They'd part soon if they survived the castle. Their lives would separate. But she could enjoy the few fleeting moments, as long as she remembered they wouldn't last.

"We should pull over after a couple miles to sleep if we can find cover," she said. "I don't think he's following us." She glanced back at the once-tempting barn.

"Okay," Grayson strained to say, straightening his spine.

"Are you okay?" Rosella asked. "Is your shoulder bothering you?" She leaned to look unsuccessfully at his arm in the moonlight.

Grayson shook his head. "I'm fine. I agree, he isn't following us."

They found an outcrop of trees, an acre or so of growth in a shallow ditch that ran between two farms. He steered the horse into the brush and found a level spot out of view. There was no sign of others lurking. They'd have a better chance of seeing anyone approach them now than when they reached the forest.

Rosella dismounted and started to gather sticks and twigs to build a fire. Dampness clung to the air and ground. The wood would smoke when burned, but beneath the bark was still dry enough to light. Rosella's mind raced to the coming winter and how she'd keep her sisters warm. Her stomach loosened as she thought of the gold sent with her sisters. Even if it wasn't at their home, they should be okay for at least this winter.

Grayson tethered the horse, removing the bit, and unloaded the bedroll and food.

The crackle of the fire blocked out the other noises and lit the space around them. Beyond lay blackness, the trees and brush blocking both the sky and their fire.

"He's laying traps for you." Rosella settled across the fire. She watched him over the flames, his yellow eyes mirroring the fire.

"You provided a diversion," Grayson said, nodding at her as he stretched out by the fire.

"More wait for us. Who knows where he sent them? Can the mirror show us?"

Grayson shook his head. "Only people I can name specifically."

"Like Lucien?"

Grayson's eyes widened.

"Where is he?" she asked. She inclined her head toward the mirror in the saddle bag.

Grayson sighed and dug it out of his sack beside him. "Show me Lucien."

The mirror shimmered in silver dissolving into blackness before reflecting a dark form laying on the ground. "Looks like the trees."

"Anything more specific?" Rosella asked. Trees covered most of the path back to the castle. She scooted around the fire closer to him and leaned against Grayson's arm to look at the mirror. She bristled at the nearness she'd created but didn't retreat, even as heat curled in her belly.

Stiffening, he cut his dark eyes to her before he turned the mirror for her to see better.

"It looks like a forest based on the growth, otherwise, no," he said, shaking his head. He started to tuck the mirror away, but stopped, and held it out to Rosella. "Do you want to check on your sisters?"

Rosella licked her lips and nodded. She took the offered mirror and stared at it. Taking a breath, she blew it out slowly before saying, "Show me my sister, Bridgette, please..."

He snickered at her manners.

The mirror shimmered and an image of her home popped into view. Bridgette stood behind their store counter, her hands on her hips, and a prim scowl darkened her face. Rosella frowned and waited, but the image shimmered out.

"What's wrong?"

"Bridgette's angry, but I don't know why," she said.

"Ask about another sister," he said, gesturing toward the mirror. He nudged her arm and leaned closer to get a look. His breath tickled her ear.

Rosella licked her lips, her focus momentarily diverted to Grayson. His warmth seeped through their shirts and coursed through her veins. With two blinks, she refocused on the mirror.

"Show me Giselle," she said, refraining from politeness and his mockery. A knowing smile tugged on his lips.

Giselle popped into view. She had an arm draped around Odette while Odette leaned into her embrace. Tears streamed down both their faces while they held hands.

Rosella's heart clenched. She should be there to offer guidance and talk to Odette's family. She should have offered more for Giselle and not been so focused on what she thought they wanted and needed, but on what their realities were.

The image ebbed out, and Rosella stared at her own reflection. The mirror tipped away from her.

"Ask about Camilla," he prompted. Gently he pushed her hands and mirror toward her.

She flickered her eyes to him and then back to the mirror nodding. She said, "Show me Camilla."

Camilla snapped into frame. She hovered in the door between the home and store, obviously eavesdropping. Angry red blotches dotted her face and her hands furled into fists.

"What is going on?" Rosella mumbled.

"Ask about Benson," Grayson whispered.

Rosella's attention shot to him.

His jaw ticked and his eyes were unreadable. He pushed his fingers against hers and the mirror. The touch sent a heated jolt through Rosella.

"What? Why?"

"Aren't you supposed to marry him?" he asked, averting his eyes and picking grass off his pants.

Rosella snorted. "Not if we could get the tax money."

Grayson sighed.

"They have it. Ask about him." He didn't meet her gaze.

Rosella rolled her eyes. "Show me Benson."

The image snapped back to the shop. Benson was on the other side of the counter.

"Oh," Rosella mumbled. She tightened her fingers around the mirror's handle.

Grayson's eyes jumped to the mirror. A snarl flicked across his lips.

Benson stood offensively, his face red and lips pinched tightly in anger. "I don't believe you," he bellowed at where Bridgette had been. "You three are liars!"

"He yelled at my sister," Rosella muttered. Acid bubbled up her stomach. She'd have words with him. No one treated Bridgette like that.

"She's sick, she'll be back." Bridgette's sharp tone belied her annoyance. "She can't travel with a fever. She didn't want us to catch it and sent us home."

"She's here by the end of the week, four days, or the land is being sold."

"We paid our taxes!" Bridgette roared.

"I convinced my father to grant you another week to wait for her," he sneered, his eyes narrowing. "No one believes she's sick, just delaying the inevitable about the land. Your sister has to pay them. She's the guardian, not you. You think a fancy carriage and someone claiming to be from a castle will fool us? How do we know this money is yours and not stolen? Your family likes to help yourselves to others' apples and trees. We know Rosella is the only one worth trusting."

Rosella stared into the mirror long after the image had dissolved. Anger thawed into frustration. Her fears had been right. They wouldn't take her sisters' word for hers. She had to get back, but they were days from the castle and even more from the town.

"He didn't believe them," Grayson said, voicing her thoughts. His eyes, dark with anger, tracked to her.

He was so close to her, their arms still touching, but she didn't notice. Her mind spun. Her sisters tried to help her out, do her job, but the town didn't trust them. They'd earned their reputation by surviving. She'd let them, but it finally caught up to them. She broke the curse, got the tax money, and they got home in time, but they were still going to lose everything. The town would see to it.

"I didn't think they would," she finally said and handed the mirror back without looking at Grayson.

"Then why'd you risk it?" he asked. "You could have gone back."

She involuntarily looked up to him. His yellow eyes scanned her face looking for something, his breaths uneven.

"I made a promise," she whispered.

His eyes met hers, and her stomach coiled. She stilled her hand from reaching for his cheek.

"I absolved it," he said evenly with a raised eyebrow.

"I promised," Rosella said louder, shifting to sit backwards with her chin up. "You held up your end. You are worth it."

His gaze flicked to the ground.

"I shouldn't have listened to Lucien," Grayson said. He pinched his brow and sighed. His body deflated.

"What?" Rosella asked.

Grayson closed his eyes upon realizing he'd spoken the thought out loud.

"Tell me what that means," Rosella demanded. When he didn't respond or open his eyes, she slapped his knee and demanded, "Now!"

"Or what? You'll pinch it out of me? Yank my ear? Or anything else you did to your sisters?"

"Is it when he spoke to you when you first met us? I know his side of it. He made sure to tell me. What did Lucien tell you?" She shifted to sit in front of him. She missed his touch instantly. Instead of focusing on it, she dug her fingers into his knees, looking for a sensitive spot.

He leaned his head back and stared up at the stars. A humorless chuckle fell from his lips.

Unable to find a spot on his knees, she placed them on his thigh to draw his attention back to her. She froze at realizing where her hands were.

When she went to pull them back, his hand covered hers. While he still gazed heavenward looking for words, he sighed. "I was going to let you four go. Let you take the items. I wasn't going to intervene at all."

"What?" Rosella asked, her retreat forgotten as she stared at him.

His fingers curled around her hands, and he finally lowered his gaze to meet hers. His eyes were bright with regret. "It's stuff. You were obviously starving and in need. I didn't need those few items."

"What did Lucien tell you?" she asked.

As she leaned in, his gaze jumped to her lips. He swallowed thickly and returned his focus to her eyes.

"He said it'd look bad to the staff, that they'd get ideas. No one would do as they were assigned. He'd been concerned about it for a while. Now, I wonder how much was real and how much was just him."

"But..." Realization dawned on her, and she finished, "He wanted to use us to break the curse. He had four people he could use."

"I see that now," Grayson said. "We had a few people over the years stumble onto our path. Maybe a half dozen or so. Lucien had been the one to see them out. He said it was part of his duties as my attaché. He had to make sure they didn't steal. I didn't think much of it."

"See them out?"

"I'm guessing they're at the bottom of the river," Grayson said, his eyes glassy in the firelight.

"His curse was broken, why would he care if the third one was?"

Rosella said. "He didn't want me to go after the third charm alone. But why?"

"I'm guessing he didn't want you finding it once he realized I was still trapped. I didn't know he had left until after he tried to poison me."

"Then why help me find it?" Rosella asked, and the truth settled on her like spiderwebs. "He wanted to destroy it, so you had no chance. That way no one, not even your most loyal staff member, could go. If he followed me, he could destroy it at the source."

The beast nodded.

Red hot anger welled in Rosella. The trickery and vileness was too common.

"I'm going to destroy him," Rosella said.

The beast hummed settled back. His eyes tracked to the mirror. Releasing her hands slowly, his fingers lingering on hers, he said, "We should sleep."

Chapter Thirty-Eight

Rosella stretched and nestled deeper into the warm bedroll. Instead of a soft layer over rocks, it was flat and warm. A heavy arm draped over her side twitched, and then tightened around her, snuggling her body closer.

Her eyes shot open, and she stared at the arm, going rigid as she tried to piece everything together. None of her sisters had arms that sinewy, or thick, and they were squishy to snuggle against, not hard.

A soft, familiar grumble rumbled by her ear. It was the sound of someone waking up and not wanting to. She closed her eyes, wanting both for the situation to be a dream and not to be.

The arm flinched and stiffened, and slowly retracted back across her and disappeared from view.

Grayson scooted away. She instantly missed his heat but remained in her sleeping position. He scrambled to his feet and, after hearing him step a few feet away, she stirred as if just waking up.

"Sleep well?" he asked, not looking at her while he dug through the food. He ran a hand through his dark, disheveled hair. The long locks dusted his shoulders. Stumble covered his square jaw.

"Better than most nights," she said, startled by the reality.

"You just needed the right bedroll," he said. Her face heated, matching the heat curling through her veins.

He handed her some bread. His hand brushed hers and sent a shock up her arm.

"I guess," she mumbled. "How about you? You sleep well?"

"Yep," he said, too high-pitched.

"How far are we from the castle?" Rosella asked. The foothill loomed in the distance. A thick canopy of trees swept across it. Green leaves shone in the bright sunlight.

He cut his eyes to her. Something flickered in them and he smiled sadly. "Probably a day and a half, if we haul."

She nodded and gulped. It's what she'd figured. It'd be two or three days to the castle and then another two or three home. Without knowing Lucien's plans, she couldn't be certain how long they'd take securing the castle. Her family would lose their house and shop.

They'd paid the taxes. She'd completed the three riddles, and they were still going to lose. Bile turned in her stomach, the acid curled up her throat. She swallowed it down, her appetite gone. She'd made her choice knowing the risk. With the gold, she'd figure a way to take care of her sisters and start over.

Breakfast was silent. Both of them were lost in thought and ate little while avoiding each other's gaze. Without a word, they cleaned up camp and mounted the horses, Rosella taking the reins.

Warmth shot through her when his hands rested gently on her hips. She bit her lip and stared forward. Her fingers rubbed over the reins. Grayson settled into his position snuggled behind her. His heat soaked through her garments, and she swallowed thickly. She tried to quiet the thoughts racing through her mind and the strange sensation snagging her heart. Foolishness. That's all it was. She needed to focus and move forward. She couldn't wish for what would never be. She needed to maintain what could be.

"Do you and your sisters have a lot of ties to the town?" Grayson asked, breaking their silence as they rode through the final farms and entered the forest that covered the foothill.

"Ties?"

"Family? Friends?" He asked it casually, but there was a hitch to his voice.

Rosella shrugged. "We were born there and grew up there."

"So yes?"

"We are friendly with the others, Bridgette is interested in Gavin, and Giselle is in love with Odette, but we don't have people who pay us social visits."

"Because of your father?" he asked.

"Partly, yes," Rosella said, bobbing her head. "My mother's father was an earl's brother. She married my father to help infuse money back into her family. He was a wealthy merchant. When he took to the bottle, her family's patience for them ran out."

"Her family abandoned her?"

"Yes," Rosella said. "His drinking drove a wedge between her family and most of the town. Toward the end, he would steal from her family to pay for his vice."

He tightened. A low growl sounded. "Then they cut you off?"

Rosella nodded. "Our father is alive, but in a work prison."

"Do you see him?"

Rosella shook her head. "I haven't seen him since he needed to sign some papers to make me executor. I don't know much about his family."

"What binds you to the town, then?" he asked gently.

She stilled, trying to find a good answer, and finally said, "It's been our home. It's what we had. We struggled to stay afloat there. I planned to run it until one of my sisters' children ran it."

"Planned?"

Rosella licked her lips and shrugged.

"Your sisters' children…" he mumbled, and then said, "You don't plan to have any?"

Rosella snorted. "No, I planned to stay a spinster. I'll provide the parental role to my sisters and the grandparent role to my nieces and nephews."

"You don't plan to marry Benson?" he asked, his voice hopeful. His fingers curled against her waist.

"No. I didn't before and now I'm definitely not going to."

Hot anger coursed through her. She blew a long breath out to settle her nerves, the spark lingering. He'd threatened and belittled her sisters. There was no recovery for mistreating them.

"You said planned..." Grayson repeated, his words slow and deliberate. "What do you plan now?"

"I don't know," Rosella whispered.

THEY TREKKED THROUGH THE DAY AND INTO THE NIGHT with Rosella at the reins. Night descended, the moon only a sliver in the dark sky, too weak to filter through the trees as they traveled deeper into the forest. Both watching for signs of others who lingered in the trees.

Despite fatigue and muscle ache, Rosella pushed on. They could make the castle by morning if they kept going, perhaps even overtake Lucien before then.

Grayson leaned in close to her ear. Tingles shimmied down her spine and warmth pooled in her belly. Her breath caught in her throat as she waited.

"We should set camp," he whispered, his lips close enough they almost brushed her ear.

"Okay," she whispered back before she remembered she didn't want to camp. Then she leaned her head in his direction, his closeness intoxicating. Sleep deprived her of her normal reserve. He shifted to lean in closer, his cheek brushing against her ear. She licked her lips and whispered, "Why are we whispering?"

He chuckled, the sensation warming and confusing her. His fingers tightened momentarily on her waist, and then he whispered, "Seems appropriate for the setting."

She smiled and nodded, her ear brushing against him.

They hovered too long in that position, and Rosella pulled away, shifting in her seat. She wasn't looking for anything, short or long term. No matter how much she wanted it. Her earlier willingness to take the fleeting moment seemed too hard when faced with his tender touch. He had a kingdom to regain, and she had a family store to try to reclaim. He was right, they needed to rest. She needed to clear her head and again hoped the rest and distance would cool her body and heart. Their paths would separate in a few days. With time, the sensations that confused her now would be cold and distant memories.

They came to a clearing and dismounted. Grayson pulled the traveling lantern from the horse and lit the wick side, bathing the path in the warm glow.

Rosella blinked and the hairs on her neck stood up. She adjusted her shoulders.

"Something doesn't feel right," she said and stepped closer to the horse, ready to remount.

Grayson looked to her and then around the forest perimeter arching over them. His brow furrowed and his hand fell to his sword.

"Should we move on?" he asked, closing the distance between them.

"It could just be my reaction to the bandit's warning," she said. Or, it could just be my imagination." Her toes curled and goosebumps ran down her arm.

He drew back and snorted. "You don't have one. You're too pragmatic."

"What does that mean?"

"You are sensible and realistic," he said. His gaze darted around the path.

She rolled her eyes. "I know what pragmatic means. What does it have to do with not having an imagination?"

"You're never riled," he said. "You look at everything logically. If you say something is wrong here, it is."

"And she'd be right," a voice called.

Rosella swore and gripped her shortsword.

"Don't bother, girly," it said. "You're outnumbered."

Four figures poured from the trees.

"How many more are in the trees?" she breathed.

"Stay against my back," Grayson said, turning around.

Rosella slid up to his back, facing the lurking thieves.

"Oh, making your lady fight?" a different voice said.

"It is a lady, right?" another mocked. "Hard to tell under the dirt and pants."

"Come closer," Rosella said, "And find out."

Grayson tensed behind her and growled at her prodding.

"Or are you a coward?" she baited. A smirk flicked across her lips.

The talker lunged toward her, a knife in both hands. Rosella parried the attack but stayed stuck to Grayson's back for both their bearings.

The thief righted themself and took a hook shot to Rosella's side. Using the opening, Rosella kicked the thief in the knee and slashed her sword at them. The blade made contact, blood weeping from the gash, coating her sword.

The person howled in pain and grabbed at their side, falling to a knee. Their hands were coated in blood and their breaths came in pants. Blood dotted the ground around them.

"You bitch," another one said and dove for Rosella. He sliced her arm before she could block it.

The sting of the blade tore at her arm. Blood darkened her shirt. She yipped and spat a curse. In pain, she slashed back out.

Her blade went wide, missing the assailant, and he grabbed at his friend and started to drag them away.

With the other two still surrounding Grayson, she stayed from a chase. Pain stung through her arm, pulling her focus. Her fingers tightened and loosened on the sword. She switched her sword to her non-dominant hand, the steel heavy in her hand.

"Kick," Grayson roared.

His horse, Henry, kicked its rear legs back, crashing into the torso of another thief who'd crept from the woods, the blow toppling them over. They lay face down and their body twitched.

"Are you okay?" Grayson asked, turning Rosella around. His hands searched her for wounds. His yellow eyes were bright with concern.

"He got my arm," she said and flinched when he touched it.

"We need to tend to it," he said. He reached for a canteen.

"I'll be fine," Rosella groused but flinched when she moved her arm. A long breath whistled out through her teeth.

"You made me let you take care of the arrows," he countered. He stuck his palm out for her arm, the canteen readied in his other hand to wash the wound.

"We had moonlight then, we don't now," she said. She tucked her arm against her frame as not to jostle it and pulled away. "It'll wait."

"Rosella," he growled, his voice filling the night, the sound vibrating through her.

"What?" she barked back. She shot him a scowl.

The horse stomped its hooves and neighed at the two.

Grayson closed his eyes and let a long breath out through his flared nose. Opening his eyes, he wiped all expression from his face.

"Please let me look at it and bandage it up," he pleaded, reaching for her again.

She stilled at the request.

"Fine," she relented. "But once we find a safer place to rest."

"Then let me help you up on the horse so you don't open the wound up more." He tilted his chin down and set his jaw.

Rosella's eyes moved to the giant horse and the height she'd have to pull herself up to mount. Her gaze flicked back to him. With a sigh, she nodded. "Give me a boost."

He laced his fingers together and helped hoist her into the saddle. Once she was settled, he mounted behind her. His frame tucked in against her. He took the reins from her hands. Careful of her cut, he wrapped his arms around her waist and held her close. She allowed herself to nestle into his warmth and protection.

Chapter Thirty-Nine

THEY TRAVELED ON FOR A FEW MORE MILES, UNTIL THE TREES eased back, and the dim moonlight peaked through the leaves. The only sound was the clomp of Henry's hooves on the trail.

Rosella sat tucked between Grayson and the horse. The strain of the last few days pulled on her muscles. Her eyes fluttered shut only to snap open again.

"Let's rest," Grayson said, his voice tight.

They stopped. With the light, they moved up in the forest to a small clearing tucked back from the path and blocked by the trees. Grayson dismounted first and offered Rosella a hand down. She begrudgingly accepted, overwhelmed and uncomfortable with her body's immediate reaction to him. Like before, heat curled through her veins and twisted in her core. A punch of desire hit her stomach and she sucked in a steadying breath. The longer she was near him, the harder it was to control.

"Sit down," Grayson said. He removed his hand from hers, misreading her reaction. His gaze drifted to the travel pack.

Rosella blinked to not respond. To not explain. It was best if she let the emotion dissolve between them. Sleep would help quench the building desire.

"I'll be fine," she said, waving him off as she turned to gather sticks and create distance. "I'm going to build a fire."

"You said I could look at it," he reminded her and moved to block her path.

"Fine," she muttered and rolled her eyes.

He dug in the travel bags and joined her on the ground with the traveling lantern.

"It'd be easier with a fire," she said.

His dark eyes flicked to her.

She swallowed hard and looked away.

"Roll your sleeve up," he said.

She did as told, biting back the bile from the pain as he laid a hand on her arm.

"Sorry." He grimaced but didn't remove his hand. He used water from the canteen to clean it, and then wrapped a strip of fabric around it.

His hands remained on her arm after he finished, his head bent over her arm.

She involuntarily met his gaze, her breath catching at the closeness. His eyes traveled from hers to her mouth. He licked his lips and blinked, his dark eyes focusing again on hers.

Rosella suppressed a shiver and looked away, breaking the trance. Standing, she brushed dirt and leaves from her clothes. Her hands trembled as she hurriedly gathered sticks.

Grayson set up the bedroll and dug out provisions as she built the fire. His lack of focus on her was deliberate, to ease what was building, give her space, and Rosella both thanked and cursed him for it. What had she been thinking earlier? It was a terrible idea to explore what lingered between them, even if she wanted to.

Exhausted, Rosella sat down. Her tired body shivered as she leaned into the fire.

"Did it get cold?" she asked, rubbing her arms.

He looked to her, an eyebrow raised. "It's been cold for a while."

"I just noticed." She raised her hands toward the fire.

"You were still in flight or fight," he said.

With his lips pressed tightly together, he handed her some bread and dried meat. He sat next to her, his leg brushing her as he settled in.

They ate in silence, unspoken words skittering between them.

"We should be there tomorrow," Rosella said to fill the void.

He nodded. "We're only a few hours out. I don't know what I expect."

She turned to him and waited for him to continue.

He swallowed, his eyes hazy as they took in the fire. "Are my parents free? Are they still cursed? Did Lucien turn the house against me? Is it worth battling him for it?"

"What do you mean?" she asked.

"It's a castle. A place to live. My parents were the rulers, not me. I just... lived there."

"Your local people were turned to wolves. They'll be freed according to the sorceress. The lands are returning."

"But what will they remember? Our lands are beyond the local villages. They go to the mountains. I didn't want people coming to the castle to find out about the curse nor us taking the curse to them. If they figured it out, it would lead to great issues. A power struggle. We had to stop our physical presence in areas so the curse wouldn't spread."

"You've been leading in your parents' absence," she said with a pointed look at him.

"I've watched the curse spread," he said "Consume more and more. I make decisions." His gaze drifted up at the canopy. "I send official letters. We collect taxes, we pay for the army that patrols. We're forgotten by those lands around us, but the areas the curse hasn't reached carry on as normal."

"Your soldiers protect the people from the troll?"

"The viscounts and earls do, yes. They send correspondences."

"Don't they want your audience?" Rosella asked.

"They knew my parents," he said and leaned back to stare at the canopy. "They were eccentric. From my understanding, they'd go through periods of great lavish parties and then years where they wouldn't listen to the nobility."

"You cared enough for your people to stop going out. You continue to pay for their needs. Keep the people happy. You keep up correspondences. Now, your lands are returning and need a strong leader more than ever to regroup. Do you want Lucien to lead your people?"

Grayson narrowed his eyes and snarled.

"Then you have more than a house to fight for," Rosella said.

He nodded and laid his hand over hers, his calloused fingers gently rubbing back and forth. His fingers then slipped around hers and held on.

She leaned against his arm as she watched the fire, letting his warmth soak into her. Her head found its way to his shoulder. He laid his head against hers.

The simple comfort could build years together, but she had mere hours. She licked her lips and swallowed the lump forming in her throat. Recent thoughts warred in her head. She could enjoy the moment. His company. Tomorrow would see to their separation, but the night and its silent cover was still theirs if she was willing to let it be. Willing to let herself have what she wanted.

"Thank you," he whispered, the words floating in the air like embers in the fire.

She tilted her head back so she could look at him.

"We'd have lost our chance," he said, smiling sadly. "We'd lost hope."

"Then Lucien did something right," she said.

He frowned and shook his head.

"My sisters are okay. You took care of them. I saw the food and stuff you loaded down for them. You paid our taxes. Lucien may have done it for only his benefit or even for the others, too, but his choice led to the curse being broken."

"You risked your life. That isn't worth the risk."

"If we aren't willing to lose, we can't make growth," she said. "I'd do it again."

"That's what worries me."

She pulled back to look at him. "Why?"

He chuckled humorlessly and sat back.

"I don't want you to get hurt," he said, choosing his words carefully.

"Pain comes with risk. So do blessings."

"You need to go home," he said, his eyes flickering into the darkness.

A painful jolt shot through her heart, and she blinked.

"You need to confirm the payment for your family," he said. "They need you."

"There's time," Rosella said. But there wasn't enough time for her to help and get back. She couldn't even make the additional time Benson had gotten from his father. They'd have to figure something out. They had enough with what Grayson sent them that they could find a new future. Whatever and wherever it would be. She had faced down a forest dryad, a troll, wolves, a siren, and bandits for her sisters. A boring spinster life could be tolerated for them, too. It'd be easier and less dangerous. She'd make sure the money they paid on the taxes was returned since they lost the house.

"You could still make it back in time," he said, his words a whisper, pulling her from her thoughts.

Rosella turned to him, their legs still touching, his hand still resting on hers. His eyes were dark pools, and his lips parted slightly. He was looking at her, but beyond her. He was seeing beyond her facade, beyond her wall, beyond the carefully constructed exterior she'd built to protect her family. He saw her.

Something stirred in her. A deep yearning. One that wouldn't be pushed away or sequestered. A warmth that both frightened and delighted her. He was a few inches away. She could close the distance, give into her interest and curiosity, or turn away and settle in for the night. There always seemed to be a fork in the road. One that led to the familiar while one offered risk and heartbreak, but also excitement and emotion.

It was safer to ignore whatever she felt. Numbness was safe and lasting, but she'd lived it so long. Accepted and welcomed it. It'd been better than the hatred and anger that'd burned for so long and drove her to protect her sisters. Drove her to turn away the townspeople. To get up each day and carve a path for her sisters in a world that wanted to use and abandon them, that wanted them to fail.

There was always time for numbness. She'd return to it in a few days. She'd live it as a spinster. Live it as the matriarch of her family.

If she took the risk, she'd never wonder what if, and the what if would eat at her. She'd never been a coward, but she sat a few inches from something she wanted and was letting fear stop her from enjoying it.

Rejection and humiliation were familiar. They were normal. They were expected. Fear was too, but it wasn't an excuse for not acting.

She shifted back to face him more directly. His eyes followed her, and his body unconsciously mimicked hers. He licked his lips but didn't move.

She stared at his lips, at the curve of the upper lip, and the subtle gap between them, at his tongue as it licked them again. His fingers tightened around hers, and her eyes moved to his. The dark pools reflected the firelight and her desire.

She reached her other hand toward his face. Leaning in, she arched up and gently pressed her lips to his.

He stilled beneath her touch, his lips stiff and unmoving.

Realization and humiliation crashed together in her. She'd been silly and lustful. She'd overstepped their friendship line. She had turned into the lust-struck maiden. She was the one reading imaginary signals and seeing feelings that weren't there. She'd turned into one of her family's suitors.

She leaned back to break the embrace when his free hand curved around her head, holding her in place. He brought her lips back to his and deepened the kiss.

He released her hand and cupped her cheek as he slipped his tongue into her mouth.

She ran her hand through his hair and fisted it as she shifted to get a better angle.

He ran his hands down her neck, shoulders, and arms then rested them gently on her hips before lifting her into his lap.

She straddled his hips and wrapped her arms around his neck. Her center pressed into his hardness.

He pulled her closer. She could feel the rise and fall of his breaths, the beating of his heart, and the shattering of her numbness.

Chapter Forty

Rosella awoke with Grayson's arm draped over her, her back pressed to his chest. She smiled and snuggled deeper into his warm embrace. He tightened his hold, caressing her arms with his fingers, and mumbled into her hair. His skin against hers sent shivers through her body, igniting in her core. The night flashed through her mind and brought a smile to her face.

Although early, the sun warmed the air and weak streaks of light lit the trees. Grayson pulled the blanket over them as a wind skimmed across the opening.

"Today, you get your castle back," Rosella said. She blinked at the realization that their time was almost done. She wouldn't regret the night, but she also wasn't ready to part ways. Her thoughts shattered when his hand ran down her side and over her hip.

"This is a good way to start the day," Grayson said. He trailed kisses along her shoulder and shifted so he was leaning over her side to face her. His golden eyes bright, and a smile tugged on his lips.

She smiled up at him and ran a hand through his thick hair.

His smile grew and he leaned down so his lips met hers. He cupped her face with his hand and deepened the kiss.

She rolled so they faced each other and arched into him, her heart racing as fire raced through her veins. He slipped his knees between hers.

A delicious reminder of the previous night. Want tightened in her stomach.

The clomp of horse hooves thundered in the distance, the rattle of wagon wheels singing along. A neigh carried on the breeze.

"What's going on?" Rosella said, breaking from the kiss, her words airy on her panting breaths.

With his eyes hazy, Grayson turned toward the path hidden behind the trees.

Rosella twisted through the thoughts racing in her mind. There hadn't been anyone out on the trails, riddled in growth for a decade, except for those Lucien had sent for them, but they weren't being covert this time.

She flicked her eyes to her shortsword lying beside the fire, readied for whatever may have come through the night. She let her breath out as the world settled around her. The morning chill nipped at her nose, the sting of coming rain lingered in the air, but more importantly, Grayson's warmth seeped from his body, warming her where they touched.

She needed to clear her mind, her senses, and focus on the current situation. They needed to make it to the castle no matter who was sent for them. Without a word, they both tugged on their boots and gear.

The clatter drew nearer, the rapid hoofbeats echoing in the trees.

"Please wait here," Grayson growled before grabbing his sword and darting for the forest line by the trail.

Ignoring his request, Rosella ran behind him, her own shortsword in hand.

A white-painted carriage with gold and red details drawn by two large bay horses came into view. The single cart barreled down the path without footmen.

"What the?" Grayson said, pulling up short. "That's a carriage from my castle."

"I don't see or hear more," Rosella said. "Is it a diversion?"

"Will you wait by Henry?" Grayson asked without taking his eyes from the carriage.

"You already know I won't," Rosella said from the tree line.

Grayson growled but didn't argue.

"He made it there already?" Rosella said. Her eyes scanned the trail in the distance. Had he pushed through the night while they rested? Lead pooled in her stomach. She let herself enjoy the evening instead of staying focused. Instead of pushing on. "Do you think they're looking for you?"

"They aren't being stealthy if they are," he said. With a growl, he leapt on to the trail.

"They won't know you," Rosella yelled, but the words were lost over the sound of the horses' neighing and jarring to a stop in front of him. She followed Grayson but hung behind a tree.

On the driver seat sat Arthur, his reddish-gray hair snarled and wind-whipped. His usually impeccable clothes were dusty and rumpled.

"Pardon us, sir," Arthur said, and his eyes darted back down the trail in the direction he had come. "We have to get out of here."

"Why?" Grayson demanded, his knuckles whitening over his sword.

Arthur swallowed, and his eyes narrowed. "No time. I'm not here for trouble. Now please, move."

A breath lodged in Rosella's throat. Arthur didn't recognize him. If he didn't, would Lucien? The other staff?

Arthur fidgeted with the reins and gave him a pleading look. His hand inched toward the musket next to him.

"Arthur," Rosella called, moving from behind the tree to a stop between Grayson and Arthur. Grayson's jaw ticked and his eyes darted back to the place she'd been hidden in behind the trees.

"Rosella," he snarled.

Rosella ignored him and stepped closer to the carriage.

"Rosella?" Arthur exclaimed. His eyes bulged and his face slackened. "Are you an illusion?"

"Arthur, you resembled a squirrel. You took my sisters back and helped me go for the third charm by getting me a horse."

"You what?" Grayson growled.

Rosella flicked her hand toward Grayson.

"Rosella... how..." Arthur trembled, his glassy eyes darting between her and Grayson.

"It's me." She splayed her fingers over her chest. She inched toward Grayson, offering him protection from Arthur if he chose to shoot.

"But... he said you died with the master."

"Lucien tried to kill me, yes," Rosella said.

"What?" Arthur said, his eyes bulging out. "No, no, no. He said the keeper killed you for getting the riddle wrong and then killed the master for following you and disobeying her orders."

"I'm here," Rosella said, and nodded at Grayson. "And the curse was broken."

Arthur's eyes tracked to Grayson, widening in recognition. His mouth opened and closed.

"Sire?" Arthur finally squeaked and tried to awkwardly bow on the carriage. "Oh master, my apologies for not recognizing you. I... You look just like your mother."

"Rosella solved the riddle. Lucien tried to kill her and keep me trapped as a beast." Grayson licked his lips, and asked, "Has he done anything to my parents?"

"They were awake before he returned. The castle is ecstatic. He's trying to convince them you've died and that they should use his counsel. That he was your most trusted advisor. That he alone helped break the curse when no one else would."

"They're awake," Grayson whispered. He blinked and his breath caught.

"Yes, Master. Everything returned to what it once was. Lucien said when you died it stopped the curse. He said we should have killed you years ago."

"Do my parents recognize him?"

Arthur grimaced and looked away. "Sofia was imprisoned for calling him a liar. She was the first of many imprisonments. They are playing along but are confused."

"Has he tried to harm them?"

"Not yet, Master, but I fear he will when they stop cooperating, which we know they will. He is not you. I think he is already plotting their death. I must get help. Some staff are trying to sequester them away for their protection."

"We have to hurry," Rosella said. She squeezed Grayson's shoulder.

Grayson cut his eyes to her. Concern clouded them.

"I'll grab our horse," Rosella said. "Then we'll get a move on."

"Rosella," Grayson started but sighed in defeat.

"What are you doing?" Arthur asked. His gaze bounced between them.

"Saving the castle," Rosella said and darted back to their campsite. Adrenaline and fear spiked her veins, pushing her forward and narrowing her vision. She let a long breath out before darting through the trees. Lucien would pay for trying to destroy Grayson.

"Wait," Grayson called, his voice echoing in the trees.

Ignoring him, she stomped out the fire, grabbed their few items and led the horse back to the trail already saddled and bridled.

Grayson frowned at her and ran a hand through his dark hair. He shook his head. His mouth opened to speak, but he shut it again.

"We'll go back with you," Arthur said, nodding to the carriage. "We have muskets."

"It's okay if you flee," Grayson said. "Protect yourselves."

"Not if you're alive, Master," Arthur said. "I won't serve Lucien, but I'll die to help you."

Grayson looked between Arthur and Rosella. Emotions warred on his face, never settling on one. Finally, he sighed but mounted the horse.

Grayson and the staff were all in danger. All willing to die. A frown flittered across her face, but Rosella grabbed the saddle to pull herself up behind him.

"Wouldn't you rather ride in the carriage?" he asked Rosella, providing his arm to help her up and a large smile that didn't meet his eyes. "It'd probably be more comfortable."

"There's stuff in there, and Merl is protecting it, but we'll make room," Arthur said. "It'll be safe and comfortable in there."

Rosella snorted and swung her leg behind Grayson. She fitted her hands on his side as they had done in their days of traveling. Arthur quirked his brow at the gesture but remained quiet. He gave Prince Grayson a nod and angled his carriage around to face back toward the castle.

Grayson grunted in resignation.

She clung to his sides as they galloped the couple of hours back to the castle, the wind whipping past them, the trees a blur. Uncertainty twisted in her stomach, but hope filled her heart. She'd bested the three riddles to save Grayson and the castle. She wouldn't let Lucien steal it.

As they neared, the overgrowth and debris were gone, reflecting the grounds that had once been. With the curse gone, the once-hidden path to the castle was wide and clean. They came to the clearing where Rosella and her sisters had originally gone off the path with wolves following them, and where she'd separated from her sisters when they went back to their town, and she went for the third charm.

Grayson came to a halt, and Arthur pulled up. Their breaths filled the air. Grayson glanced over his shoulder at Rosella, but he avoided making eye contact.

She curled her fingers into his side and nodded. "Let's go," she murmured. Her eyes skimmed the scenery, and she found the towering white spires of his castle that pierced through the treetops and into the sky.

"Are you sure, Sire?" Arthur asked, his fingers fidgeting over the reins. His lips curled down into a frown.

"Yes," Grayson said. A sad smile darkened his face.

"What are we doing?" Rosella asked.

"Lucien will see the horses," Grayson said and dismounted. "We need to be careful."

Rosella followed him down and brushed her pants off.

Before she stood back up, Grayson wrapped his arms around her waist and put her in the carriage.

"What are you doing?" she screamed and whirled around. She was alone in the carriage except for some clothes and gold and silver items.

Merl and Arthur stood behind the master; their eyes averted and hands fisted at their sides.

"I can't lose you," Grayson choked and pulled the door shut. His yellow eyes shimmered in the dim sunlight.

"We have to go together!" she screamed and kicked the door. Emotion clogged her throat and she swallowed. Her breaths came in heaves, and she kicked the door again. "Let me out!"

"I can't... you have to be safe. I'm sorry... you're more important..."

"I'm going!" Rosella's shrill voice bounced off the carriage walls. "I promised. She said we had to do it together. Grayson! Let me out!"

She pounded on the door and tried to ram it open, but he'd laid something on the outside to keep it closed.

"Rosella, I..." Grayson's voice broke. "Please stay safe."

Rosella slid to the floor, holding her head.

The carriage rattled to life and pulled away.

Chapter Forty-One

Rosella rested against the door, the vibrations jarring her and matching her annoyance.

He'd shoved her away. Sent her away.

She'd helped him. He'd helped her. He'd been a partner. Someone who gave as much as she did. Yet, he was done with her.

She pulled her lip between her teeth and was reminded of their kiss and their night. If she could have that every night, she wouldn't be so against getting married. But it definitely meant she wasn't marrying Benson or any of the other suitors. The thought of any of them touching her like that caused her to wretch. Once this was all over, she'd settle in for her spinster life. But first, they had to battle for the castle. Even if he didn't want her help, he needed it.

The carriage hit a bump, tossing her hard against the floorboard. Blood tanged her mouth. She pushed her hair from her eyes and looked around again for something to pry the door open, to no avail.

They were going at a fast clip, but it wasn't enough. If Grayson went in now, without her, she'd never make it back to the castle in time.

Why'd he have to be an idiot and send her away? Try to be protective? She could help him.

She pounded on the carriage for the umpteenth time. And then gave it a kick for good measure.

Arthur ignored her, and the carriage rocked as he picked up speed.

"I thought we were friends," Rosella yelled through the side.

Arthur didn't respond.

"He needs help!" she screamed. "He'll go in alone!"

The horses continued on, the carriage creaking at their fast speed. He likely wouldn't pull over until they were in her town, not giving her a chance to get out and get back to the castle.

She plotted the course as they banged along. The time it'd take for her to make it from her house back. It was a two-day travel at top walking speed if she didn't rest. If she could get a horse, that'd cut it down to less than a day. That was her only option. She needed a horse and she needed to get back to Grayson. She scanned over the items tossed in the cart with her, protected only by the garments that they'd been wrapped in. Any one of them would be enough for a stable of horses. She just had to find a willing seller.

The carriage came to a jarring stop. Rosella braced against the door, straining to hear anything. There were voices, most of them curious. Too muffled to recognize with certainty. They were in a town. She hoped it was hers.

"Miss Rosella," Arthur squeaked. "I'm going to let you out."

Rosella waited, but nothing happened. "When?" she barked.

"As soon as you promise not to take it out on me," Arthur said. "I had to follow Master's orders."

"Arthur, I'm not mad at you. I'm mad at him. I'm going back to that castle, beat Lucien, and then throttle Grayson for locking me in this carriage."

"I can't let you out if you say that."

"What?" Her fingers gnarled into fists, and she yelled a growl.

"He said you can't come back," Arthur said. His voice beseeching. "He was adamant I had to keep you safe."

"Arthur, let me out now, or I'll make a scene for the ages," Rosella growled.

Arthur paused.

"I took on three keepers," Rosella warned. "I'll get out of this carriage. We know I will. You can either help me or I'll fight you, too."

"Yes, Miss Rosella," Arthur said. A scraping sound rubbed against the wall as he removed the blockade.

Rosella sprung from the carriage and whirled around. Townspeople were gathered around, gawking at her and the expensive carriage. She looked a fright in her travel gear, caked in dirt and blood. Wounds still stained her shirt and skin, but she didn't bother to shy away.

Arthur had stopped them in front of her store. The familiar beacon was no longer a site of refuge but stood in dreary reminder of all that was at stake. All she could lose beyond the clapboard siding and meager contents that couldn't feed her family.

A notice was posted to the door—AUCTION. She didn't bother reading the details beyond it. The village had taken her money and were now taking her home. Something inside her broke. She'd be damned if another person tried to tell her what to do. Try to take what was hers. She'd fought three magical keepers and survived. She'd traveled over new lands, to the mountains, and seas. She could take on whatever the petty town had to offer.

She pushed inside and bellowed, "Sisters!"

Camilla jumped up from her nap chair, a musket in hand, her hair strewn about. Bridgette pushed in from the house. Both wore their normal linen gowns, their new dresses likely stored away.

"Rosella!" they both cheered, but then frowned at seeing her face.

"Sleeping with a musket now?" Rosella eyed up the antique piece that likely came from the castle and noticed a sword dangling from Camilla's waist in a scabbard.

Camilla patted her musket. "They told us we have to vacate, but we said no. We paid our filthy taxes. I've delayed anyone entering for two days."

"We'll deal with that later," Rosella said. "We have more important issues right now."

"What happened?" Bridgette asked. "Did you break the curse?"

"Yes," Rosella said. "Where's Giselle?"

"Yes!" Camilla said. She thrust a fist the air and let out a victory cheer.

"Giselle is talking with Odette," Bridgette said. Her eyes darted back toward the house.

"I'm only saying this story once, go get her."

Bridgette leaned back in the other room, and yelled, "Giselle, Rosella is here."

Footsteps pounded in the hall and both Giselle and Odette appeared in the entryway, tears streaking their reddened faces. Rosella figured they were saying their goodbyes. One more failure to add to her list. The heaviness of their lives settled on her chest.

"Rosella, are you okay?" Giselle asked. She sniffed and wiped her nose.

"No!" she roared.

"How hurt are you?" Bridgette asked, stepping closer, her eyes jumping between the different blood stains. "We can send for a doctor. We have gold and treasure from… from the castle. They gave it to us. We can pay for a doctor."

Rosella seethed. Her nose flared out, and a large, heaving breath shook her frame. "I broke the curse. Lucien tried to kill me. Grayson and I escaped. Lucien took the castle. Grayson locked me in a carriage and sent me back here."

"Why'd he send you back if Lucien is at the castle?" Giselle asked.

"That's the part that you're questioning?" Odette asked, her face ashen. She swung her gaze between the sisters' faces.

"I already explained what happened twice, and Bridgette did once," Giselle said, rubbing Odette's shoulder.

"I confirmed it, too," Camilla added.

Bridgette, Odette, and Giselle shot her a dark look. "There weren't any banshees," Giselle growled.

"Tomato, to-mat-o."

"There are no two versions of the truth!" Giselle seethed.

"Girls!" Bridgette yelled. "Why did he send you back if Lucien has the castle?"

"He doesn't want my help," Rosella said. Her anger rimmed her eyes with tears, threatening to spill. She let out a shaky breath and rubbed a hand through her snarled hair.

"It's not that, ma'am," Arthur squeaked at the entryway, rolling his fingers around his thumbs.

"Then why?" Bridgette demanded. Her gray eyes pinned him with a sharp stare.

"He's afraid Lucien will kill Rosella this time. He stabbed her at the cave. He can't have you die. He'd do anything to protect you."

Her sisters gasped. They spoke at once, the words colliding together into a shriek.

"Arthur," Rosella exclaimed. "How do you know that?"

"He told me while you got Henry. Miss Rosella, he just wants to protect you."

"WAIT!" Camilla roared louder than her sisters. She pounded her fist into her other hand. "He did what, now?"

"Master is trying to protect Miss Rosella," Arthur stammered.

"Oh, I get what the beast did," Camilla said. "I completely understand that." She waved off Rosella's angry look. "What? I do! The guy has it bad for you. But Lucien is dead meat. He stabbed Rosella. Left her for dead. No one messes with my sister. NO. ONE."

"Agreed," Giselle and Bridgette said in unison. They gave each other a knowing look.

"Oh, no," Arthur whimpered. "I'm going to get in trouble."

"No, you're not." Rosella reassured him. "We'll tie you up and take the carriage."

"No need," Arthur said, shaking his head. "I already figured you would want to return. I know my promise and I know yours. I got you back here, but only a fool would think I could keep you here. I spoke with some men in town and acquired fresh horses. Ours can't make the trip in any haste."

Rosella smiled. "Arthur, you're really making up for helping him kidnap me."

Arthur blushed.

"Let's go," Camilla said, twirling her finger in the air.

"But the store," Odette said.

"It'll be fine, or not," Camilla said. "You can watch it, though. We have something more important to handle. I need to explain to Lucien with my fists that he doesn't get to mess with my sister."

"I want to go, too," Odette said, standing tall. "I want to help before…"

She sniffed, and tears streamed down her face.

"Her wedding is at the end of the week," Giselle sniffed, her face swollen from shed tears.

Rosella's eyebrow lifted in question.

"Please," Odette asked. She squeezed Giselle's hand.

Rosella smiled softly. Maybe she could still fix something for one of her sisters. "Okay, Odette, you can join us."

"I'll get more horses," Arthur said.

The five women followed Arthur outside. The town had emptied out of their stores and homes to surround the carriage, squawking and pointing at the ornate contraption.

"Rosella," Benson called, pushing through the crowd. With hasty steps, he covered the distance. Freshly oiled, his hair glistened in the sun. "What happened to you?"

Rosella turned her gaze to him, and he stepped back. His smile dimmed into a cautious grimace.

"Where's your father?" she demanded. With a sneer, she looked behind him.

"My father?" Benson asked.

"I don't have time to deal with you," Rosella said, hands on her hips. "I want to speak to your father, now. We paid our taxes. I sent a letter." She lifted her chin in challenge and peered down at him. She pointed to the sign on her door. "I want to make sure it is settled and that is removed."

"Looks like Rosella is going to handle it her way," Camilla snickered behind her hand. Her green eyes lit with amusement.

Bridgette went to scold her but rolled her lips between her teeth to stop herself from joining in the laugh.

"But you weren't here to file it," Mr. Trible said, stepping out from the crowd. With his chin in the air, his lips quavered into a triumphant sneer. He wore black breeches, a white shirt, and an ornate blue jacket trimmed in embroidery. Benson stepped behind his father. "You missed the deadline. And per your agreement, you won't contest the auctioning of it."

Rosella narrowed her eyes, hatred twisting in her veins. Her lips flickered into a snarl. Little changed. Greedy men were still bullies. Weak men were still fearful.

"Did you take the money from my sisters?" Rosella said, stepping toward him.

"I, uh," he stammered. He opened and closed his mouth, his face reddening. "You had back taxes that needed to be paid. They were your obligation."

"Are the taxes paid?"

"Yes," he squeaked.

"From the funds my sister gave you?"

His eyes darted around the town, but no one would speak up for him. Many shot him a knowing look. Benson averted his eyes.

"I take that as a yes. That means, my family is no longer in arrears. We are paid in full, and on time. I won't contest an auction, as there won't be one for my land." She opened the carriage and pulled out a silver candlestick. She tossed it to him. "Here, here's some interest to cover any new imaginary fees you just came up with."

While he fumbled to pick it up and brush the road's dust from it, Rosella tore the notice from the door. She wadded it up and tossed it at his feet, too.

"Lock the door, Camilla," Rosella said while staring Mr. Trible down.

"Yes, ma'am," Camilla saluted and followed directions with a smile.

"How do I know this isn't stolen?" he sneered. He waved a manicured hand at her dirtied garments while clutching the candlestick close to his chest with his other hand. "I mean, look at you. We can't accept your crime tokens as payment for our legal and just debts."

"You had no problem accepting the payment my sisters sent in. No problem using them to pay taxes."

"Sir," Arthur interrupted, his humble voice gone and filled with deep tammar. Although almost a foot shorter than Mr. Trible, Arthur bristled his shoulders and sneered down at him.

"And who are you?" Mr. Trible snarled with little more than a flick of his gaze at him.

"I am Sir Arthur of Castle Redrock," he said. "I speak for his Royal Highness Prince Grayson Redrock that the items in her sisters' care and in the carriage belong to Miss Rosella Belle. You accepted them from her sisters as payment for Rosella and her family's taxes. You used them as means to pay for all amounts, including arrears and current. Acknowledge here and now she is free and clear, or I will inform my master you have taken his property untowardly."

"She handed it to me," Mr. Trible bellowed, pointing at Rosella, the candlestick still in his grasp.

"As an additional un-owed payment on the funds you already took," Arthur said, narrowing his eyes. "Funds paid for services these women completed for the kingdom."

Mr. Trible's eyes darted to the women, and back to Arthur. His eyes narrowed and a dark grin curved his lips. "What type of services?"

"Retrieving charms belonging to his Royal Highness," Arthur said, stepping forward. "If you are insinuating anything other, I will stop you now. They are the most respected guests of our kingdom, and we will defend their honor."

"What could they possibly do?" He waved a dismissive hand at the four women. "They're four poor, pitiful orphans who steal."

"Our dad's still alive," Camilla growled. "Just worthless."

"Sh," Rosella and Bridgette said in unison.

"Are you ready to state here and now in front of these witnesses, that their property is cleared and theirs with no contingencies?" Arthur asked, ignoring Mr. Trible's question. "Or are you going to return all the items they paid for the taxes?"

Mr. Trible paused, his eyes darting for an unseen answer.

Arthur continued, "Or will I need to send down troops to retrieve you for theft and my master's belongings you are keeping illegally if you take their property with the claim taxes are unpaid?"

"Fine," Mr. Trible seethed. His gaze flickered to his son, and he shook his head. "It's their property."

Benson scowled and kicked the ground.

"Good day, sir," Arthur spat.

Rosella stifled her cheer as her sisters taunted Benson. The victory, though all she had wanted originally, was dull in comparison to what lay ahead. They had a castle to save. If she survived, she had a home to return to. Her sisters would have an anchor and safe place. If they made it. She knew better than to not let her sisters go. They'd proven already they'd just follow her. It'd be easier to just accept it than try to outmaneuver them.

Arthur smiled at Rosella and her sisters, and then turned to another man as he arrived. "Are our horses ready?"

Rosella turned to find Gavin waiting for them.

"Yes, sir," Gavin said. "I have five ready to go."

His brown eyes darted to the women, and then Arthur. He added, "I didn't know it was for the Belle sisters."

"Is that an issue?" Arthur asked, raising an eyebrow.

"No, not at all," he stammered. He ran his brown fingers through his black hair as he snuck a peek at Bridgette. "I'll just be a moment. I'm going to get two more."

"Thank you, I was going to request a sixth for our new guest," Arthur said, nodding toward Odette. "But we don't need two."

"I'd like to go, too," he said, and peered back to Bridgette. "If that is okay?"

Bridgette's eyes brightened with joy as she almost shouted, "Yes, that is fine."

"Thanks, Gavin." Rosella smiled at him. Maybe she could make things right for two of her sisters.

With the additional horses retrieved, the seven mounted and galloped toward the castle.

Chapter Forty-Two

THE SEVEN REACHED THE EDGE OF THE FOREST. NIGHT edged on the horizon, clawing at the remaining sun, and casting the land into darkness. Unlike before, wolves didn't follow them. Ahead, the castle perched, finally visible miles away with the curse lifted, the twisting towers and spirals covered in regrowth and rejuvenation, the spires glowing in the setting sun, belying nothing about the betrayal unravelling inside.

"They'll see us coming up the road," Rosella said, staring at the cleared grounds visible from the castle. Instead of broken and weathered relics, fountains and statues decorated a splendid garden bursting with blooms. "When the curse broke, it removed a lot of the debris that we could have used as cover."

"I know a way around," Arthur said. He pointed to a small animal path that cut parallel to the castle, winding through the forest. The rough trail was barely wide enough for a person, much less a horse. Tall trees guarded the path, the branches swooping across the space.

"Will they see us?" Rosella asked.

"Doubtful, unless other servants joined Lucien. The last time it was used was during one of his parents' parties. That was almost two decades ago. We'd sneak intoxicated or unruly guests out of view."

"I really want to see one of their parties," Camilla said, a grin curving her lips. Her eyes cut mischievously to Rosella. "You'll need to reinstate them immediately."

Bridgette sent her a dark glance while the others ignored her.

"Well, after we take down Lucien. Then we can celebrate."

Bridgette let out a long breath. "Do you think other staff joined him?"

"None had when I bolted, but there was a lot of confusion and joy. It wasn't servants helping Lucien. He brought his own people. Townsmen or thieves, or both. The staff is loyal to His Highness but they also trusted Lucien. He was master's attaché. A trusted advisor. I never thought he'd bring harm to Prince Grayson. They grew up together. Lucien was never forthright or disrespectful, but his disdain for Master's parent is known. I don't think any staff would join over Master but I also didn't think Lucien would do this."

"How many are we going to face?" Rosella asked. She and Lucien hadn't been to any villages while they went for the curses, but that didn't mean Lucien didn't know where some were. Or what had been restored with the curse lifted.

"He had a few dozen with him. None of the staff had joined yet, but we aren't equipped to fight. We still have a few soldiers, but they are out of practice."

"How'd he get his troops?" Rosella asked.

"Probably said there was a beast here or offered money," Arthur said. "He likely stashed treasures from the castle and used those. With the troll killed, many are hoping to be heroes, too. He likely touted the kill as his own, ma'am. If he can claim the throne, he'll have the treasury. Your village suffered a dismal harvest. Others have, too."

"Oh, he probably took credit for the troll kill and showed them the body," Camilla whispered. She cracked her knuckles.

"He wouldn't have had time to dig it up," Bridgette said. "But villagers being hateful and scared makes sense. If he said he killed the troll, they'd follow him to kill another beast."

"So I inspired them?" Rosella asked, swallowing down bile. She'd rallied troops for Lucien?

"No, fear and hatred inspired this," Gavin said. "It sounds like Lucien knows how to inspire through intimidation and terror."

"Well put," Arthur said, nodding. "The staff knew better. Merl and I ran when we heard his goon seize Sofia for disagreeing with Lucien when he told the king and queen that he alone broke the curse. She said he'd been a coward who ran away while Rosella did it."

"His parents believed Sofia or Lucien?" Giselle asked.

Arthur snorted. "They could see while cursed. It was meant to bring them more pain, which it did. But they saw much. Lucien's lies aren't supported."

"So why didn't he just kill Grayson's parents when he returned?" Camilla asked. She tugged her tangled hair from a branch as they crept down the path. "Wouldn't that be easier?"

"They were already awake," Arthur said. "The staff has been diligent with their recovery. They aren't left unattended. We knew something had to have happened, but Lucien said you were both dead. I thought that meant the curse was broken when Grayson died. Lucien confirmed that. He led us to believe... It doesn't matter. What matters is protecting Prince Grayson."

"Didn't Lucien try to convince you to join him?" Rosella asked.

Arthur snorted. "Yes, he hoped we hated the master as much as he did."

"But you didn't?" Gavin asked. His brown eyes darted between Bridgette and Arthur.

Rosella stilled, her eyes sweeping to Gavin and Odette, both absorbing the information with wide eyes. Neither had questioned the fantastical tales the others had spoken about freely: humans as animals, curses, and not aging. Instead, they followed them through a forest to a castle no one knew about to take on a murderer.

"You're taking this well," Arthur said with a nod of approval.

"The world is full of weird." Gavin shrugged. "Did you hate him?"

Arthur smiled and said, "No, we didn't hate the master. In the beginning, we respected his parents. They had led for decades. Yes, they squandered resources, but they still cared about the wellbeing of the kingdom. That changed a few years before Prince Grayson's birth. Many of us wanted to leave. Duty had locked us there for many years, but as they drained the suffering towns and threw more and more parties, the temptations grew. Then the castle was cursed. Bound in our animal forms, we watched the master grow up without the horrid guidance of his parents. We taught him proper etiquette. Merl taught him to read. We raised him to be the prince. A good prince. One who cared beyond more than just amassing wealth and displaying it. He fixed much of what his parents had done in those few years. He wanted to break the curse so much, but we couldn't let him leave. As he matured and changed into the form you saw, his hope vanished. He did his duties to his people, but just waited for the end. The last few years were the hardest. The hope in his eyes burned out... until you four arrived."

"He's a good man," Rosella said. She sucked in a breath and blew it out through her teeth. Lucien had lied to her. Tried to get her to see Grayson as the monster. And yet it had been Lucien plotting against her sisters, planning to use them. He was the one willing to kill people to claim the throne. She needed to focus on Grayson. Protecting him and the castle, and then imprisoning Lucien. "Grayson's kind and considerate... even if he's a stubborn fool, too."

"So, are you two going to hook up?" Camilla asked. Her bright eyes cut to Rosella, a wicked smile on her lips. "You seem pretty fond of him. You've called him a good man, and you never do that. You went to finish the curse after he absolved you, and you're mounting a coup to help regain control of his castle. I'd say you more than respect him."

Rosella snorted a cough, her face flushing. She rubbed a hand down her hot neck. There could never be anything between them. He was a prince and had a kingdom to run. She was a poor merchant and needed to look after her sisters.

"Camilla," Giselle scolded, and then turned a teasing smile to Rosella. "Don't forget, Rosella plans to be a spinster for all her days. Playing mother to us and grandmother to our children. She doesn't have time for her own love affair."

"That's boring," Camilla said. "I bet he'd be fun to—"

"Camilla," Bridgette roared. Red darkened her cheeks, and her fingers curled into fists as she stared at Camilla.

Gavin chuckled, covering it with his hand.

"What?" Camilla asked innocently. Batting her eyes, she laid a hand over her chest. "I don't understand what you thought I meant?"

"What would you like me to do?" Rosella demanded. "Do you want to turn around and go back home? Should I go burrow behind the cash register and start knitting while Lucien takes over the castle? I made a promise."

Her sisters snorted laughs.

Gavin and Odette shared a confused look.

Arthur smiled affectionately at Rosella and gave her a nod.

"Oh, we know," Camilla mocked.

"You could just let yourself be happy," Giselle added. "If you married him, then you wouldn't have to worry about us stealing because he's loaded. And you'd actually have a relationship you'd be happy in."

Rosella's mouth fell agape. Words failed her as her mind swarmed.

"I second that," Arthur said and gave a mockingly stern look right back at Rosella. "You are well suited."

Rosella's stomach twisted and her vision tunneled.

"We agree," Bridgette said and nodded toward Camilla.

"Whoa," Giselle said. "We all agree on something."

"And you, Miss Rosella?" Arthur asked, his eyes hopeful. "How do you feel about that?"

"My feelings do not matter in this situation," Rosella gritted out. "It is not going to happen. We need to focus on getting into the castle and stopping Lucien. We're in possible line of sight now. Be quiet and stay on guard."

"Nice dodge, Roz," Bridgette said dryly.

"This discussion isn't over," Camilla said and pointed two fingers at her eyes and then at Rosella.

"I wouldn't be so lucky," Rosella mumbled.

THEY CREPT THROUGH A SERVANT'S PASSAGE CUT INTO THE stone base of the mountain that led to the cold cellar. The boarded-up door was dry-rotted and gave no fight when they tugged it away. Inside the corridor, cobwebs laced the air. Critters skittered around the dirt pathway. Darkness encased them, the hall offering no light.

Familiar with the passage, Arthur plucked a torch from a sconce and lit it. The dusty air sprang to life, sizzling the webs and scattering bugs in all directions. The flame flickered, lighting the path for them, but the black vastness sprawled around them.

After a ways, the tunnel turned warmer as they neared the kitchen.

"We'll come in by the butler's pantry," Arthur whispered and pointed to a small hoist. The rickety antique was still solid but aged from nonuse.

"Will this hold?" Rosella asked, testing the wood.

"Yes, ma'am," Arthur said. "It's a short distance to the back pantry."

"And the staff is where?" Giselle asked. "Will they see us?"

"Lucien moved anyone who protested or looked about to protest to the dungeon," Arthur said. "Some of us fled before he could round us up."

"Like where we were supposed to be," Bridgette murmured, rubbing her arms.

The memory settled over the group, chilling the air and silencing them.

"What?" Gavin asked. He reached out a hand to Bridgette and turned his dark gaze to Arthur.

"That was Lucien's idea," Rosella said. "It was part of his plan."

"What?" her sisters said, turning to her.

"Lucien suggested it because it'd look good to the staff," Rosella said. "Lucien saw four possible people to break the curse if one failed. One last attempt to break the curse."

"He did?" Bridgette asked, looking to Arthur.

"It wasn't like the master to intervene," Arthur said. "He always left it to us. We were quite shocked by the decision."

"Grayson now thinks Lucien led the other visitors to the ravine where they died by the hands of the first keeper," Rosella said.

Arthur frowned as realization darkened his face.

"I really hate this Lucien guy," Gavin said.

"Join the club," Camilla said, furling her hands into fists.

They each rode in the hoist, and as Arthur said, they arrived in a pantry used for storage. Although deserted, the space was clean and tidied. They crept through the corridors to the abandoned kitchen.

Dishes and utensils were scattered around, food left in clumps on the counter and floor.

"What a mess," Giselle said.

"Stupid," Bridgette said. "If the goons plan to stay, they'll need provisions."

"Don't bring logic to this fight," Camilla said.

"Where do we go?" Gavin asked.

"Let's free the servants, first," Giselle said. "They can help us."

Rosella's stomach rolled. She didn't want to delay helping Grayson.

"You all go and help them," Rosella said, stepping away from the group. She had a feeling where Grayson and Lucien would likely be.

"What are you going to do?" Bridgette asked. She frowned and crossed her arms. "We should stay together."

"She's going to rescue her man," Camilla said and made kissing noises. "Go get him."

"I'm hoping for the element of surprise," Rosella said, stiffening to not respond to Camilla.

Arthur looked between them. "I'll lead them to the dungeon to rescue the others. Use the servant's passages to go undetected."

"Won't Lucien use them?" Rosella asked.

Arthur cursed and tsked. "It's possible, but he sees himself as the master now and the tunnels would be beneath him."

"If he's smart, he'd set up traps in them," Bridgette said.

"Is he smart?" Camilla asked.

"He's devious and conniving," Rosella said. "It's best to air on the side of caution."

"I don't like you going alone," Bridgette said.

"I faced three keepers. He will be my fourth one."

"But he almost killed you once already," Arthur said, wringing his hands. His eyes darted around the room. "Perhaps it is best if we stay together. The master would prefer that."

"He also preferred sending me back to the village. He was wrong on that too."

"Please be careful," Giselle whispered and hugged Rosella. "We've almost lost you too many times. I don't want one to be the last."

The sisters all embraced, swaying in their normal fashion.

"Meet us at the fireplace we sat at the first night here if you can't find him," Bridgette said. "We'll check there first after getting the staff before trying to find you in the castle."

Rosella nodded in agreement. She sucked in a breath and licked her lips.

"Keep each other safe," Rosella said and headed for the servant's staircase.

Chapter Forty-Three

Rosella's heart slammed in her chest. Her breaths racked her frame. The castle, void of movement, sat tense and still, waiting. The air clung with hope and uncertainty. Each room showed the aftermath of those who had come with Lucien. Furniture was toppled, items smashed, and everything was muddied. It'd take weeks to clean it, and she doubted some of the treasures could be restored.

With cautious steps, she followed the path through the hallways and into the next wing. Men's voices carried throughout the castle, their raucous laughter echoing in the corridors. Her gaze flicked around the new area. It was one she hadn't been in before, and was likely used to host large balls. The golden marble floors, once polished, gleamed through the dirt tracked on top of it. Velvet drapes were tied back, welcoming in the rising moonlight that arched across the floor. Gashes gnarled the paintings, the people staring back at her begging her to do something.

Licking her lips, she took a steadying breath. She needed to be readied. She needed to be prepared to do what was necessary, no matter if it meant she crossed a line she had vowed not to. One her family was known for and had forever changed them. She wasn't entering this drunken or with ill intent. Justified or not in her actions, she would protect Prince Grayson and his staff.

She followed the men's joyful bouts to a familiar section as they looted in a symphony of crashes and shattering glass. The shadows draped around her, offering some safety as she inched closer. Peering into the grand dining room, memories flooded back. It'd only been a week or so since she dined with Grayson. He'd barely had any traces of his humanness left, but he'd sat by her. They'd eaten and talked together. He had been more concerned for her safety and the wellbeing of his staff than his own future.

Now, townsmen were shattering dishes and looting silver while making disparaging comments about a beast and taunts about what they planned to do with his carcass.

Though Grayson no longer resembled a beast, Lucien and Prince Grayson's parents would recognize him for who he was. With that thought, she quickened her step and crept around the entryway into the room with the men, circling the light's dark perimeter in the shadow.

She went further into the heart of the castle and heard more voices.

A group of six men lounged in a parlor, smoking from pipes, and leaving dirtied prints on the furniture and decor. They snorted in satisfaction as one coughed on his inhale. Steins of likely mead littered the tables, leaving rings and sticky messes. The men wore antique pistols and swords as medals of a greedy and hate-filled mission on their worn and faded clothing.

Each group she came across was gorging on the luxuries of each room. Destroying delicate pieces, devouring delicacies, and pillaging for their gain. Lucien hadn't hired an army. He'd brought in a distraction that was promised riches. They weren't focused on being heroes but lining their pockets with treasures. Hope bloomed in her chest that she'd find Lucien and Grayson without having to engage in a battle. Like the townsmen she knew, with their promises and words blown away when offered riches and luxuries, these men didn't care for honor.

Crossing into the next section, she stood next to the west wing. Plastered walls trimmed in gold, paintings, and golden sconces circled the grand staircase. Red carpeted steps circled the girth of the room, the dark, rich wood spindles carved in elaborate fantastical designs. However, the long corridor had slashes running the length of the plaster, through the paintings and the wooden wainscoting. His cretins were destroying what Lucien hoped to claim. His palace was an aftermath of looting. He hadn't thought through the usefulness of a fearful drunken mob versus hired men.

"What are you doing?" an unfamiliar voice called behind her. Labored steps approached, the uneven pace of an old injury distorting the gait. "You pretty little thing looking for some fun? I got some for you."

Rosella blinked and let out a breath. In a quick motion, she unsheathed her shortsword, whirled around, and lunged at the voice, not caring who it belonged to. None of the town goons were going to help her. Any showing interest would only try to harm her.

The beefy man had an unruly brown beard with specks of food and spittle in it. His beady blue eyes narrowed in on her. His oversized belly hung over his brown pants and pulled on his linen shirt. He carried an axe in one hand and a crystal goblet sloshing wine in the other. His clouded eyes said he had had more than one drink already. She didn't allow the memories to flood back in, but she let the anger and fear fuel her muscles.

He stumbled at her attack, dropping his goblet and axe as she plowed into him with her shoulder, her sword going wide. His wine darkened the floor and his axe clattered to the ground, shattering the goblet. He recovered quickly and grabbed her arm, whirling her around, their boots crunching on the glass bits.

He threw her against the wall, pressing his stomach and more into her. His face was a few inches above her. Sweat and dirt smeared across his face, and his teeth were brown and cracked. He dug his fingers into her arm and pressed harder into her with a moan.

"I'm going to have fun with you," he said. He licked his lips and then ran his tongue up along her cheek across her scar. "I'm going to feel you tight around me as I fuck you and you're gonna scream."

Bile rose in her throat. Fear, blood red and bright, blinded her and stole her breath. Acid churned in her stomach. The memories flashed in her mind. The night her father killed her mother. The night she slashed his shoulder, rendering it useless.

The man laughed when she dry heaved.

"That pretty little mouth is going to have fun too," he said and grinded into her. "I'm going to tie you down and have fun over and over again."

She pushed the memories aside. The sleepless nights making sure her father didn't cross the threshold, the scars that decorated her body from the nights he tried. Her father had never succeeded. And neither would this man. Still holding her sword, she couldn't physically arch it to hit him with the blade, but instead she jabbed the hilt into his lower back by the kidney.

He reared in pain, releasing her from the surprise, and growled.

"I'm going to take you here!" He stumbled forward, spittle flying from his mouth, his meaty hands clawing for her.

She whirled around, readying for the attack. With her arms free, she pushed him back in his daze and drove her knee into his groin.

His eyes bulged and his body caved forward. He gasped for air; a long, wheezy breath escaped his mouth. He fell forward, scrabbling for her.

She swung her sword in defense, catching his arm. Blood spurted from his arm, soaking his shirt, and he howled in pain as he clutched his arm to his chest.

"So much for stealth," she growled. She whipped her head around, looking for would-be heroes for him or fortune seeking fools. A shaky breath escaped her lips.

He made another grab for her foot, and she stumbled forward. Bracing herself against the wall, she cursed as her stomach twisted and her heart slammed into her chest. She'd allowed a distraction.

He pulled her across the floor toward him, his fleshy hands grabbing at her garments and legs. With each squeeze and dig, he inched her closer and closer.

She spat and said a prayer for forgiveness as she plunged her sword into his gut. She pushed until it hit bone, the vibration sending nausea through her. She wanted to wretch.

Lurching forward, he gargled, blood bubbling from his mouth, his hands fumbling for the sword's hilt. She pushed it deeper, past bone, until his movement stopped and his body lay limp.

Taking a moment, she let the world settle around her. No one had come running. She had killed a man. The world hadn't ended, and the castle was still under siege. She pulled her sword back out and wiped it on his back, returning his blood to him.

"Why did you have to be such a filthy creature?" she said to his back. Her eyes stung with tears and her nose flared. Her fingers sought for her scar, but she only smeared blood across it and then tangled her fingers in her hair.

She trembled, staring at the lifeless form before falling back against the wall. Sobs stuck in her throat and she gasped for air. She blinked to stop the tears.

"I'm sorry," she whispered to the hall. She repeated it to the heavens and finally let her tears fall.

After a few moments, she sniffed and wiped at her face, and swallowed down the emotion from bubbling over. She would do it again and more if necessary.

She looked both directions in the hall. Nothing stirred. No one came running to answer his cries and no one slammed doors to hide from her. She looked back to the west wing, to Grayson's quarters.

There wasn't time for pity, for her or him. It'd only distort her senses, distract her.

She pushed herself up. With a final sniffle, she looked down at the dead man and his weaponry. She took his knife and axe. He wouldn't need them anymore.

Chapter Forty-Four

As she neared the study, voices filtered through the closed door and items clattered to the floor and against the wall in a cacophony of sound. Hope twisted in her veins, and she curled her fingers around her sword's hilt.

She sucked in her breath and pressed against the wall. Her heartbeat rammed against her chest and clogged her ears. She closed her eyes to focus on the sounds. She couldn't distinguish the words, but Lucien's voice was clear. A hot jolt of anger pierced her heart and focused her mind. He was a wall away.

Without a view of what was going on in the room, she'd be entering blindly. If he had other men with him, she'd be trapped, too. Unlike with the keepers who had magic, he had thugs.

She listened for more voices, but the muffled sounds blended together, and she couldn't tell the lower registered voices apart nor tell how many were there.

She knew of no other entrance. She rubbed her thumb over her knuckles and took a deep breath. Holding her shortsword at the ready, she carefully turned the door handle. When the tongue depressed completely, she inched the door open, keeping her eyes moving between the floor for shadows and her head level for attack.

When the door was open enough for her to peek in, she moved just her face to investigate the room, making sure she could shut the door and run if needed.

The room was only lit by the ascending moonlight. Long shadows swayed in the room, leaving a halo of light around a group of men.

Lucien wasn't alone.

She sucked in a breath and her mind and body stood still, a whirling sound in her ears. Her muscles contracted, her fingers curled, and her body screamed to run to Grayson's aid. Heat pulsed through her heart and into her body, willing her to move forward. To defend him.

He was braced against the wall and blood swatches dotted the floral wallpaper around him. His face was swollen and smeared with blood. He held his right arm, blood soaking through the fabric and leeching onto his torso. His deep heaves rocked his frame and his bloodied mouth hung open as he panted for air.

Lucien stood before him, a sword stretched between them. Four men flanked him, each with weapons trained on Grayson.

No one noticed her as she pushed the door open further. She moved into the room and left it open in case she needed to turn and run.

Grayson's eyes momentarily lifted at the motion and widened in surprise, but he quickly caught the action and pretended to cough, the wheezy, watery sound bringing chuckles from the men surrounding him.

Rosella swallowed back the acid clawing at her throat and averted her eyes from him. Neither of them could be distracted now.

"How did you break the curse?" Lucien demanded, tilting his head. His blond locks stayed in place with oil.

"I didn't," Grayson panted.

"You left the castle; you should have permanently been a monster!"

Grayson's body deflated, his strength dissolving before her eyes. How he was still standing was beyond her.

"Is there another riddle?" Lucien sneered, cocking his head back and anchoring his feet to the floor.

"No," Grayson said.

"Where's Rosella? Looking for another charm to help you?" A smirk darkened Lucien's face.

"She's gone," he whispered, his face shifting to the floor. He flinched and sniffed. His long locks fell against his face.

Lucien chuckled darkly.

A snarl rippled across Grayson's lips but he only lifted his eyes to glare at Lucien.

"At least her death was quick. Unlike yours. Where's the mirror?" Lucien demanded.

"Gone too." Something flickered across Grayson's face—anger or resignation—and his body heaved with his haggard breaths.

All that was between her and Lucien was the thick door and disgusting men. She'd go through them if she needed to.

"What did you do with it?"

Grayson forced his eyes up to meet Lucien's and smirked.

Hope surged through Rosella that he was still there, still not internally defeated even if physically.

"What's so funny?" Lucien said.

"You," Grayson spat.

Lucien butted his sword's hilt into his gut.

Grayson crumbled to his knee, cradling his chest as he winced and sucked in breath. Blood darkened his teeth.

"This castle is mine," Lucien growled. "This kingdom is mine. You are nothing. Never were."

Rosella took out the looted knife and axe she'd taken from the man in the hall. She braced her feet in the floor and readied her attack.

"Everything here is mine, now," Lucien growled.

"Not yet," Grayson croaked.

"What's stopping me?" Lucien taunted.

"Me," Rosella spat and flung the knife and axe at the goons behind Lucien.

Two fell to the ground. The one hit with the axe made gurgling noises and then went silent. The knife-wounded one howled and grasped for the knife in his back but couldn't reach it.

The others left him to writhe.

Instead of the expected guilt, numbness ebbed at her heart. Perhaps she had more of her father in her than she thought. Or perhaps she'd become frozen to it with all she'd done in the past weeks. If she survived, perhaps the guilt would come. But she doubted it. They chose to harm and torture Grayson.

"Rosella," Lucien said, looking over his shoulder at her, his blue eyes cold. "I had a feeling you might show up."

"Interesting, since you left me for dead," she said. Her fingers tightened around her sword, the cold metal familiar and comfortable in contrast to the fervor coursing through her.

"But you have a hard time dying. You didn't see the bigger picture." Lucien turned to face her. "We could have been something."

"Still don't see it."

"You chose a monster instead!" Lucien spat. "He's a beast. His whole family is. Making us do their bidding while they squirreled away treasures and lived the life of luxury."

The two men on his side stepped toward her.

"Isn't that what you're trying to do for yourself now?" Rosella said. Her eyes never left his gaze, but she noticed the other men in her periphery.

Lucien sneered. "I deserve it. I've paid my time."

Just like the men in the village thinking they deserved her sisters' hands in marriage or the right to her property. They'd done nothing for it but felt entitled and vindicated in their own warped rationales.

"What about the other servants in the dungeon? Didn't they do their time, too?"

"They haven't worked like I have," Lucien said.

"You mean like sending unexpecting visitors to the bottom of the ravine?"

"You shouldn't say things without proof," he snarled.

"Why'd you help with the curse?" Rosella asked.

"I had to break the curse. Nothing else worked. I wanted to be human again. Killing him and his parents hadn't worked."

"What?" Rosella sputtered. Her breath caught in her throat.

"I've poisoned them, tried to set them on fire, and even suffocate them," Lucien said in dismay. "But nothing has worked."

"You did what?" Grayson wheezed. His body shuddered and he coughed.

Lucien raised an eyebrow but didn't turn around. "The curse locked them as beasts but protected them, too."

"You let the sorceress in," Rosella said. "Aren't you the one that convinced him to punish my sisters? Didn't he normally not do anything when others stayed?"

"Who told you that?" Lucien spat and whirled around to look at Grayson. "I see you two were getting chummy. Did you spread her legs too? Was she willing with you? You know it's only to use and control you, right? Get your riches? Pay her taxes and set her sisters up in luxury?"

Darkness flickered behind Grayson's golden eyes, and he bared his teeth. Blood oozed from his mouth.

Lucien turned back to Rosella, a wicked smile darkening his face. "Then maybe I have the leverage I need after all."

Rosella stepped closer, gauging the three men.

"Stand him up." Lucien waved to the men by him without taking his eyes off Rosella. "Make sure you don't turn your back on him."

"Your plans aren't going to work," Rosella said, but uncertainty wormed into her heart. It was her against four armed men, all with their own greed and hatred fueling them.

"Who's going to stop me?" he asked. "I'll destroy your world. I know your weakness. All three of them. And possibly a monstrous fourth."

Rosella swallowed back the fear clawing at her throat. He knew too much about her. She'd kept her life private, but he knew what she valued, what she cared for, what she'd sacrifice to save.

"You are weak," Lucien continued. "Sure, you took on three keepers, but that was pride running its course. You hate yourself. You don't feel worthy. You don't value yourself at all. You've built a life for your sisters, all while cleaning up their disasters. You even came here and volunteered for their punishment."

"A punishment you wanted bestowed," Rosella seethed.

"Hm," he said, drawing his lips into a thin line. His eyes flashed with anger and his jaw ticked. "I'm flattered. Really. Here you were talking about me while alone with him."

Rosella scoffed.

"I'm in your thoughts and yet you were foolish again, giving your help to those unworthy. I could have offered you a throne. My hand. My bed." Lucien's hand thumped his chest.

"I already turned you down," Rosella said.

"Yes, you did, and for what?" Lucien bellowed. He threw his hands behind him as he yelled, "For him? He doesn't deserve what you are."

"What am I?" Rosella challenged.

"A tool," Lucien said as a twisted smile spread across his face. "A weapon. A person who can accomplish almost anything when her family is at stake. I'm sure they're here. Somewhere. Waiting to get caught. My way to control you, make you into my personal force, is simple."

Rosella blinked but stilled her face and reactions. He was baiting her. Waiting for her to slip up.

"What do you want?" Rosella asked.

"See, you're already trying to figure out how to keep them safe. So predictable."

"You already plan to take the castle and throne."

"I've done that," Lucien seethed. "His parents can acknowledge me as the rightful heir, or they'll catch death."

"The curse is broken," Rosella said. "There is no other part of it."

"I disagree," Lucien said.

"Why?" Rosella asked, genuine confusion clouding her face. "Everything has been restored."

"Yes, to the eye," Lucien said, nodding. "But he broke a cardinal rule of the curse."

"Leaving the castle?" Rosella asked.

"Yes," Lucien said. "He followed us, and the curse should have been locked in then. He should still be in beast form. Especially with her dead... Wait... You survived. Did the siren survive, too?"

Rosella's jaw ticked as she restrained all other reactions.

"That witch survived, didn't she?" he said, spittle flying from his mouth.

"So, you want to know what the missing part is?" Rosella asked.

"Yes. There is a payment owed for the curse being broken when he left. That's how magic works."

"The sorceress created the curse, she can undo it," Rosella repeated what the sorceress had said, but uncertainty gnawed at her stomach. Lucien made too much sense with everything else she'd seen.

"No, magic has rules," Lucien said "He broke them. We'll be punished again." His face contorted with his rage, marring his handsome features.

Rosella allowed her eyes to dart to Grayson. He had doubled over as far as the men's grip went up. They strained against his size and bulk. His raspy breaths were weak, and sweat dripped from his face, but he was listening to Lucien.

He agreed, too. Something was off.

"What do you want, then?" Rosella asked. "What will it take for you to let him go and not harm him?"

"Rosella, no," Grayson choked out.

Lucien smiled. "I want the final piece solved. Or..."

Rosella didn't want to ask, but she knew he was waiting. "Or what?"

"I'll carve him in front of you. I'll show you what happens when you defy me, and then I'll carve your sisters." He paused, his eyes clouded for a moment in thought. Then added, "Or make them my mistresses. I wouldn't mind riding them a few times."

Rosella dry heaved and red dots danced in front of her eyes. She clenched her fists to keep her anger in check. He wanted her to let loose. To be careless and reckless.

"You could have had me," Lucien said, fanning his fingers over his chest. "But you chose a beast."

"I didn't want you," Rosella said, her mind already reeling. Could there be a fourth riddle?

"We could have been great," he said, disappointment emphasizing his words. "You took on a dryad, troll, and siren. We could have ruled this land. You'd have been queen and destroyer. But, you chose the wrong side."

"Did a fourth paper appear?" Rosella asked, ignoring his tirade.

"What?" Lucien said, flinching.

"Each time a part was broken, a new riddle appeared."

His eyes darted around the room, seeing nothing as he processed her words.

"There is a fourth riddle," Lucien said.

"What is it, then?" Rosella said.

His eyes narrowed and he sneered. "You're toying with me. She gave it to you, didn't she?"

"What? You tried to kill me. You threw the last piece into the ocean. It's lost forever. It's how the next riddle was unlocked. One appeared when the charm was brought back and he touched it. I don't have another riddle."

"She survived and gave you the fourth riddle. What is it?"

"I don't know," Rosella said. "She didn't give me anything."

"Cut him," Lucien said to the men, gesturing behind him.

"No!" Rosella screamed. "I won't help if you hurt him."

"Yes, you will," Lucien assured her. "You'll get a taste of what will happen to your sisters if you don't."

"Where, sir?" one asked.

"His face," Lucien said, drawing an imaginary line in the air toward Rosella's scar. "Give him a matching one to Rosella's."

A man did as instructed, slicing a line from Grayson's cheek to his chin, coating the blade in his blood. Crimson wept from the wound, running down his cheek and into his shirt.

Grayson's face pinched and his eyes shut tight at the pain.

Nausea waved through Rosella, and anger coiled in her stomach. She swallowed back the hatred clawing at her throat.

"Stop it," Rosella seethed. "I already said I'd help, but you can't hurt him."

"Then what is the riddle?" Lucien demanded.

Rosella licked her lips and willed her mind to come up with a lie.

"Wait," Grayson choked out, drawing their attention.

Lucien's brows furrowed and he rocked back on his heels.

"It's too late to bargain," Lucien said without turning around.

"She gave me the riddle," Grayson said, his breaths barely above the sound of air. "She didn't want Rosella to know since she solved the first three. It was mine alone for not following the order to stay in the castle."

Lucien looked to Rosella and then Grayson.

"Did she?" Lucien questioned Rosella.

Rosella shrugged, doubt sitting heavy on her heart. They hadn't been apart in the cave. He hadn't been distracted by it, trying to figure it out.

"What is it?" Lucien demanded, tilting his chin down.

"First, she goes free," Grayson said and nodded at Rosella. "Once she's off the grounds, I'll tell you."

"Oh, and you say I'm the conniving one," Lucien said, chuckling mirthlessly. "I guess they need another demonstration. Give him a matching one on the other side."

"Lucien, wait," Rosella said.

He turned back to her with amusement. "Looks like they both want to admit to having the riddle."

Rosella shook her head. "I don't have the riddle. I didn't lie. But we can figure it out."

"How?" Lucien demanded.

"Let's think about the riddles and charms," Rosella said, inching her foot forward speck by speck as she spoke, her brain grasping on shards of the past few weeks.

"What about them?"

"We went into a ravine for a pearl, a mountain for a rose, and an ocean for a tear."

"They're all based on local lore. There're many tales of the land."

Rosella brushed away his words with her hand. "A ravine is low, cut deep from water. The mountain a high point, and the ocean expansive."

"So? The objects that broke the curse are a pearl, rose, and tear."

"But look at the pattern. Low, high, far... we need close," Rosella said, grabbing at anything that made sense.

"Close as in...?" Lucien asked, his interest piqued.

"My guess is it's in the castle or on the grounds," Rosella said. "Close."

"A lore with the castle? What is it? There aren't any." Lucien stilled. His gaze slid to Grayson. "A beast, perhaps?"

"There was a pearl, rose, and tear," Rosella said. "They are all naturally created."

Commotion in the hall pulled their attention to the open door.

"We found three of them," a man said, helping another to restrain Camilla while others restrained Bridgette and Gavin.

"There's another," Lucien said. "You'll like her. You'll have fun with her beauty in bed."

"There's actually two." Another set of men appeared, dragging Giselle and Odette behind them.

Her sisters' protests clouded out her thoughts and her stomach churned as it filled with lead. Lucien had everything of hers and she couldn't give him what he wanted to free them, but it was unlikely he would anyway. Not after everything that had transpired. There was only one way this would end.

"So, Rosella, are you going to find me the fourth charm? You can't win. You know this. I have your family and your lover."

"Can't win," Rosella muttered, the word familiar but not right. Her thoughts crystalized, and the word "winless" echoed in her brain.

"What?" Lucien spat. His eyes widened and his lips curled into a grin. "Did you figure it out?"

"Winless," Rosella echoed and reached for her necklace. The siren had said it was for a winless situation.

"What are you doing?" Lucien asked and drew his sword. The weapon hung between them, the blade darkened already with another's blood. "What do you know?"

Rosella barely noticed as the words cycled through her brain.

"I may have the riddle after all," Rosella said, and pulled the locket out. The face of the bauble was still lit with gems, the image making clear sense. All the charms she needed were there, along with their locations. The pearl moon at the end of the river, a rose on a mountain, and a siren with a tear. Nothing was added on the image, but on a hunch, she opened the locket. The metal faces swung apart. Inscribed on the left side where three verses. All the pieces together.

She read out loud, "'What you start will end, With a heart that cannot mend, A curse suspended for a beast, That's lied in wait shall be released.'"

But she didn't read the last lines out loud. "Let your sword fly, Your heart will be your eye."

She paused at the last line. Let her sword fly. On the facing side of the verse, was a painted image of a woman throwing a glowing sword. She blinked. The woman looked like her with auburn hair, dark eyes, a black tunic, and a shortsword.

"What is it?" Lucien demanded.

"The riddle," Rosella said. She smiled. "And I know what it means."

"Then get on with it!" Lucien roared.

She licked her lips and then recited the two lines in her mind. "Will end... so you were right. There was a final piece. We have a heart that cannot mend. Most likely something in the castle... or maybe a room. A curse suspended for a beast..."

"We need the third verse," Lucien said, interrupting her. "'What you start will end, A heart that cannot mend...'" Lucien paused and pointed at Grayson. "That's him, a heart that cannot mend. The curse is suspended and will be released!"

Lucien pumped his fist in the air and sauntered to stand in front of Grayson. "I won. The castle is mine, Rosella is mine. You are a disgusting beast and will die one. The curse was only suspended. You'll die like a filthy beast."

"You're wrong, Lucien," Rosella said. "*You're* the beast."

Lucien turned to face her as she flung her sword at him, hoping the lines were true.

Her sword glowed gold as it sailed through the air. Directed by magic, it sliced through his heart, engulfing him in a wave of gold magic.

The light expanded, bulged, and then disappeared. In its wake, Lucien was lifeless on the floor, his human form distorted and twisted. Her shortsword stuck out of his body, but instead of red blood, black oozed from its incision.

The locket glowed and hummed, the images shifting. A new image appeared over the text, one of Grayson. He was in his human form wearing a black tunic with a crest similar to her family's, but additional swirls accentuated it. His tangled black hair was pulled back, and his yellow eyes glowed. The image of her holding the sword morphed into a new one of her. She wore a black tunic, but crests were woven into the design matching Grayson's. Instead of a frown, she matched his smile.

She instinctively closed the locket and saw the cover had changed, too. The mountain, river, and sea remained, but a castle nestled on the mountain instead of the moon, rose, and tear. The castle's white stone face was made of pearls and emeralds and rubies dotted around it as gardens.

She lifted her eyes to look around the room. Grayson, the two men flanking him, and behind her, her sisters, Gavin, Odette, and their captures all stared at her.

"Roz," Bridgette murmured. She shoved the goon away from her and rubbed her wrists.

"The curse is over," Rosella whispered and let the locket drop back to her chest.

"Over?" Bridgette echoed back to her.

Rosella cleared her throat and stood up straight. She walked up to Lucien. She said a quick prayer and pulled her sword from him. His body withered and collapsed as if it had rotted from the inside. "If you were hired by Lucien, you have one minute to be out of the castle before I come for you with my sword."

Without pause or hesitation, the hired men ran from the room, leaving the others in their wake.

"See to it they're all gone," Rosella called to her sisters, and she made her way over to Grayson. Her breaths stilled, her body trembled, and pain panged in her heart.

Free of the two men and with no fear to prop him up, his body slumped to the floor and his eyes blinked, the motion slowing as did his breaths. More blood wept from his body, pooling around his form.

"I should have listened." He grimaced, a sharp breath rattling his frame. "Gone in together."

"Stay with me," Rosella ordered, a sob rocking her body, and tears blurring her eyes.

"Rosella," he breathed before crashing to the floor.

"Grayson," Rosella screamed, hot tears streaming down her face and dampening her tunic. "Do not leave me!"

Chapter Forty-Five

Rosella watched through the towering windows as the sun set and rose almost a dozen times. Autumn slowly warmed the trees on the distant hills. Rich reds, oranges, yellows, and purples splashed across the land, the sentinel pines resilient and steady as winter approached.

When the last riddle resolved, the destruction Lucien had caused reverted back, and the ruffians were tossed from the castle. While the staff had kept it pristine, they had renewed fervor for the returned majesties and a distraction from the unconscious Prince Grayson. The staff cycled through the room, offering help that was declined, and disturbing Rosella as she kept watch.

She'd sent her sisters home. They had a store and home to tend to, but she figured they had stayed in the castle and just out of her sight. It wasn't hard; she hadn't left Grayson's room since they'd carried him there.

She'd cleaned his wounds, stitched them in her normal crooked pattern, and watched. She watched his chest rise and fall with each labored breath, watched as the sun warmed his skin and night cast him in shadows.

She turned him regularly with the help of anyone close by so he wouldn't get bed sores. She fed him broth and water. The slow, meticulous process took hours. She'd forgotten about food for herself multiple times, but Sofia or Merl always brought her something. Based on the selections, her sisters were picking the food.

Her current tray sat barely touched in the corner, the soup already cold. Settling a blanket over her lap, she smoothed out the simple blouse she wore with her leggings. She sipped her tea and reached her other hand out for his. She folded her fingers on his hand, tucking his fingers in her palm, rubbing gently. Carefully, she lifted his hand back to her lap. Rosella picked up the book she'd been reading. A classic fairytale.

She opened it to the page she'd left off on, and started reading aloud, her voice filling the room and blocking out her thoughts.

As she flipped the page, his fingers tightened around hers. She startled, upsetting the book and knocking it to the floor.

His fingers tensed again, and she turned to him. His face scrunched as he shifted on the bed and flinched, a soft groan escaping his lips.

"Grayson," she whispered, the name like water on her parched tongue.

His eyes twitched and fluttered open, his yellow orbs finding hers.

"Rosella," he choked out, the word rusty and harsh. His lips curled up before he groaned.

"You're awake." She leaned closer to him and curled her fingers around his. Her eyes searched his face, trying to find any illusion or trickery. Had she slipped into slumber or had her prayers been met?

He looked around the room, confusion darkening his face. He swallowed before returning his gaze to her.

"Are you okay?" he asked, taking in her exhausted appearance.

"I'm fine," Rosella said. "I was so worried about you." Her lip trembled, but she smiled down at him. Tears rimmed her eyes as relief eased her muscles.

"Lucien?" Grayson choked.

Rosella shook her head, and said, "He's dead." The guilt had never come. Instead, only concern for Grayson.

Grayson's eyes darted to her. "The curse?"

"The locket she gave back. It had the last riddle. He'd been right. There was another one, but it was meant for Lucien."

"Everyone else?"

"All the staff beside Lucien are safe. The mob was run out. The castle is restored. I sent my sisters home, but I am certain they are still here, hiding from me."

He narrowed his eyes, his face pinched. "How long have I been here?"

Rosella pursed her lips and sighed. The days had bled together. "About ten days, give or take."

"You stayed?" he murmured.

"I had to make sure you woke up," she said and patted his hand. "I..." Her voice broke off and she looked away.

He tightened his fingers around hers, again.

She looked back to him, forcing a watery smile. "I am so happy you're awake."

He searched her face for something he wouldn't voice.

"Your parents will be so happy you're awake. They've been infuriating. They've wanted regular updates. Been asking endless questions." Cold numbness settled through her. He would return to the life he was born to, as would she. Apart from each other.

"My parents?" Grayson choked.

"It's been a long time, but yes, your parents," Rosella said. He would finally get a chance to know them. The decades had passed, but he was given a second chance.

"I..." Grayson grimaced and shook his head. "I don't think I want to see them."

Rosella rubbed his arm with her free hand. She'd heard the stories, the three sides. Lucien, the staff, and his parents. The truth lay somewhere in between, but Lucien's version contrasted the other two. She also heard what the sorceress had said. Lucien had already been looking for a way as a young teen to claim the throne.

"Is Lucien the one that told you the stories about your parents and what happened with the sorceress?"

Grayson thought for a moment, and slowly nodded. "He did, but the others mentioned it, too."

"Did they hear it from him?"

Grayson's eyes widened. "I'm not sure."

"I don't know what parts, if any, are true," Rosella said. "I know your parents did other things the servants weren't fond of, but they heard everything going on since the curse went into place. You need to talk with them."

"Have you?"

Rosella nodded. "When they aren't asking what I need, they ask if you've woken up. We've talked a bit about the curse. About before. During..."

He looked away and shuddered his eyes. His fingers tightened around hers again.

"Grayson," Rosella said, causing him to look back. She took a moment to savor his face, memorize his eyes. "Take your time with it. You don't have to do anything right now. There is a lot for everyone to learn."

His eyes drifted shut and he relaxed back into sleep.

She watched him a bit longer, hoping he'd wake up while also hoping he'd remain asleep.

The sun shifted behind the curtains, and she quietly stood up. Leaning over, she kissed his cheek.

"You are a good man," she whispered to him. She blinked to stop the tears, but they spilled over, anyway.

Gathering her book and tunic she exited the room and closed the door.

Chapter Forty-Six

"I don't understand why you left," Bridgette said, standing in front of the counter with her arms folded over her chest. She wore a gown from the castle, emerald green with chiffon overlay. Gavin stood next to her in simple pants and shirt, his hands in his pockets. He sheepishly smiled at Rosella.

Rosella furrowed her brow and looked around the store. "This is our home." She'd returned to her normal black breeches and blouse and her position by the cash register. Her heart had tried to return to the normal numbness before the castle, but a heaviness had settled in. When she allowed her mind to drift to Grayson, a sharp spike tore through her façade, stealing her breath and sending pain through her limbs.

"So?" Camilla said from her chair. She was back in her worn and comfortable linen dress but held a plush blanket from the castle. A few items from the castle decorated her nook. Her fingers nimbly embroidered the dress collar in her lap. "You can visit."

"What would I do in the castle?" Rosella scoffed. She ran a rag over the spotless counter and chipped at imaginary dirt with her fingernail.

"Do we need to have the talk?" Camilla asked, turning in her chair to stare at Rosella over her shoulder with a raised eyebrow.

"Oh, haha," Rosella said. She rolled her eyes. "I have a job. A purpose here. I take care of the store."

"You use that as a front to watch us," Camilla said, waving her off.

"Uh-huh," Giselle said, coming into the room with Odette next to her. Giselle wore an older garment of red along with muck boots and an apron while Odette wore a dark gray dress of the current fashion.

"Have you told your family yet?" Rosella asked, looking between the two.

"Nice distraction," Camilla coughed and tossed her head back to stare at the ceiling.

Odette shook her head and looked to the ground.

"They know the wedding is off?" Rosella asked.

Odette and Giselle shared a look, and then Odette nodded.

"What does that look mean?" Rosella asked, pointing between them.

"I may have given Odette's family one of the silver statues from the castle," Giselle said.

"Okay?" Rosella asked. "Why?"

"It covers the dowry they paid," Odette said.

"And?"

Odette and Giselle shared another look.

"Just tell me so I stop asking," Rosella said.

"And the rest is part of a promise to let me wait a few years to make a decision," Odette murmured.

"They agreed?" Rosella asked, her eyes widening.

Giselle shrugged. "Why wouldn't they have?"

Rosella raised an eyebrow.

"I am very convincing," Giselle said, bringing her folded hands to her chin and batting her eyelashes.

"That you are," Rosella said with a smile. "I'm glad that you have more time."

"So, let's get back to you," Bridgette said, leaning on the counter. Resting her elbows on the surface, she placed her chin on her clasped hands.

"How about we talk about the dowry to Gavin's family instead?" Rosella said.

Bridgette flushed and ran her tongue over her teeth. She glared at Rosella and shifted back off the counter to put her fists on her hips.

"My family doesn't want a dowry," Gavin said, moving to stand beside Bridgette. His manners didn't allow him to wrap an arm around her yet. "I've already spoken with them."

Rosella narrowed her eyes. "Why? It's tradition. It's customary."

"I'm not getting paid to marry Bridgette," he said, and blushed when she smiled at him. "I am marrying her because I love her and want to spend my life with her."

"You're too cute," Camilla said and gagged. "Maybe we want to pay you to take her off our hands. She's mouthy, you know. We don't want her back."

Bridgette walked over and cuffed Camilla on the back of her head. Camilla flinched and cradled the assaulted spot.

"And handsy," Camilla said, and ducking added, "Wait, you might like that."

Giselle and Rosella laughed, and Bridgette jumped across the back of the chair to clutch Camilla. She tangled her fingers in Camilla's hair, grabbing chunks and yanking back while pushing Camilla's head in the opposite direction.

"Ow, don't pull my hair," Camilla wailed. She grabbed Bridgette's arm and pulled her over her shoulder, wincing as Bridgette clung to her hair, so she landed with her butt on the floor.

"I'll pull your face, then," Bridgette said and clawed at Camilla's face.

Rosella looked to Gavin, and asked, "Changed your mind on the dowry?"

He smiled, and then looked back at Bridgette with fondness.

"Oh, he's in deep," Giselle said. "He's too blind to see the truth."

"Let's hope he stays that way," Rosella said and went to pull Camilla off of Bridgette.

"OW! YOU BIT ME!" Camilla roared and lunged on top of Bridgette.

Rosella grabbed Camilla's dress's collar and yanked her backwards.

Camilla growled and continued to kick and reach for Bridgette.

Bridgette righted and pushed herself to her feet. She braced her hands on the floor, ready to push off, when Giselle wrapped her arms around Bridgette's torso, anchoring her to the ground.

"At least Roz is finally smiling," Giselle grunted as Bridgette strained to get away from her.

"What are you talking about? I smile." Rosella huffed and yanked Camilla harder back toward her chair.

"Sure, okay," Camilla said and gave Bridgette and Giselle an eye roll. "Do you hear these lies?"

The two nodded in agreement. All three sent Rosella withering looks.

"You four change sides in one fluid swoop," Odette said, resting against the counter with a broad smile.

"Just don't cross us," Camilla said, pulling away from Rosella and smoothing her skirt down but letting her shirt and hair stay rumpled.

"So, you really have no intention of going back to the castle?" Odette asked.

"No," Rosella said. She looked around the shop and, not finding anything to focus on, she pushed past her family and walked into the house.

The others followed and Rosella growled.

"Avoiding your feelings won't make them go away," Bridgette said.

"It'll just make you a cantankerous old goat," Camilla said. "You're halfway there now."

"You're too young to be a spinster," Giselle said. "And you already found someone you love and who loves you. Don't be a fool."

"What are you talking about?" Rosella asked, her eyes bulged in surprise and annoyance.

"Which part, hun?" Camilla asked. "The too young? Yes, you really are. You aren't our parent. You're two years older than me and six years older than the youngest. Though you act a good twenty more."

Rosella rolled her eyes. "I didn't say I was old."

"You don't realize you love him, do you?" Bridgette asked, reaching out and holding Gavin's hand.

He smiled at her and gazed at her with glossy eyes.

Rosella rolled her eyes again, longer and more dramatic at the romantic display, and pushed the dining chairs in farther until they tipped backwards. "You're making stuff up."

"Holy cow," Camilla said, her eyes large as she followed Rosella's actions. "She really doesn't know it."

"How can I love him and not know it?" Rosella scoffed, but pink stained her cheeks.

"Because you don't want to," Bridgette pushed. "You're not used to it. It scares you. You don't feel worthy of it."

"That's bull. I know you three love me." Rosella folded one arm over her torso and waved the other at her three sisters.

"Oh, that's so different and debatable," Camilla said. "Most days I do, but there are some days, uh-uh."

"We do love you, but we're not in love with you," Giselle said. She squeezed Odette's hand before releasing it to wrap her arm around Rosella's shoulder.

"What?" Rosella barked. She shrugged to remove Giselle's hands, but Giselle squeezed her tighter.

"Love is so basic," Giselle explained. "We use it to describe so many feelings of the soul."

Rosella rolled her eyes.

"You love us unconditionally," Giselle continued. "We completely ignored your request at the castle to put the stuff back. We got caught. You fought for us and risked your life to save us."

"You'd do the same," Rosella countered.

"Of course, we love you and your broody ways unconditionally, too," Camilla said.

"But you have romantic, lifelong gooey eyes love with Grayson," Giselle added.

"No." Rosella shook her head but already knew it was a lie.

"Roz, he let you go," Bridgette said. "He did what was best for *you*. You and your happiness were his foremost thoughts. You chose to find the third charm. Because you care about him."

"I promised I would." Uncertainty twisted in her stomach. She had promised him, but was it more?

"He said it was absolved," Bridgette countered.

"It was my promise."

"So stubborn," Camilla said. "How do you explain staying in vigilant watch for ten days?"

"He was injured."

"You didn't leave his room," Bridgette said dryly.

"I did too," Rosella said and then cursed inwardly, uncertain if she had left the room.

"Other than to use a chamber pot?"

Rosella sighed and ran a hand through her hair.

"He's a friend," Rosella growled.

"Who you happen to be in love with and who loves you back," Giselle said.

"I don't know what you're talking about." Rosella threw her hands in the air and let out a growly breath.

"You two spent days together," Giselle pressed.

"I spent days with Lucien, too," Rosella said and grimaced.

"Did you like Lucien's company?" Giselle asked with genuine curiosity.

"He was okay until he tried to kill me," Rosella said and shrugged. "Like having a cawing bird around."

"He never came on to you?" Camilla asked.

Rosella snorted. "He made comments on the way to find the third charm, and I told him to stop."

"But not the other times?"

"The first charm, he freaked out on the climb down and ran away when he thought I drowned. We only rode horses together."

"We remember," Bridgette said dryly.

"He left you?" Gavin asked.

"He also tried to kill her," Camilla said. "We are upset by both, but the killing is worse."

"Yeah, I get that," Gavin said.

"The troll was a couple days, though," Giselle said. "Did you enjoy that time?"

Her sisters gave her a knowing look.

"I was focused on getting the charm," Rosella said. "He wanted to rest too much. I was focused on speed."

"No, you just don't sleep," Bridgette said.

Rosella rolled her eyes at the frequent reminder.

"What about with Grayson?" Giselle asked. "Did you enjoy your time with him? Did he show romantic interest?"

Rosella stilled and tried to act aloof, her arms awkward and her face twisting with emotion without her consent. Their kisses and night together stirred in her veins and sent pulses to her heart and brain.

"Oh, did you see that change?" Camilla said, pointing a finger at Rosella's face.

"Something happened," Giselle said, rubbing her hands.

"Spill," Camilla demanded.

Rosella frowned. She didn't want to share those moments. She loved her sisters, but she didn't want them to ask questions. Questions she didn't want to answer because she'd have to lie to them and herself and say it meant nothing. That it had just been circumstance and actions of the moment. Lust and adrenaline. She didn't want to admit her heart had been involved. Or that she missed him. Or that she loved him.

Chapter Forty-Seven

Rosella stared at Mr. Trible and waited for him to stop ranting. He'd been trying to get her audience for the two weeks since she returned.

"I assure you," Rosella said when he paused to take in a breath, "I have no intentions of marrying your son, nor have I ever."

Benson's face crimsoned, and he looked to his father.

"Your sisters told him," Mr. Trible started, his eyes bulged, and spittle flying. "They said if he looked after the store..."

"He offered to look after the store," Rosella corrected.

"With the assumption you were looking at wedding apparel," he spat. "For a wedding with him."

"If I was or was not looking at wedding apparel does not mean I meant for a wedding with him."

"You owe our family," Mr. Trible said.

"For what?" Rosella asked, moving to straighten a shelf of new perfumes.

"You used him as a bridge to save your failing business," he yelled.

"Failing?" Rosella asked, looking around at the covered shelves, made good with the provisions from a few items from the castle. With the curse lifted, travelers once again traversed the forest they once thought haunted. The late fall harvest promised to be abundant, and the town was hopeful.

"We kept it afloat," he said, puffing his chest out and lifting his chin.

"Afloat?" Rosella laughed. "There weren't any sales. If there were, he kept all the money. The store was worse off after he watched it."

She folded her arms over her chest and met his gaze evenly.

"Are you calling him a thief?" Mr. Trible challenged.

"Absolutely not," Rosella said. "I, however, do not owe you anything other than a thank you at most."

A knock resounded off the door, and Rosella turned to see a man dressed in black attire, a droopy face, and a miserable expression. The tax collector had finished out his business and was set to head off to the next village.

"Sir," she said, opening the door for him.

"Madam," he said, tipping his hat. His eyes flicked unamused to the Tribles. "Are you open?"

"Yes, how can I help you?" she asked, returning to her post by the register, providing a counter buffer between her and Benson and Mr. Trible.

"I heard you had currant wine," he said and scanned the shelf behind her.

"Yes, freshly stocked," Rosella said, pulling down a bottle.

She rang him up, offering him a smile that turned into a smirk when she met Mr. Trible's gaze.

After tipping his hat, the tax collector exited the door but stepped back when a shadow fell across him.

He mumbled and sloppily bowed before holding the door open. His lips curved into a frown, but his eyes lit with interest.

Rosella watched as he stepped back, and confusion gripped her stomach when Arthur stepped past the man. He wore fresh livery, and his hair was combed back and coiffed.

"Arthur?" Rosella exclaimed. Her mind spun on the many reasons Arthur could be in her store, but she couldn't move past the idea that he'd brought bad news. Her excitement petered and she forced a smile.

"Rosella," he said, his face lighting up with a grin.

Her heart thudded in her chest and she sucked back a breath.

"You were the horse person," Benson said, stepping in front of Rosella.

"Horse person?" Arthur said with an impish smile. "No, no, I was a squirrel."

"What?" Benson barked. His lips curled back in a grimace.

Rosella snorted a laugh, some of her tension easing.

"I am the one who provided proof the items collected for the taxes were obtained legitimately," Arthur said and gave him a derisive look. "Thus, the Belle sisters kept their home without unneeded marriages."

"It is great to see you," Rosella said and skirted the counter to embrace him.

Arthur returned it, color staining his cheeks.

"What are you doing here?" Rosella asked. "Is everything all right? Is Grayson doing okay?"

She felt Benson and Mr. Trible shift behind her, their presence meant to be intimidating. Little did they know they couldn't match a person who served a beast.

"Master is physically well. His body has recovered."

Rosella smiled, her stomach untightening.

"I came to see you," Arthur said, taking her hands in his.

"Really? Well, I'm happy to see you." She beamed. "Would you like to stay for dinner?"

"What?" Benson sputtered, his gaze bouncing between them. His mouth moved but no other sound came out.

Arthur's eyes lit up.

"I am sure my sisters would be thrilled," Rosella said, smiling wide. "I think Camilla has some chicken and potatoes. Giselle found a few late season berries. I think Camilla is making pie with them."

"May I also join?" Grayson's voice called.

Rosella stilled and blinked, her mouth suddenly dry. She licked her lips and turned back to the door.

Grayson stood in the doorway, taking up the entire frame. He wore a black tunic, with red strands running vertically down the front. His dark hair was pulled back, but a few tendrils had worked free. His mouth twitched between a smile and a grimace, his only sign of nerves, as his posture was rigid and commanding. His yellow eyes were solely focused on her.

Once she locked eyes with him, she couldn't look anywhere else. Warmth flooded her body.

"Grayson," she murmured, the name a hoarse whisper on her tongue.

Her heart stamped in her chest.

Benson jostled past her, rocking her on her feet and bringing her out of the trance. Mr. Trible joined his son, and they stood proudly in front of her. Despite their shorter stature, they angled their heads to look down at Grayson.

An amused smile skittered across his face as he looked past them to Rosella.

He stepped into the shop, the door closing behind him with a jangle.

The Tribles squared their shoulders, and Mr. Trible sneered, "And who are you?"

Rosella rolled her eyes, and said, "Prince Grayson."

"Prince?" Benson said and looked back at her. Doubt clouded his eyes. "He doesn't look like a prince."

She raised her eyebrow and shrugged her right shoulder. Their disbelief didn't make it untrue.

Mr. Trible's eyes enlarged, his head slowly lifting as he took in the tunic and the silver-embellished collar with his family's crest. Recognition dawned on his face.

"Soon to be King Grayson of Redrock," Arthur added.

Grayson shrugged and stepped to the left. A smile tugged on his lips.

Rosella matched his step, and seeing the sign of trespassing, Benson stepped over, too.

"Your father is going to abdicate his throne?" Rosella asked.

"Mind your place," Mr. Trible asked, flustered by the knowledge he was in the presence of royalty. "You should not question him. Where are your manners?"

"I never had them," Rosella said without looking away from Grayson. A small grin curved on her lips to match Grayson's.

"Wait... He's... he's King Lyleford and Queen Artemis' son." Mr. Tremble ran a quavering hand over his head, bowing awkwardly. "Your Highness..."

Benson flinched, his eyes darting between everyone in the room like they were all in on an elaborate prank.

"My father has decided he spent enough time idly," Grayson said, ignoring Mr. Trible. "Since things were running without him, all things considered, he's decided he'd rather pass the crown down."

Rosella nodded. Prince Grayson was another metaphorical step away from her. The chasm was too wide to cross.

"I wish you the best," Rosella said, her heart suddenly heavy. "You already made a great ruler."

"How do you know him?" Benson hissed, stepping in Rosella's path. He crowded her space and leaned over to try to catch her eye.

"Benson," Mr. Trible scolded. He inclined his chin to bow.

Benson scowled but gave a half-hearted bow.

"This is my master, Prince Grayson of Redrock," Arthur said, stepping forward. "We were telling the truth of the Belle sisters' support of our kingdom."

"You know royalty," Mr. Trible twittered, his eyes dancing around the room unfocused. "How is that possible? We have royalty in our town!"

Benson's scowl deepened and his cheeks flamed purple.

Rosella ignored Benson; her gaze fixed on Grayson.

"May we speak privately?" Grayson asked.

Rosella's heart stalled before thudding against her chest. Her mind screamed at her to run, that he couldn't offer what she wanted, but her heart held her to the spot. He had come here. Personally. A thank you could have been sent by any member of the staff. But he came. Despite her efforts not to get her hopes up, her lips curled into a smile.

"Yes," Rosella said, disregarding Benson, his father, and propriety as she gestured toward the door leading into the family section.

"I'll keep watch on the store," Arthur said and bowed.

Chapter Forty-Eight

Rosella pushed into the room and groaned at seeing her sisters acting nonchalant inside.

"How long?" Rosella breathed.

"How long what?" Camilla asked.

"Were you listening?"

The sisters shared a look, and Bridgette said, "When we saw the carriage pull up."

"You clean up very nicely," Camilla said, giving Grayson an appreciative glance.

He gave a puzzled look. His brows knit together but he remained straight in posture.

"We can go to the kitchen," Rosella said and stepped forward.

"You could go to the bedroom," Camilla said. "It's easier for us to hear without having to cram into the door jam. You may also enjoy it more."

Rosella closed her eyes. "You could just let us talk privately and not eavesdrop."

"What fun would that be?"

"Here works," Grayson said, his glance bouncing uncertainly to her sisters. "They'll hear no matter where we go."

"You missed her, didn't you?" Camilla said, and leaned closer, a smile spreading across her face.

"Yes," he answered immediately. His warm eyes watched Rosella.

"Aw," the three sisters said in unison.

Rosella's heart fluttered and butterflies dominated her stomach.

"We tried to convince her to go back to the castle," Camilla said, leaning back against the table and giving Rosella a stern look. "But some people are stubborn."

Grayson's expression fell, and his hand fidgeted. His jaw ticked and his eyes turned to the floor.

"She's got a weird notion that you are too different," Bridgette said and stepped backwards out of Rosella's reach.

Heat crept across Rosella's cheeks. She shot her sisters warning looks, her eyes dark and her lips pressed tightly together, but they only smiled in return.

"What do you mean?" Grayson asked Bridgette.

"We're merchants.," Giselle said and stepped forward to stand between Rosella and Grayson, her hands extending to both of them. "You're royalty."

"So?" Grayson asked.

"See?" Giselle scoffed. "See! He doesn't care."

Rosella sucked in a wobblily breath. More than anything, she wanted to reach out and take his hand. Feel his warmth. Meld into his touch. But it was foolishness. Even if only a few feet separated them in the room, too many unsaid words created an uncrossable chasm.

But he was in her home.

With the curse broken. Promises kept.

They owed each other nothing, and yet he stood before her.

"What are your intentions with our sister?" Camilla said, joining Giselle as a blockade.

"Camilla and Giselle," Rosella seethed, anger and embarrassment warring through her. Heat twisted in her throat, robbing her of breath.

"Yes, what are they?" Bridgette added, finishing off the inquisition line.

"My intentions are to ask her to return with me to the castle and to ask for her hand in marriage," Grayson said. "But if she doesn't want to come back to the castle, I will leave it be."

Rosella stood still, the world ebbing out around her. His words washed over her like a warm wave and left her breathless and disarrayed.

He wanted to be with her.

He returned her feelings. And not just one stolen night on a trail.

Could they work?

Her sisters babbled around her, making happy, giddy sounds.

They jumped around, shaking her and laughing.

"Told you so," Giselle sang and danced back to Grayson, who appeared as unsure as Rosella felt. Giselle grabbed his hand and he let her lift it. She twirled under it, and then let it fall as she danced back to Rosella.

"I did not mean to intrude," Grayson said, his eyes locked with Rosella's. "There are no obligations. I will see myself out."

With glassy eyes, he turned and walked toward the door.

He was leaving. Without her. Her heart slammed in her chest. Crashing and cracking. The sharp splinters stealing her breath. Hesitation rooted her feet to the ground.

"What are you doing?" Bridgette yelled in Rosella's face.

Camilla grabbed her cheeks and pinched.

"OW," Rosella roared, her trance dissolved, and slapped her sister's hands away.

"He's leaving, you idiot," Camilla said, her face ashen. "Do you want him to leave?"

"No," Rosella whispered. Her helpless eyes flicked to her sisters.

"Then go stop him," Bridgette pleaded.

"Let yourself be happy," Camilla said.

Rosella nodded, and on legs of jelly, walked through the door Grayson had escaped through. In the store, the Tribles were quiet as he entered, their eyes following his every step. With his long stride, Grayson was already at the door when Rosella entered, and it swung closed behind him.

"Wait!" Rosella screamed and ran toward the door.

Before she reached it, Grayson had reopened it. His face pinched in confusion and pain.

He met her gaze, his eyes shiny and the rims red.

Hope and warmth flooded through her. Without a doubt, he was the future she wanted. She'd defied the town, gone after three keepers, broken a curse, and destroyed Lucien to free the castle. She'd taken on the world to carve out her happiness with her sisters supporting her despite her attempts to sabotage it.

She was her last hurdle to happiness.

"What's wrong?" he asked, stepping back into the store, his hand reaching for his sword. His eyes darted around the room for the threat.

Rosella closed the distance between them. She lifted her hands to cup his cheeks and brought his face to hers. She stepped on her tiptoes and crashed her lips into his.

Without hesitation, his hands flew around her waist and pressed her closer, kissing her back.

"What are you doing?" Mr. Trible roared. "This is highly inappropriate and disgusting behavior."

Rosella ignored him and let her tongue sweep into Grayson's mouth. He groaned and deepened their kiss.

"You two should really get a room," Camilla said.

Her sisters stood behind her, peering over her shoulder. All three had smiles.

Rosella chuckled and stepped back but stayed within Grayson's embrace.

"You two should really leave," Camilla said to Benson and his father. She pointed two fingers at them and gestured to the door. "You are not wanted or needed, and you really bring the mood down."

Arthur stepped forward, extending his arm to the door. The Tribles pushed out of the door in a huff.

"I'm glad you two have the *showing* down, but consider using words, too," Bridgette said and pulled the curtains on the store. "This village isn't ready for you."

Grayson smiled. "Rosella, I love you and I want to be your husband."

Rosella smiled back, and said, "I love you, too."

Camilla coughed. "Do you want to be married to him?"

Rosella looked to Grayson, who looked at her to answer.

"Yes," Rosella said, the truth of it sizzling in her veins. Instead of a settled-for future, she could have one she never allowed herself to dream of. One built on love and not duty.

"About time," Camilla said and pulled a bottle of currant wine from the shelves. "I'll put it on your tab." She nodded at Grayson.

"With Rosella going to the castle, who'll watch the store?" Giselle asked.

Rosella opened her mouth, but Bridgette cut her off. "Gavin and I would like to run the store."

"Oh, yeah," Camilla said. "That means I don't have to."

Giselle raised an eyebrow. "Why would we ask you to?"

"I'm next oldest."

"But the least mature," Giselle said.

Camilla shrugged, and said, "Well, when you and Odette get back from your travels, you can visit us at the castle."

"Us?" Bridgette asked. "You're going?"

"Oh yes," Camilla said. "I can help plan the wedding for the end of the week, and

they'll need a nanny when the time comes."

Rosella gulped, the color draining from her face. "End of the week?"

Grayson's hand tightened around her. She leaned into his frame, already finding familiar comfort and enticement. There was no reason to delay what they wanted. End of the week would work.

"Yep, and then hopefully by the end of the year, I'll be an aunt," Camilla said, nodding.

Rosella's limbs went numb, and she licked her lips. "How about some time married first?"

Grayson leaned in close so only she could hear, "We'll have fun practicing."

Rosella laughed. Inviting heat warmed through her and settled low in her belly. It would be one of the perks of marriage.

"I heard that," Camilla said. "And I approve."

Acknowledgments

As with all my stories, this one would not exist without the foundation my mom and sister built. My mom's endless support of whatever hobby I was interested in (and buying some VHS tapes more than once when they wore out) and the countless hours my sister and I spent building worlds and characters will forever inspire me. Miss you, sis. Also, my partner's complete and odd support is crucial. He can't really explain what I am doing (he gets the writing part, just not why I would want to or how much work goes into drafting, revising, and everything else) but he'll nod and say, "go for it!" And, my four-legged family. My cat and senior puppy kept me company the entire time I fast drafted, revised, and edited this manuscript. My cat even sat on my keyboard and typed for me when I became too focused.

A special thanks to those who helped along the way. Madelyn, MadHope Editoral, for critiquing, reading opening pages back when I had no idea how to move forward, copyedits, and proofreading. Tory Hunter, Tory Hunter Editorial, for multiple readings, sound advice, and endless encouragement. My readers: Emilie (always so encouraging!), Lili (you always crack me up), Bree (our first time working together), and Shannon R. Lir (who not only read the manuscript but also had to listen to me while I revised it. She also has an amazing romantasy series you should check out).

About the Author

Amelia J. Rivers is a bitter cinnamon roll who lives in the Midwest with her husband, a legion of demonic cats, and a pampered dog. Data diver by day, writer by night. She also spends as much time with her nieces as she can. She is an emerging author of paranormal fantasies. This is Amelia's third book.

- Author website
- Join Newsletter
- All links